Delores Fossen, a *USA TODAY* bestselling author, has written over one hundred novels, with millions of copies of her books in print worldwide. She's received a Booksellers' Best Award and an RT Reviewers' Choice Best Book Award. She was also a finalist for a prestigious RITA® Award. You can contact the author through her website at deloresfossen.com

Multi-award-winning author **Leslie Marshman** writes novels featuring strong heroines, the heroes who love them and the bad guys who fear them. She called Denver home until she married a Texan without reading the fine print. Now she lives halfway between Houston and Galveston and embraces the humidity. When Leslie's not writing, you might find her camping at a lake, fishing pole in one hand and a book in the other. Visit her at lesliemarshman.com,Facebook.com/lesliemarshmanauthor, Instagram.com/leslie_marshman or @lesliemarshman on Twitter.

Also by Delores Fossen

Sheriff in the Saddle
Her Child to Protect
Safeguarding the Surrogate
Targeting the Deputy
Pursued by the Sheriff
Safety Breach
A Threat to His Family
Settling an Old Score
His Brand of Justice

Also by Leslie Marshman

Resolute Justice

Discover more at millsandboon.co.uk

MAVERICK JUSTICE

DELORES FOSSEN

SCENT DETECTION

LESLIE MARSHMAN

MILLS & BOON

First Published in Great Britain 2022
by Mills & Boon, an imprint of HarperCollins*Publishers* Ltd
1 London Bridge Street, London, SE1 9GF

www.harpercollins.co.uk

HarperCollins*Publishers*
1st Floor, Watermarque Building,
Ringsend Road, Dublin 4, Ireland

Maverick Justice © 2022 Delores Fossen
Scent Detection © 2022 Harlequin Enterprises ULC

Special thanks and acknowledgement are given to Leslie Marshman for her contribution to the *K-9s on Patrol* series.

ISBN: 978-0-263-30349-0

0722

MIX
Paper from
responsible sources
FSC™ C007454

This book is produced from independently certified FSC™ paper to ensure responsible forest management.

For more information visit: www.harpercollins.co.uk/green

Printed and Bound in Spain using 100% Renewable electricity at CPI Black Print, Barcelona

MAVERICK
JUSTICE

DELORES FOSSEN

Chapter One

The car was following her.

Delaney Archer was sure of it. She was sure, too, that the black SUV was quickly eating up the distance between them. When it caught up with her, the person inside would try to kill her.

Her too-fast heartbeat throbbed in her ears, and she shook her head, trying to will away the dizziness. She had to stay focused. Alert. Because her life depended on it. If she ran off the road, the killer would have her.

Lightning rifled through the black sky and lit up the sign that told her she was still five miles from the town of Clay Ridge. Too far. And on the rural road, there was nowhere to turn around and try to get back to her house in Lubbock. Besides, it wouldn't be safe there, either. The SUV would just follow her, and since she'd be alone at her home, she would be an easy target.

The thunder came several seconds after the lightning. A thick rumbling groan that sounded like a primal warning. One that she tried hard not to allow to fuel the panic that was racing through her. Just a couple more minutes and then she could see her fiancé, Cash Mercer.

Cash would make all of this better. He always did, and more than ever she needed him. He'd know what to do about the person following her. Cash could stop it because he was the sheriff of Clay Ridge.

She took the road toward Cash's ranch and checked her rearview mirror again. Even with the rain and her spotty vision, Delaney could see the SUV make the turn right behind her. He stayed close. Too close.

Delaney added more pressure to the accelerator and sped through the deep puddles that had already collected on the road. The wipers slashed over the windshield, smearing the rain on the glass so it was even harder for her to see.

Praying, she maneuvered her car around a sharp curve. The tires squealed and shimmied with the excessive speed, and she checked the mirror again. The other vehicle stayed right with her, its high beam headlight glaring into her eyes.

It certainly wasn't safe to race through a storm at one o'clock in the morning while she was dizzy and feeling off, but she didn't want to face a killer on a deserted country road. She had no weapon. No way to defend herself. Worse, she was exhausted and was worried she wouldn't be able to stand, much less fight.

"A quarter mile to go," Delaney mumbled when she saw the pond and cluster of cedars that marked the beginning of Cash's property.

Delaney made the final turn and sped through the cattle gates that fronted the ranch with its acres of pasture, house and outbuildings. She glanced behind her. And everything inside her went still. Because there was nothing there. No SUV. No headlights. No one.

When her chest began to ache, Delaney released the breath that'd backed up in her lungs, and she stared into the rearview mirror. The empty darkness behind her should have made her feel elated and safe. It didn't.

Mercy, had she imagined that someone was following her?

No. She couldn't have been mistaken about something like that. She just couldn't have.

Delaney slowed down and clamped her teeth over her bottom lip to keep it from trembling. Why did everything seem slightly out of focus? And wrong. Something was definitely wrong. But what? She couldn't think through the haze to try to figure it out.

More lightning veined across the sky as she came to a stop in front of Cash's place. It was dark. Not even the porch light was on. He was obviously in bed, but that wasn't unusual. He didn't keep late hours since he was usually up early to deal with the ranching chores before going into the sheriff's office.

The cold spring rain pelted her when she got out of the car, but Delaney managed to make her way across the yard. Each step was an effort. She was dizzy. So dizzy. And she was soaked by the time she used her key to let herself inside the house.

She leaned against the wall and peeled off her wet dress, surprised that she wasn't wearing any underwear. It took her a moment to recall that she'd left everything but her purse at the hospital.

Yes. The hospital in Lubbock.

She'd dressed in a hurry so she could get out of there. But why?

Because someone had wanted her dead. That was why she'd panicked when she'd seen the SUV following her. Except maybe there'd been no SUV. She shook her head again and pushed all of her questions and worries aside. The answers would come to her later after she'd rested.

She tossed her dress over the back of the chair in the living room. Drops of rain slid down her face, and she swiped at them with her equally wet forearm. Discarding her soggy shoes, she made her way down the hall to Cash's bedroom.

Delaney pushed open the door, and thanks to another slash of lightning, she was able to see him lying on his stomach in bed. He had a patchwork quilt covering the lower half of his body. The storm raged outside, the rain pounded on the tin roof, but it didn't disturb him. He looked peaceful.

Without taking her gaze off him, Delaney stepped closer. He stirred, his left hand brushing against the empty pillow next to him. *Her* pillow. Her place. Right there next to Cash.

She stood there for several moments, and despite the chill from her damp skin and the bone-weary fatigue, she just admired the view. And what a view it was. The rich black hair that swept against his neck. A solid back and shoulders that were corded with muscles he'd earned through years of hard work.

Even though Delaney couldn't quite see his angled face, she knew it was rugged, tanned and a little weathered. Not model-perfect by any stretch of the imagination, and that suited her just fine. Cash Mercer was definitely a cowboy. *Her* cowboy.

Delaney lifted the covers and slipped into bed next to him. He stirred again. Rolled to his side, and he automatically pulled her into his arms. He was warm. Solid.

And he was also naked.

"Cash," she whispered and snuggled to him.

His body slid against hers. Bare skin against bare skin. His breath brushed over her face.

Delaney leaned in and located his mouth. The taste of him jolted through her like the lightning outside. It soothed her and made her feel as if everything was right with the world. She pushed aside the SUV that had followed her, the storm, the hospital and all the other confusing thoughts that darted through her head. She was safe now and right where she belonged.

Cash made a sleepy sound of arousal just before he deepened the kiss. He took her mouth, claiming it. The dizziness went up another notch, but at least this time she had an excuse for the whirling in her head. Cash's kisses always knocked her a little off-kilter—in a good kind of way.

She slid her hand down his chest and felt the firm muscles and the moisture that had rubbed off her own body. She gently circled his nipple with her fingertips and was rewarded when he grunted with pleasure.

"Delaney," he mumbled.

Just the sound of Cash saying her name was enough to send the fire roaring through her blood. She loved him, and she needed him.

She pulled him to her. The mattress shifted, easing him on top of her. Delaney took advantage of the new position and wrapped her legs around him.

"Cash," she murmured on a rise of breath.

Every muscle in his body went board-stiff.

He levered himself up slightly and stared down at her. Alarmed, Delaney caught on to his shoulders and tried to see his face. No such luck. The room was pitch-black, and this time the lightning didn't cooperate and give her a glimpse of his expression.

Cash's hoarse voice cut through the drone of the rain. "Delaney?"

His tone made it seem like a question. She almost laughed. *Almost.* "Who else would be climbing into your bed at one in the morning?"

He didn't answer her. She felt his heart hammer against her chest. Hers was doing the same, and neither of them seemed to be breathing.

"Is this a joke?" he asked. Cursing, Cash rolled off her and bolted to his feet.

"What do you mean?" Delaney did some silent cursing of her own. Why was he acting like this?

"What the devil do you think I mean?" Cash grabbed a pair of boxers from the dresser and yanked them on. "What are you doing here? You're naked, for Pete's sake."

Despite the dizziness, Delaney sat up though she had to lean her back against the headboard to keep from slumping. "I wanted to see you."

"Why?" And it wasn't exactly a carnal invitation, either. It was more like a challenge.

A wave of panic started to crawl up her spine. "I've been sick, Cash." She almost told him about the SUV that had followed her but decided that could wait. They apparently had more important things to work out. "I was in the hospital."

"Hell." He added some raw profanity under his breath. "Why didn't you say that right off? Why were you in the hospital?"

"An allergic reaction to some meds." And there was more, but she was too tired to get into that now. "I'll feel better after I've had a good night's sleep."

"Sure." Cash scrubbed his hand over his face. "I'll

make up the bed in the spare-room for you." He started out the door.

"Wait. The spare room? Why would you want me to stay there?"

He slowly turned back around to face her. This time the lightning did its job. It slashed through the sky and gave her a glimpse of his face, and the bewildered expression on it. "You have something else in mind?"

Yes, she did. "We're engaged, Cash. I didn't figure you'd have any objections if we slept together. What's the matter with you anyway?"

"Engaged?" he spat out. Then he went still, the silence hanging in the air for several long moments. "What the heck are you talking about?"

That panic turned into a full-fledged roar. The muscles in her stomach tightened. Her breath became thin. "What's wrong?"

"You tell me, Delaney. I don't know where you got the idea that we're engaged. We're not. In fact, I haven't seen you in over a year."

No.

That wasn't true. It couldn't be true.

But she couldn't get the words of denial to leave her mouth. Almost terrified at what she might see, Delaney reached over and turned on the lamp. She didn't dare look at Cash. Not yet. Instead, she glanced down at her left hand.

There was no engagement ring on her finger. Nothing. Not even a faint line to indicate that it had ever been there.

A ragged groan tore from her throat. "Oh, God."

Chapter Two

All Cash could manage to say was another "hell."

Delaney sure had a way of capturing his complete attention, but in this case, that wasn't a good thing. A year ago, it would have pleased him big-time if Delaney had shown up in the middle of the night and crawled naked into his bed. But not tonight. Something was wrong.

He walked to the bed and pressed the back of his hand to her forehead. No fever. His gaze met hers, and in the depths of those cat green eyes, he saw a whole lot of confusion and panic. Of course, he hadn't needed to look into her eyes to realize that. She was clearly disoriented.

Cash studied her milky complexion. She was too pale, and there were dark circles beneath her eyes. Even though he'd been half-asleep when he kissed her, he hadn't detected any alcohol on her breath. No. She wasn't drunk, but that was one of the few things he could rule out.

"I'll call the doctor," he let her know.

He reached for the phone, but Delaney caught his arm. "Please don't. Not yet. Things are…sort of whirling around in my head. Just give me a minute to catch my breath, and I'll be all right."

Cash didn't think a minute would help much of anything for her. Nor would simply catching her breath. Whatever was wrong with her was no doubt serious.

"What kind of allergic reaction did you have that landed you in the hospital?" he asked.

Delaney glanced down at the plastic hospital bracelet strapped on her wrist. "It was to some pain meds."

Cash bit off some profanity. "And they discharged you like this, while you're still out of it?"

"No." A tear slid down her cheek. She didn't even seem aware of it and didn't try to wipe it away. "I'd been in the hospital for days. At least I think it was days." She paused, her forehead bunching up. "But I wasn't discharged. I left on my own because I was scared."

His concern went into overdrive. "Scared? Of what?"

Delaney shifted her gaze to his, and she hugged the quilt to her body. "We're really not engaged?"

This wasn't a conversation he wanted to have now, but it was probably best not to put it off. He'd consider this groundwork and then he could get answers about that hospital stay.

"No," he said, trying to keep any trace of emotion out of his voice. "We were engaged a while back, but we broke things off about a year ago."

"Sweet heaven." Delaney started to cry in earnest, the tears spilling from her eyes.

Cash considered reaching for her, but she moved farther away from him. And he let her. She seemed to be coming to terms with a whole bunch of stuff. The broken engagement, yes, but also why she'd come to his house in the middle of the night.

"I remember now," she said through the broken sobs.

"I remember. We argued a lot about my father. I left because I didn't think we could work out things."

Yeah. And that about summed up their entire four-month-long engagement. Delaney and he had spent hours, maybe even days, arguing about her father, Gil, a small-time rancher who hadn't wanted his little girl getting together with the likes of Cash. That was because Gil blamed Cash's father, Sheriff Jeb Mercer, for tearing his family to pieces. Gil hadn't been shy about voicing his objections as often as he got a chance, along with pressuring Delaney to end things.

Delaney had caved.

And until tonight Cash hadn't seen her since she'd handed him back the engagement ring and told him it was over between them.

Delaney drew his attention back to her when she draped the quilt around her shoulders and started to get off the bed. "I'll just be going."

"I don't think so." He stopped her from getting up. "You're staying put. I'll call my doctor and see if he'll make a house call. If not, I'll drive you to the Clay Ridge Hospital."

"No," she insisted, and her response was loud and fast. "I don't want anyone to know where I am. Someone followed me, Cash. I saw the headlights in my rearview mirror when I was driving out here."

Cash eased down on the bed next to her. He hated the fear he heard in her voice, and he hated even more that he didn't know if there was a real reason for it or not. After all, she'd thought they were still engaged. Maybe the person following her was just part of the disorientation caused by the allergic reaction.

"Look, the person behind you on the road was probably one of Matt O'Brien's boys," Cash explained. He kept his tone calm, hoping it would calm her as well. "They're always out late at night."

She frantically shook her head. "It wasn't one of Matt's sons. I swear it wasn't."

Because she seemed on the verge of panicking, he slid his arm around her. "You got a good look at the person?"

"No. But this isn't the first time he's followed me. It's been going on for a while now. Weeks."

Hell. Weeks. If that was true, then no wonder she was terrified. "You've let the police in Lubbock know about this?" Since he'd heard that was where Delaney lived these days, that would be the thing to do.

"They know," she assured him.

There was nothing uncertain about that response. He checked her eyes. They seemed clearer than they had been just minutes earlier, and she no longer seemed as confused.

"Why would this person be following you?" he asked.

Delaney hesitated. For a moment. Then two. "He wants me dead."

Cash had braced himself for her to say almost anything. Not that, though. He battled to keep his emotions in check, but it wasn't easy to do after hearing that.

"Start from the beginning," he insisted. "Tell me about this man you believe wants you dead."

He could tell she was doing her best to try to compose herself. And she failed. Cash didn't miss the tremble of her bottom lip or the soft shudder of her breath. She managed to assemble a veneer to mask her fear—

and whatever else she was feeling—but that veneer looked ready to crumble at any moment.

Delaney moistened her lips. "Last year, when I was still working as a public defender, I was given a manslaughter case. The victim was a young woman who was killed during a domestic dispute."

It didn't take long for Cash to flip back through his memory. That'd happened shortly before Delaney had broken off their engagement. "I remember. You were pretty stressed out about it."

"Yes, I was." Her words were deliberate, as if she were choosing them carefully. "The defendants were brothers—Webb and Ramone Bennison. Even though they had separate trials, I was the attorney for both of them. Webb was accused of manslaughter for killing the woman, Beatrice Stockwell, who was his live-in lover. Ramone was charged as an accomplice."

Cash tried to keep the knot from tightening in his stomach. He knew all of this already. Knew that she had been a public defender in Lubbock. She'd gotten the job right out of law school when she was barely twenty-four. Neither her father nor Cash had approved of the move, but Delaney had been determined to do a job that she thought would make a difference. After all, she'd said, everyone deserved to have a good lawyer.

But Cash knew there was a lot more to it than that.

Guilt and blame were greedy monsters that could suck the life right out of you. He had firsthand knowledge of that. He'd failed to keep his kid brother safe, and as a result, Joe had been kidnapped as a toddler and never seen again.

Delaney felt the guilt, too, but hers had a whole different twist to it. When she was sixteen, her father had walked in on her date, Aaron Skyler, trying to rape her. Gil had gone after the boy.

And in a blind rage, Gil had killed him with blows from a baseball bat.

That had led to Gil's arrest by none other than Cash's father, Sheriff Jeb Mercer. Jeb had charged Delaney's father with excessive force resulting in manslaughter since he'd outweighed the boy and Aaron hadn't been armed. In fact, Aaron hadn't even fought back and had been trying to run out of the house when Gil had confronted him.

The charges had been controversial. So had the conviction, and Gil had gotten some jail time. He had also ended up losing his ranch. Added to that, after his release, Gil had needed several stays in rehab as well as mental health facilities when depression had taken over.

"Webb Bennison was my first manslaughter case," Delaney continued a moment later. He saw her mouth tremble again and barely resisted the urge to pull her closer. "And I lost it."

"Because Webb was guilty," Cash quickly pointed out.

She lifted her shoulder but then nodded. "There was a lot of evidence against him. Still, Webb thought I could have done a better job of defending him."

"You couldn't have," he assured her.

She made a sound as if she didn't quite buy that. "Maybe, but Webb was convicted. His brother, Ramone, was acquitted. Webb went to jail, but three weeks ago he escaped during a routine transfer. It was some kind of paperwork mix-up. They literally let him walk out of there."

This time Cash didn't manage to bite off the profanity. Damn it. He hadn't heard about Webb's escape, but then Webb had never lived in Cash's jurisdiction. He wouldn't have gotten any kind of alert for it.

As soon as he got Delaney settled in for the night, he needed to make two phone calls. One to the doctor. The other to a cop friend in Lubbock to find out everything he could about the search for Webb. No wonder she was so worried about being followed. Or killed. Webb had been a huge nightmare from the moment he'd come into Delaney's life.

Breathing out a weary sigh, Delaney pushed her fingers through her wet hair. "For a couple days after Webb's escape, I thought he was dead," she explained, her voice wavering. "The Rangers found his burned car near Marble Falls. It'd gone over one of the bluffs. They were sure he died, but I've seen him since then. Just glimpses. But I know it's Webb."

That knot in his stomach got much worse.

Telling him all of this seemed to sap what was left of her resolve. Her eyes watered, and Cash saw her blink back more tears. Again, he had to resist holding her, but that wouldn't end up being good for either of them. There was a darn good reason Delaney and he were no longer together.

Her father, Gil.

And that reason was still around in spades. It had taken Cash too long to get over the crushed heart Delaney had left him with, and he didn't want another round of that. Still, the attraction was there. And that was his cue to shift his focus back to stopping the threat.

"You're sure it's Webb Bennison who's stalking you and not his brother?" he asked.

It took her a moment to compose herself, and she finally nodded. "I'm sure. No one has seen or heard from Ramone in a while. He disappeared after his acquittal. Besides, if he'd wanted to stalk me, he wouldn't have waited all these months."

That didn't mean Cash would write the man off. Maybe both brothers were in on this.

"And then there's the letter," Delaney added. "Webb sent it last week. He said he was going to kill me. He didn't sign it," she added before he could ask. "But I'm sure it's from him."

"What exactly did the letter say?" Cash pressed.

She paused, swallowed hard. "Just that he intended to torture me, to make me pay for not doing my job." She shuttered. "The crime lab has the letter now, but I saved a copy. It's at my house in Lubbock."

He nodded. "I want to see it tomorrow. And I also want to get one of my deputies involved in the search for Webb," he informed her. Deputy Jesse McCloud was as good a cop as they came, and he would work hard to piece all of this together.

Cash tipped his head to the guest room. "Why don't you try to get some sleep? In the morning we'll figure out what to do about all of this."

Cash braced himself for Delaney to object, for her to tell him that she didn't want to wait. Or to sleep. But the objection never came. She gave a weak nod and started toward the guest room. "Thanks for everything, Cash."

"You're welcome."

He'd hardly gotten out the last syllable before she interrupted him. "But that doesn't mean I want you to pull your Cash-the-protector routine. Webb's my problem. Not yours. Now that I'm thinking clearer, I know

I shouldn't have brought this to you. I shouldn't have come here."

The corner of his mouth hitched. Well, it sure hadn't taken her long to stand her ground. But then, it rarely did.

"Cash-the-protector," he repeated under his breath. So that was how Delaney thought of him and none too fondly, either, judging from her smart-mouth tone. Well, it didn't matter. He didn't need her approval to help her out with this.

He was about to turn on his security system when his phone rang. Heaven knew who was calling this late, but it probably wouldn't be good news.

"Sorry to bother you," the man said. "I'm Kevin Byers, a private detective. I work, or rather I *worked* for Delaney. You're Cash Mercer, her ex-boyfriend?"

"Yeah." He checked to make sure Delaney hadn't come out of the guest bedroom. Thankfully, the door was still closed. "Listen, Delaney's already turned in for the night. Can this wait until morning?"

"I hadn't called to speak to her anyway. I just wanted to make sure she was there and that she was all right. When I found out she'd left the hospital, I was worried about her."

There was something about the man's tone that set Cash's teeth on edge. Maybe it was plain old-fashioned jealousy. The guy certainly seemed concerned about Delaney. Concerned in a too-concerned kind of way.

"She's fine," Cash said curtly.

"Well, good. Uh, I guess you know I've been trying to find this Webb Bennison. Delaney hired me to do that, but then she fired me."

"Not a surprise if you couldn't find him," Cash grumbled.

Cash could almost see the man scowl. "No, but there's a reason why I haven't located him. Delaney doesn't have a stalker."

Now it was Cash who scowled. "She says she does."

"I know. But I'll tell you what I told her. I looked for this Webb every day for nearly three weeks, and never once laid eyes on him. In fact, no one has, including the entire Lubbock Police Department or anyone in the other law enforcement agencies searching for him."

"Delaney's laid eyes on him," Cash quickly pointed out.

There was a moment of uncomfortable silence on the other end of the line. "So she claims, but only her. No one else. And that should tell you something."

Cash didn't know this man, but he definitely didn't like him. "What should that tell me, other than the fact the guy's been careful?"

"Webb Dennison's dead," he insisted. "Delaney's suffering from acute delirium. Did she tell you that?"

"She mentioned it." Not in those exact words, of course. But Cash had gotten the gist of it when she mistook him for her fiancé. Still, she'd quickly recovered her grasp on reality.

"The only stalker after Delaney is the one in her own imagination," Byers added. "She didn't tell you everything, did she?" he asked before Cash could say anything else.

"What the hell does that mean?" Cash countered.

From the other end of the line, Cash heard the PI drag in a long, weary-sounding breath. "Delaney wasn't just in the hospital, Sheriff Mercer. She was under psychiatric observation. And she didn't just walk out. She escaped."

Chapter Three

The sunlight stabbing through the window woke her.
Delaney forced her eyes open, but it took several hard
blinks just to be able to focus. Even then she felt as if
she'd just spent the night being tossed around on a carnival ride.

She glanced at the room. Got her bearings. And then
she groaned.

What in the name of heaven was she doing here in
Cash's spare bedroom? Delaney struggled with the answer much as she'd struggled to focus. She remembered
leaving the hospital because she was scared Webb Bennison was there, that he was coming after her. She'd
driven to the ranch during a bad storm…

Oh, mercy.

And then she'd stripped off her clothes and climbed
into bed with Cash. She did that while he was naked,
thinking he was still her fiancé. Worse, they'd kissed
and come within a heartbeat of making love.

Cursing herself and the fog in her head, Delaney
threw back the covers. She had to find Cash because
she obviously owed him both an apology and an explanation. But when she caught a glimpse of herself in the

mirror, she knew that talking to him would have to wait. She didn't intend to face him while she was stark naked.

He probably thought she had lost her mind. Heck, maybe she had. Others certainly thought it was true, and it was why she'd ended up in the hospital.

Delaney rummaged through his dresser and came up with a Christmas red terrycloth robe. It was probably a gift that he'd never worn, since Cash wasn't the bathrobe type.

She washed her face in the adjoining bathroom and tried to comb some of the tangles from her shoulder-length hair. She finally gave up, located a rubber band in one of the drawers and pulled the unruly mess of curls into a ponytail. One last glimpse in the dresser mirror confirmed what she'd already guessed: she looked how she felt—hungover and horrible.

The scent of coffee greeted her when she stepped into the hallway, but Delaney came to a quick stop when she heard the serious tone of Cash's voice.

"No," he insisted. "I want Buck and Ted riding fence today. Have them call me immediately if they see anything or anyone suspicious."

Security measures. Part of her was pleased that he believed there truly was a stalker after her. Another part of her, a much larger part, hated that security measures were even necessary. She shouldn't have brought this to his doorstep.

"Jesse's coming out soon," Cash added to the person on the phone, "and if he agrees we should add more men to keep watch, we will."

Delaney had hoped her situation wouldn't seem so downright scary after a good night's sleep. However, the fear was just as bone-deep as it had been when she'd first realized that Webb was stalking her and—worse—that he'd been at the hospital at the same time she was.

Delaney walked closer to the sound of Cash's voice, stopping in the doorway of the kitchen. She glanced at the dress she'd been wearing when she'd arrived the night before—it was now dry and draped over a chair at the table. Cash had his hip leaning against the counter, and despite the intense conversation he was having, his gaze snared her right away. The long, lingering look he gave her stole her breath.

She cursed herself. Cursed him, too. She didn't need this now. An attack of raging hormones. She wasn't some teenage girl with stars in her eyes and rocks in her head. She was a grown woman with more than enough problems that she didn't have time for anything else. Especially a good, old-fashioned case of lust. And that was all there was to it, she assured herself. Lust. Any deeper feelings she'd once had for Cash were long gone. They had to be gone.

Too bad there were times like now, when her body, or her heart didn't quite believe that.

Cash was dressed in the cowboy cop mode. Jeans, a gray T-shirt, boots. His black Stetson was hanging on a peg next to the back door. Rather than stand there and continue to gawk at him, she helped herself to a cup of coffee, sat at the table and waited for him to finish his phone conversation.

"I'll let you know what Jesse says," he relayed to the person on the other end of the line. He ended the call and turned toward her. "How are you feeling?"

"Fine," she quickly answered and hoped she sounded believable.

Apparently, she failed to convince him, because he

scowled at her lie. "How are you feeling?" he repeated, and this time it was more of a demand than a simple question.

Delaney took a deep breath. "I'm fine, considering that my head's pounding and I have a killer stalking me." She took a long sip of her coffee and prayed it wasn't decaffeinated. She needed all the help that she could get with this blasted headache. "By the way, I'm sorry about last night."

He just stood there and looked at her. It didn't take long for that penetrating stare to unnerve her.

"Things got mixed up a little in my head," she added.

Cash's frown deepened.

"All right, they got mixed up a lot. I had this problem with some medication. An allergic reaction to a new pain pill for the bad headaches I get." Delaney paused. "Did I tell you this already?"

Cash nodded. "But what you didn't tell me was that you'd been under psychiatric observation and left the hospital without telling anyone."

"Oh," she said, knowing that he was going to want to hear a lot more than just that vague response. But Cash continued before she could get the explanation right in her head.

"Yes, *oh*. It took me a while to get the info, but care to know what I learned?" Cash didn't wait for an answer. "When you collapsed on the sidewalk outside your office in Lubbock two days ago, someone took you to the ER, where you were diagnosed with acute delirium, brought on by sleep deprivation and stress. Do you remember that?"

"Yes," Delaney admitted.

What she wouldn't admit was that she hadn't actually remembered all of that until now, until he'd just spelled it out for her. There were still some gaps in her memory, and it scared her spitless to think what might be in those gaps.

"Once the ER doctors had you stable," Cash continued, "they placed you under psychiatric observation because you were having hallucinations and possible paranoia. You were *combative*—their word," he emphasized. "And they believed you could harm yourself and maybe even others."

Delaney practically jumped to her feet. "It wasn't paranoia, and I wouldn't have harmed myself or anybody else. And the only reason I was *combative* was because they wouldn't listen to me. Webb's stalking me. He wants to kill me." She stopped. The short fit of temper had drained her of what little energy she had. "But I understand how that could sound like paranoia."

"And the hallucinations?" he pressed.

On a sigh, she sank back down onto the chair. "I thought I saw Webb in the hospital, and I screamed for help. That was possibly a hallucination," she admitted when Cash just continued to stare at her, "but I honestly believed Webb was there. He wanted to taunt me, to let me know that he could get to me anytime he wanted."

The muscles in Cash's jaw stirred, and he sat down across from her so they were eye to eye. "The doctor who treated you wants you to go back—"

"No." Delaney didn't have to think about that, either. "Yes, there's security, but Webb could get past that. The windows are locked on the ward where I was, and if he came into my room, I'd be trapped. He's a big man, and I'd have no way to fight him off."

Delaney steeled herself up to hear Cash's argument.

But he simply nodded. Then he cursed. His jaw muscles went to war with each other again.

"Your doctor who did the psychiatric evaluation said it might be a day or two before all the symptoms go away," Cash explained as if he didn't like the information any better than she did. "He also said it was vital for you to get some rest in a comfortable, nonthreatening environment."

A burst of laughter left her mouth, but it wasn't from humor. "That's impossible. Not with Webb out there." Delaney gulped down more coffee. If the caffeine was going to work, it was sure taking its sweet time. "But not to worry. I don't plan to get naked and climb into bed with you again. I'll just get dressed—thank you for drying my clothing, by the way—and then I'll drive into Lubbock and speak to the cops there."

That earned her a glare. "You're not thinking about leaving, are you?"

"No," she said honestly. "I'm not thinking about it. I *am* leaving." She kept a firm grip on her cup to keep her hands from shaking. "I can't stay, Cash. Webb might learn that I've come to your ranch. That means I've put you and everybody else around here in danger."

He huffed, tapped the badge that was lying on the counter. "I'm a cop. I'm trained to deal with danger."

"This isn't your situation to deal with," she reminded him. "If I'd been thinking straight, I never would have come here."

He made a rough sound of displeasure and crammed his hands into the pockets of his jeans, making them snugger than they already were. Something Delaney wished she hadn't noticed.

"I won't let you go," he insisted. There wasn't a shred of compromise in his tone.

Her chin automatically came up. "I don't think you have a choice."

Because she didn't want to look at his narrowed amber brown eyes, Delaney got up and walked to the window. Outside, there were a few ranch hands milling around the barns. She quickly scanned their faces to make sure Webb wasn't among them.

He wasn't.

For the moment, she was safe.

Too bad that moment couldn't last for at least a couple of weeks. She was past the just-being-weary stage and had moved on to exhaustion. That comfortable, nonthreatening environment, even though it wasn't possible for her, sounded like paradise.

"Do you think Webb will quit stalking you simply because you leave here?" Cash asked.

"No." When her fingers began to ache from the tight grip, she put her coffee cup on the counter. "But this is my problem, and I'll—"

"Wrong. It's my problem, too." He swore under his breath. "Delaney, I can't just let you walk. You're not well and you look like you're ready to fall flat on your face." Cash paused and then huffed. "Please stay."

Delaney scowled at him. How dare he *please* her. Especially now. She felt raw and vulnerable, and a *please* could cut straight through the defenses she'd put up against him. "I can't let you do this."

He stepped closer, his boots thudding against the Saltillo tiles on the floor. She gave him a hands-off scowl. Which he ignored. Cash reached out and hauled her into his arms.

"Give me some time," he whispered right against her ear. "I don't want you driving out of here while you can hardly see straight and with that monster after you. If you stay, we can possibly put an end to this, here and now."

Delaney felt her hard-fought resolve slip a considerable notch. Before she could stop it from happening, she lowered her head to his shoulder. "I'm just so tired of all of this," she confessed.

"I know." His arms tightened around her.

She managed to choke back the tears but had no idea how long she could keep them at bay. The bone-weary fatigue seemed to seep all the way to her soul. And therein lay a huge problem. She couldn't allow her fatigue and her situation to draw her closer to Cash. She just couldn't.

There was a knock at the door, and Cash immediately stepped away from her. Delaney pulled in her breath to steady herself. It didn't help. Her heart was already pounding.

"I'll see who it is," he told her. "Just wait here."

Delaney did stay put, but only because she didn't think she could convince her legs to move. Mercy, she had to get a grip.

She cursed her body, and herself, for even allowing that embrace to happen. She didn't have time or the energy to deal with an attraction to a man, any man, but especially Cash. Their history put a high price tag on physical attraction, and it was a cost that Delaney didn't want to pay again.

"I want to see her," she heard a male voice demand.

Not Webb. But she recognized the speaker. It was Kevin Byers, the private detective she'd hired.

And fired.

She hurried into the living room, where the men stood in the doorway. It was obvious from the stern look on Cash's face that he wasn't pleased with this visit. Or surprised.

"Delaney," the PI greeted. His mouth tightened when he glanced at her bathrobe. Or rather *Cash's* bathrobe. "I've been trying to reach you."

"Really? I haven't a clue why. You no longer work for me."

Byers didn't budge from his position by the door. Probably because Cash was practically blocking his path to keep him from entering any farther.

The two men were certainly a study in contrasts. Cash was dark—his complexion and hair genetic legacies from his Lipan Apache grandmother. Byers, on the other hand, had pale skin, and his hair was the color of the moon. Their clothes were a huge contrast, too. Cash might have been a cop, but beneath it, he was all cowboy in his jeans, boots and work shirt. Byers wore khakis, a crisp white shirt and aftershave so thick and musky that she smelled it all the way across the room.

Byers kept his attention firmly on her. "I had to come. And you know why, Delaney. I had to put an end to this nonsense and make sure you get some medical attention. There's no stalker after you."

She saw the muscles in Cash's jaw jump. Thankfully, he'd seen proof to the contrary. At least in a way he had. Last night, Cash had seen her terrified. Certainly that had convinced him that Webb was after her?

Well, maybe it had.

"There is a stalker," she assured Byers. But that was

all the assurance she intended to give him. "I want you to go. There's no reason for you to be here."

That seemed to be the only impetus Cash needed to latch on to Byers's arm. "You're leaving. Now."

Byers held his ground and waved a sheet of paper in the air. "I have proof there's no stalker."

Cash's gaze rifled to hers. He didn't say a word, but in that look, there were questions.

"Then your so-called proof is wrong," Delaney told Byers. "Webb followed me last night. And frankly I'm a little tired of you telling me what is and isn't happening in my life. Webb's real. His threats are real."

Byers simply handed her the paper. "It's a copy of the lab report for the letter you say you received from Webb. A friend of mine at the lab managed to get the report for me."

Delaney felt a cold hard knot tighten in her stomach as she took the paper from the man. She had no idea what the report would reveal, but from the glimmer of victory in Byers's eyes, it wasn't good. After all, Byers was convinced she'd fabricated Webb and his threats.

Cash went to her side. "Do you want me to toss this guy out of here?"

"Not just yet." But she might take Cash up on his offer later. Or as riled as she was, she could do it herself.

Delaney scanned through the technical words used for the analysis until she got to the summary at the bottom. She took in the words, the impact of them nearly knocking the breath out of her.

"Oh, God," she managed.

"It's your DNA on the sealed part of the envelope," Byers provided. "It's not merely from you touching it.

You licked the envelope. You sealed it. I think that says it all, don't you, Delaney?"

She shook her head. How could her DNA possibly be on that envelope? It'd been a letter from Webb. Not that he'd signed it, of course. And the threat had been veiled with comments hinting that they would get together very soon. Still, Delaney had known it was a threat.

"Delaney?" she heard Cash say. "Are you okay?"

She didn't even attempt a lie this time. "No." She handed him the report. "This isn't right. Webb sent me that letter. I swear he sent it. This report is wrong."

She must have sounded frantic, because Cash laid the report on the table and gave her a reassuring glance. There was nothing gentle, however, about the scathing look he gave Byers. "You're leaving. Do you want to walk out of here on your own, or do you need me to give you some *encouragement*?"

"I'll go," Byers assured him. "But I think you should get Delaney professional help. She's having some kind of breakdown. The cops won't be pleased when they learn she filed a bogus report."

Cash jerked open the door. "You just wore out what little was left of your welcome." He muscled his shoulder against Byers and pushed the man onto the porch. Cash slammed the door in his face.

"She needs help," Byers yelled. "Do us all a favor and make sure she gets it."

Delaney didn't release the breath she'd been holding until she heard Byers stomp off the porch and drive away. She waited. Waited for Cash to question her about the report, and her sanity. However, he didn't say a word.

"Byers thinks I belong on the psychiatric ward." Delaney squeezed her eyes shut a moment. "And after the police read that report, they'll agree with him."

"Not necessarily. It wouldn't be the first time a lab has come back with inaccurate results. We can have the envelope retested, and it'll prove what you've been saying."

Delaney replayed everything he'd just said. Cash believed her. He didn't think she'd lost her mind.

Relief rushed through her. Followed by the dread. Was this the real reason she'd come home—because she needed someone to accept that what was happening to her was real and not just in her head?

He pushed a wispy strand of hair off her cheek. "I get the feeling there's some tension between you and the PI," he commented. "And I don't think it's because the man has seriously bad taste in aftershave." Cash made a face, fanned the air. "Might take a while to get the stench out of here."

Delaney gave a nervous laugh. "I hired him last month and then fired him nearly a week ago."

"Because he doesn't believe there's a stalker." Cash paused. "But there's more to it than that."

The man was a pro at reading her. It made her wonder why she hadn't just spilled everything before Byers had shown up. "Byers wanted a relationship. I wasn't interested, and I don't think he likes to hear no for an answer."

Cash didn't say anything for several snail-crawling moments. "You're sure it's not more than that? He seemed, well, determined to get back at you."

She heard what was beneath his words. A PI should have thicker skin. And the truth was—it had felt like more. She just wasn't sure what. Or why. But Byers's reaction to her firing him was just off.

"I knew I should have punched him," Cash grumbled when she didn't say anything.

His tone was in jest but not completely. Delaney had no trouble hearing the underlying threat. Cash would have stood up for her, and that brought her back full circle to the point she'd been trying to drill into her head. They couldn't do anything that might test, or tempt, the precarious barriers they'd built between them.

Those barriers were necessary.

For reasons she didn't want him to know. Reasons *he* couldn't know. Because then Cash would want to right that wrong, too.

Delaney took both a mental and physical step back from him. "I need to get some things from my house in Lubbock."

"I'll go with you," Cash insisted.

She didn't even try to talk him out of it. The truth was, since Cash was insistent on helping her, she really didn't want to go outside alone because Webb might still be out there. Or even Byers. But she couldn't let that possibility stop her from coming up with a plan of action.

For starters, she had to figure out a way to convince the cops in Lubbock that the threat was real. That her life was in danger. That her DNA on the envelope had been planted or something. And she had to do it fast. Despite Cash's *hospitality*, she couldn't continue to stay at the ranch and put him in danger.

She took her dress and shoes to the bathroom to put them on, only to remember that she still didn't have underwear. Something that Cash already knew since he'd obviously gotten her dress off the floor and put it in the dryer. No way would he have not noticed that there were no other items of her clothing lying around.

Delaney dressed as fast as she could and saw Cash waiting for her when she came out of the bathroom. Specifically, he was waiting and watching at the window. No doubt making sure no one was about to ambush them.

"I've alerted the ranch hands," Cash let her know. "They'll be on the lookout for Webb."

"Thank you," she said, truly grateful for his help.

But having the hands be on the lookout wasn't enough. If Webb wanted to get onto the ranch undetected, he could probably figure out a way to do it. The ranch was a big place with plenty of ways in and out.

"And you're thinking I can't help you do what's necessary to stop Webb," Cash added, looking her straight in the eyes. "But I will. Promise," he added.

Promise. That was one of his favorite words. Sometimes he said it with a slathering of sarcasm. Other times, there was enough sexual heat in it to trigger them falling straight into bed. But now it was just that. A promise. He would help her, and in doing so, he would put his life on the line.

Delaney wouldn't argue with him about that. Not now anyway. But she needed to come up with a better plan than the one that was playing out right now.

Her car was still parked out front, but Cash stopped her when she started toward it. "One of the hands checked it out, and the battery's dead," he told her. "You'd left the door open and the parking lights on when you got here."

Delaney huffed in frustration, but it didn't surprise

her. She'd really been out of it the night before. It was a miracle that she'd even managed to get to the ranch.

"We'll take my truck," Cash added.

His dark blue pickup was parked in the driveway on the side of the house, and they headed in that direction. They had nearly reached it when she heard a sound.

A growl.

Delaney's gaze whipped toward the road. Just ahead, barely yards away, were five Dobermans. How they'd gotten so close without her seeing them, she didn't know, but these were no pets. They had their teeth bared.

And the dogs were already charging right at them.

Cash shoved her toward the truck, and the moment he had the passenger's-side door open, he pushed her inside. He followed her, with Delaney dragging him in, but one of the dogs snapped at his leg. He kicked at it, forcing it to move back, and Cash bolted into the cab of the truck with her. He slammed the door shut just as the other dogs lunged at them.

"Did you get bit?" she blurted out.

"No." He moved out of her grip and took out his phone. "Brent," he said when his ranch hand answered. "We've got five Dobermans in the front yard, and they're not very friendly."

"Yeah. I just got a call from one of the hands at Eagle Hill," she heard Brent say. "The dogs belong to the new owner, and they got out."

Eagle Hill was a nearby ranch, but she hadn't known there was a new owner. The place had been unoccupied the whole time she'd been with Cash.

"The owner's driving around looking for them,"

Brent went on, "but I'll text the hand and have them get over here ASAP."

However, before Cash could even end the call, a red truck barreled up the road and came to a quick stop. A man hurried out. He was well over six feet tall and had a bulky build. He whistled, and the dogs immediately turned and hurried to him. With a snap of his fingers, the dogs jumped into the back of the truck.

"Sorry about this," the man called out, and he started toward them.

Cash got out, facing their visitor, and Delaney stepped out behind him. Even when the man got closer, she couldn't see much of his face because of the angle of his hat, but there was something about his voice that turned her blood to ice.

Using his thumb, their visitor pushed back the brim of his hat, his gaze zooming right in on her.

"Delaney," he said, smiling.

But she definitely wasn't smiling. Delaney knew she was looking at the face of a killer.

Chapter Four

Ramone Bennison.

Cash cursed under his breath when he instantly recognized the man, and slid his hand over the gun in his shoulder holster. After all, Ramone might be a free man, acquitted of helping his brother murder a woman, but Cash wasn't at all sure the guy was innocent. Especially considering those attack dogs.

Cash also stepped in front of Delaney, but not before he felt the muscles tense in her arm.

Hell.

Seeing Ramone was no doubt like stepping back into a nightmare for her. Nightmares of the threats from Ramone's brother, Webb. Considering what had been going on recently with Delaney, those threats likely seemed even more menacing than the dogs.

Ramone shifted his attention, and then his smile, to Cash. "The gun's not necessary," he informed Cash.

Cash didn't move his hand, and he didn't buy into Ramone's friendly tone and smile. Not with what had to be buckets of bad blood between Delaney and the man.

"What are you doing here?" Delaney demanded, and Cash had to hand it to her—she sounded a lot stronger than she probably felt.

Ramone hitched his thumb in the direction behind Cash's property. "I'm your new neighbor. I bought Eagle Hill, the old Henderson ranch."

Cash shook his head. "I was told the new owner was a guy named Frank Taylor."

"He's my business partner," Ramone quickly explained. "He bought the ranch, but I'll be running it. At least I will once I get it fixed up."

That didn't sound aboveboard. Then again, Cash figured he'd suspect any-and everything the man said or did.

"Why the hell would you buy a place so close to me?" Cash snapped. "Because I sure as hell don't believe you didn't know Delaney's connection to me."

The breath Ramone released was long and sounded weary. Of course, weariness could be faked, and Cash knew this could be some kind of sick game of cat and mouse that Ramone and Webb were playing with Delaney.

"The ranch was a good price, a good investment," Ramone said. "And yes, I knew we'd share a property line. Once I was settled in, I'd planned on coming over to let you know I have no ill will or bitter feelings for Delaney or you." He paused a heartbeat, his gaze sliding between Delaney and Cash. "Besides, last I heard Delaney and you weren't even together."

No, they weren't together, but Cash had no intention of confirming that to a man who might be out to harm her. He wanted Ramone to believe that Delaney would have all the protection she needed if Ramone and Webb came after her. And she would. Well, she'd have it from Cash anyway.

"Delaney," Ramone continued when neither Cash nor

she said anything. He shifted his gaze to her. "There's no reason for you to be worried about me being here."

A burst of air left her mouth. A hollow laugh, definitely not one from humor. "Your brother wants to kill me."

Ramone lifted his shoulder in a noncommittal shrug and glanced behind him at the dogs. Maybe to make sure they were staying put. They were.

"Maybe you want to kill me, too," she added.

Ramone shook his head. "No. I don't. And FYI, I believe Webb's dead," he threw out there like gospel. "I think if he were alive, he would have already gotten in touch with me. He hasn't."

"You and I don't share the same opinion." Delaney stepped to Cash's side, no doubt so she could face Ramone head-on. "I believe Webb's taunting me and that he plans to murder me."

No shrug this time. Ramone stared at her a moment. Then he nodded. "I hope you're wrong about that. But if Webb's alive like you think, well, he'll probably be holding a grudge."

"And you're not holding one?" Cash fired back.

Ramone smiled again. "I didn't kill anyone, and I didn't help Webb kill anyone. And the jury agreed. That's why I'm a free man. So, no grudge for me, not toward either of you." His smile faded, and he shrugged. "As for my brother, things weren't solid between us after the trial. You could say I'm having a little trouble forgiving him for dragging me into the mess that landed him in jail."

Cash didn't believe that for a second. Blood was blood, and yeah, he personally didn't have that kind of connection with his own kin, but he thought that Ramone and Webb might still be tight.

Ramone sighed as if frustrated by what he believed Cash was thinking, and then he tipped his head to the dogs. "I'd best be getting them back. Sorry about the Dobermans getting out. They're all bark, no bite, but I'm sure it was...unsettling." He seemed to savor the word. "It won't happen again."

"It'd better not," Cash snapped, and he made sure that sounded like a warning from a cop. "Because if they get out again, I'll come after you. That's a promise." The last bit was much more than a warning. It sounded very much like the threat that it was.

Cash gave Ramone a hard stare until the man drove away, and then he got Delaney back in the truck. He'd already had plenty of concerns about this drive into Lubbock, but dealing with Ramone skyrocketed those concerns.

"Please don't tell me I have no reason to be worried," Delaney muttered. "Because I'm not buying that it's a coincidence that Ramone bought the ranch as a good investment."

Cash wanted to try to reassure her that all would be well, but he didn't want her wearing rose-tinted glasses. Not for something like this. Rather, he wanted her to stay alert and focused. Like now. As he drove away from the ranch, both of them glanced around to make sure they weren't being followed.

Or about to be attacked.

"I'll keep an eye on Ramone," he assured her. "And I'll check on the sale of the ranch. If there's anything, and I mean anything, off about it, I'll use it to file charges against him."

He got that started by pressing the button on his steering wheel to make a quick, hands-free call to his office, and Jesse answered on the first ring.

"Ramone Bennison just showed up at my place," Cash told his deputy. "He claims he bought the old Henderson ranch."

Jesse muttered some profanity, his voice pouring through the truck. "You think Webb's there with him?"

"Maybe, but if he is, I'm betting he'll keep his sorry butt well hidden. Ramone had to know that once word got out about him being the owner, then anybody in law enforcement would look at it as a possible hiding place for Webb."

But Cash immediately rethought that. Maybe law enforcement wouldn't look because they thought Webb was dead.

"What do you need me to do?" Jesse asked.

"Contact the Texas Rangers and tell them about Ramone. Then dig into the sale of the property and into any paperwork you can get your hands on. If there's dirt to find, I want it found." He could use that dirt ASAP to get the man out of Clay Ridge.

"Will do," Jesse answered. "You want me to see if I can set up some kind of surveillance in case Webb is at the ranch?"

Cash considered how to go about that. "Yeah. Arrange for security cameras, but keep them on my property so we don't have to get a warrant. There are a couple of spots where you should be able to get a visual of Ramone's house."

"Thank you," Delaney murmured.

There was no need for her gratitude. Even if Delaney and he hadn't had a history together, he would have wanted to keep an eye on Ramone. Anyone who'd been charged with such a serious crime would automatically be on his radar.

Cash had just ended his conversation with Jesse when his phone rang, and he frowned when he saw the name of the caller on the dash screen of his truck. Leigh as in Leigh Mercer. She was not only his sister, but she was also sheriff of the nearby town of Dark River.

Most brothers probably weren't surprised to get calls from their siblings, but the two of them weren't exactly close, and she rarely had reason to get in touch with him.

"A problem?" Cash said the moment he answered.

"Is Delaney with you?" Leigh immediately said.

Of all the questions he'd thought his sister might ask, that hadn't been one of them. Leigh knew Delaney, of course. They'd all grown up together in Dark River, but like Cash, Delaney had moved away when she turned eighteen.

"I'm here," Delaney volunteered. And Cash was glad she had. It would signal Leigh not to say anything sensitive about an investigation in case his sister was calling cop to cop.

Leigh muttered something he didn't catch, but he didn't have to hear exactly what she'd said to pick up on the frustrated tone. That probably had something to do with his and Leigh's last visit.

Shortly after Cash's breakup with Delaney.

After getting many nudges and calls from their father and friends, Leigh had drawn the short straw and come to Cash's house to check on him. He'd been surly and on his way to getting drunk. In other words, not his finest hour, and Leigh might be making sure he wasn't about to have a repeat of that.

"How'd you know I was with Delaney?" he came out and asked his sister.

"I just got a visit from a PI," Leigh explained. "Kevin Byers."

Cash wasn't sure whose groan was louder—his or Delaney's. "I fired him," Delaney said. "And he's not happy about it."

"Yeah, I picked up on that right away." Leigh paused. "Any truth to what Byers said? Because he's claiming that you escaped from a mental hospital and that you need help. Help that Byers doesn't believe Cash will give you because you've convinced him that you're right as rain."

Now Cash cursed. "Byers shouldn't have gotten into all of that with you."

"Agreed. But he did. He said since Delaney grew up here in Dark River and he knew we'd been friends that I might have some influence over her."

"Influence to do what exactly?" Cash snarled. "Get Delaney to turn herself over to him?"

"Yes. He thought I'd be willing to talk her into it. Of course, I have no intentions of doing that. And while I don't want to poke my nose where it doesn't belong, I'm calling to ask if there's any way I can help."

For an instant, Cash got a flash of Leigh and him as kids. They hadn't been close even then. Too many bad memories and family turmoil for that. But even with the turmoil, Leigh had usually been on his side. And vice versa.

"Does anyone in the crime lab owe you any favors?" Cash asked. "Because I need a letter retested."

"The letter that Webb sent Delaney?" Leigh quickly provided. That was also info she'd no doubt heard from the PI.

"That's the one," Cash verified. "I believe Webb sent it, but according to Byers, Webb's DNA wasn't on it. Only Delaney's."

"All right," Leigh agreed a moment later. "I'll call in some favors. By the way, after I explained to Byers that I wouldn't help him, that anything Delaney might have done isn't even in my jurisdiction, he said with or without my help, he intended to have her arrested for making a false claim and manufacturing evidence."

"That's not gonna happen," Cash snapped.

Because an arrest could get her killed. If he couldn't legally stop Delaney from being taken, then he'd do it illegally. That'd make him an outlaw, a maverick, but it'd be damn worth being on the wrong side of the badge to keep her alive.

"I'll go ahead and call the lab guys so they can get started on the letter right away," his sister said. She paused again but continued before Cash could thank her. "Something's wrong with Jeb."

Cash felt his chest tighten. Then again, that was his usual reaction to hearing his father's name. The fact that both his sister and he called him Jeb instead of *Dad* or *Father* pretty much said it all. Yeah, that family turmoil was a mess that had lasting effects, and at the center of that turmoil was Jeb.

"Define *wrong*," Cash insisted.

"He needs heart surgery. And no, I don't have the details because Jeb won't give them to me. You know how he is," she added in a mumble. "I just thought I should tell you."

Cash did indeed know how Jeb could be. Until his recent retirement, Jeb had been the sheriff of Dark River for over forty years. He'd been *the* law in Lubbock County. Jeb had also doled out that law with a hard hand and very little compassion.

Even when it came to his own kids.

Cash knew that Jeb still resented the hell out of him for not staying in Dark River to take over as sheriff. No way though would Cash have stayed under Jeb's thumb. But Leigh had.

Well, sort of.

She'd stayed and been elected sheriff after Jeb's retirement. It didn't matter that she was darn good at the job, either, because Jeb had made it clear that he'd wanted that particular badge to go to one of his sons. Either Cash or Joe, the son who'd been kidnapped as a toddler. Jeb had always held out hope that Joe was not only alive but that also someday he'd return and take over the reins of the law in Dark River.

And just like that, Cash got sucked back into more memories of the shambles that'd once been his life.

He cursed and wasn't able to keep that profanity to himself. Some of the words flew right out of his mouth. Leigh obviously knew how he felt, because she made a sound of agreement. She probably got sucked into the memories a lot since she was right there, right in the mix with Jeb, in Dark River.

"I'll let you know if I find out anything else about Jeb. And I'll make that call to the lab," Leigh said, clearly changing the subject.

"Thank you," Delaney spoke up. "I'm sorry about Byers bothering you. I'll call him and demand he back off."

"No need," Leigh assured her. "I told him that my-self. Stay safe," she added before she ended the call.

"Are you okay?" Delaney immediately asked him.

"Yeah." Cash took a moment, hoping that moment would make him seem more okay than he was feel-ing. When that didn't work, he just shoved it all aside. Something he was used to doing. Dealing with any kind of news about Jeb often required shoving things aside.

"You understand complicated relationships with fa-thers," Cash threw out there.

"Yes," she agreed in a whisper.

Delaney kept her attention out the window. Specifi-cally, on the side mirror where she'd be able to see any-one following them, but Cash had heard the soft sigh she released. Not a sigh of regret. Just resignation.

"Things are the same between Jeb and you?" she asked.

"Pretty much." Cash wasn't sure he should reopen this particular can of worms, but he went with it any-way while he took the exit to her house. "How about you? How are things between Gil and you?"

"Pretty much the same," she echoed. Delaney tore her attention from the side mirror to give him a long look. "My father doesn't know about the trouble I've been having. Or that I was in the hospital. I need to keep it that way."

Cash thought about that for a moment. "There's lit-tle to no chance he'd hear it from me, but Byers might contact him."

She groaned, shook her head. "After I pack some things at my house, I'll pay a visit to Byers and warn him to stay out of my business."

Cash would be making that visit with her, and if

necessary, he'd use the badge to get the PI to back off. Byers had no official reason to be involved in Delaney's life. At least no reason that Cash knew of, and what the man was doing was a form of stalking.

Which brought him to his next concern.

What with her recent health scare, and with Webb, Ramone and now Byers causing her some grief, Cash didn't want Delaney trying to fix this on her own.

"Are you going to argue with me about staying at my place?" Cash came out and asked.

She opened her mouth, closed it and groaned again. "I don't want to put you in the middle of this. Plus, there's my father," she added before he could tell her the middle was exactly where he wanted to be.

Cash tried not to let that feel like a sucker punch. But it did. Always would. "You don't want Gil to know you'd be staying with me, even if it was to keep you out of harm's way?" Oh, yeah. There was plenty of bitterness in his tone.

"I don't want him to know about the harm's way," she emphasized. "It'll be easier all around if I find some other place to stay."

Well, hell. She was going to argue with him about that after all.

"I can stay with my father," Delaney added.

Once Cash got past the second sucker punch—this time of annoyance—he decided that maybe this was for the best. Not her going to her father but not wanting to stay with him. After all, Delaney clearly didn't want to get involved with him again, and that meant he'd be a fool to create a situation where they'd be under the same roof.

While she was packing her things, he'd make some

calls and see about getting her into protective custody. He'd find someone who'd be willing to bend whatever laws were necessary to keep her from being arrested or killed. She needed to be with someone who knew how to keep her safe. That would get her out of Webb's path. Byers's, too.

And out of his own path as well.

Because there were other memories, too. Memories of Delaney naked in his bed. Memories that could end up causing him to make another huge mistake by giving in to the heat. Best to cool down that heat some by going with the "out of sight, out of mind" approach.

Mentally repeating that reminder and hoping it would soon sink in, Cash turned onto Delaney's street. Definitely not out in the sticks as his place was. This was a neighborhood of homes that had been built in the 1920s and then remodeled over the years.

In Delaney's case, the dark gray Craftsman-style house with the white shutters and pristine yard had once belonged to her grandmother. Delaney loved the place. When they'd gotten engaged, she'd told him that she would keep the house and maybe turn it into her law office.

Cash hadn't objected to her plans for merging their lives. After all, her work was here in Lubbock, and it wouldn't have been a long commute to the ranch, so it was a good plan. A plan that had gone to hell in a handbasket when Delaney decided to bend to her father's demands.

And that was yet something else he needed to push aside.

Cash pulled to a stop in her driveway and had a look around. Not an ordinary look but rather one where he was searching for any signs of Webb. But there was nothing. In fact, the street was empty, and he certainly didn't see anyone lurking in any of the yards.

He got out and walked to the passenger's side so he'd be right next to Delaney as they made their way up the porch. Again, there were no signs of trouble here and nothing seemed out of place.

"I need to disengage the security system," she said, taking out her phone. She frowned, though, when she pulled up the app for the controls for the system. "It's off. Not just the system, but the locks are off, too."

Cash had a look for himself and saw the red X where there should have been a green dot. "How long has it been since you've been here?" he asked.

She hesitated, shook her head. "Before I was put in the hospital."

So a couple of days. "Maybe you forgot to turn it on when you left," Cash suggested. The allergic reaction to the meds could have played into that happening. No way had she been thinking straight when she'd gone to his place and climbed into bed with him.

"I don't forget to do that. I mean, it's automatic, like putting on a seat belt. I use the app to lock the door and set the alarm." She looked at him, her eyes pleading for him to believe that. "Other than last night when I left the hospital, I've been careful because of Webb. I didn't want him to be able just to walk in."

Yeah, he got that, but she certainly hadn't been careful last night. She could have been so disoriented that she'd forgotten even something that was rote. It could be something as simple as that, but he still stepped in front of her when she reached for the door.

"Let me open it," he insisted, drawing his gun.

Her eyes widened, but she gave a shaky nod. He considered having her wait in his truck while he went inside and checked out the place, but that had its risks, too. If Webb was truly trying to get to her, he would likely try it when she was alone. That included when she might be in a vehicle by herself.

Cash glanced over his shoulder, just to make sure they weren't about to be ambushed, and he tested the knob. Definitely unlocked. With his gun ready, he stayed positioned in front of Delaney and eased open the door. And the moment he saw the foyer wall, he knew that all was not well.

There, painted in red, was a warning that turned his blood to ice.

Delaney, there's no place for you to hide. Sooner or later, I will get to you.

Chapter Five

Delaney would have staggered back a step had Cash not caught her arm to steady her. In the same motion, he shifted her behind him and lifted his gun while his gaze darted all around the foyer and to the rooms beyond.

"Webb," she said on a rise of breath. Delaney looked, too. Because she had no doubt who'd left that threatening message. No one else hated her enough to leave something like that.

Delaney, there's no place for you to hide. Sooner or later, I will get to you.

"If I'd come home last night instead of going to your place…" she muttered, but she didn't finish that. No need for her to spell out that Webb could have had her then and there. As dizzy and disoriented as she'd been, she wouldn't have been able to fight him off.

"Stay right next to me," Cash instructed. "We'll go back to the truck so I can call this in."

"You're not going to look through the house for Webb?" she asked. Not that she wanted him to do that. No. She didn't want Cash to run into Webb, who could be lying in wait.

"Not now. If Webb's here, I don't want to take him on while you're with me."

The thought of that terrified her. Because Webb might be the one who did the *taking*. If Webb was still inside, he could kill Cash, and it would be a bonus for him, a way of getting in another jab at her to murder someone who'd been such an important part of her life.

"You need backup before you go through the house," she insisted, and Delaney would hold him to that. She wouldn't let him do the search alone.

"Let's go," Cash insisted.

With his gun still ready, he backed out of the house, adjusting his position every step so he could keep watch and continue to use his body to shield her. She kept watch, too, but didn't see anyone. However, she did hear something. The sound of an approaching vehicle.

Cash must have heard it as well, because he pivoted fast, taking aim in the direction of the sound while he pressed her back against the front exterior wall. She felt his muscles brace, preparing for what might be a fight. Delaney tried to do the same. She might not have a gun, but she had no intention of just standing there if Webb came for her.

Part of her welcomed a showdown with the snake who'd turned her life upside down. Because maybe Cash and she would be able to end the danger. Maybe it would all finally come to a stop.

She released the breath that was causing her lungs to ache when she saw the truck that pulled into her driveway. Not Webb. "It's my father," she muttered at the same time that Cash spat out, "Gil."

Cash grumbled something else that she didn't catch, but she was betting it was profanity. Her father was likely grumbling the same words, too, because he was scowling when he stepped from the truck. A scowl no doubt meant for Cash.

As usual, Gil was wearing jeans and a work shirt. Emphasis on *work* since he was a hand at a ranch just outside of Lubbock. His boots were scuffed. His cowboy hat, more than a little battered. Both were items that Delaney had offered to replace many times over, but he'd always refused.

Also as usual, she felt the mix of emotions at seeing him. The love she felt for him. And the guilt. Both were equally strong, but most times, like now, it was the guilt that won out and consumed her. Just as it was consuming him.

Before that night nearly a decade ago, her father had been a ranch owner. It hadn't been especially big, but it'd been profitable. More importantly, it'd been in his family for generations. And afterward, after he'd killed because of her, he'd become the shell of the man she saw walking toward her now. There were things that she wished she could go back and change, but that fateful night was at the top of her list.

"What's wrong?" her father asked, shifting his attention to her. "Why are you with Cash?"

Delaney had a quick debate about how much to tell him. The full truth would worry him. Maybe *more* than worry him. But it would be hard to keep this sort of thing from him. Best to fill him in on the basics and go from there.

"I'm with Cash because it would have been too risky for me to come here alone. Webb broke into my house and left me a message," Delaney said. She tried to tamp down her fear, but it was still there, as bright and glaring at the message Webb had left her. "Cash was about to call it in to the local cops."

Her father froze in midstep, his scowl morphing to one of concern. "Are you okay?"

Obviously, Cash knew the question wasn't meant for him, because he went ahead and called Lubbock PD. He made it quick, and all the while he continued to keep watch.

There was a good reason for that.

Webb could use her father's arrival as a distraction to try to gun them down. Of course, any bullets that flew right now would have a much greater chance of hitting Cash and her father than her since both of them were obviously trying to keep her covered.

"The cops will be here in about ten minutes," Cash relayed to her.

"Dad, you should go," Delaney told him. "I'll call you once they've finished searching the house."

Gil didn't hesitate. "I'm not leaving." Not a trace of a scowl remained, and his forehead bunched up in worry.

She sighed and tried to think up an argument that she could use to get him to go. But Delaney knew there wasn't one. If she mentioned the possibility of an attack from Webb, that would only make him dig in his heels even more. She hadn't seen traces of the rage her father had had when he'd killed Aaron Skyler, and she didn't want to risk bringing that to the surface again. If her father went looking for Webb, he just might find him.

And Webb might kill him.

Webb wasn't a teenage boy who could be easily beaten down. He was big and strong. And mean. Her father would be no match for the man.

"What'd the message say?" Gil insisted.

Again, she debated what to say and what tone to use. "It was just a taunt," she settled for saying, and she kept her voice level. "Something that he knew would rattle me."

It had worked, too. All the nerves in her body seemed to be firing just beneath her skin. Something that she prayed her father wouldn't be able to tell. She needed this part of the situation defused so she could concentrate on finding Webb and stopping him. She couldn't do that if she was worried about her father.

"A taunt," Gil repeated like profanity, and he paused so long that Delaney thought he might demand to know the exact words that Webb had used. He didn't. "I'm worried about you," he continued a moment later. "You were in the hospital and didn't even tell me."

Delaney groaned because she so didn't want to have this conversation now, but she also didn't want it to come down to Cash trying to force her father to leave. "How'd you find out?"

"A better question would be why I didn't hear it from you," her father argued. Except there wasn't much of an argument in his tone. However, there was hurt. Loads and loads of it.

Because Delaney could see and feel that hurt and his concerns about her, she softened her voice. "I didn't tell you because I didn't want you to worry. How'd you find out?" she repeated.

"A PI you'd hired called me," he said after hesitating.

Great. Just great. No way could she tamp down her temper this time. Byers was at it again, and that gave her another slam of anger. She was definitely going to have a conversation with the man.

"Byers also told me you were at Cash's," her father

went on. "Since you weren't answering your phone, I was going to leave you a note. I figured sooner or later, you'd have to come home."

She wasn't answering her phone because she'd left it when she'd sneaked out of the hospital the night before. Delaney had taken her purse, but her phone hadn't been in it. Apparently, someone on the staff had taken it when she'd been placed under observation.

"Why'd you go to Cash and not me?" Gil asked, and yes, the hurt had gone up some significant notches. "He's Jeb Mercer's son," he said as if that were the ultimate insult.

Which, to her father, it was.

Cash cursed. "I had nothing to do with being his son, and FYI, Jeb and I aren't exactly in a cozy father-and-son relationship."

"You've got his blood," her father fired back. No hurt now. This was anger, his usual reaction when it came to Jeb or anyone in the Mercer gene pool.

"And so what? That means I'll arrest some guy for going after the SOB who tried to rape his teenage daughter?" Cash shook his head, muttered more profanity. "I'm a lot of things, Gil, but I'm not Jeb Mercer."

Gil kept his gaze nailed to Cash. "The Mercers ruined me," he accused, his voice trembling now. "I shouldn't have gone to jail for what I did. I shouldn't have lost nearly everything I loved, and every time I see one of them, it brings back all those bad memories."

She knew he wasn't lying about the memories being bad. She'd heard his shouts when he was caught up in a nightmare and had watched him try to push back the darkness by drinking until he passed out.

And it was all her fault.

Gil scrubbed his hand over his face before he dragged in a shaky breath and looked at Delaney. "I need you to come home with me."

She couldn't do that, couldn't give Webb a reason to go after her at her father's place. "I'll be staying with a friend," she said. "Not Cash," she added when Gil's gaze shifted to Cash. "I'll be all right."

Her father studied her expression as if trying to suss out if what she'd said was true. Part of it was. But the "I'll be all right" wasn't anywhere close to being a certainty. The message left for her on the foyer wall was proof of that. If Webb could get past her security system to do that, then he would continue to come at her.

"I can't go through this again," her father muttered, and then he clamped his teeth over his bottom lip as if he hadn't meant to say that.

Delaney went to him and pulled him into a hug. "I'm sorry—"

"Don't." He moved out of her grip and backed away from her. "I can't go through this again."

She didn't try to touch him again, but Delaney did study his eyes. "Do you mean you can't deal with Cash and me? Because if so, I'm not with him."

The corner of Gil's mouth lifted in a dry smile. One that was touched with venom when his attention drifted toward Cash. "I can't watch this happen."

"Delaney is right," Cash said on a frustrated huff. "We're not together."

But he was talking to the air because her father had already turned and stormed back to his truck. She watched as he sped out of her driveway and took off down the road.

Delaney wanted to go after him, to tell him he was

wrong, but mercy, she was too tired to deal with her father right now. Soon, though, she'd need to go see him and try to smooth things over. But not until she was sure that she wouldn't be bringing danger right to his doorstep.

"We need to wait in the truck," Cash reminded her. "You shouldn't be out in the open like this."

Because she knew that was true, Delaney hurried to the truck with him, and once they were inside, he motioned for her to lower herself to the seat. She did but frowned when he didn't do the same.

"You're not getting down," she pointed out.

"Because I have no intention of letting Webb sneak up on us." He stopped, shook his head. "But he'd be an idiot to do that. If he's watching the place, he'd know that I've already called for backup. My guess is that he's long gone."

Yes, but she doubted Webb had gone far. Maybe he was with his brother in Clay Ridge, where he could take the time to plot how to keep tormenting her. If so, then she hoped Webb would be caught by the security cameras that Cash's deputy was setting up. Then Cash could arrange to go in and have both Ramone and him arrested.

However, Webb could go elsewhere, and the reminder of that slammed into her.

"Webb might try to get to me through my dad," she blurted out. Delaney nearly sprang off the seat, but Cash eased her right back down.

"I was going to ask Lubbock PD to offer Gil protection. Anyone else Webb could use to try to lure you out?"

Delaney silently cursed that she hadn't already gone over all of this. "My assistant, Melanie Adams."

In fact, she needed to contact Melanie and fill her in on what was happening. Melanie often worked from home, where she lived with her parents and two younger siblings, but that didn't mean Webb couldn't find a way around them.

"Melanie Adams," Cash repeated as if picking through his memory. "I remember meeting her shortly after you hired her. I'll ask for protection for her, too. And you, of course." He paused, glanced down at his phone when it dinged with a text message.

He frowned, then cursed.

"Webb," he snarled, getting her attention.

He showed her the text he'd just gotten from an un-known caller. If you want to find me, go to Delaney's house. I left something that oughta give her a night-mare or two.

Delaney felt another wave of fear slide over her. "Webb," she agreed.

Cash continued to frown. "The text was delayed. The person sent it over an hour ago."

She'd had that happen a couple of times, especially on drives from Lubbock to Clay Ridge, and it made her wonder when Webb, or someone he'd hired, had bro-ken in and left that message. The paint smell had still been strong, so maybe it'd happened right before he'd sent the text.

"If the text hadn't been delayed, I would have left you at my ranch and come here with a couple of local cops," Cash muttered. "So why wouldn't Webb have wanted you to see the message for yourself?"

Good question, and Delaney didn't like the possible

answer. "Maybe Webb wants to get me away from you because he thinks it'll be easier to kill me that way."

Cash made a sound of agreement. "You told your father you'd be staying with a friend. You told me you'd be staying with him. Where exactly are you planning on going?"

She opened her mouth but had to close it. Because she didn't have an answer for that. Not yet anyway.

"I get it," Cash continued when she didn't say anything. "You're worried about Webb having a go at me."

Yes, but it was more than a worry. It was a fear that was already eating away at her. Webb had killed once, and given the chance, he would again.

"I can take care of myself," he assured her. "And I can make sure your father's taken care of, too. Promise."

She had no doubts, none, that Cash would do that. But it would come with a huge price tag. A price tag that he wouldn't want, but it would be there. Because she would owe him for protecting her, and even more, she would owe him for the heat that would grow because of the two of them being thrown together like this. She could already feel the pull of the strong attraction between them. And she couldn't push away just how much she wanted to be in his arms.

But it couldn't happen.

If it did, she'd have another layer of guilt in her life. Because if she was with Cash, it could cause her father to try to kill himself. Again. She'd already cost him way too much, and she couldn't risk him losing his life.

Delaney was about to explain to Cash that she would indeed make some calls. She would arrange for security for both her father and her as well as finding a safe place for both of them to stay. But she didn't get the chance to do that because of the black-and-white patrol car that turned into her driveway.

Cash huffed, likely because he'd wanted to hear what she had been about to say, and he holstered his gun before he opened his truck door. "Stay put," he warned her. "They'll have to talk to you, but I want that to happen at the police station."

So did she, and maybe the Lubbock cops would believe her when she insisted that Webb Bennison was responsible for this.

Cash stepped out, shut the truck door and made it just one step before all hell broke loose.

The blast ripped through her house.

Chapter Six

One second Cash was standing, and the next moment, he was flying through the air. He landed hard, the pain shooting through his chest and jaw, but he forced himself to move. Fast. Even though he wasn't sure what had just happened, he did know one thing for certain.

Someone had just tried to kill Delaney and him.

Cash managed to get to his feet, and he whirled around to check on Delaney. His heart rocketed to his knees when he saw the huge chunk of her home's burning roof on top of his truck. It had caved in the metal, and the flames were whipping through what was left of the windshield. Which wasn't much. But that wasn't the worst of it.

The worst was that Delaney was still inside the truck.

Behind him, there were shouts from the cops who'd just arrived on scene. One of them yelled for Cash to get back. He didn't listen. No way would he leave Delaney in there to be burned alive.

Obviously, Delaney didn't have plans for that, either, because she shoved open the passenger's-side door and practically spilled out into his arms. Cash caught her, pulling her away from the flames, and it was barely in the nick of time. Because the rest of the front windshield caved in, sending a wall of fire and glass right onto the seat where Delaney had just been sitting.

Beating out the embers that were smoking and sparking on her clothes, Cash dragged her away from the truck and into the center of the yard. He glanced up and got his first look at the house.

Hell.

The front of the structure was gone, obviously blown out by some kind of bomb. The rest of the place hadn't fared much better. What was left of the roof was groaning and creaking—ready to collapse—and the thick flames were eating their way from the floor to the ceiling.

"He blew up my house," Delaney muttered.

Cash was reasonably sure that she was in shock, but he didn't know if she'd been physically hurt as well. There were some small cuts and a bruise on her face, and he hoped that was the worst of it. However, she could have internal injuries. There was no telling what may have hit her when the building exploded.

"We have to move," Cash told her. The wind was sending the thick black smoke right at them, and Delaney was already starting to cough. They had enough to worry about without dealing with smoke inhalation.

"Get away from there!" someone yelled. Maybe one of the cops, and it was highly likely the shout was meant for them.

Cash hauled Delaney to her feet and pulled her against him, sheltering her from the heat of the fire, while he forced her to turn and start toward the cops. Cash could see them now, two of them, and they were frantically motioning for Delaney and him to move.

And Cash soon learned why.

Behind them, what remained of the fiery roof came crashing down, and it spewed smoke, flames and debris right at them. Cash could feel the scalding heat and knew it could hurt them both, so he scooped up Delaney and started running.

"I'm Cash Mercer, sheriff of Clay Ridge," he called out when he saw the alarm on the cops' faces. Alarm in part because Cash still had hold of his gun.

The two cops certainly didn't relax, but they hurried toward them to help Cash get Delaney away from the house.

"You're Delaney Archer?" one of the cops asked her. He was tall and lanky, in his early thirties, and had thinning brown hair. According to his name tag, he was N. Jenkins.

Coughing, she nodded, and Cash put her on the back seat of the cruiser when the second cop opened the door. This one, P. Chavez, was Hispanic and built like a heavyweight boxer.

Along with giving both Delaney and Cash some once-overs, Chavez and Jenkins continued to keep an eye on the fire. It wasn't spreading, but there was still a chance of that, especially if the winds picked up.

"What happened here?" Chavez asked, and he directed that particular question at Cash.

"Webb Bennison," Delaney answered before Cash could say anything. "He did this. He's done a lot of bad things."

Chavez and Jenkins exchanged a look that made Cash want to curse. Because Cash could see the skepticism flash in their eyes. Word had likely gotten out that the FBI thought Webb was dead, but the message on the wall of the foyer was proof that he was very much alive.

Except there was no longer a foyer wall. Which meant there was no longer any proof.

Cash wanted to kick himself for not getting a photo of what their attacker had written. That way, the lab could have examined it to see if there was anything that he'd missed, but his priority had been getting Delaney out of there. Good thing, too, because if they'd stayed inside, they would have been killed in the explosion.

"Someone left Delaney a message, a threat," Cash emphasized, "painted on the wall of the foyer. It said, *'Delaney, there's no place for you to hide. Sooner or later, I will get to you.'*"

The cops exchanged another glance. "You saw this threat?" Chavez asked him.

"I did," Cash verified.

"And why are you here with Ms. Archer?" Chavez pressed after a short pause.

Cash had no intention of telling them that a dazed and out-of-it Delaney had shown up at his house the night before, but if they ran a background check on him, which they would certainly do, they'd learn the connection. Best to hear it from him so Chavez and Jenkins didn't think he was hiding something.

"Delaney and I were once engaged," Cash explained. "She came to me for help because Webb Bennison has been threatening her."

Cash heard the wail of the sirens, lots of them. Fire department, more cops, maybe even an ambulance. Soon, the place would be overrun by the first responders who would all be trying to do their jobs. Jobs that might not include pinning all of this on a man they believed to be dead.

Dragging in a long breath, Chavez shifted his attention to Delaney. "Ma'am, you've seen Webb? You know for certain that he's the one who did this?" He tipped his head to the fire.

Delaney took a long breath as well. "I didn't see Webb, but I know he's the one doing this." Her voice cracked, and Cash could see that she was trying to steel herself up. "He could have killed us."

"And Webb has a reason to murder Sheriff Mercer?" Jenkins asked.

"No," she answered, but then Delaney shook her head. "Maybe Webb wants Cash dead because of his connection to me."

Judging from the questions the cops were asking, they already knew about Delaney defending Webb. And that probably took her down a notch or two in their eyes. Everyone might deserve to have a lawyer, but cops didn't always have a lot of respect for those who defended criminals. That didn't mean they wouldn't do their jobs and investigate this. But Cash would do his own investigation. He had to find Webb and put him back behind bars before he could get to Delaney again.

When the ambulance pulled up in front of the house, Jenkins motioned for it to come closer. "The EMTs are going to take you both to the hospital to be checked out," he told Cash and Delaney.

"No," Delaney insisted. "I'm fine."

Cash figured her most recent hospital stay under psychiatric observation was playing into her quick response. He understood it, but he wanted Delaney checked to make sure she truly was okay.

"I should see a doctor," Cash said, rotating his shoulder as if it were hurting. It was. Actually, his chest and jaw were aching, too. Not enough for him to be carted to the hospital, but if he went, Delaney would come with him.

She stood, and there was alarm in her eyes. In fact, she no longer looked in shock. Just concerned, and that concern was all for him. Cash felt a little guilty about playing that particular card, but along with the ploy causing Delaney to get an exam, it would also get her the heck away from what was left of her house. She didn't need to be here, to see the proof of what Webb had just tried to do to her.

Except maybe it wasn't Webb.

As a cop, he had to look at all angles, and it was possible someone else had done this to make it look as if Webb were responsible. Ramone, for instance. If Webb was truly dead, then maybe Ramone was doing some extreme gaslighting to get back at Delaney for not keeping his brother out of prison. But there was another possibility here, too.

The private investigator, Byers.

With all the calls, visits and tattling Byers was doing, it seemed to Cash that the PI was obsessed with Delaney. Maybe that obsession had taken an even darker turn that had led to an attempt on her life. Byers could have ditched his insistence that there was no threat to Delaney because it wasn't getting him what he possibly wanted—access to her. Then Byers could create the threat himself.

Yeah, that was definitely something Cash needed to check out.

As the fire department moved in to try to contain

the flames, Cash led Delaney toward the ambulance. He holstered his gun, but he kept watch because the person who'd set that bomb could still be around. Watching. Waiting for another chance to kill them. But Cash didn't see anyone who set off his cop alarms.

But there was one person who had today. And that had been Gil. Cash didn't want to think the worst of Delaney's father, but it was hard not to do just that. Along with spending time in jail, Gil had also been in and out of mental institutions, and while Cash didn't see the man doing anything to hurt his daughter, there was the potential for Gil to go off the deep end and do something to try to hurt Jeb Mercer's son.

Hell.

He hoped that wasn't the case, that he'd just been put off by the man's venom over the bad blood with Jeb. But it was yet something else Cash needed to check off the list. If Gil had sent the text that'd gotten delayed, he could have done that, believing that Cash wouldn't take Delaney to her house until he was sure it was safe. He didn't know if Gil had any kind of explosives training or knowledge, but that went on Cash's to-do list as well.

The EMTs helped them into the ambulance, and when one of them put Delaney on the gurney, Cash took the seat next to her.

"What is it?" Delaney asked.

She reached out and touched Cash's hand, and that was when he realized she'd likely been staring at him while he was lost in thought. Thoughts about her father blowing her house, and maybe Cash himself, to smithereens.

Cash didn't plan to spell that out to her now. Not when she was still trembling from nearly being killed.

It would only put a wedge between them because she'd feel the need to defend her father. Right now was a really bad time for wedges.

"I don't want you to give me a hassle about staying with me," he said. "I want you in my protective custody."

Even with everything that had just happened, Cash could see that she did indeed want to give him that hassle. Not because she didn't know the depths of the danger. No, she knew that all right. This was about her trying to keep him safe. Which was a load of crap. He was a cop, and this was his job.

Or rather Cash was making it his job.

A hired guard or the local cops didn't have the emotional investment he did. Of course, it was an *investment* he shouldn't have. But hey, it was there all right. Always there. And Cash just wasn't going to fight it when he knew he'd do everything to keep Delaney safe.

She might have seen that resolve in his eyes, because she finally nodded, and her grip tightened on his hand. "If you get yourself hurt protecting me, I'm going to be really mad at you."

Cash smiled. "Ditto," he said, and then he did something stupid.

He brushed his mouth over hers.

Talk about a wedge. Delaney went stiff, pulling her hand from his, and she got a panicked look in her eyes. A look Cash totally understood. They shouldn't be kissing. They shouldn't be doing anything to give in to this relentless heat that not even an explosion and near death could cool down.

Thankfully, they both got a quick distraction when the EMT's phone rang, the sound shooting through the back of the ambulance. But only a few seconds later, Cash was rethinking the *thankfully* part. The EMT looked plenty unsteady when he handed his phone to Cash.

"It's Jenkins," the EMT relayed, "the cop who responded to Ms. Archer's house. He wants to talk to you."

Cash didn't ask if the cop had told the EMT why he'd called. He just took the phone and hoped they weren't about to get another dose of bad news. However, the feeling in his gut told him to brace for the worst.

"Sheriff Mercer," Cash answered.

"I figured I'd give you the news and you could pass it along," Jenkins explained. "We just got a report about Ms. Archer's assistant, Melanie Adams. She's been kidnapped."

Cash felt the initial slam of adrenaline, but he tried to keep his expression neutral so that Delaney wouldn't panic. "Do you have any details of how it happened or who took her?" he snapped.

"According to an eyewitness, a man wearing a ski mask dragged her out of the office at gunpoint and forced her into a truck."

Cash silently cursed. Because he could see it all playing out. And he knew Melanie had to be terrified.

"The eyewitness didn't get the license plate or a description of the truck, for that matter," Jenkins continued, and then he paused. "But according to the message left inside the office, the man who took her was Webb Bennison."

"What message?" Cash demanded.

"I'm sending a photo of it now," Jenkins assured him. Cash avoided eye contact with Delaney while he waited for the dinging sound to indicate the photo had loaded. Like the message left in Delaney's foyer, this one was also written in red paint with the words scrawled across six or more feet on the wall.

Words that would tear Delaney to pieces.

Chapter Seven

This is your fault, Delaney. I took Melanie because of you. Love, Webb.

Even though Delaney had barely gotten a look at the picture that Officer Jenkins had sent Cash, a glimpse was all she needed for the message to be burned into her mind.

A message that was true.

It was her fault that Webb had kidnapped Melanie. She'd been so caught up in dealing with the aftermath of her escape from the hospital that she hadn't warned Melanie. Something she should have done right after the dizziness and the disorientation had worn off. It didn't matter that it was what Delaney had planned to do. No. That didn't matter at all.

The bottom line was that she hadn't acted fast enough, and because she hadn't, Melanie was now in the hands of a killer.

"You should keep watch," Cash said, pulling Delaney out of her thoughts. Something he'd been doing a lot since they'd left Lubbock and started the drive to his ranch in the truck he'd rented.

Delaney was keeping watch. Making sure they weren't being followed. Checking to see if they were about to be ambushed on the country road. But with the weariness scraping her raw all the way to the bone, it probably looked to Cash as if she were about to zone out on him. Part of her wanted to do that, to escape so that she didn't have to feel this fear she had for Melanie. But the fear wasn't the only thing she was feeling. There was plenty of anger, too. Anger at herself and especially at Webb for taking his vendetta out on an innocent woman who'd only been doing her job.

It'd been nearly eight hours since Delaney had seen a picture of that message Webb had left at her office. The ambulance had taken them to the hospital, where she and Cash had gotten their minor burns and cuts treated. After that, two cops had driven them to the police station to give their statements.

Delaney had put herself on autopilot to go over all the details that the cops had wanted. Just getting it done, going over all the things about Webb that she wished were only part of her past and not playing into what was happening now.

Because Webb was indeed part of what was *happening now*, Delaney had also used Cash's phone so she could make some security arrangements. She'd hired a PI/bodyguard to go to her father's house to stay with him. Gil hadn't appreciated the guard and had told her so when she'd called him. However, since she had also filled him in on the explosion, he knew there was the possibility of danger spilling over onto him.

"You think it's a mistake for me not to be with my father?" she asked, knowing it would cause that flash of worry in Cash's eyes.

It did. Maybe because he knew Gil wouldn't welcome him into his house even if it meant she'd be safer with Cash around. But as Delaney studied Cash, she thought there might be something more.

"Other than the obvious, what exactly are you worried about?" she added to her question. "Do you think my father wouldn't put my safety above his hatred for you?"

"Maybe," Cash answered after a very long hesitation. "Not purposely, though. I don't think he'd intentionally put you at risk." He paused again, studied her. "Do you?"

Delaney opened her mouth to give him a quick no, but she didn't think she was mistaking Cash's tone. *He* thought it was possible that Gil could hurt her.

Even though Delaney didn't especially want her thoughts to go in that direction, she played around with some possible scenarios that could have caused Cash to ask that particular question.

"You believe that if my father starts drinking it might lead him to do something dangerous?" she suggested. "Like try to lure Webb out to stop him from coming after me?"

And just her saying that aloud made her realize it was true. Oh, mercy. It was true.

Her father had a temper, a really bad one that stayed contained most of the time. But if he unleashed it with the help of some alcohol, he could want a showdown with Webb. One that Gil would lose. Webb was a lot younger and lot stronger. Not to mention a lot more desperate.

"I need to use your phone," she insisted.

Cash pulled it from his pocket and handed it to her. "You're calling your father?"

"No, the PI I hired."

No need to clarify that she hadn't meant Byers. She'd learned her lesson with him and had gone with a large agency, one with a sterling reputation, and they had assigned Trevor Salvetti, who also had bodyguard training. Salvetti had gone straight to her father's house and now answered her call on the first ring.

"This is Delaney Archer," she said. "I need you to make sure my father doesn't get out of your sight. He might try to leave and contact Webb Bennison."

"He hasn't tried that so far," Salvetti assured her. "But I'll definitely keep my eye on him. FYI, he's not happy about me being here."

"No," she agreed. Delaney had known that would be his reaction, but she could deal with his anger as long as he was safe. "Uh, he hasn't had anything to drink, has he? I mean alcohol." She mentally cringed because this was definitely going behind her father's back, but she had to be sure the situation hadn't sent him back over the edge.

"If he has, I haven't seen any signs of it," the PI answered, "but I'll keep my eye out for it."

Thankfully, Salvetti didn't press her on the details of why she'd asked the question in the first place. Good thing because Delaney didn't want to spell out that her father was a mean drunk who often made bad decisions.

"Any word on your missing assistant?" Salvetti wanted to know. Delaney had filled him in on that when she'd hired him.

"No. Not yet." But Delaney held on to the hope that Webb would be contacting her soon with some kind of ransom demand.

Not money.

No, that wasn't what Webb wanted. He wanted her,

and Delaney suspected Webb would demand a trade—
her for Melanie. That would be their best-case scenario
unless the cops managed to find Melanie soon. It was
entirely possible that Webb would just murder Melanie
to make Delaney suffer. And it would. It would cut deep.

She ended the call with the PI and handed Cash back
his phone. Delaney avoided eye contact with him because she didn't want him to see that she was barely
holding on by a thread. But he must have sensed it
anyway.

"I know you're worried about Webb possibly going
after your father or vice versa," Cash said. "But I get
the feeling there's something more. Something about
Gil that you're not telling me."

Delaney wanted to curse. Cash was a good cop, but
she hadn't wanted him to pick up on the nerves simmer-
ing beneath the obvious. Because, yes, there was plenty
about her father that she hadn't told him.

She kept her gaze on the road as Cash made the
turn off the interstate and took the exit for Clay Ridge.
"My father doesn't always think straight when he's been
drinking."

Cash made a quick sound of agreement. "Got that.
And you're concerned the not thinking straight could
cause him to take a risk with Webb. Got that, too, but
there's more to it than that," he quickly added. "What's
going on with your father?"

She could read the subtext. Cash wanted to know
why she continued to keep close ties with her father
when it was obvious their relationship was strained and
at times even toxic.

"He defended you," Cash continued when she didn't

say anything. "You blame yourself because he went to jail—"

"It was all my fault," she blurted out before he could start laying out the reasons why she shouldn't feel guilty. "I knew Aaron Skyler was bad, and I took him to the house anyway."

"You sure as hell didn't take him there so he could rape you," Cash snarled.

"No," she quietly agreed.

But she'd known Aaron would likely want to make out with her, and she'd wanted the same. At least she had until he'd started to push her for more and she'd said no. Aaron hadn't accepted her "no," and had started tearing away at her clothes. Aaron had done that after he'd punched her in the face. By the time her father had come in, she was bruised, bleeding and terrified.

"And you didn't ask your father to kill Aaron," Cash added. He'd softened his voice as well.

"No," she repeated. "But he did kill him and then went to jail for it."

Cash huffed, then sighed. "And just like he said— seeing me is a reminder of what happened. I can curse my DNA for the umpteenth time. I know I'm the spitting image of how Jeb looked when he was in his thirties. I bring back the bad memories for your father. You know that, and that's why you try to shelter him from me. That's what tore us apart, and it'll keep on tearing—"

"My father tried to kill himself," she blurted out.

Judging from the shock she saw on Cash's face, this was one bit of info that he hadn't heard. Then again, Delaney had worked hard to keep it under wraps because she'd known Gil wouldn't be able to face the pity or the looks that he was a broken man.

"I never heard anything about this," Cash muttered.

Delaney nodded. Sighed. She hadn't intended to tell him, not like this anyway, but maybe it was time for him to know. But she had to take a deep breath before she continued.

"He tried twice," she explained. "Booze and sleeping pills both times. The second time was worse than the first, and he barely survived. That's when he told me he'd rather be dead than have to see me with you."

Cash groaned and then cursed. "When did he tell you that? When the hell did this happen?"

Again, she needed a deep breath. "Right before I ended our engagement." And that was all she had to say for Cash to fill in a lot of blanks.

Yes, her father was the reason she'd broken up with him. Yes, she'd been terrified of a third suicide attempt, one that would end his life. Or worse.

"I was the one who found my father after both attempts," she continued. "With the second one, he was groggy, and mumbling. Maybe talking out of his head. But he mentioned that it might be better off if we were both dead. You and me," Delaney clarified, pointing to Cash. "Later, I asked him about it, and he said he didn't remember. But I think that when he's been drinking he sometimes wishes you and I weren't around. After all, I'm also a reminder of the night he killed a boy, and you're a reminder of Jeb and his arrest."

Cash stayed quiet for several long moments before he cursed. "You should have told me this," he snapped.

As expected, there was plenty of anger in his voice. With reason. Cash now knew that she'd broken off their engagement to save her father.

Maybe to save Cash, too.

Delaney didn't want to believe that her father would go to such a dark place that he'd try to kill Cash, or her, and then end his own life, but believing Gil wouldn't have hurt or killed Cash had seemed a huge risk to take. Of course, if she'd told Cash, he would have tried to help her work it out. She had loved Cash too much to put that on him.

When Cash cursed again, she thought that maybe he was about to verbally blast her for holding back about Gil's suicide attempts. But when she looked up, Delaney realized the cursing wasn't for her or their situation. It was because there were two vehicles parked in front of his house. There were also two men standing by those vehicles, and while Delaney didn't recognize one, she did the other.

"That's Kevin Byers," she snapped.

It was now her turn to curse. She hadn't had time to go by his office and tell the PI to back the heck off, but she could certainly do that now. Just seeing him here at Cash's ranch washed away some of the bone-weary fatigue caused by the adrenaline crash, and Delaney likely would have bolted from the truck when it came to a stop if Cash hadn't taken hold of her arm.

"And who's the second man?" Cash asked.

She shook her head, glared at Byers through the windshield. "I've never seen him before."

He was short and beefy with a wrestler's build, and he was wearing a dark gray suit with the jacket unbuttoned. He turned, causing the light to glint off the badge clipped to his belt. The badge she recognized.

It belonged to an FBI agent.

Delaney felt her stomach tighten. *What now?* The day had already been plenty bad enough, and she prayed the agent wasn't there to give her bad news about Melanie.

Byers and the man with the badge weren't the only ones in Cash's front yard. Two of his ranch hands were there, too, and both were armed. They were obviously keeping watch, and the hands moved toward them when Cash and she got out of the truck. One of them was Stoney Quates, who'd worked for Cash for years, and judging by the strong resemblance, the younger man was his son.

"They insisted on waiting for you," Stoney told Cash, and the hand obviously wasn't pleased about that. Probably because the ranch was basically on lockdown right now.

"I'm Special Agent Van Curley," the FBI agent volunteered, his voice no-nonsense and all lawman. He spared Cash a glance before nailing his attention to Delaney. "Ms. Archer?" He didn't continue until she gave an acknowledging nod. "You and I need to talk."

"I need to talk to you, too," Byers insisted. As usual, the man reeked of the aftershave he obviously favored, and the scent only made Delaney's stomach even more unsettled. "Now," he added like an order that he was dead certain she would obey.

Delaney didn't roll her eyes. Instead, she narrowed them. "We have nothing to discuss," she warned Byers. "In fact, I don't want you here, and I don't want you contacting people about me. My business with you is finished. If you don't stop hounding me, I'll file a restraining order."

That caused Byers's own eyes to narrow. "You're conning people to make them believe you're in danger. You're not. You're making false claims that are tying up the law enforcement officers who need to be concentrating on finding Webb Bennison's body so they can put this all to rest."

Cash riled her when he stepped in front of her. Delaney wanted to blister Byers with a glare and a response, and she didn't need help for that. Still, Cash obviously felt the need to do the same.

"Delaney was nearly killed when someone blew up her house. Then someone kidnapped her assistant. Webb Bennison, probably. Delaney *is* in danger, period, and you're not welcome here. Leave or I'll arrest you for trespassing."

Byers didn't budge. "It's Delaney's DNA on the envelope of the so-called threatening letter she got from Webb," the PI snarled. "Go ahead. Ask Special Agent Curley here. He'll tell you the same."

Curley sighed, nodded. "The lab reran the test. It's her DNA, all right."

"And someone could have set her up," Cash pointed out. "It's not that hard to get someone's DNA. From her trash. From a water glass she used at a restaurant." Cash shifted his attention back to Byers. "In fact, you could have done that because she fired you."

She could practically see the temper bubbling up in Byers, but then he seemed to rein in the anger. "I could have done that," the PI admitted, "but I didn't." He groaned and squeezed his eyes shut for a moment. "I just need all of this to go away. I need to put it behind me."

That was a lot of emotion for a mere case that he'd no longer been hired to do. "What are you talking about?" Delaney demanded.

But Byers shook his head, waved her off and hurried toward his vehicle.

"You know him well?" Curley asked, his attention on Byers as he sped off.

"No," Delaney answered. "I hired him to find Webb, and then I fired him."

Curley's forehead bunched up. "Did Byers develop feelings for you?" Curley pressed, but then he waved that off. "Sorry, the hazards of the job. It just seems to me that you two might be together." He motioned to Cash and her. "And I was thinking Byers might be jealous. The kind of jealousy that sends someone into a rant like we just witnessed."

Cash made a quick sound of agreement and drew in a long breath. He didn't shift his attention off Byers until the PI's vehicle was no longer in sight. "Why don't we take this chat inside?" Cash asked, but he didn't wait for Curley to agree. He took hold of Delaney's hand and led her to the front door. "I don't want Delaney standing around outside to give someone the chance to attack her again."

Curley made his own sound of agreement, and the three of them went in when Stoney opened the door for them.

"Nobody else has been here today?" Cash asked the ranch hand.

"Nobody," Stoney confirmed. "You want me to wait in here with you until your *company* leaves?" He cast an uneasy glance at Curley.

"No, it's okay. I want you on the porch in case Byers comes back."

Stoney muttered, "Will do," and he headed back out to the porch.

Delaney didn't waste any time getting her point across to the agent. "If you're here to arrest me for making a false report, then you're making a huge mistake. I didn't send myself that threatening note, and I didn't blow up my house or kidnap my assistant."

. "I believe you," Curley said without even a second of hesitation.

She had to do a mental double take and bite off the rest of the argument she'd been prepared to deliver. "You believe me," Delaney repeated, her voice thick with relief. But there was also some skepticism.

She wasn't anywhere close to being steady right now, but it was possible the agent was placating her to get on her good side. Perhaps because he thought it would encourage her to confess to any wrongdoing.

"Yes," the agent verified. "Webb's a killer, and if he's alive, I could see him going after you like this."

"If he's alive," she repeated, and some of the frustration returned. "You think he's dead?"

"I think he *could be* dead," Curley corrected. "His brother could be behind the attacks and threats."

"Especially since Ramone is now my new neighbor," Cash tossed out there. "Along with his business partner, he bought the ranch next to mine."

Curley's eyes widened with surprise. Obviously, he hadn't gotten the word about that yet. "You're sure?"

"Dead sure. Ramone paid Delaney and me a visit this morning. He played nice. Well, nice enough," Cash amended, "considering he has dogs that have probably been trained to attack. Dogs that got loose and came onto my property, where they could have hurt Delaney."

Curley took a moment, clearly processing that, and grumbled some profanity. "The FBI has been keeping tabs on Ramone since his brother's escape. Obviously, though, we haven't been careful enough if we missed something like that. You believe Ramone is here to taunt Delaney?"

"Or try to finish her off for Webb," Cash said, but then he was the one to mutter a curse. "Sorry," he added to Delaney.

It had spiked her heart rate a couple of notches to hear Cash spell it out like that, but Delaney had already come to that same conclusion. Ramone might be the sole threat, the person responsible for all the horrible things that had been going on. Maybe he was doing that because his brother was indeed dead, and Ramone had taken it upon himself to exact revenge.

"I had a deputy put up security cameras on the property line I share with Ramone," Cash continued a moment later. "The deputy's monitoring the feed so we'll know if Webb shows up."

"I'd like for you to share anything on that feed that could be connected to this investigation," Curley insisted. And it was indeed an insistence. "I can get a court order," he added when Cash paused.

"No need," Cash assured him, his stare boring into Curley. "I'll share, but if I get one whiff that you or anyone in your agency is coming after Delaney for false reports and such, my cooperation with you will end in a snap."

Judging from the flicker of annoyance in the agent's eyes, Curley didn't care much for that, but he didn't get a chance to voice his objection because Stoney called out to them.

"Boss, you got a visitor," the ranch hand announced, opening the door a fraction.

"Is it the PI?" Cash snapped.

"No. Uh, it's your dad."

Cash got the same surprised expression that Curley had when he'd found out about Ramone buying the adjacent ranch. Unless things had changed since she'd broken off their engagement, Jeb Mercer didn't make a habit of coming out to visit his son.

"Excuse me a minute," Cash muttered, and he tipped his head for Delaney to follow him to the door. Perhaps because he didn't want to leave her alone with Curley in case the agent started to interrogate her.

Cash opened the door wider, but he positioned himself so that he was standing in front of her. Still protecting her. Though she doubted Jeb would be a threat. Still, a sniper could fire into the doorway, and that was a reminder for her to keep watch. And to make this visit short if Cash wasn't planning on inviting Jeb inside.

From over Cash's shoulder, Delaney saw Jeb step from his truck. He looked a lot older than he had the last time she'd seen him, and from beneath his Stetson, she could see the sides of his hair were mostly gray. Still, he managed to look formidable, maybe because he'd taken on a bogeyman status because of what he had done to her own father.

"I'm here on business," Jeb said, probably noting the extreme disapproval in Cash's eyes.

Because she had her arm next to Cash's, she felt his muscles stay tight. "What kind of business?"

Jeb shifted his gaze to Delaney. "I thought you'd want to know. I found your assistant. I found Melanie."

Chapter Eight

"You found Melanie?" Delaney said, her breath rushing out with the words.

She might have rushed out to Jeb, too, if Cash hadn't held her back. Cash didn't want Webb or anyone else to get an easy shot at Delaney, and her going out into the open would definitely make it easier.

"Where? How?" Cash asked Jeb, and he also wanted to know how his father had gotten involved in this. Jeb was no longer the sheriff and lived miles from Lubbock, where Melanie had been kidnapped.

"I got an anonymous call," Jeb explained as he walked to the porch. He made a sweeping glance around the yard. The kind of glance a cop would make. "The caller said a missing woman, Melanie Adams, was at the end of my road. I went down there and found her. She was tied up and gagged."

"She's alive?" Delaney blurted out. Her breath was gusting now, and Cash could practically feel the hope coming off her in waves.

Jeb nodded. "She has some cuts and bruises. A broken finger, too. I got her to the hospital and had the security guard stay with her. I considered calling you but figured I'd better drive out and give you the news in person."

Cash mentally went through everything Jeb had just told them, and he got hit with a whole mountain of concerns. Not only was he troubled by what Leigh had said about Jeb's health problem, Cash was also concerned that the anonymous call could have been a hoax to lure Jeb out so he could be taken and then used to "negotiate" with Delaney and him.

Or Jeb could have been gunned down.

Webb or whoever was behind the attacks might not realize that Jeb and he didn't exactly have a loving relationship and could have planned Jeb's murder as a way to punish Cash for helping Delaney. Thankfully, none of that had happened.

Cash's next round of questions and concerns dealt with the big picture. A puzzling big picture. Why the heck had Melanie's kidnapper left her by Jeb's ranch? And why hadn't the kidnapper just killed her? Cash had figured the point in taking the woman was to use her as a sort of ransom to get to Delaney. But maybe this had been just another taunt. If so, Cash would take it. Delaney, too. Because a taunt was a hell of a lot better than Delaney's assistant being dead.

"I need to get to the hospital," Delaney insisted. "I have to see Melanie."

Cash had known she was going to want to do that. He would have wanted the same thing in her place. But the problem was getting Delaney safely to and from Dark River. Maybe that had been the point of Melanie's abduction—to get Delaney into a position where she could be attacked, killed or taken.

None of those possibilities were acceptable.

"I can follow you to the hospital," Jeb offered.

"So can I," Agent Curley spoke up. He'd obviously heard the conversation.

Cash didn't bother with introductions. He focused on the best way to go from here to there, and having two backups might not guarantee Delaney's safety, but it would get her there faster because he wouldn't have to wait for one of his deputies to arrive.

"Thanks," Cash told both Jeb and Curley, and he turned back to Jeb. "Was Melanie able to tell you anything about her kidnapping?"

Jeb shook his head. "She was pretty shaken up. In shock, you know."

Cash had figured that was the case, and he knew that Delaney was shaken up as well. "Give me a minute with Delaney," Cash said, speaking to both Jeb and the agent.

Curley nodded. "I'll wait in my car." He stepped around them to go outside and toward his vehicle.

When Jeb headed back to his truck, Cash closed the door so he could lay out some ground rules for Delaney and try to steel her up for what could turn out to be a gut-wrenching visit with Melanie. However, he didn't even get a chance to start because Delaney went straight into his arms. The sound she made was part sob, part relief.

"Melanie's alive," she whispered, her voice hoarse and clogged with everything she was feeling.

Cash sighed and brushed a kiss on the top of her head. He hated to remind her of this, but it had to be done. "Going to see her could be a trap."

"I know. But Melanie's alive."

Yeah, that was definitely a good bottom line. Added to that, Melanie might be able to give him details about who'd taken her. She might be able to ID Webb as her kidnapper. If so, that would convince any naysayers who were still clinging to the notion that Webb was dead.

As if she'd just remembered something, Delaney's head whipped up from his shoulder. "Webb could go after her again."

Cash could give her some reassurance on this. "Jeb said the security guard's with her, and I'll text Leigh to have her assign a protection detail." Something that his sister had already likely done since Leigh was a damn good cop.

"We can't let Webb hurt her again." There was a frantic edge to Delaney's voice now, and he saw that edge mirrored in her eyes. She'd been through the wringer over the past couple of days, and something like this—even though it was good news about Melanie being alive—could break her.

"We won't," he assured her. "Melanie will be guarded, and when she's released from the hospital, she'll be moved to a safe house."

While she blinked back tears, Delaney searched his face as if she was trying to make sure he was telling her the truth. He was. But what he was holding back was that Melanie might already be broken. Some people just couldn't come back from a trauma like this, and Cash was betting that her captor hadn't made any part of this ordeal easy for her.

"We'll get Melanie the help she needs," Cash settled for saying.

Delaney continued to stare at him for several moments, and then she finally released the breath she'd been holding.

And then she kissed him.

Cash sure hadn't seen that coming, but her mouth landed on his, giving him a quick hit of her taste and the heat. Oh, yeah. This was a hit all right, and she didn't stop with just a celebratory peck. This was a full-fledged kiss, long and deep. The kind of kiss they'd usually shared right before they'd landed in bed.

He felt the heat slide through him. Felt his body start to nudge him to take the kiss and run with it. Straight to the bed. But the timing sucked. And that was why Cash forced himself to ease away from her.

Blinking, Delaney looked up at him, her breath gusting against his mouth. She looked like a woman coming out of a dream. A hot woman. One he wanted way too much.

"We should go," Cash said, not only as a reminder to her but also for himself.

She nodded but didn't move. Delaney kept her gaze fixed on him. "I'll never forget what you've done for me. For Melanie," she added.

And that was the perfect thing for her to say to slap him out of his own dream state. Delaney was grateful, and that was the reason she'd kissed him. Well, the heat had probably played into it for her, too, but it was gratitude that had started this particular ball rolling, and that gave Cash another reminder. She'd broken up with him for a reason.

Because of her father.

That reason was still there. Delaney wouldn't be able to live with herself if being with him again caused Gil to take his own life. That meant the kisses and the heat were just a torment right now. One that could complicate things when more than ever he needed a clear head.

"Let's go," he said, drawing his gun.

Cash stepped out onto the porch and glanced around before he led Delaney to the rental truck. As he'd done with their previous trip, he had her sink lower in the seat so she wouldn't be an easy target, and he pulled out of his driveway with both Jeb and Curley following them. Maybe, just maybe, having the close proximity of the other vehicles would discourage someone from attacking.

While he kept watch, Cash used the hands-free function to send a text to Leigh, asking her about the protection detail. As expected, he got a quick response with just one word. Done.

Good. That was one thing off his plate, so he then called Jesse to get his deputy started on a few things.

"You're okay?" Jesse immediately asked.

Cash understood his deputy's edgy tone. Jesse had it for a good reason since he knew all about what had gone on at Delaney's house.

"You're on speaker," Cash informed Jesse. "And Delaney's right here with me."

Of course, that meant Cash wanted Jesse to be mindful of the way he responded, but it caused Delaney to huff. Obviously, she didn't want "mindful," but she was getting it anyway.

"Delaney's assistant is alive and in the Dark River Hospital," Cash explained to Jesse. "Delaney and I are on the way to see her now."

Again, Jesse was quick with the question. "You need backup?"

"No, I have it." And Cash made an uneasy glance in the rearview mirror.

He wasn't exactly comfortable being around Jeb or an FBI agent who might or might not believe Delaney had created a hoax threat. But if it came down to it, Cash figured both men were capable of helping him fight off Webb.

"The FBI wants a look at any suspicious feed from the security cameras," Cash explained. "I'm guessing there hasn't been any or you would have called me."

"I would have," Jesse assured him. "Other than a few ranch hands and the dogs, no one appeared on the camera, but the house is big, and if Ramone knew we were filming him, he could have sneaked out back."

Cash had already come to that same conclusion. There was a barn not far from the house, and Ramone could have slipped in there and left out the back to get to one of the old ranch trails that threaded through the property. From there, he could have had a vehicle waiting for him. A vehicle that he could have used to get to Delaney's, where he left the message and set the explosion.

"Is there anything in Ramone's background about him having experience with building bombs?" Cash asked.

"Nothing, but that doesn't mean he didn't learn that particular skill."

No, it didn't. Which meant Cash wouldn't be taking Ramone off his suspect list anytime soon.

"I did find out something else," Jesse continued a moment later. "Something on that PI you asked me to run a check on."

"Kevin Byers," Cash supplied. He had indeed asked Jesse for a check, but Cash also intended to do some digging of his own. "What'd you find?"

"Well, it's nothing criminal, but it's definitely interesting. Did you know Byers has a connection to Webb? A *personal* connection," Jesse emphasized.

That got Delaney's attention. "Personal? How?" she demanded, taking the questions right out of Cash's mouth.

"This didn't come out in Webb's trial," Jesse explained, "but I found Byers mentioned a couple of times on social media pages that belonged to a friend of Beatrice Stockwell."

Cash instantly recognized the name. She'd been Webb's girlfriend, and Webb had been convicted of killing her during a heated argument.

"This friend, Sasha Mondale, also posted pictures of her together with Beatrice and Byers." Jessie paused. "I contacted Sasha, and she claims Beatrice and Byers were having an affair right around the time Beatrice was killed."

Delaney shook her head. "Webb never mentioned this. Did he know?"

"According to Sasha, he did," Jesse answered.

Delaney huffed. "Why didn't Sasha report that to the cops? It would have gone to motive for Webb killing Beatrice."

"Because Sasha doesn't trust cops. And because Sasha said she was too scared to tell."

"Scared of Webb?" Cash pressed.

"No." Jesse paused a heartbeat. "Of Byers. In fact, Sasha doesn't believe Webb's guilty. She believes Byers is the one who murdered Beatrice."

"Byers," Delaney repeated.

She got a sick feeling in the pit of her stomach. Sick because this was a man she'd been stupid enough to hire. But was he a man who could have also killed? Delaney wasn't so sure of that. She'd seen his temper, and he was a bully, but he'd never been physical with her.

"Webb never confessed to killing Beatrice," Cash muttered. "Did he ever admit it to you?" he asked, and Delaney knew the question was meant for her.

"No. Not an actual confession, but there was a smugness to his denial." And that smugness had carried over into what he'd anticipated the outcome of his trial would be.

Webb had believed with 100 percent certainty that he would be found innocent.

When that hadn't happened, he was enraged, and Delaney had thought she'd seen the true colors of a killer. Unlike Byers, Webb had pushed her and even tried to take a swing at her before the bailiff had restrained him. Webb had shown he could be violent.

But what if he hadn't murdered Beatrice?

That would also account for the rage. Webb could have blamed that miscarriage of justice on her. So it was possible that Webb had been innocent. Of murder, anyway.

"I'll need to talk to Sasha," Delaney insisted.

"I thought you might want to," Jesse said. "I'll text Cash her contact info right now." Seconds later, Cash's phone dinged with the incoming message from Jesse. "Remember, though, that part about her not trusting cops. I'm pretty sure her mistrust extends to lawyers, too."

"Is Sasha credible?" Cash asked. "Is it possible she's got a reason for saying Byers murdered Beatrice?"

"Don't know. She doesn't have a police record, and she appears to be law-abiding. Still, she could have a grudge against Byers. Heck, maybe he was her ex-lover, and she wants to get back at him for having an affair with Beatrice."

That was possible, but Delaney still wanted to talk face-to-face with the woman. How she could make that happen, she didn't know. Cash would agree to a phone conversation, but it'd be a risk for her to meet with Sasha. Unless Delaney could talk the woman into meeting her at the police station. Cash might go along with that as long as he could be there with her.

Cash ended the call with his deputy, and for a few moments, he was quiet, but Delaney figured he was mentally trying to work all of this out. Just as she was trying to do.

He took the exit for Dark River, and Delaney saw the sign. Only five miles. Not far, but this was still a farm road with lots of places for an attacker to hide.

For Byers to hide.

"How and why did you hire Byers?" Cash finally asked.

Delaney wanted all of this out in the open, so she could try to make sense of it, but it still wasn't an easy subject for her. For one, it brought back memories of Webb. It also made her feel like a fool for ever allowing Byers into her life.

"I got the threatening letter," she explained. "And I was also positive someone was following me. So I called a few lawyer friends and asked them for recommendations for a PI. The cops were investigating the letter, but I wanted more. Someone to push hard to find out who'd sent it and who was following me. I figured a PI could do that, and yes, I know that sounds like a slap to the cops, but..." She stopped and lifted her shoulder.

"Cops don't always have time to follow through on threats, especially when there's been no escalation of violence," Cash finished for her.

She nodded before she continued. "I was in the process of narrowing down the list of PIs that I'd gotten when Byers came to my office. He rattled off the name of one of my friends and said he'd heard that I was looking for a PI."

"You didn't verify that with your friend or vet him?" Cash pressed.

Yes, she definitely felt like a fool. "No. I was really shaken up, and I just wanted quick answers. If Webb was following me, I wanted it to stop." She muttered a profanity. "You don't have to tell me how stupid I was—"

"Not stupid," Cash interrupted. "You weren't thinking straight." He dragged in a long breath. "And Byers might have taken advantage of that. Hell, he could have been the reason you weren't thinking straight to begin with, because maybe he was the one following you."

That put ice in her blood, and her stomach didn't just tighten. Everything inside her twisted and knotted. "You really think Byers could be the person trying to kill me?"

Cash stared at her. "What was it he said back at my house? *I just need all of this to go away. I need to put it behind me.*"

Yes, Byers had indeed said that, and it had confused her. Delaney had thought that maybe Byers had meant the bitterness over their failed working relationship, but maybe it was a whole lot more than that.

"You think Byers is feeling guilty because he might have gotten Beatrice killed?" she suggested.

Cash nodded. "If he didn't do the actual killing, Webb might have murdered her if he found out about the affair with Byers. Something like that could make a man obsessed with getting justice."

True, but Byers wasn't obsessed with Webb. The obsession seemed to be for her.

"But if Byers killed Beatrice," Delaney said, "then he could be enraged at me for not getting Webb an acquittal. Maybe that only deepened Byers's feelings of guilt because Webb was behind bars and he wasn't."

However, that didn't explain why Byers would insist that Webb was dead. Or try to pin those threats on her. Again, it could be guilt, not wanting to deal with the fact that Webb might not be "dead" if he hadn't ended up in prison in the first place.

And that went straight back to Delaney.

She wanted to play around with that idea some more, but Delaney pushed it aside when Cash pulled into the parking lot of the Dark River Hospital. Curley and Jeb parked on each side of Cash's rental truck, and they all got out together. The three lawmen flanked her as they hurried inside.

"Melanie's in room 111," Jeb told them. He stayed back while they went to the room.

Delaney was relieved to see an armed deputy standing guard outside the door, and she would thank Leigh for that first chance she got. Obviously, the deputy recognized Cash because he stepped aside.

"I'd like to talk to her when you're done," Curley reminded them, and as Jeb had done, he stayed back in the hall when Cash and she went into the room.

Delaney saw Melanie in the hospital bed, and she felt another avalanche of emotions. Normally, there wasn't a strand of Melanie's long blond hair out of place, but right now it was a tangled mess.

And there was blood in it.

Delaney could also see the cuts and bruises. So many bruises. Melanie's face was covered with them, and her bottom lip was split. There was a splint on her right hand, no doubt to stabilize the broken finger.

"I'm okay," Melanie insisted, probably because she could see that Delaney was shaken to the core. "The doctor said my injuries are superficial."

The physical injuries probably were, but Delaney knew Melanie would be living with this nightmare for a long time. So would she.

Delaney went to her, maneuvering around the IV, so she could lean down and give Melanie a hug. She kept it light, barely making contact, because Delaney didn't want to add to the pain that Melanie was no doubt already feeling.

"I'm so sorry," Delaney whispered, and even though she fought the tears, they came anyway.

"This isn't your fault," Melanie muttered, and she was crying, too. And also shaking. Delaney could feel her trembling as she stroked Melanie's arm. "This is the fault of the man who took me."

The man. Not Webb. Delaney tried not to let her disappointment show when she pulled back from the hug, but she'd hoped—prayed even—that Melanie would be able to name Webb as her abductor.

Cash stepped closer. "Melanie, you remember me?" he asked.

Melanie nodded. "Cash Mercer. You're a cop, and your father's the one who found me."

Cash nodded, too, and eased even closer. "Yeah, and

I want to make sure Delaney and you are safe." He kept his voice low and steady. None of the emotion that Delaney was feeling, but she was certain the emotion was there. Cash was just tamping it down to keep Melanie calm.

"Are we safe?" Melanie asked, her bottom lip quivering.

"You are," Cash assured her.

Delaney wanted to hang on to that, to believe it was true. And in Melanie's case, it probably was. After all, she was alive, and she could have been killed at any point during her captivity. The person who'd taken her hadn't done that, so it likely meant he wouldn't try to kill her again.

"My sister's the sheriff here in Dark River, and she's assigned deputies to protect you," Cash added, and then he paused. "I know this is hard, but anything you can tell me about your kidnapping might help. Do you know who took you?"

Melanie shook her head, a fast jerky motion as if she was trying to fight away the images of what had happened to her. "He came up from behind me. I guess he broke in through the backdoor or window in Delaney's office and then sneaked up on me. The front door was locked because we didn't have any appointments scheduled. I was there to catch up on some paperwork."

"You were at your desk?" Delaney asked, hoping to ease Melanie into the rest of the explanation. It sickened her though to think that Webb or whoever had done this had used her own office door to break in.

"Yes," Melanie confirmed. "I heard footsteps, but before I could turn around and look, it was too late. He bashed me on the head and knocked me out."

"But you're sure it was a man?" Cash pressed.

"Positive." Melanie stopped and took several shallow breaths. "When I came to, my hands were tied and I had on a blindfold, but he was carrying me so I could feel his chest muscles. It was a man," she added in a mutter.

Webb and Ramone were certainly strong enough to lift a woman and carry her to an escape vehicle. But so were plenty of men. In fact, Webb could have hired a thug to do the job for him.

"What else do you remember?" Cash asked.

"Not much. He kept me blindfolded, even when he was hitting me." Melanie cringed, fought for composure as she sat up. "He didn't use his fists. I think it was a leather sap or maybe a billy club. He just kept hitting me," she said, the words rushing out with a fresh round of tears.

Delaney gathered Melanie into her arms. "It's okay. You're safe now," she reminded her.

"I know," Melanie said on a sob. "And I know it's important that I tell you all of this, but I didn't see his face, and he never once spoke to me."

That last part was interesting. And perhaps telling. Maybe he hadn't spoken because Melanie would have recognized his voice. She almost certainly would have recognized Webb's, because Melanie had been in court every day when Webb was on trial. Ditto for Ramone's.

"I don't know where he took me," Melanie continued a moment later. "I think we stayed in the car or truck the whole time until he put me by the side of the road. I figured he was going to leave me to die because I was there for hours before Mr. Mercer came and rescued me."

"Hours," Delaney repeated, looking at Cash.

He was probably thinking the same thing she was.

Jeb would have immediately responded to the call about a woman being at the end of his road. So why hadn't the kidnapper called Jeb sooner if he'd already released her?

Maybe the person who'd taken Melanie wanted to be certain that he'd have time to get away. After all, Jeb was a former lawman, and it was possible Melanie's abductor hadn't wanted to take a risk that Jeb would spot him. The abductor also wouldn't have wanted anyone else noticing him near where he'd left Melanie. That made sense, but it still left her with two big questions.

Who'd taken Melanie and why?

Yes, taking her had tormented Delaney, but the torment would have been much greater if Melanie had been held captive longer. Each minute would have been agony for both women, and the agony would have been intensified if the kidnapper had taunted Delaney with calls or photos so that she'd know the pain and terror Melanie was going through. That would have been much greater punishment than leaving her assistant on the side of the road.

Of course, the ultimate punishment would have been for the kidnapper to kill Melanie. Delaney was beyond thankful that hadn't happened, but she had to wonder why Webb wouldn't have taken that final step and ended Melanie's life.

"Any idea why this man would have left you near my father's ranch?" Cash asked.

Melanie shook her head again. "Like I said, he didn't talk, and I don't know your father." She paused. "You think he did?" She shifted her gaze to Delaney. "Does Webb know Cash's father?"

"I doubt it. Jeb never visited me when Cash and I were together." Now it was Delaney who paused. "But

Jeb was the sheriff of Dark River for a long time. Decades. So it's possible that Webb or Ramone had some kind of run-in with him."

"I'll ask Jeb about that," Cash assured them.

"There's something else," Melanie said, getting Delaney's attention. "I don't know if it's important…"

"Anything you remember could be important," Cash told Melanie when she stopped.

Melanie's bruised forehead bunched up. "I remember his smell," she said. "Strong aftershave. I mean, really strong." She stopped again, probably noticing that both Cash and Delaney had reacted to that.

"Byers," Cash and Delaney said in unison.

Cash pulled out his phone. "I'll get him in for questioning now."

Chapter Nine

Cash cursed under his breath when he saw the latest text from Jesse. A text to let Cash know that no one had been able to get in touch yet with Byers.

The PI hadn't been in his office and wasn't answering his phone. In fact, no one had seen him since he left Cash's ranch the day before. Cash seriously doubted Byers was the victim of foul play, but it was possible he was avoiding being brought in for questioning.

That was why Cash had issued a BOLO, for everyone to be on the lookout. Cops all over would be keeping an eye out for Byers. If Cash got lucky and the PI was found, he could haul his butt in for an interview as a person of interest in Melanie's abduction. Maybe even for attempted murder in the bombing at Delaney's house.

Cash sipped his third cup of coffee and considered that for a moment. A strong aftershave wasn't exactly compelling evidence, but paired with the fact that Byers had purportedly had an affair with Webb's lover, it was enough for the BOLO and an official interview.

Not enough for an arrest, though.

Not nearly enough.

Then again, maybe Byers hadn't done anything to

warrant an arrest. Maybe this all came back to Ramone or Webb, and perhaps one of them had doused himself with aftershave to make sure Melanie didn't pick up on any other scents that might be linked back to them.

Like the smell of a ranch, for example.

A ranch had some pretty distinct odors, and it was possible Webb had driven Melanie to his brother's ranch, beat her to torment Delaney and then taken her to Jeb's place. But Cash had trouble with that theory. Because there was a piece that just didn't fit.

Why had the kidnapper left Melanie at Jeb's?

That was the question that had gone around in Cash's mind all night, and it had cost him some sleep. Of course, the biggest reason he hadn't slept had been Delaney. She'd stayed in his guest room, and his body hadn't wanted to let him forget that she was just across the hall. But he'd ignored the ache he had for her, because she hadn't needed sex. She'd needed rest, and he was hoping she had gotten more than he had. However, one look at her when she stepped in the kitchen, and he knew that she hadn't.

Wearing loaner jeans and a pale blue shirt that Cash had gotten from his sister, Delaney went straight to the coffeepot, poured a cup and cooled it down with some tap water so she could chug it like medicine.

"Melanie and I have been emailing this morning," she said, staring down into her cup. "It's early, but she's awake."

It was indeed early, only half past six, and the sun wasn't even up yet. But Cash suspected Melanie hadn't had a peaceful night's sleep, either.

"How's she doing?" Cash asked.

Delaney sighed. "About as well as can be expected, I

suppose. She's been sending an email to me about every ten minutes since midnight."

Cash wasn't surprised about the emails. He'd loaned Delaney a laptop and made sure that Melanie had one as well so they could do just that. He figured they needed to have those email chats and that it would help soothe them both. Well, as much as they could be soothed, considering there was a snake who wanted to do Delaney even more harm.

"I've arranged for the safe house for Melanie," Cash told Delaney. "She'll be moved there once doctors release her."

Hopefully, a release that wouldn't happen until Melanie had agreed to speak to a counselor. The kind of trauma she'd gone through could eat away at her if she didn't get help.

It was the same for Delaney.

Cash was still deciding the best way to convince her to speak to a professional. She'd probably fight it after the experience she'd had with the reaction to the meds, but she needed it to get past what had happened. What she needed more, however, was safety, and that was at the top of Cash's to-do list.

"I thought you might come to my room last night," she said, finally lifting her gaze from her coffee to meet his.

"Trust me, I considered it. *Strongly considered it,*" he emphasized. "But I thought you needed rest more than you needed me."

Delaney didn't jump to agree with him about that, and it gave his body a very bad message. A message that Delaney might need him to the point where he could haul her off to bed.

With both hands still wrapped around her mug, she went to him. Her eyes never left his when she leaned down and kissed him. Even though he'd seen it coming, the jolt of it still hit him damn hard.

A punch of pure lust.

It was something he often felt for Delaney, but it had a dangerous edge to it now. They were also revved from the danger and looking for an outlet to deal with the fact they'd nearly been killed in the bombing. But Cash didn't want to be an outlet. Not when it could cost them focus.

And more.

There was that whole issue with Delaney's father. Cash could dive into the kiss headfirst. Could probably do that hauling her off to bed as well. But doing those things would come with a huge price tag, and he wasn't sure he should just offer up his heart for another stomping. Still, he didn't pull back, *couldn't* pull back, when Delaney deepened the kiss.

That tore down any shred of resistance, and Cash put aside his coffee cup so he could hook an arm around her and draw her even closer to him. Mouth to mouth and breath to breath. She didn't make any attempt to move away from him. Just the opposite. She practically dropped her cup on the table next to his, slid her hands around his neck and kept on kissing him.

Cash forgot all about high price tags, stomped-on hearts and clouded judgment. Hell, he wasn't sure he could even think straight, but he knew something for certain. He wanted Delaney, and he was willing to pay whatever price there was to have her.

Obviously, Delaney was dealing with her own needs for him, because she moved right onto his lap when

Cash guided her there. Now they were kissing and touching A lethal combination for foreplay, but this felt a whole lot more than just foreplay

She tasted hot. Like things forbidden. Things he should resist. But wouldn't. Couldn't. And she felt as good as she tasted. Her body trembled beneath his touch, and her breath hitched when he slid his hand down the front of her shirt to cup her breasts.

Cash had been out of it when they'd done all the touching and kissing two nights ago after she'd shown up at his house. But he wasn't out of it now. He was feeling and taking everything in. Her silky skin. Her scent. The little sounds of need that were coming from her throat.

He got more of those sounds when he flicked his thumb over her nipple, and she pressed her forehead to his. "I know this is a bad idea."

So did he. Cash wasn't disputing that, but he could justify that a round of good, sweaty sex would clear the air between them. It would burn off some of this aching need they had for each other.

Or not.

It was just as possible that sex would only cause the need to soar, but Cash didn't see he had much of a choice in this. He wanted Delaney, and he wanted her now.

He lowered his arm from her waist to her butt, pushing her center right against his erection. It was a fit that nearly took off the top of his head, and it would have almost certainly led to more kissing and more touching if he hadn't heard the sound over the throbbing in his ears. Not one of Delaney's silky moans of need. No. It was his phone ringing.

Cash cursed the interruption. He wanted to ignore the call and finish things with Delaney. But he couldn't do that. Not with an active investigation where her life was at risk.

"We'll pick this up later," he grumbled. "Promise."

He eased Delaney back, breaking the intimate contact between them. Ignoring the protests of his body and the groan of complaint that Delaney made, he took his phone from his pocket. One look at the screen, and he knew it was a call he'd have to take.

"It's Byers," Cash relayed to Delaney.

She groaned again but moved off his lap as Cash answered the call. He also put it on speaker.

"You put out a BOLO on me?" Byers snarled the moment he was on the line.

"I did." Cash also snarled, and he knew his tone was a heck of a lot meaner. "You're a person of interest in Melanie Adams's kidnapping, and I need to interview you."

That must've stunned Byers into silence, because he didn't make a quick comeback. "What are you talking about?"

"Melanie Adams," Cash repeated, speaking slowly. "She's Delaney's assistant, and you're a person of interest in her abduction and assault."

"You've lost your mind." Byers was back to snarling. "I didn't kidnap her. I don't even know her."

"Well, she knows you." And Cash decided to try to press some of the PI's buttons. "Or rather she got a whiff of you. That aftershave you wear is distinct. You probably should have showered before you kidnapped anyone."

"I didn't kidnap her," Byers practically yelled. "I don't have any reason to do that."

"Oh, yes, you do," Cash argued. "You want to get back at Delaney. But I can't figure out if that's because she fired you or because you despise her."

"That's nonsense—"

"Beatrice Stockwell," Cash interrupted, stopping what would have no doubt been a tirade. And, yeah, it stopped Byers, all right.

"What about her?" Byers asked. The snarl was gone, and in its place was a quiet kind of concern.

Cash had no intention of ratting out Beatrice's friend Sasha. He couldn't be certain that Byers wouldn't fly off the handle and go after the woman. So he kept things simple.

"You had an affair with Beatrice." Cash stated it as fact. "An affair that was going on while she was still living with Webb. Don't bother to lie and deny it because I have proof. That's why there's a BOLO out on you. That's why you'll be coming in for questioning. First, by me, but I'm betting the FBI will want in on this."

There was a long silence, and Cash would have loved to see Byers's expression. Part of him wished he'd waited to drop this at the interview, but Cash hadn't been sure that Byers would actually show up in Clay Ridge. Byers might just go on the run. If he did, at least Cash would have had this chance to confront him. To let Byers know that he was sussing out the reason the PI was so adamant about Delaney being guilty of sending that threatening letter.

"Yes, I had a relationship with Beatrice," Byers finally said. "But that has nothing to do with Delaney or her assistant."

"You're sure about that?" Cash taunted. "Because I have a theory that you're riled about Delaney not getting Webb acquitted of the murder charges. And I think you're riled because in your guilty little mind, you know Webb is innocent. You know that because you're the one who murdered Beatrice."

"I did not," Byers shouted, and he spewed out a string of profanities. Cash just let the man wind himself down. "I didn't kill anyone. Webb murdered Beatrice, and I wanted justice for her. Justice that didn't happen because that SOB Ramone is a free man."

Bingo. There it was. The little nugget that Cash had been waiting to hear. Obviously, Delaney had, too, because she was staring at the phone. She released a long, hard breath.

"That sounds like motive for the attacks and threats against Delaney," Cash told Byers. "Ramone is free, and you want revenge. You've decided that Delaney is the target of your revenge."

Again, there was a long silence. "Are you going to arrest me?" Byers came out and asked.

"That depends on what you say during your interview. I want you at the Clay Ridge PD at one o'clock this afternoon. If you're not there, I'll get a warrant for your apprehension and arrest."

"I'll be there," Byers snapped. "With my lawyers. You're not getting away with this, *Sheriff.* I won't be your scapegoat."

Byers ended the call abruptly. No surprise there. Cash hadn't expected the PI to stay on the line as long as he had. A smart man would have ended the call the moment he realized he was in legal hot water.

"You really believe Byers could have been the one who killed Beatrice?" Delaney asked.

Cash heard the slight tremble in her voice. Saw the worry in her eyes. Not worry for Byers. But worry because Webb might have been innocent after all. And she would blame herself for an innocent man being sent to prison.

He stood, went to her and pulled her into his arms. This wasn't the hot and fast embrace when she'd been on his lap. He hoped his arms would give her some comfort. What he had to say possibly could, too.

"There was enough evidence to convict Webb," he reminded her. "You didn't send him to jail. A jury did."

She nodded, sighed. "As his lawyer, I really did do everything I could to make sure he wasn't convicted."

"I know you did."

And because she needed it, he kissed her again. Yes, this was for comfort, but still he deepened it. It didn't send them into the rush to haul each other off to bed, but when he eased back, Cash was pleased that she was a little breathless.

"Better?" he asked.

"Your kisses don't make things better," she muttered.

"Ouch," Cash joked. Well, partially joked. It did sting.

"I mean they don't make this better." She motioned toward his phone. "Your kisses make me wish all was well, that Melanie hadn't been hurt and that we could be cocooned in our own bed."

That took away some of the sting, and he smiled. Kissed her again. Too bad they couldn't do the cocoon thing because his body was still aching for her. He probably would have tried to soothe that ache with another kiss, but his blasted phone rang again. Some of his annoyance vanished, though, when he saw Jesse's name on the screen. His deputy could be calling because of trouble.

"Is everything okay?" Cash asked the moment he answered.

"I just got a call from Lubbock PD," Jesse explained. "They canvassed Delaney's neighbors after the bombing, and they all claim they didn't see anything suspicious. But one of her neighbors pulled a double shift at work, and didn't hear about the bombing until he got home. He called the cops a little while ago to tell them he had seen someone go into Delaney's house."

Cash latched on to the hope that this could be the break they needed to ID Webb. "Please tell me the neighbor got a good look at the guy."

"Oh, he did," Jesse verified. "He said he thought the guy could be there for repairs or such, but that he got a bad feeling about it. That's why he took out his phone and snapped a picture."

"A picture," Delaney repeated in a whisper, and there was plenty of hope in her voice, too.

"I'm sending you the image now," Jesse explained.

A moment later, Cash's phone dinged, and the photo loaded. He enlarged it, zooming right in on the man who was at Delaney's front door. The guy's head was turned, as if he was looking around for someone who might spot him, and the angle gave them a good view of the man's face.

Hell.

Chapter Ten

Delaney could have sworn her heart stopped. It just stopped. And the breath rushed from her body.

Because it was a picture of her father.

"When was the photo taken?" Cash asked Jesse.

"About two hours before the bomb went off," his deputy promptly answered, which told Delaney it was a question he'd already asked Lubbock PD.

She frantically picked through the memory of the conversation Cash and she had had with her father, and recalled that Gil hadn't said anything about going to her house during that time.

Nothing.

Gil had told them he'd come to her house to leave a note, because he was worried about her, but he hadn't said anything about going there two hours earlier. But maybe he had done just that and then had forgotten to mention it.

"Does the neighbor know if Gil actually went into the house?" Cash pressed.

"He said he did. The neighbor considered calling the cops then and there, but he said the guy had a key, so he figured it was okay."

Cash looked at her, and she understood what he

wanted to know. Did her father have a key? "Yes, he had a spare key," Delaney answered.

"The neighbor isn't sure how long Delaney's father stayed in the house," Jesse went on, "but he was still inside when the neighbor left for work. The neighbor estimates that was at least ten minutes, because he was watching out the window while he was having his coffee."

Cash muttered something that she didn't catch and scrubbed his hand over his face. His expression was a mix of dread and frustration. And she knew why. Even if her father had done nothing wrong, Cash was still going to have to talk to him. That wouldn't be pleasant for any of them.

"See if Lubbock PD will give you the neighbor's name so Delaney and I can talk to him," Cash told his deputy. "I'll get it touch with Gil now and see what he has to say about all of this."

Cash ended the call with Jesse and handed her his phone. "Go ahead and press in your dad's number. If he hears my voice first, he might just hang up."

She couldn't argue with that. He probably wouldn't take a call from Cash. But there was the possibility Gil would do the same to her. Their conversation at her house hadn't ended all that well. Still, that wasn't going to stand in the way of getting the answers they needed. She had to know why her father had gone into her house and if he'd seen that threat that'd been painted on her wall.

Or if he'd been the one to leave the threat.

Delaney pushed that disturbing possibility aside and pressed in Gil's number. She held her breath, waited, but he didn't answer. Not on the first ring, the second or even the third. Finally, he picked up. Except it wasn't her father.

"Trevor Salvetti," the PI greeted.

Since Delaney hadn't expected him to answer, it took her a couple of seconds to regroup. "This is Delaney. I need to speak to my father."

"Welcome to the club," Salvetti muttered. "I was about to call you to let you know that your father sneaked out during the night."

"Where is he?" Delaney blurted out.

"I have no idea. He left his phone, probably so it couldn't be traced. I don't even know when he left. Around midnight, he said he was headed to bed, and he went to his room. When I didn't hear him stirring this morning, I went to check on him, and he was gone."

Delaney wanted to curse. Or yell. The reason she'd hired a PI was so her father would be safe, and now he wasn't. In fact, it was possible that something horrible had happened to him.

"Could Webb have kidnapped him?" Delaney came out and asked. As much as she hated to hear the answer, she had to know.

"I don't think so. There's no sign of a struggle, and it appears he went out through the window in his bedroom." The PI groaned. "I'm so sorry about this. Gil didn't show any signs of running, or I would have kept a closer watch on him."

Her father had no doubt purposely made sure not to telegraph any moves to make the PI suspicious. But why had he run?

And better yet, where the heck was he?

"Did Gil take his truck?" Cash asked, and then he

identified himself so that the PI would know he was talking to a cop.

"No. It's still here. Unless he had another vehicle stashed somewhere nearby, he left on foot."

That only caused Delaney's fears to skyrocket. Her father lived over two miles outside of town, and if he'd walked, Webb could have spotted him and taken him. Of course, there was no proof that Webb was actually after Gil, and Delaney had to hang on to that. If she didn't, the panic was going to eat away at her until she couldn't think straight.

"Did your father ever mention that he's had blackouts?" Salvetti asked.

"No," she answered without hesitating. If he had, she would have remembered. "I know he still drinks, and sometimes he passes out from it."

"It's more than that," Salvetti said. "We were talking last night before he went to bed, and he told me he'd had a couple of blackouts, times when he'd woken up and didn't know how he'd gotten there."

Sweet heaven. That terrified her even more. "Could that have happened last night? Could he have had so much to drink that he left the house without realizing what he was doing?"

"I doubt it. I couldn't find any bottles of booze in his room. Plus, if he'd been drunk, I doubt he would have made such a clean getaway. He probably would have stumbled or even fallen when he crawled out the window."

That was true. Her father wouldn't have gotten drunk and then cleaned up the liquor bottles. Still, that didn't rule out foul play. After all, Webb had managed to break in through her office to get to Melanie. Webb could have done the same at her father's house, especially since Gil didn't even have a security system.

"I'm taking his phone and heading out to look for him now," the PI explained. "If I spot him, I'll call you. It would help if you could text me the names of any friends he might have gone to."

"He doesn't have any friends," Delaney said on a sigh. It sounded pitiful, but it was the truth. "I can give you the contact info for his boss."

"I've got that, and I'll drive over to the ranch and ask if anyone's seen him." The PI paused. "If Gil's actually on the run, though, he probably wouldn't go where he knows we'd look."

True. And that meant he could be anywhere. Midnight was hours ago, so he could have already had at least a six-hour head start. He could have gotten into Lubbock, and from there, ended up heaven knew where.

"Any idea how much money Gil would have had on hand?" Salvetti asked.

"Probably not much," Delaney admitted. "I think he lives pretty much paycheck to paycheck." Still, he could have squirreled away enough for a hotel or a bus ticket. But that brought her back around full circle.

Why would he have done that?

Why would he have run from the PI she'd hired to protect him? Or maybe her father was actually running from her.

"Call me if you hear from him or find out where he is," Delaney emphasized, and she ended the call so she could hand Cash back his phone.

Cash sat there, the muscles tight on his face and with a hitch in his breathing. Like her, he was obviously trying to work out Gil's motive for running, and judging from the profanity he muttered, he wasn't having any better luck with that than she had. Or maybe Cash had come up with a reason he knew she wasn't going to like.

"I need to get someone over to your father's house," Cash finally said. "A cop, maybe a CSI."

Her chest suddenly got very tight. "You think Webb kidnapped him?"

Cash looked her straight in the eyes. "It's possible that Webb lured him out…"

"But?" she prompted when he stopped and muttered another curse.

He took a deep breath before he continued. "I also need to know if there are any signs that Gil built a bomb in his house."

Delaney had no choice. She dropped down into the chair. Because if she hadn't, she would have fallen flat on her face.

"I'm not saying for sure that Gil blew up your house," Cash continued. "But it's something that needs to be ruled out."

She managed a headshake. "Why would you even consider he's done this?"

Cash slid his hand over hers. "Because of the timing of that text I got. *If you want to find me, go to Delaney's house*," he recited. *"I left something that oughta give her a nightmare or two."*

Delaney felt another wave of fear slide over her. "Webb sent that text," she murmured.

"Maybe. Probably," Cash amended. "But I have to rule out that your father sent it to lure me to your house so I'd be there when the bomb went off. I need to question him, Delaney," he quickly added. "I need to bring him in for an official interview."

"Like Byers," she said. Mercy, it felt as if her throat had clamped shut, making it hard for her to breathe. "They're both suspects."

"They're both persons of interest who I need to rule out," he corrected.

But there was a flip side to that, and Delaney knew it. If he couldn't rule them out, then they were indeed suspects.

"Even if you find my father, he won't want you to interview him," she reminded Cash.

Cash nodded. "I'll have Jesse or one of the other deputies do it. But first, we have to find him." He texted Jesse, and Delaney saw that Cash was requesting a BOLO on her father.

"You really believe there's a possibility that my father could have wanted to kill you?" she asked. Delaney tried to tamp down the tremble in her voice. And she tried to blink back the tears that were threatening to spill.

"You tell me," he said. Not as a challenge. His voice was gentle. His words, a plea for her to go back through that conversation they'd had outside her house.

She got up, went to the window and stared out while she considered everything she'd just learned. Her father's blackouts. Him leaving his phone behind. The anger that had been in his voice and on his face when he'd confronted them at her house. And there was no doubt about it—that had been a confrontation. Then, there were his own words.

I can't go through this again.

I can't watch this happen.

Had her father's hatred for Cash and the possibility of them getting back together sent Gil over the edge?

As much as it twisted away at her, there was only one answer. An answer she had to give Cash.

"Yes, it's possible," she admitted.

She stood there, watching the beautiful sunrise come up over the pastures. A beauty that didn't ease the ache inside her one bit. Because, yes, it was possible.

And more.

Much more.

Had her father also left that horrible message for her on the foyer wall? She didn't want to believe it was possible, but Delaney couldn't put blinders on and hope that he was innocent. That way of thinking could get Cash killed. Because if her father had truly lost it, then she wouldn't be his first target.

Cash would.

She was trying so hard to fight back those blasted tears that she didn't hear Cash walk up behind her. However, she felt his arms when they went around her. This embrace didn't have the heat, but it was very much needed. Cash had always been a rock for her, and right now, she needed someone to lean on so she could get through this. She'd need him even more if it turned out that her father had intended to kill.

"I swear, I won't read anything into what you're doing right now," she said, pressing the back of her head to the crook of his neck.

She felt him go a little stiff. "What do you mean?"

"This." She ran her hand over his arm. The arm that was giving her so much comfort. "I know you're caught up in the emotion of us nearly being killed, but it doesn't erase what I did to you."

He didn't ask her to clarify what she was referring to. No need. She'd crushed Cash when she'd ended their engagement, and she hadn't told him the truth of why she'd done it, because she hadn't wanted him to confront her father. It was only going to make this situation more bitter if it turned out that Gil was the one behind the attacks.

"You still have feelings for me," he threw out there.

She did. No doubts about that. But it was more than feelings. Delaney was still in love with him, but now wasn't the time to drop that bombshell on him. Especially since it could mess things up even more than they already were.

Cash's phone rang again, the sound slicing through the silence. And the moment. Cash eased back and frowned when he saw the screen.

"It's from Dark River PD," he muttered.

Delaney whirled around, her attention going straight to his phone because this could be about Melanie. Thankfully, Cash put the call on speaker.

"Sheriff Mercer," the woman said when Cash answered. "I'm Deputy Dawn Farley. I work for your sister, and I'm on guard duty at the hospital. We've had an, uh, incident."

"Is Melanie all right?" Delaney blurted out.

"I'm guessing you're Melanie's boss?" the deputy asked.

"Yes, I'm Delaney Archer," she snapped, annoyed that she had to wait even a second for what could be critical info. "Is Melanie all right?" Delaney repeated.

"She's safe," Deputy Farley assured her.

That should have at least helped Delaney tamp down the surge of adrenaline, but it didn't. "What kind of incident?"

"Someone sent her flowers," the deputy answered

after a heavy sigh, "and the card said—and I'm quoting—*I'm not finished with you. Let's play again real soon.*"

Oh, mercy. Delaney's legs went weak again, and she steadied herself by leaning against the kitchen counter. But she also felt something more than the wobbliness and the fresh adrenaline. There was anger. Hot and raw. Because Melanie didn't deserve to be put through this.

"Who delivered the flowers?" Cash asked.

"A man named Noah Carson. He's not much more than a kid, Sheriff. And he's not behind the threat. He's just the person who makes deliveries. But get this, the person who ordered the flowers didn't do it over the phone. It was a man, and he did it in person at a Lubbock florist. He came in last night right before the shop was due to close, and he asked that the flowers be delivered first thing this morning."

Everything inside Delaney tightened. Because she was afraid the deputy was about to say her father had placed the order. But Delaney just couldn't see him making that kind of threat. If Gil was behind the attacks, then he'd have no reason to taunt her with Melanie.

"Please tell me you've got a good description of the man," Cash said.

"I've got a good description," Deputy Farley verified. "Your sister had a couple of Lubbock uniforms go to the florist, and after hearing the clerk describe the guy, they showed her Webb's picture. The clerk says she's about ninety percent sure that Webb was the one who bought the flowers."

Delaney got a quick hit of relief that it hadn't been her father, but the relief vanished as fast as it had come.

Because this was proof that Webb was alive. Alive and trying to make her life a living hell by using someone like Melanie.

"Are there security cameras in the flower shop?" Cash asked.

"No. But Lubbock PD is checking to see if Webb appeared on any of the cameras from nearby shops. He paid cash," the deputy continued, "so he didn't leave a paper trail, but the clerk said when he left he got into a black truck that he'd parked right out front. Sorry, he didn't get a look at the plates, but he noticed a big crack across the front of the windshield."

That wasn't the best of descriptions when trying to track down a killer, but maybe it'd be enough for someone at Lubbock PD to spot the truck. And Webb.

"Which direction was Webb heading when he left?" Cash pressed.

"East," the deputy readily provided. "But there's a big intersection less than a half mile from the florist. Lubbock PD will have a look at traffic cams. We might get lucky."

Yes, and they desperately needed some luck. "Please don't let Webb get to Melanie again," Delaney said.

"I won't. But this will probably speed up her going to the safe house. She's just too spooked to stay here, and I don't blame her. It'll be a lot easier to keep Webb away if we're not in a hospital where there are plenty of strangers coming and going."

Delaney agreed. She just hoped that Melanie was well enough to make the trip.

"Keep me posted about anything Lubbock PD finds on those cams," Cash added to the deputy before he ended the call.

"I won't be able to see Melanie once she's at the safe house, will I?" Delaney asked him.

Cash shook his head. "It'd be too dangerous. If Webb managed to follow us there, it could put both you and Melanie in danger."

She'd known that was what he would say, but it still gnawed away at her. Melanie had gotten hurt because of her, and Delaney wouldn't even be able to comfort her. Then again, maybe that was for the best. She wasn't sure how much comfort she could give when every nerve in her body was firing on all cylinders.

Delaney tried to calm those nerves so she could process all the info spinning in her head. Webb's sighting meant he was definitely involved in Melanie's kidnapping. More involved in everything that had happened. If she went with that theory, then Webb had been the one who'd left that message for her in the foyer. So maybe her father's visit meant nothing.

Except that he hadn't said anything about it.

Maybe his visit had been part of one of his blackouts? She prayed that was it. Because a blackout was far better than the alternative, that her father had plotted to murder Cash and had nearly gotten them both killed in the process.

"I want to go ahead and update Curley about this," Cash said, drawing her attention back to him. He went through his dispatcher to get the agent's number and made the call.

Curley answered right away, and Cash filled him in on the flowers. And then told him about her father's disappearance.

"I can help," Curley volunteered. "Let me see if I can speed up the process of getting that traffic cam feed. I can also nudge a few contacts to try to get someone out looking for Gil." He paused. "You think he left because he's guilty of something?"

That was the million-dollar question. Too bad Delaney didn't know the answer.

"I need to rule him out," Cash said. "Ditto for Byers. I need to make sure they didn't have a part in this."

"Can't say about Delaney's father," Curley answered, "but something popped on Byers."

"What?" Cash and she asked in unison.

"I got access to Delaney's medical report on her allergic reaction to the medication."

Of all the things Delaney had thought the agent might say, that wasn't one of them. "Why?"

"Because I didn't like the timing," Curley readily admitted. "I just thought it was too pat that you'd have that reaction right about the time Webb was taunting you with those threats."

"I agree," Cash said. "What'd you find out, and how does this connect to Byers?"

"According to the doctor who treated Delaney after she collapsed, he thought she'd taken some kind of drug that caused disorientation and maybe hallucinations. The lab results that just came back confirmed it. It was a strong anti-seizure medication."

Delaney frantically shook her head. "I don't have seizures, and I didn't take anything like that."

"Not knowingly," Curley agreed. "But I believe someone switched your meds. You had the bottle in your office, right?"

"That's right. I keep it in my center desk drawer, and I have another bottle at home." And she stopped. Because Melanie's kidnapper had broken in through her office. Webb or someone else had also gotten into Delaney's home to leave that message in the foyer. If he'd done that once, he could have done it to replace the meds.

Her stomach was twisting and knotting again, too, and it sickened her to think that someone had not only broken in but had tampered with her meds. The person who'd done that could have killed her.

So why hadn't he?

Because this was yet more taunting? In this case, it had gone well beyond that because she'd ended up in the hospital.

"So why do you think Byers is connected?" Delaney asked the agent.

"Because he does have seizures," Curley explained. "And the specific medication that was in your system is the one he's been prescribed."

Chapter Eleven

Cash ended the call with Agent Curley, and he did the only thing he could do. He pulled Delaney into his arms and tried to give her what comfort he could. Which probably wasn't much.

Every detail they learned had to feel like another blow to her. Webb, Byers or whoever the hell was doing this was nipping away at her. Bite after greedy bite. Cash wanted to promise her that he'd end these taunts. The threat. But first he had to learn who was responsible.

"Byers," Delaney said with her head on his shoulder.

Yes, Byers was definitely high on the suspect list, but Cash didn't want to zoom in only on the PI. Shifting the investigation solely to Byers could turn out to be a big mistake along with letting a killer get a chance at, well, killing.

"Webb could have stolen Byers's meds and put them in your pill bottle," Cash pointed out.

Her father could have done that as well, but Cash couldn't see Gil going in that direction. If Gil was the culprit, then Delaney wasn't the target. Cash was. But that didn't mean it wasn't her father who set the explosive. Webb could be the one responsible for everything else.

"It's possible that Webb even knew about Byers's seizures," Cash went on. "We don't know if Beatrice told Webb anything about her side lover."

Delaney eased back, her eyes meeting his, and she nodded. "If Webb found out about the affair, he could have beaten or threatened her until she gave him info about Byers. Once Webb had a name, he'd be able to do some research." But she stopped and shook her head. "It's not easy to hack into medical records."

"He wouldn't have had to hack. It was several days before Webb was arrested for Beatrice's murder, and Webb could have used that time to stalk Byers. He maybe even broken into Byers's office or home. He could have broken in again after he escaped jail and stolen some of the meds then. Byers might not have even noticed."

Delaney stayed quiet a moment, obviously trying to work that through, and she finally nodded. Then she sighed. It wasn't a weak sound, though. It had some anger in it.

"Webb is playing a very sick game," she said. Her voice was no longer shaky. "And I want him to pay for everything he's done."

Cash couldn't agree more. He just hoped he could find Webb before the man could do any more damage. Ditto for finding her father. For starters, though, maybe he could get some answers from Byers when he interviewed him at one.

And that brought Cash to another concern.

"I can get one of my deputies to interview Byers," he said. "But I'd prefer to do it myself."

"Of course," she readily agreed. "I want to be there. I want to hear what he has to say, especially when you ask him about the meds."

Cash wasn't surprised that she'd want to be in on that. After all, those meds had caused her all kinds of trouble. But being at the interview could be trouble, too.

"We could be attacked on the road," he pointed out. "In fact, Webb might be waiting for us to drive to the station."

Delaney paused only a heartbeat. "I still want to be there."

Cash wasn't surprised by that, either. There was plenty enough fight in Delaney for her to want to see this through to the end. But he was going to have to take some serious precautions, and that started with a call to Jesse so Cash could get backup for the drive. However, before he could contact his deputy, his phone rang, and this time the name and number on the screen were familiar.

"It's Leigh," he relayed to Delaney. "Please tell me you have good news," Cash added to his sister once he'd answered the call.

"Well, it's news. Not sure you'll think it's good, though."

That caused Cash to groan. "What is it?"

"Lubbock PD got a fast hit from the traffic cams on that black truck with the cracked windshield. The one Webb got in outside the florist," she added. "The cams picked it up a couple of times, and they got a good enough image to confirm that it was Webb behind the wheel."

Even though Cash had expected the news, it still

packed a wallop. And it confirmed that Webb had a part in at least the threats and the taunts.

"The plates are bogus," Leigh went on. "No surprise there. I suspect it's also stolen and that Webb will be ditching it soon."

Cash figured the same thing. Webb had to have known there was the possibility that he'd be spotted on camera. Heck, he probably wanted that since it played into the fear he was trying to build for Delaney. But now that he'd been spotted, Webb couldn't risk the cops noticing those bogus tags and pulling him over.

"There's more," Leigh continued a moment later. "The last of the traffic cams show that Webb took the exit that could lead to Clay Ridge. *Could*," she emphasized. "He could have gone up a mile or two and circled back. He might not be anywhere near Clay Ridge right now."

No, but Cash had the sickening feeling that Webb would eventually end up here. After all, Webb meant to come after her. If he didn't have confirmation that Delaney was indeed in Clay Ridge, then he could easily find out.

"Uh, one more thing," Leigh said a moment later. "You'll hear it sooner or later, so I wanted you to hear it from me. I'm engaged to Cullen Brodie."

Cash didn't laugh. Or groan. But a couple of months ago, that was exactly what he would have done. There was a long-standing feud between the Brodies and the Mercers. It was a Texas version of the Hatfields and McCoys. There was no way in hell that Jeb or Cullen's father, Bowen, would approve of such an engagement, but Leigh and Cullen had obviously managed to put that aside.

Something that Cash wished Delaney could do.

Her father's bad blood was with Jeb, but Cash doubted Bowen would be thinking suicide over his son's engagement to Jeb's daughter. Nope. Bowen would just be pissed off, maybe even disown Cullen, but obviously Leigh and Cullen hadn't allowed that possibility to get in the way of Cullen popping the question and Leigh accepting.

"Congrats," Cash told his sister. "You're happy?"

"Yes," Leigh said so fast that it caused Cash to smile. His sister wasn't known for her big displays of affection. Probably because she'd learned to hide her feelings from all the hurt Jeb had caused. "I love Cullen," she added, sounding very much like an over-the-moon bride-to-be.

"I'm happy for you," Delaney muttered, drawing Cash's attention back to her.

Oh, man. There was hurt in her eyes, and he knew it went back to their own engagement. The one she'd broken to save her father. Delaney was probably indeed happy for his sister, but this brought back the old painful memories. Not just for Delaney but for him, too.

"Thanks," Leigh answered. "For about two seconds, I considered not accepting Cullen's proposal because I knew the trouble it'd cause for our families. Just for about two seconds." She paused. "But I'm not giving up Cullen over bad feelings that should have been put to rest years ago."

Leigh didn't add that she thought it was something they, too, should consider, but Cash could almost hear the words come out of his sister's mouth. Wise words, indeed. And it almost felt like a personal challenge to

Cash, for him to find a way to have Delaney back in his life and not have it ruin her relationship with Gil.

"I'll call you if I get anything else on the traffic cams," Leigh assured Delaney before ending the call.

Cash put his phone away, took a deep breath and looked up at Delaney. She still wasn't rock-solid, but it was probably best if he didn't hug her again right now. The air seemed charged between them. It was practically zinging with emotions, and yes, heat. Best to keep his hands and mouth off her and dive into the work.

"I want to go through all the reports from Lubbock PD," he explained. "I need to find out if their bomb experts have been able to get anything from the explosives that blew up your house."

She nodded. "You mean like a bomber's signature."

That was indeed what he meant. There wouldn't be trace or fibers. Not likely anyway. But bomb makers often had a specific style that could sometimes be used to ID them. It was possible that Webb had made the bomb, but since he didn't have any experience in that area, he could have hired someone. Someone with a signature. If they found the person who'd made the bomb, it could lead them to Webb.

"What can I do to help?" Delaney asked. "Give me something to do," she amended. "I can't just sit around here and do nothing."

He understood that. Cash didn't want too much thinking time for anything other than the investigation. "You can read the reports from your neighbors as to what they saw and didn't see yesterday before that bomb went off. Maybe something one of them said will ring a bell."

It was a long shot, but right now everything they had fell into that particular category.

Cash set up Delaney with a laptop at the kitchen table. However, they'd barely gotten started when his phone rang again. Not Leigh this time but rather Stoney, his ranch hand.

"You got a visitor," Stoney said when Cash answered.

"Not Byers," he grumbled. And if it was the PI, Cash intended to arrest him.

"No. It's your new neighbor." There was plenty of disdain in Stoney's voice. "Ramone Bennison's here."

That sent Cash and Delaney to the living room so they could look out the front window. It was indeed Ramone, and he was sitting in his truck in Cash's driveway. Stoney and his son were there, too, and both were armed with rifles.

"What the heck does he want?" Cash asked.

"He said he needs to talk to you, and that it's real important," Stoney answered. "Ramone said he's got something to tell you about his brother."

DELANEY STARED AT RAMONE, who was staring back at them. He didn't have the dogs with him this time, and it appeared he was alone in the truck. Of course, she couldn't help but think that maybe he had hired thugs—or Webb—hiding low on the seat.

But an attack like that would be stupid.

After all, Cash was armed and so were the two ranch hands who were keeping their attention nailed to Ramone. If Ramone was foolish enough to try to fire shots at them, he'd soon be a dead man.

Cash was studying Ramone, too, and he swore under his breath. "Did he happen to say why he didn't just call me with this *real important* information?" he asked Stoney.

"I asked, and he said this needed to be face-to-face," Stoney answered. "You want me to send him on his way or insist he call you?"

Cash stayed quiet a moment, obviously considering that, and while he was still thinking it over, Ramone stepped out from his truck. He put his hands in the air, maybe to show them he wasn't armed. Or at least he didn't have hold of a weapon, but that didn't mean he wasn't carrying.

"Webb called me," Ramone shouted, looking straight at Cash. "You need to hear what he had to say."

"He's not coming in the house," Cash concluded several long moments later. "And you're not going out there with me."

Delaney caught on to his arm. "But you're going out there?"

"Yeah." Maybe because of the sudden alarm on her face, he brushed a kiss on her mouth and added, "Not in the yard. I'll have Ramone come to the porch."

That would prevent a sniper from getting an easy shot, but there was still the possibility that Cash could be gunned down.

"You can demand that Ramone meet you at your office this afternoon," she suggested. "If he has info about Webb, then it'd be obstruction for him to refuse to tell you."

Cash made a quick sound of agreement. "But I don't want to wait hours to hear what he has to say. He could give me something now that could get Webb back behind bars."

Delaney couldn't dispute that. It was entirely possible that Ramone would indeed want his brother back in jail. But it was also possible that brotherly ties ran deep enough that Ramone would help Webb. Maybe by feeding them false information. Maybe by helping Webb kill Cash by drawing him out into the open.

"I'll be careful, and I won't be long," Cash assured her. He dropped another kiss on her mouth. "Move back from the door." He tipped his head to the kitchen. "Wait in there."

She didn't want to wait or leave him, but it wasn't smart for her to be right in the doorway when Cash opened it. Even if it didn't lead to her getting shot, just her mere presence would be a huge distraction for Cash. Right now, she wanted him focused on Ramone so he could hear whatever the man had to say and then come back inside the house.

"Can you leave your phone with me?" Delaney asked since he was still on the line with Stoney. "That way, if you speak up, I'll be able to hear at least some of the conversation."

Cash nodded. "Did you get that, Stoney?" he asked his ranch hand.

"I got it. I'll try to stay turned toward you and our visitor so that Delaney can hear."

Good. It wouldn't guarantee Cash was safe, but at least she'd know what was happening.

Delaney took Cash's phone, and while watching Cash from over her shoulder, she went to the kitchen. The house had an open floor plan, so she saw him as he disarmed the security system and opened the door. She caught just a glimpse of Ramone walking toward the porch before Cash shut the door behind him.

"This had better be important," Cash immediately warned Ramone.

"It is. Webb called me," she heard Ramone say. "I'll give you the number he used, but he said it wouldn't do any good to try to trace it because he was using a burner."

No surprise there. Webb wouldn't be dumb enough to use a phone that could be traced back to him.

Ramone rattled off the number to Cash, and Delaney hurried to the fridge so she could jot it down on the dry-erase board hanging there.

"Webb asked me to help him," Ramone continued. "He said he needed money and a vehicle. I told him I'd help, but that it'd take me an hour or two to get the cash. He's due to call me back in about thirty minutes."

Delaney felt the quick jolt of hope. She hadn't expected for Cash to get much from Ramone, but this could be the beginning of Webb being apprehended.

"Where are you supposed to meet Webb?" Cash demanded.

"He's coming to my ranch later this morning," Ramone said without hesitation. He muttered something she didn't catch. "Look, he's my brother, but I can't get mixed up in this. If I help him, I could end up in jail, and I've just now started to get my life back together."

"Yeah, you would have ended up in jail," Cash verified. "That's why it was smart of you to come to me."

Delaney agreed with that if Ramone was being on the up-and-up. She wasn't sure he was, and it would be a huge risk for Cash to be sucked into meeting Webb when it could all be a trap. Cash had no doubt already considered that, but she figured it was a risk he'd take.

And that twisted her up again.

Cash would put his life on the line to get Webb, to make sure she was safe. But if something went wrong, and he was hurt

That thought broke off when she heard a sound behind her. The sound of the back door opening.

Delaney whirled around and came face-to-face with her worst nightmare.

Smiling, Webb barged his way inside and put a gun to her head. "Shh," he said, his hot breath raking against her cheek. "Don't say boo, or you'll get lover boy killed."

Chapter Twelve

Cash studied Ramone's expression and body language. Looking for any signs that the man was lying. If he was, he was darn good at it, because Cash only saw the nerves and the face of a very troubled man.

"Webb's calling you back to confirm you have the money and the vehicle?" Cash asked.

Ramone nodded. "And then his plan is to drive to my place. He said he wants to ditch the truck he has now because the cops know about it."

Yeah, they knew all right, but it still made Cash wonder why Webb had parked and driven the truck so that it could be caught on the security cams. If that had been his plan all along, then why had he waited to call his brother and ask for another vehicle? Why hadn't Webb set that in motion before the florist? Or just skipped a personal appearance at the florist altogether?

Something definitely wasn't right.

"I figured I'd tell Webb that it was okay to come and get the money and a truck," Ramone continued. He kept his gaze pinned to Cash, but Cash did some glancing around, to make sure this wasn't a ploy for Webb to get in position to gun him down. "But maybe you and some of your deputies could be there to take him when he shows up. *Take him alive*," Ramone emphasized. "I don't want to be the reason my brother gets killed."

Cash couldn't give him guarantees about that. Webb would almost certainly be armed, maybe with a gun that he'd gotten from Ramone. Maybe one he'd stolen. Either way, Webb wouldn't just give up in a peaceful surrender.

"Webb knows that Delaney's been staying here," Ramone added. "And no, I didn't tell him. He might have guessed or somebody could have told him."

Any of those were possibilities. Webb might have also had them under surveillance when they were at her house. It wouldn't have been hard to figure out she was staying with him if Webb had seen them together.

"I don't want him going after Delaney." Ramone groaned, shook his head. "I don't want another dead woman on my conscience." He stopped, his eyes widening as if he'd said too much.

Which he had.

Ramone had just come close to confessing that he'd been an accessory to murder. But since he'd already been tried and acquitted for any part in Beatrice's death, double jeopardy applied, and he couldn't be tried for it again.

"Call me once you have everything set up with Webb," Cash instructed. "We'll work out the details as to how to handle this. Tell him not to come through for at least three hours because I need some time to prepare."

That included making sure Delaney was safe, because Cash didn't want this sting operation to be an opportunity for Webb to try to get to her. The moment that thought entered his head, Cash could have sworn someone put ice in his veins.

"Stay here," Cash ordered Ramone. "Watch him," he added to Stoney, and hurried back into the house.

He tried to tamp down his suddenly crashing heartbeat. And the Texas-sized worry that went along with it. He assured himself that Webb couldn't have sneaked onto the ranch and gotten past the hands.

But he could have.

Webb could have done just that.

"Delaney?" Cash called out the moment he was inside. He figured that once he heard her voice or caught sight of her he could tell this bad gut feeling to take a hike.

That didn't happen.

Because he didn't hear her voice. Nor did Cash see her when he ran into the kitchen. She wasn't there, but his phone was lying on the floor.

And the back door was wide open.

A dozen possibilities went through his head. None good. Delaney wouldn't have left unless something had gone horribly wrong. Or unless she'd been taken.

He scooped up his phone, shoving it into his pocket. His heartbeat revved up even more, and Cash drew his gun as he hurried to the back door. Holding his breath and praying, he peered out, bracing himself in case someone shot at him. Nothing. No gunfire. No Delaney. And there wasn't a ranch hand in sight.

His gaze darted around the grounds, and he spotted some smoke. Two ranch hands, Buck and Ted, were using feed sacks to beat down a small fire. Since the ground wasn't dry and that wasn't a spot where one of his workers would use open flames, Cash figured someone had set it. Probably to draw the attention of the ranch hands. Something it had succeeded in doing.

"Delaney?" he called out, knowing his shout would alert anyone waiting to attack him. But it also alerted the ranch hands.

"Everything okay, boss?" Stoney answered from the front of the house at the same time that Buck said, "Somebody dropped a cigarette butt on some hay. Don't worry. Me and Ted got it out."

Oh, but there was plenty of reason to worry, and it had nothing to do with a cigarette fire.

"Delaney's gone," Cash told them, and he hurried out into the yard. "Ted, get inside the house and search every inch of it. Buck, look in the barn to make sure she's not there."

Cash wanted to hold on to the idea that maybe something had spooked her, and she'd gone some place to hide. But she'd had his phone. If there'd been signs of trouble, she could have simply told Stoney, and he could have relayed that to Cash.

He fired more glances around and was gearing up to call out for her again when he spotted something. Movement in the grove of pecan trees on the east side of the ranch. The trees were tall and with plenty of low-hanging branches, giving someone lots of places to hide.

Cash headed in that direction.

"Delaney?" he shouted, and then he went with his gut. "Webb?"

And this time he got an answer. Someone fired a shot at him. It missed, smacking into the ground just to his right. Cash scrambled to the left, ducking behind a storage shed.

"Boss?" he heard Stoney yell.

"Call for backup," Cash shouted back. "I want deputies out here now. And don't let Ramone out of your sight," he added. "Webb's got Delaney."

Cash heard Ramone say something, but he tuned him out. He tuned out everything and pinpointed his focus to the pecan grove.

Glancing around the shed, Cash saw more movement, and while he couldn't make out Delaney and Webb, Cash was sure it was them. Since Delaney wasn't calling out for help, that meant Webb either had her gagged or was holding her at gunpoint. Maybe both.

Cash had to fight the urge to go running straight toward her. Had to fight the thought that Webb could and likely had already hurt her. Webb would enjoy hurting her, but obviously the man didn't want her dead yet or he would have killed her in the kitchen.

That didn't help the twisting and turning in his gut.

"Webb?" Cash yelled. "If this is a kidnapping, you've got demands. What are they?" He kept his voice all cop while he hurried to the other end of the shed where he hoped he'd have a better view.

And he did.

There, in the shadows of those branches, Cash could make out Delaney. She was standing in front of a man. Webb probably. Or rather she was forced to stand in front of him. Cash spotted the choke hold the man had around her neck. Along with the gun. He'd been right about Webb holding her at gunpoint.

Hell.

The fear scraped over him, flesh to bone, and in that instant Cash knew he'd do anything to save her. *Anything.* But to save her, he had to stay alive.

"Backup's on the way," Stoney shouted to him.

It wouldn't take long for his deputies to arrive. Less than twenty minutes. But that might be too much time if Webb had plans to take Delaney from here. The man must have had a vehicle. Or maybe he'd hitched a ride with his brother, who'd dropped him off at the end of the road. If so, if Ramone had a part in this, Cash would personally make sure he paid for what Webb was doing to Delaney.

"Well, Webb?" Cash tried again. "What are your demands?"

He didn't expect Webb to answer. But he did.

"I'm thinking it could be fun if Delaney watches her lover boy get gunned down," Webb said.

The man's tone was joking, but this wasn't anything to laugh at. Cash suspected that was exactly what Webb would try to do. Gun him down so that Delaney would have to see it.

Cash dropped down on his belly and started crawling. Thankfully, there were a lot of things between him and the pecan grove, and Cash used them for cover. First, some shrubs. Then an old watering trough.

"Well, Sheriff?" Webb mocked. "What do you think about dying today? Are you up for it?"

Cash didn't answer. He didn't want to give away his position as he moved as fast as he could, staying low and continuing to pray.

"Cat got your tongue?" Webb asked several moments later. "Oh, well. I wasn't in the mood for chitchat anyway. But I will give you a chance to say goodbye to Delaney. She's going with me right now before your deputies get here and try to mess with my fun."

Fun. Cash wished he could tear this sick SOB limb

from limb. Webb wanted to hurt Delaney all because she hadn't kept his guilty butt out of jail.

Cash levered up a little once he reached the edge of the pasture fence. He got a better view of Delaney. At her face. He expected to see sheer terror there, but he saw the anger, too. And the determination that she was not going to let Webb take her without a fight.

He watched as she slammed her elbow into Webb's stomach. Webb cursed her, grunted and fired a shot. Not at Delaney. But at the shed. Maybe because he thought Cash was still there.

Delaney's expression turned to pain, no doubt from the gunshot blast so close to her ear. Cash knew from experience that it would make her temporarily deaf and might even cause some permanent damage.

That didn't tamp down Cash's temper any, but it made him realize he couldn't wait another second. Because Webb might forgo having his fun and turn the next shot on Delaney. Webb might not put up with her attempts to resist the abduction.

Cursing and tightening his choke hold on Delaney, Webb turned, heading in the direction of a trail that led out to the road. The moment he had his back turned, Cash made his move.

And he moved fast.

He ran hard, eating up the distance between Webb and him. Webb must have heard it, too, because the man whirled around, already bringing up his gun to take aim at Cash.

But Cash was just a second faster.

Cash tossed his own weapon aside, and in the same motion, he latched on to Webb's right wrist. He wrenched Webb's hand up so that the shot he fired went into the air. Cash elbowed Delaney to the side, getting her out of the way in case Webb managed to get off another shot.

Webb cursed again, the words vile and filled with rage. Cash didn't bother with his own curse words. He had one goal. Just one. To stop Delaney from being killed. With as much momentum as he could manage, Cash rammed his body into Webb's.

And he knocked Webb to the ground.

DELANEY DIDN'T HAVE time to react. Didn't have time to stop Webb or try to break her fall. She fell, hard, her head smacking against one of the trees. She was already in pain from Webb's choke hold and the gun blast, and the impact only added to it. Still, she'd take the pain because it meant she was alive.

But maybe not for long.

The fear hit her heavy in the chest. In the heart. Because the fear wasn't for herself but for Cash.

He'd seemingly come out of nowhere, and in a blur of motion, she had seen him drag Webb to the ground. Where they still were. Even though her vision was spotty, she could hear the sounds of the struggle. Fist against flesh. And she wasn't sure who was winning. Webb was not only a lot bigger than Cash, he had perhaps managed to hang on to his gun in the fall.

"Cash?" someone shouted, and she thought it was Ted, one of his ranch hands. "Are you okay?"

She wanted to know the same thing, and Delaney forced herself to get to her feet. It wasn't easy to do. Her head was spinning and everything seemed out of focus, as if her vision had been smeared with oil. Still, she could see Webb and Cash. Could see the life-and-death struggle that was going on.

Cash had both his hands clamped around Webb's right wrist. She'd been right about Webb hanging on to his gun. He had it, his finger poised on the trigger, and Cash was using all his strength to stop Webb from taking aim at her.

And Webb was making him pay for it.

Webb was pounding his left fist into Cash's side, obviously trying to break Cash's grip so he could try to kill them. Delaney had no intention of letting Cash fight this battle alone.

She glanced around, looking for something she could use to stop Webb, and she spotted Cash's gun on the ground. She scrambled to it, scooped it up. And took aim. Except she immediately realized she couldn't risk firing a shot. Not with Cash and Webb moving around. Any shot she fired now could hit Cash.

She caught some movement from the corner of her eye, and Delaney shifted toward it in case this was Ramone or someone else coming to help Webb. But it was the ranch hand, Buck. He had obviously run there because he was out of breath. He was also armed, and like Delaney he took aim, but he didn't have any better chance of a shot than she did.

Since she couldn't shoot, Delaney went after Webb's arm and the fist he was using to pummel Cash. She kicked Webb, causing him to howl in pain. He shifted but so did she, and she just kept kicking and stomping on any part of him she could reach.

The sound of the blast stopped her.

Webb had pulled the trigger.

Delaney's heart crashed against her ribs, and her

breath stalled in her throat. *No.* Cash couldn't be shot. He couldn't be hurt. Or worse.

Yelling, and letting the rage ram through her, she stooped lower, and she saw the blood. It was on both Cash and Webb, so she couldn't tell which one of them had been hit.

Delaney clawed at Webb and scored his face with her nails before she took hold of his gun. He still had a fierce grip on it, but she couldn't let him get off another shot. Cash must've had the same plan, because he rammed his forearm into Webb's jaw and nose. More blood flew, and Delaney had the satisfaction of hearing the cartilage crunch from Webb's broken nose.

Webb called her a vicious name and reached out, trying to grab hold of her throat. Cash stopped him. Grunting from the exertion, Cash twisted Webb around, slamming him back onto the ground. Buck rushed forward to stomp his boot onto Webb's right hand, and Delaney kicked aside Webb's gun.

In the back of her mind, it registered that she'd just disarmed a killer. A killer who wanted Cash and her dead. But she felt no relief whatsoever. Because the damage had already been done.

There was so much blood.

While Buck kept Webb pinned in place, Delaney had her first real look at Cash. And her heart dropped. A lot of that blood was on the front of his shirt. Soaked through to the skin.

"I wasn't shot," Cash blurted out.

She shook her head and lifted her gaze to his face. She could feel every muscle in her body trembling.

"I wasn't shot," he repeated. "Most of the blood is Webb's."

Delaney shifted her attention to Webb, who was now on his back. His breathing was labored, and he had almost no color in his face. However, there was plenty of color on his shirt, and Delaney could see that Cash was right. Most of the blood was indeed Webb's. She wasn't sure how it'd happened, but the bullet Webb had fired hadn't hit Cash.

It had hit Webb.

Now the relief came, and even though she didn't want to take her eyes off Webb, she threw her arms around Cash. She thought that maybe he needed that as much as she had. But it didn't last.

At the sound of approaching footsteps, they both whirled around. Cash snatched his gun from her and took aim. Her body braced for a fight, but bracing wasn't necessary because it was Jesse, Cash's deputy.

"Are you okay?" Jesse asked, glancing at Cash, Buck and her.

She was far from being okay. Delaney figured she was probably in shock, and her ears were still throbbing in pain, but at least they weren't seriously hurt. Well, Webb was, but her pity meter for him was below zero.

Cash turned to her and gave her a quick once-over, no doubt to verify that she hadn't been injured. She did the same to him. Or rather she tried. But it turned her stomach to see that blood all over the front of his shirt. Blood that could have been his if Webb had managed to turn the gun on him.

"I'm the one who needs help," Webb complained. "If you let me keep bleeding out, I'm gonna sue your butt." He added a sick, hollow laugh. One that made Delaney glad that she'd kicked him and broken his nose.

"Call for an ambulance," Cash told Jesse. "And then

check to make sure Ramone hasn't gone anywhere. I want a deputy on him ASAP because he and I are going to have a conversation."

Delaney wanted in on that talk, too. It was entirely possible that Ramone had been a decoy, and that his visit was meant to be a distraction to draw Cash out of the house so that Webb could break in through the back door. The same way he'd gotten to Melanie. If Ramone had helped with either of the break-ins, then Delaney wanted him arrested.

"You think he'll live?" Buck asked, staring down at Webb.

"Hard to say," Cash muttered, and he used the pair of plastic cuffs that Jesse handed him to restrain Webb's wrists.

"You think I'm gonna get up and run when I'm bleeding like a stuck pig?" Webb snarled, and he laughed again. This time, though, he also coughed, and his color was definitely draining.

Delaney had never seen anyone die, but she thought that might change. Still, Cash tried to staunch the flow of blood by pressing his hands to Webb's chest. It didn't seem to help.

"Care to make a deathbed confession?" Cash asked him.

There was blood on his teeth when Webb grinned. "I haven't done anything wrong. I'm an innocent man."

That gave Delaney a whole new jolt of anger. She leaned over him, glaring right into his eyes. "You just tried to kill Cash, and you dragged me out of his house at gunpoint. You kidnapped and beat Melanie. And you blew up my house, nearly killing Cash and me in the process."

Webb met her eye to eye. "Now, you see, sweetheart, that's only partly true." He stopped, coughed, then grimaced. The pain was etched all over his face. "Care to guess which part is a big fat lie?" Even now, there was a taunt in his voice.

A taunt that gave her already raw nerves another jab. "All of it's true," Delaney insisted, and she prayed that it was.

Because if Webb had committed all those crimes, then it meant this was over. No more looking over her shoulder. No more danger.

Webb's next laugh was weak and filled with his hoarse breath. "No, sweetheart. You're wrong. I did try to kill you, and I'm the one who took Melanie. I dumped her by Jeb's house so I could mess with you and your lover boy's heads. But I didn't set that bomb. Not my style. I prefer, uh, hands-on. Plus, it would have been over way too fast. I like to take things slow when it comes to you."

The chill that came was winter-cold and rippled over her skin. "You set the bomb," she insisted.

Webb smiled that jeering smile, and even now, it packed a wallop. And so did what he said.

"Poor Delaney," Webb murmured. "Sweetheart, I'm not the only one who wants you dead."

Chapter Thirteen

Cash slipped his arm around Delaney's waist and got her moving away from Webb. There was no reason for her to stand there and let him continue to taunt her.

"Watch him," Cash instructed Jesse though he knew his deputy would do just that.

Webb might be hurt, was likely dying from the gunshot wound to the chest, but Cash didn't want the man to get a chance to do something else to harm Delaney.

"Oh, let her stay and listen," Webb joked. His voice was thankfully weaker now, and once Cash had gotten Delaney a few yards away, he could no longer hear Webb at all.

"Webb's lying," Delaney muttered. "He has to be lying. He was the one who put that bomb in my house."

Maybe. It would be just like Webb to lie about something that would cause the worry to eat away at Delaney. And that was exactly what his words would do.

Poor Delaney. Sweetheart, I'm not the only one who wants you dead.

Because that might be true. There was Byers to consider, and her father, too. Maybe Gil didn't actually want her dead, but if he'd set that bomb, then he could do something else reckless that would get her killed.

Byers was a different kettle of fish, however. He might indeed actually want to kill Delaney, and that was why Cash needed that interview with him. Unfortunately, Delaney might not be up for the trip. She was trembling, and the adrenaline crash would soon leave her spent. Along with that, she had a new set of nightmares to deal with now that Webb had come so close to killing her.

If Webb wasn't working alone, however, if someone else did indeed want "poor Delaney" dead, then Gil and Byers weren't the only ones on Cash's suspect list. Right now, his top suspect was in his front yard, and Cash didn't have to wait to talk to him. He spotted Stoney holding Ramone at gunpoint.

"What happened?" Ramone called out. "Is that really Webb back there?"

Cash ignored him, for the moment anyway, but it seemed there was genuine surprise and worry in his voice. Of course, those were emotions that could be faked, and Cash wasn't ready to believe that it was a coincidence that both Ramone and Webb had showed up at his ranch around the same time.

Nope, he wasn't buying that one little bit.

But he also wasn't going to put Delaney at risk. Just in case Webb had told the truth about someone else wanting her dead. That someone else could be Ramone, and it didn't matter that he was being held at gunpoint, because he could have hired a sniper to try to finish the job his brother had started. That was why Cash took Delaney back into the house.

He led her through the kitchen, hoping that just the sight of the scene wouldn't trigger flashbacks of her abduction. Cash moved fast, keeping hold of her hand, and he took her to the front door.

"Nobody's inside the house," Ted said, "I searched the place." He was in the doorway and also had a gun aimed at Ramone.

"Good," Cash said, adding a mumbled thanks. "I need you to go to the pecan grove and see if Jesse needs any help. More deputies and the ambulance will be here soon."

In fact, it would be a different kind of chaos in just a matter of minutes. His ranch was now essentially a crime scene with one man injured and another about to be interrogated.

"Stay behind me," Cash instructed Delaney. He moved into the doorway after Ted left.

Ramone's eyes widened when he saw Cash. Or rather when he saw Cash's blood-soaked shirt. "You're hurt?" Ramone asked. "Did Webb do that?"

"The blood is your brother's," Cash said, and he didn't bother to cushion the news because he needed to see his reaction.

Again, Ramone's surprise seemed like the real deal. Then again, he'd been standing out here a while where he'd had plenty of time to rehearse his responses. A rehearsal that Ramone would know was critical if he didn't want to be charged as an accessory to the dangerous stunt his brother had just tried to pull off.

"Webb's dead?" Ramone asked, and he swallowed hard.

"He's shot," Cash corrected, keeping the hard edge to his voice. He knew his eyes and expression were all cop. "Not sure if he'll make it."

Again, he watched for a reaction. This time, Ramone

closed his eyes for a moment and muttered something under his breath that Cash didn't catch.

"Want to tell me what part you had in Webb's plan to kidnap and murder Delaney?" Cash demanded. "Or was it your plan and you brought Webb here to carry it out?"

Ramone was shaking his head before Cash even finished. Frantically shaking it. "I didn't know Webb was here, and I damn sure didn't have anything to do with his plan. I've got no beef against Delaney."

"But you knew that Webb was here to take her?" Cash argued.

"No." Ramone's answer was fast and practically a shout. "I wouldn't do that. If I'd known he was going to hurt her, I would have found a way to stop him. I wouldn't have helped him. You have to believe me."

Cash didn't have to believe anything right now. Delaney had just been put through hell and back, and someone would pay for that. Webb, definitely. But maybe Ramone, too.

"I swear, I didn't know Webb was going to do this," Ramone went on. In the distance, there was the howl of sirens. "He called and asked me for money and a vehicle. That's it. I didn't even know he was in the area."

"And when's the last time you saw Webb?" Cash threw out there, hoping to get Ramone to slip up and admit that he had indeed been in contact with his brother.

But Ramone only shook his head again. "It's been months. I went to see him in prison, but that was around Christmas. I haven't seen him since."

Cash intended to push to find out if that was true. Maybe the security cams at the back of his ranch had picked up something. Like Webb's arrival shortly before Ramone's visit to tell Cash about his brother's demands for money and a vehicle.

The sirens got louder, and several moments later, an ambulance and a cruiser pulled into Cash's driveway.

"That way," Cash directed the EMTs when they hurried out. He motioned toward the pecan grove. "A man's down. Gunshot wound to the chest. He's a dangerous fugitive and will stay restrained. Jesse will go with you in the ambulance."

As expected, no one gave him any flak about that, and he turned to the three deputies who stepped from the cruiser. Clark Whitlow, Dave Garcia and Marcella Hendrick. All three drew their weapons.

"Clark and Marcella, I need you to take him to the sheriff's office," Cash instructed, tipping his head to Ramone.

"But I didn't do anything," Ramone snapped. "I had no part in what my brother did."

"You need to be interviewed," Cash insisted. "It's procedure."

Obviously not pleased about that, Ramone shot him a glare. "I came here to help, not to be arrested."

"You're not under arrest," Cash assured him. Not yet anyway. "But if I find out you helped Webb, you will be."

That intensified Ramone's scowl, and Cash heard the man curse him as the two deputies led him to the cruiser.

With that ball rolling, Cash turned to Dave, the remaining deputy. "Jesse will go with Webb in the ambulance, so I need you to secure the crime scene. I need to stay with Delaney for now, and I don't want her anywhere outside. Not until we're sure Webb doesn't have any hired help."

Dave nodded, his gaze drifting to the cruiser as it drove away. "What about Webb's brother? Did he *help*?"

"To be determined. For now, go to Jesse, and call me if Webb has said anything that isn't a lie or a taunt."

Of course, Dave might have trouble distinguishing a lie from the truth, but if there was anything questionable, his deputy would relay it to him. And he'd do that over the phone. That was one call that Cash wouldn't be putting on speaker. No need for Delaney to hear any more of Webb's garbage.

With his deputies on their way, Cash stepped back inside, shut the door and armed the security system. He'd have to disengage it if Dave, Jesse or the EMTs came to the house, but for now, he wanted the extra precaution. If there was truly a hired-thug out there, Cash doubted the guy would try to break in, but then he'd never thought Webb would try it, either. Better to be safe than sorry.

And he was plenty sorry.

He'd left Delaney alone while he'd gone out and talked to Ramone. Alone and unsuspecting that Webb would get in and take her. He should have set the security system then. Or better yet, he should have demanded that Ramone go to the sheriff's office and report the call he'd said Webb had made to him. He damn sure shouldn't have put Delaney in a position where she could have been hurt or killed.

"You're beating yourself up," she said, reading his thoughts. She touched his arm, rubbed lightly. "Don't."

"I should have done more to protect you." He groaned and started to scrub his hand over his face. That was when he realized he still had Webb's blood on him. Not just on his hands but on both his shirt and jeans.

Cash grumbled some profanity. "I need to bag my clothes. You, too. They probably won't be needed since I caught Webb in the act of committing a kidnapping, but it's procedure."

She nodded, sighed. The kind of sigh that let him know Delaney was starting to see the big picture. Webb might be in custody, but what had gone on here this morning would need to be investigated.

"Leigh sent over another pair of jeans and a top," she said, heading toward the guest room.

Cash followed her, not with plans to stand around gawking at her while she undressed, but because he didn't want her alone. Unfortunately, some gawking might happen. It was hard to convince his eyes, and other parts of him, that Delaney was hands-off.

He was about to tell her that he wanted her with him when he changed, but his phone rang. Delaney was in the process of unbuttoning her shirt, but she froze. Judging from her suddenly stark expression, she was expecting bad news.

And it might be.

That would fall into the "to be determined" category, too, because it was her father

"Gil," Cash said, putting the call on speaker. He hoped that didn't turn out to be a mistake and that Gil wouldn't say something that would only add to the shell-shocked look in Delaney's eyes.

"I need to talk to Delaney," Gil insisted.

"Where are you?" Cash countered before Delaney could say anything.

"That's none of your business."

"Well, you see, it is," Cash assured him. "I've got a badge, remember, and I need to question you about a few things."

There was a long silence. "I need to speak to my daughter," Gil finally said, and there was nothing friendly about his tone.

Delaney didn't speak until Cash gave her a nod, and then she repeated Cash's question. "Where are you? And don't you dare say it's none of my business." Some of her shock had vanished, and her voice was a snarl.

"I'm safe," Gil told her after another long pause.

"I hired a bodyguard to protect you, and you snuck out of the house. Where are you?" Delaney didn't shout that last part, but it was close.

"A friend lent me his truck, and I'm driving around." There was nothing friendly or pleasant about his response. "And for the record, I didn't ask for a bodyguard and don't want one. In fact, I don't want you butting into my life. Just leave me the hell alone."

Delaney pulled back her shoulders. "Have you been drinking?" she came out and asked.

"I'm not going to discuss that with you." But his words were slurred just enough to make Cash believe the answer to that was yes.

Delaney sighed, shook her head. "Then tell me if you had anything to do with that bomb in my house."

Cash expected a fast denial from Gil. One filled with rage. But that didn't happen.

"I can see where your loyalties lie," Gil said, his voice practically a whisper now. "Cash has turned you against me."

"He hasn't," Delaney assured him. "But I want you

to answer the question. Did you have anything to do with that bomb?"

However, she was talking to the air because Gil had already ended the call.

Cash quickly contacted dispatch to see if they could trace the call, but he figured Gil had made sure that wouldn't happen by using a burner. Still, they might get lucky. Maybe their luck would extend to Gil not hurting anyone if he truly was drinking and driving.

The moment he'd finished with dispatch, Cash's phone rang again. This time it was Jesse, and he answered it right away. He didn't put it on speaker, but Delaney was plenty close enough that she'd likely hear anyway.

"I'm in the ambulance," Jesse said, "but there's no hurry for us to get to the hospital. Webb just took the last breath he'll ever take."

WEBB WAS DEAD.

It had been several hours since Jesse had told them the news. Two hours for it to sink in that she no longer had to worry about a man who'd terrorized her, gone after people she cared about and had then tried to kill Cash and her.

Webb was dead.

Delaney kept repeating those words to herself in the hope that her body would finally believe it and would start settling down. Everything inside her still felt revved and raw. Every one of her nerves was much too close to the surface, putting her senses on hyperdrive. That was why she gasped when Cash came into the guest room, where she'd been pacing.

Her reaction caused him to sigh, and slipping his

phone into his pocket, he went to her and pulled her into his arms. Something he'd been doing a lot since he'd rescued her from Webb. The close contact helped, but she had to wonder just how long it would be before she stopped feeling on edge. Maybe not until she knew for certain that Webb had been lying.

I'm not the only one who wants you dead.

That had to be a lie. It just had to be. Because if it wasn't, she might never have any peace.

She eased back just enough to look up at Cash and study his eyes. Even though it wasn't anywhere near bedtime, he looked exhausted. Probably felt it, too. But at least he was no longer wearing clothes soaked with Webb's blood, and he smelled like the fresh soap from his shower rather than the scents from the fight.

Jesse had picked up their clothes and bagged them in case they were needed. The deputy had also brought Delaney several loaner outfits and had taken their statements. As part of procedure, Cash put himself on administrative leave. It was just a formality. No one believed he'd murdered Webb in cold blood, but until all the reports were filed, Cash wouldn't be able to do anything official.

Including interview Byers.

That had been moved to the following morning, and while Cash and she would be able to listen in, Jesse would actually be doing it. That would give the deputy time to get the report from Curley on Byers's medication, something that Jesse could maybe use to get Byers to confess that he'd tampered with her meds.

If he had actually done it, that is.

Delaney hadn't specifically asked Webb if he'd switched the medications, and she wished she had.

Webb might have lied and said no, but it was just as possible that he would have admitted to it.

"I had the doctor drop off a sedative," Cash said. "I didn't figure you'd take it," he added when she started shaking her head, "but I wanted you to have the option. I doubt you'll get much sleep without it."

No, she wouldn't get sleep, and she might even consider taking it if she thought it would keep the nightmares at bay. But she doubted anything could do that.

"I'll be okay," she said. Which was a lie on so many levels.

There'd be nightmares even if she was awake. Her father was out there somewhere maybe doing harm to himself or someone else if he was driving around drunk. And she couldn't push aside that Cash had come so close to dying today.

"If Webb's gun had shifted—" she muttered. But she didn't get a chance to finish because Cash lowered his head and kissed her.

That was yet something else he'd been doing a lot since the fight in the pecan orchard. He'd been kissing her so that she wouldn't have the flashbacks. And it worked. For the moments when his mouth was on hers, Delaney was able to push everything aside and feel something good. Cash's kisses definitely qualified as good.

Then he eased back, studying her. "That put a little color back in your cheeks," he said.

The corner of his mouth hitched into a smile. A smile that didn't quite make it to his eyes. Probably because his thoughts were along the same lines as hers. After all, she'd come close to dying today, too.

"I don't want to think about what would have happened if you hadn't gotten to me in time," she whispered.

Again, he stopped her with a kiss. But this one was different. It didn't have the feel of a gesture of comfort. There was some heat to it, and only got hotter when Cash deepened it.

Delaney felt the need start to slide through her, and mercy, it was good. The opposite of what she'd been feeling for the past couple of hours. Cash had always had a way of doing that, turning things around for the better, and he was definitely doing that now.

He lowered his hand to her back, nudging her closer until they were body to body. The kiss continued, meshing with that extra punch of having her breasts against his chest. It caused the heat to leap up even more, surrounding her so that this time when Cash started to move away, Delaney was the one who pulled him back to her. This time, she was the one who deepened the kiss.

Oh, his taste was so familiar. Like a soothing balm on the pain and fear. He could make that all go away. Make her just focus on one thing.

Him.

He made a sound, a groan that came from deep within his chest, and he broke the kiss. "You're not up to doing this," he said.

"I certainly feel up to it." And to prove it, she gave his midsection a bump with hers. But then she stopped when it occurred to her that they might not have time to land in bed. "Your deputies are still here?"

He shook his head. "The hands are patrolling the grounds, but I sent the deputies back to work."

So that meant no one would likely come to the door.

If there were signs of trouble, one of his ranch hands would call him.

"With Byers's interview rescheduled, we don't have to go anywhere until morning," she reminded him. "I'd rather have you than a sedative."

She could see the quick debate in his eyes. The heat, too. He probably didn't want to lose focus by hauling her off to bed, but if so, that was a fight he lost because he kissed her again. And this kiss jumped straight to foreplay.

This time it was Delaney who made a sound. A purr of pleasure vibrated through her, and she melted against Cash. He took full advantage of the melting by moving that wildfire kiss to her neck. She felt so many things when he kissed her. The need. The ache for him. And the love. That was always there, too, and it was probably the reason she hooked her arm around his neck and started backing him toward the bed.

Cash moved with her, but he didn't let up on the kisses. Thank goodness. He went lower, kissing the bare skin of her throat and chest that the vee of her borrowed shirt exposed. He certainly started some fires there as well, and then spread even more when he touched her.

He moved his hand between their bodies. Cupping her right breast and swiping his thumb over her nipple. That caused her to purr again. And moan. She thought it wouldn't be long before she started to beg.

They fell back onto the bed, and in the same motion, Cash went after her shirt. His fingers worked fast to open the buttons, and he had it off her in no time.

The kisses started up again.

His mouth and tongue on her stomach, while he unhooked her bra. Once he'd freed her breasts, he kissed her there, too.

Her mind blurred from the heat, and Delaney savored the delicious feel of him taking her to the only place she wanted to go. But she didn't want to do this particular trip alone. Nope. Cash was going to be with her, and that meant getting him out of his clothes.

It wasn't easy to undress him. Mainly because Cash was doing the same thing to her, along with kissing every inch of her that his mouth encountered. He shimmied off her jeans, then her panties, and all while he was still fully dressed.

Delaney went white hot when he dropped some of those kisses between her legs, and she knew if she didn't do something fast, this would be over way too soon for her.

Again, she didn't want this to be solo, so she went after his shirt with a vengeance. It wasn't easy to get him out of his shirt, but it was so worth the effort to get her hands, and her mouth, on his bare chest. Kissing him like this brought back so many memories. Good ones. And for a little while, they could push aside all the bad things that had happened.

He grunted with pleasure when Delaney tackled his belt and zipper, but when she pushed his jeans off his hips, he stopped her.

"Condom," he growled.

For one heart-stopping moment she thought he was calling this off, that he was going to push her away. But instead he fumbled in his back pocket, located his wallet and got a condom. She remembered he always carried one there and was thankful for it. She didn't want to postpone this. She wanted Cash now.

Now happened as soon as he'd gotten the condom on. As if starved for her, he kneed her legs apart and pushed into her. Delaney had to fight hard not to climax right then and there. This was pleasure in its purest form. This was the kind of heat that continued to flame higher and higher with each stroke Cash made inside her.

Those strokes came harder, faster, deeper. Until Delaney could no longer hang on. Until her body gave way and tossed her over the edge.

Cash was right there, taking that plunge with her.

Chapter Fourteen

Cash scowled at the text he'd just gotten from Jesse.

We need to talk about Byers and Ramone.

Hell. That couldn't be good. Especially since it was nearly 9:00 p.m., which meant Jesse should have been off shift.

Cash eased out of bed, pulling on his jeans and shirt but not bothering to button or zip them. Moving as quietly as he could, he stepped out of the guest room so he wouldn't wake Delaney when he called his deputy. She was sleeping—peacefully, from the looks of it— and Cash wanted her to stay that way.

The fact that she hadn't even stirred with the ding of the text told him that she was well past being exhausted. He probably was, too, but apparently sex with Delaney worked better than a good night's sleep and a handful of energy pills. He was both revved and sated.

And worried.

Worried about Delaney's safety. About her father. About their future. Heck, they might not even have a future. That was a worry, too. But for now, Cash put all of that on the back burner and went into the kitchen to make the call to Jesse.

"How bad is the news?" Cash asked his deputy the moment Jesse answered.

"Well, it's not good," Jesse began. "Byers is refusing to come in for his interview, and he left you a message through his attorney. If you want to question him, then issue a warrant for his arrest."

Cash groaned. He hadn't wanted to go this route, especially because everything he had against Byers was circumstantial, but a warrant would compel the man to come in, and one way or another he needed to be interviewed. That connection he had with the meds Delaney had been given had to be addressed.

"His lawyer told me that he'd advised Byers to come in and clear up this matter," Jesse went on. "But Byers is refusing."

That left Cash with no choice. "Issue a warrant. Have him come in midmorning tomorrow." By then, Cash could decide if it was safe enough to take Delaney with him or if they'd go with the plan of having Jesse do the interview.

"That should rile Byers even more than he already is," Jesse commented. "And speaking of riled, Ramone's madder than a hornet. He's threatening to sue us for harassment."

That wasn't a surprise. Cash had already had a conversation with Jesse shortly after he'd finished the interview with Ramone, and Jesse had told him then that Ramone had been none too happy about being "hauled in" and treated like a criminal. All while he was grieving the death of his brother.

Cash might actually have some sympathy for the

man if he could confirm that Ramone had had no part in the things that Webb had done. According to his earlier conversation with Jesse, his deputy hadn't been able to make that confirmation. Now that some hours had passed, though, Cash had let all of this settle in his mind and had come up with some new conclusions. Ones that they could hopefully back up with evidence.

"What's your gut feel about Ramone?" Cash asked. "Did he help set up Delaney's kidnapping?"

"Still not sure," Jesse said, but then paused. "There's plenty of anger in that man. The kind of anger that seethes and twists. I pressed him about that anger being directed at Delaney, but he insisted that he has nothing against her. You're the one he's riled about."

Yeah, Cash had gotten that message loud and clear. However, that didn't mean Ramone wasn't hiding how he really felt about Delaney. Because admitting his hatred for her would go to motive.

Cash turned when he heard the footsteps, and a yawning Delaney stepped into the kitchen. Her hair was mussed, and she was wearing one of his T-shirts, so big it practically swallowed her. Still, she managed to look amazing.

"Issue the warrant," Cash repeated to Jesse. "Then go home and get some sleep."

"Will do," Jesse assured him and ended the call.

Cash slipped his phone in his pocket and went to her. "Sorry, I didn't mean to wake you."

"It's okay. I feel more rested than I have in a long time." She came up on her toes and kissed him. She kept it light, then eased back to meet his eyes. "Please tell me you're not regretting that we had sex."

No regrets about that, but Cash didn't believe it had

just been sex. That was where he had regrets. Because he wasn't sure Delaney and he could get past their troubles to have a life together. A life not filled with family drama.

Or danger.

Cash still wasn't sure Webb's death had put an end to that.

"No regrets," he said, and he pulled her back to him for another kiss. A much longer one that stirred the heat and made him ache for her all over again. The heat and ache came to an abrupt halt, though, when she stopped and looked up at him.

"Why do you need a warrant?" she asked. She kept her body pressed against his. Kept her mouth close enough that her breath hit against his lips.

"It's for Byers. Apparently, he doesn't want to come in for questioning."

That put some concern in her eyes, and Cash cursed Byers for it. "It's the only way he'll come in, and he needs to be questioned about those meds."

She nodded, and more concern showed on her face. "When Webb said he wasn't the only one who wanted me dead, do you think he was talking about Byers?"

That was possible, but it wasn't what Cash said to Delaney. "Webb could have said that just to spook you. A way of getting in one last dig."

"It worked," she muttered.

Silently cursing because he knew that was true, Cash pulled her tighter into his arms, and he considered just scooping her up and hauling her back to bed. But The slash of headlights outside the front windows stopped him, and he automatically moved in front of Delaney.

Instead of leaving her in the kitchen—a mistake he'd

made earlier—he took hold of her hand, hurrying to the guest room to get his weapon and holster. While he was pulling on his boots, his phone rang, and he saw Stoney's name on the screen. Cash knew that the hands had divvied up shifts for keeping watch of the house, and apparently Stoney was on guard duty.

"Who just drove up?" Cash asked.

"I'm going out to check on that now," Stoney assured him.

Before his ranch hand could say more, Cash heard the shout, and he knew who'd come to pay them a visit.

Gil.

"Delaney, I need to talk to you," Gil shouted. His words were slurred, and when Cash peered out the front window, he saw Delaney's father staggering toward the house.

"My dad," Delaney muttered, and this time the worry in her expression went up a huge notch. She didn't go for the door, something that Cash thought she might do. Instead, she watched from over his shoulder. "He's drunk."

Oh, yeah. Well, unless he was putting on an act, but if so, it was a darn good one. Gil stumbled and would have fallen on his face if Stoney hadn't caught him.

"Get off me," Gil grumbled, pushing at Stoney, but Gil's shove missed Stoney by a couple of inches.

"Delaney?" Gil continued to shout. "I need to see my daughter. You can't keep her from me."

Cash could indeed keep her away from him, but Delaney was worried about her father, and if she truly wanted to see him, Cash doubted he could talk her out of it.

"I have to tell Delaney goodbye," Gil yelled. "I need to tell her this is the last time she'll ever see me."

"Oh, mercy," Delaney muttered, and Cash heard her slow intake of breath. "He's going to try to kill himself again."

"Maybe," Cash conceded. But this could be some kind of trick similar to what Webb had pulled when he'd sneaked into the house.

"Boss, what you want me to do with him?" Stoney asked, letting Gil fall to the ground. Groaning and cursing, Gil landed on his back.

Cash had a quick debate with himself and considered calling his night deputy to come out and take Gil into custody, but one look at Delaney, and he knew he had to do more than that.

"See if you can get him to the porch," Cash instructed, and he glanced at Delaney. "I'll let Gil in the house if that's what you want, but I'll search him for weapons and cuff him."

He figured Delaney would balk about the cuff, but after only a couple of seconds, she nodded. It made Cash wonder if she'd truly accepted that her father might have had a part in setting that bomb. Then again, maybe she was just at a point where she wasn't ready to trust anyone who could be a person of interest in this investigation.

Cash hurried to the closet and got a pair of plastic cuffs from a supply bag he kept there. He went back to the window and watched Stoney drag Gil to his feet. Not easily. Gil was a big man, and wobbling all over the place, but the ranch hand finally got Gil to the porch.

"Stay right behind me," Cash told Delaney.

She did exactly that as he used his phone to disarm

the security system and open the door. Cash reached for Delaney's father, pulling the man inside. Not just into the foyer but away from the door and into the living room. The first thing Cash smelled was the strong stench of alcohol. If Gil wasn't truly drunk, then he'd doused his clothes with what smelled like cheap whiskey.

With Stoney standing guard, Cash got Gil on the floor and frisked him. No weapon, other than a pocketknife that Cash tossed onto the coffee table.

"No need for this manhandling," Gil complained. He threw a punch at Cash. It missed him, but Gil knocked Cash's phone from his hand, and it skittered across the hardwood floor. "I just need to talk to my girl."

Ignoring Gil and the phone, Cash spun Delaney's father around and cuffed his hands behind his back. Once he was sure the man was secure, he looked at Stoney. "Shut and lock the front door. I need you to patrol the yard and make sure no one came here with our drunk visitor."

Stoney nodded and headed right out, doing as Cash had instructed. Since his phone was somewhere on the floor, Cash hurried to the foyer and used the keypad by the door to rearm the security system. He didn't want any repeats of what had happened with Webb.

"Give me one good reason why I shouldn't haul you off to jail," Cash snarled, coming back into the living room and standing over Gil.

Gil looked up at him and blinked hard as if trying to focus, when his attention landed on Delaney. "My girl," the man said, and tears filled his eyes. "I'm sorry. So sorry."

"For what?" she asked, her voice trembling.

But Gil didn't get a chance to answer. The power went off, plunging the room, and the house, into total darkness.

DELANEY FROZE. HER body did, anyway. But the thoughts started to race through her head. Bad thoughts. And she automatically flashed back to the moment when Webb had grabbed her and put a gun to her head.

Was that about to happen now?

Had someone managed to get inside the house?

Worse, had her father arranged this drunken ruse so that someone could get in and kill Cash and her?

Delaney wanted to demand to know if Gil had indeed done something like that, but her instincts were telling her to stay quiet. If her father was in on this, he already knew her location in the room, but there was no reason to telegraph it to someone who'd come with him.

She went stiff when someone took hold of her arm, and Delaney started to fight back so that she wouldn't be kidnapped.

"It's me," Cash said.

He pulled her to his side, and she heard the slide of his gun against the leather of his holster when he drew his weapon. She also heard other sounds. Footsteps. Someone shuffling around, and she wished Cash had his phone so he could use the flashlight on it. The last she'd seen it, it was on the floor, and right now she couldn't see her hand in front of her face much less the floor.

Cash tensed when a low sounding beep began to pulse through the house. "It's the backup to the security system," he whispered.

She hoped that meant the alarm would sound if

someone broke in, but Delaney knew it could mean something else.

Someone could have already gotten inside.

That sent her heart pounding, but she tried to tamp down the panic and fear. Neither emotion would do them any good right now.

With his left arm around her waist, Cash started to step back with her. Leading her to the corner of the living room, she realized. Away from the doors and windows.

Away from her father, too.

"What about Gil?" she asked, trying to keep her voice as soft as possible.

"He's staying quiet," was all Cash said.

Yes, he was quiet, and Delaney considered that he might have passed out. Well, if he was as truly drunk as he'd seemed, that was possible. But her father also might not want them to know where he was. Even though he was cuffed, that wouldn't stop him from getting to his feet and doing whatever it was he'd come here to do.

She thought of Cash's phone, of the way her father had knocked it from his hand. Had that been intentional? If so, it'd been a good move on his part because now Cash had no way to call for backup. He could shout for Stoney, who was almost certainly nearby, but a shout might come at a high price if it caused a killer to pinpoint their location and shoot them.

There were more sounds of movement, and as Delaney's eyes began to focus in the dark, she thought she saw a blur of motion. Cash must have seen something, too, because he turned his body, and she thought that maybe he shifted his gun in that direction.

Mercy. This couldn't be happening. Not again. And

it was worse than when Webb had taken her out of the house and to the pecan grove. There'd been places outside for Cash to take cover, but right now both of them were exposed, especially if someone was wearing night vision goggles.

Cash put his mouth right against her ear. "I need to get my phone."

She nodded. Delaney thought it was somewhere by the living room chair that was close to the foyer. Obviously, Cash thought that, too, because he started to inch them in that direction, all while staying close to the wall.

"Duck down," he instructed when they reached a window.

Delaney did, and with the same snail's-crawl pace, they moved to the other side. Then they repeated the maneuver as they got past the second window.

With each step, her eyes adjusted even more, and Delaney could see the shapes of the furniture and the arched entrance that separated the foyer from the living room. She glanced around on the floor, searching for both her father and Cash's phone.

She didn't see either.

Cash muttered some profanity, his voice hardly making a sound, but she clearly heard the frustration. They needed that phone.

With his arm still around her, Cash eased her down lower until they were in a crouch. Delaney could see more shapes and shadows, but there just wasn't enough moonlight filtering in through the windows for her to see anything on the dark hardwood floor.

"There's a flashlight in the kitchen," Cash murmured.

She remembered it being in the drawer next to the

fridge. It wasn't far away, but with the darkness and the possible threat, it suddenly seemed miles away. They needed the light not only to find the phone but so she could also check on her father. Delaney wanted to see his face, and she thought that with just one look she might be able to tell if he'd had any part in all this.

Still crouching, Cash got them moving toward the kitchen, but they'd hardly made it a few inches when he cursed again. He let go of her so he could pick up something, and Delaney quickly realized it was the plastic cuffs. Maybe the ones that'd been on her father, but if so, they'd been cut.

That dropped her heart to her knees.

The odds were her father couldn't have cut them off himself. Which meant he'd had help. An accomplice. Or perhaps he was the accomplice here and had just helped someone get into the house. Someone who could try to kill Cash. Delaney didn't want to believe that her father would intentionally make her a target, but then she remembered what he'd said right before the electricity had gone off.

I'm sorry. So sorry.

She'd thought he was apologizing for being drunk and showing up at Cash's, but it could have been a whole lot more than that. He could have put something in place that could lead to her murder. Or rather her attempted murder. Because Delaney had no intention of just allowing someone to kill Cash and her. She'd fight and fight hard—even if it meant that fight was against her own father.

Cash tossed the cuffs aside and got them moving again. As they inched their way to the kitchen, Delaney listened. And kept watch. She no longer heard footsteps, and there were no more of those shuffling sounds. Sounds that had probably been someone cutting those restraints from her father's hands

But where was her father now?

And better yet, who and where was the person who'd freed him?

Delaney braced herself in case Cash and she ran into that person. But they didn't. They made it all the way to the kitchen without her seeing or hearing anything.

When Cash reached the kitchen drawer, he fumbled inside and came up with a small flashlight. He passed it to her, no doubt so his hands would be free if he needed to shoot or fight.

"Go ahead and turn it on," Cash instructed. "But keep the light aimed at the floor."

Good idea. They might be able to use the light to find the phone before her father or someone else saw it and zoomed in on them. Of course, maybe the person had already done the zooming in. Maybe he was just waiting for a clean shot.

Even though her fingers were trembling, Delaney located the flashlight switch and turned it on. The light spilled over the kitchen floor, and that was when she saw something. Dark-colored drops on the white tile.

And she immediately knew what it was.

Blood.

Chapter Fifteen

Cash looked at the blood and cursed. Blood drops that led from the kitchen straight to the back door.

Hell.

This situation had gone from bad to worse because he figured that blood belonged to Delaney's father.

All those shuffling sounds and footsteps had probably been someone "helping" Gil get out of the house. Maybe Gil had been in on the plan. Maybe not. But even if Gil was hurt, it didn't mean he wasn't going to help someone else try to kill Delaney and him.

"My father," Delaney whispered, her breath rising. Cash could hear the panic in her voice.

Cash held her back. He certainly didn't want her rushing out into the backyard, where she could be gunned down. The killer might have counted on her doing just that, and perhaps that was why Gil's blood was on the floor.

"I need a phone," Cash muttered. He had to call for backup. Maybe an ambulance, too, depending on how badly the bleeding person was hurt.

He glanced around, peering into the darkness, and didn't see anyone. Cash didn't hear anyone, either. That didn't mean someone wasn't inside. Still, he was armed and had a flashlight that he could use to locate his phone.

Maybe.

It was possible that Gil or the person who'd gotten him out of the house had also taken the phone. That way, it would buy these SOBs time to do whatever it was they planned to do. Obviously, it wasn't just to gun Delaney and him down, or that would have happened when the person got Gil out.

But Cash had to add another *maybe* to that theory.

Gil and his accomplice/abductor could have wanted to get Delaney's father out of the way before any shooting began. That way, Gil would either be protector or used as a pawn by having this attack pinned on him. That definitely wasn't a settling thought.

"Stay right next to me," Cash told Delaney.

She gave a shaky nod, dragged in an even shakier breath, and he hated that she was having to go through this all over again. This was worse than Webb grabbing her, because now she had the added worry about her father. Delaney had to know that he could be bleeding out right now.

Or Gil could already be dead.

If her father had helped orchestrate this ploy for someone to get to her, then maybe his usefulness was over and done. His accomplice knew the only way to tie up a loose end was by killing Gil. But if so, why hadn't the person just murdered Gil in the living room? Why cut off his restraints and get him out?

Cash didn't know the answer to either of those questions, but he sure as hell hoped to find out soon.

In case someone was watching the house, Cash turned off the flashlight and got Delaney moving back toward the living room. However, they'd only made it a few steps when Cash heard something he definitely hadn't wanted to hear.

The slight creak of the front door opening.

He stopped, positioning himself in front of Delaney but also keeping his body at an angle so he could continue to watch the back door. He didn't want this to be another ruse where someone distracted them so that someone else could sneak in and attack them from behind.

Cash hoped the footsteps he heard in the foyer belonged to Stoney or one of his other ranch hands, but he didn't want to risk calling out to verify that. If he was wrong, it could get Delaney and him shot.

Without saying anything, Cash eased Delaney back so he could maneuver her to the side of the fridge. It wasn't bulletproof, but it was easy cover. It was also close enough to the back door in case they had to attempt a quick escape.

The footsteps stopped in the living room, and Cash figured the person was doing the same thing he was. Listening. Maybe waiting, too, for Delaney and him to make the first move.

Cash tightened his grip on his gun and took aim as best he could, but he had no idea exactly where this "visitor" was. And he couldn't just blindly shoot, either, in case it was one of the ranch hands. So Cash stood there, his heart pounding, and the adrenaline surging through him. Preparing him for the fight. Except Cash didn't want a fight, not with Delaney right next to him.

No.

He wanted to take out this killer when he was sure

Delaney was safe. Unfortunately, Cash had no idea when that would be.

Cash detected some movement. Not footsteps. But something else. And a few seconds later, he realized exactly what that *something* was. Movement from someone who was trying to kill them.

A gunshot slammed into the fridge just on the other side of where Delaney and he were standing.

Cursing, Cash automatically pushed Delaney down, and it wasn't a second too soon. Another shot came, and this one tore through the fridge as if it were paper. The bullet exited and penetrated the wall and went into the pantry.

Cash wanted to return fire. To stop this SOB in his tracks. But to shoot, he'd have to leave cover. Where he'd be an easy target. If he got killed, Delaney would be a sitting duck.

Cash had a quick debate as to what to do, and he decided it was too risky to stand their ground. Obviously, the shooter had an idea of where they were. Maybe because he was using night vision. He could stand where he was and keep firing until he hit one or both of them.

"Stay low," Cash whispered to her, and he hoped she could hear him over the sound of the third blast.

He didn't waste any time. With them in a crouch, Cash got Delaney to the back door. He eased it open, looked around. And prayed. He didn't see anyone, but of course, a second gunman could be out there, waiting for them to do exactly what Cash was about to do.

"Move to the right side of the porch," Cash added to her.

The moment Delaney and he were outside, he picked up the pace and got them moving as fast as he could to the porch swing. Again, it was lousy cover, but if the gunman came onto the back porch, Cash would have a shot—especially since the moonlight made it easier for him to see. Plus, Delaney and he could drop down into the yard if things took a bad turn.

Things did indeed take a bad turn when Cash saw more dark-colored drops on the porch. More blood. He was sure of it. And these drops led off the porch and into the backyard.

The fear crawled through him when he heard Delaney gasp, and for one heart-stopping moment he thought someone was about to grab her. Or worse. That someone was about to shoot her. But when he followed her pointing finger to the yard, Cash saw the reason for the gasp.

Someone was lying facedown on the grass, only a few yards from the shed.

It was a man, and Cash was pretty sure that was blood he saw on the back of the guy's shirt.

"My father," she whispered.

While he kept an eye on the back door, Cash leaned a little so he could get a better look at the man. And his chest tightened, vising his ribs until he thought they might crack. Because it wasn't Gil.

It was Stoney.

Hell. His ranch hand was down.

Cash wondered if the blood in the kitchen and on the porch could be Stoney's. He wasn't moving, and with all that blood, he could be dead. Cash hadn't heard a gunshot in the backyard, but that didn't mean someone hadn't fired using a silencer. Of course, there were plenty of other ways to kill, and it was possible that Stoney had been stabbed.

Delaney made a soft gasp when there was some movement in the kitchen, and Cash volleyed his attention between the yard and the door. That was because the person in the kitchen could be a decoy or something. Someone meant to distract them so the killer could come at them from somewhere on the grounds.

Cash cursed himself for not grabbing a knife from the kitchen. If he had thought of it, Delaney would have had a weapon in case it came down to a fight. However, he prayed that things wouldn't get that far. He took aim at the door, and if any one of their suspects came out, he'd be ready to put a stop to this.

The door creaked open just a couple of inches, and Cash dragged in his breath. Waiting. Listening. And steeling himself up to do whatever necessary to keep Delaney alive.

A hand jutted out from the opening, and in the blink of an eye, the person tossed something onto the porch. It thudded onto the wood planks and then rolled. It wasn't until it got closer to them that Cash realized what it was.

"A grenade," Cash spat out.

He didn't wait for Delaney to react. Hooking his arm around her waist, Cash tumbled off the porch with her. They landed hard on some rocks and shrubs, but he quickly pulled Delaney to her feet and got them running.

DELANEY HAD ONLY gotten a glimpse of the grenade that had been thrown out on the porch, but a glimpse had been more than enough to confirm that Cash and she were in huge trouble.

They couldn't stay there and wait to be blown to

bits, but running out into the yard meant they could be gunned down.

Still, they ran.

Cash made sure of that. He kept a firm grip on her arm, and moving fast, they headed for the side of the barn. They nearly made it there, too, when the blast tore through the air.

Delaney staggered and risked looking back. The porch had been ripped apart, and bits of the wood and railing were flying across the yard.

Cash dragged her to the side of the barn, positioning them back-to-back and in a crouching position. "Keep watch. If you see anyone, let me know."

Delaney nodded, and with her breath gusting, she fired glances around, looking for the person who obviously wanted them dead. But she didn't see anyone. Well, no one other than Stoney, who was still facedown on the ground. Thankfully, the ranch hand was out of the way from the falling debris, so he likely wouldn't be hit. However, he also hadn't moved, which couldn't be a good sign.

Maybe because he was dead.

Delaney had to shove that possibility aside because it would scrape her nerves raw, and that wouldn't help anything. She needed to stay focused, alert. That was the only way they could stay alive.

As bad as the grenade had been, at least it would alert the ranch hands, and one of them would certainly call the cops and maybe even an ambulance. If they could make a call, that is. Delaney had a sickening thought, one that clawed its way up her throat. If the killer had murdered or injured Stoney, he might have done the same thing to the other ranch hands.

Oh, mercy.

There were three other hands somewhere on the grounds. Maybe even in the bunkhouse. They'd been vigilant, standing guard and patrolling the grounds, but that didn't mean someone couldn't have sneaked up on them one at a time.

Had her father done that?

Delaney still didn't want to believe he'd had any part in this, but she had to accept that he might have helped set it up. Maybe he'd done that without realizing what the would-be killer planned to do. Maybe her father had figured out that she was the target, and tried to fight back. That could explain the blood.

And maybe she was just hanging on to false hope.

Either way, she needed to find her father and discover if he was the reason this attack was happening. Of course, for her to get those answers, Delancy needed to find him alive.

She thought of the blood in the kitchen and on the porch. It wasn't a huge amount, so maybe he didn't have a life-threatening injury. Or maybe it wasn't his blood at all. That twisted away at her, too, but Delaney had to consider that her father might be the attacker here and that anyone in his path was a possible victim.

A second blast thundered through the silence, and Delaney could have sworn that it shook the ground beneath her. She didn't dare look back to see how much damage this one had caused. She kept her attention pinned to the back of the barn and the pasture that spread out behind it.

And then she saw it.

Some movement on the ground at the back of the barn. She pinned her gaze there and considered alerting

Cash. But it could be nothing. And Delaney didn't want to pull his attention from the house, especially since that was where the grenades had come from. Their attacker could still be inside, but it was just as possible that he'd already gone out through the front door. If so, then Cash would be able to see if he came to the backyard to try to finish what he had started.

Delaney saw another flutter of movement by the barn, and she heard something. It sounded like moaning. The kind of moan a person would make if they were in pain.

"Someone's back there," she whispered to Cash.

Cash immediately spun around, pinning her against the barn. Using his body to shield hers. Delaney didn't want him doing that. Risking himself for her, but now was hardly the time to tell him that she couldn't lose him. She just couldn't.

There was another moan, this one louder than the first, and Delaney saw more movement. Because of the heavy shadows, she couldn't be certain, but she thought it was another man. Maybe one of the ranch hands.

Maybe her father.

She forced herself to stay put, and she tamped down her instincts to go to him. To make sure he was okay. She couldn't do that because it could be a trap.

That possibility tightened every muscle in her body, and she held her breath for so long that her lungs began to ache. Cash stayed in place, protecting her, while he volleyed glances between the house and the back of the barn where the person was still moaning.

Delaney focused straight ahead. At the shed. At Stoney. At the groves of trees that rimmed the pasture. There wasn't nearly enough light for her to see if anyone was lurking in those trees, but it would be a good spot for a sniper. Of course, a sniper might not be needed at all if the person who'd thrown those grenades got close enough to Cash and her to toss another one at them.

"I'm going to try to get us to the bunkhouse," Cash whispered.

That made sense, because even if the ranch hands were all down, there'd likely be a phone in the bunkhouse. Or other weapons they could use to defend themselves. But the bunkhouse was behind the barn, and there were plenty of places where they could be attacked along the way. Still, just sitting here wasn't a smart move. Another grenade could come their way at any second.

"Stay low and keep watch," Cash whispered to her. "I'll deal with whoever that is on the ground."

Delaney considered how that might play out. Perhaps with a gunfight. But then she heard something else. Something that sent an icy shock through her entire body.

The sound of dogs growling.

Chapter Sixteen

Cash had prayed things wouldn't get any worse. But the sound of those barking, snarling dogs meant that Delaney and he had to get out of there fast.

Judging from the sound of the barks, these were Ramone's Dobermans. Maybe the dogs had gotten loose again, but Cash thought it could be a lot more than that. Ramone could have set them loose as a way of finishing what he'd started by throwing those grenades at them.

"Let's go," Cash told Delaney, pulling her to her feet.

She'd already started moving toward the back of the barn, away from the dogs, but directly toward the man who was lying on the ground. There were barn doors at the rear that they could slip through and get away from the Dobermans, but first Cash had to deal with the guy on the ground. If it wasn't one of his ranch hands, then it was possibly someone involved in the plot to kill Delaney and him.

Behind them, Cash heard the dogs gaining ground. They would no doubt attack, and that had Cash considering if he should make a stand and try to get them to back off. The problem with that was while he was dealing with the Dobermans, the person who wanted them dead could just pick off Delaney and him. In fact, the dogs could be a ruse making it easier for that to happen.

Cash kept them running until they reached the man, who was now trying to sit up. Not one of his hands.

But Gil.

Delaney's father was still moaning, and there was a cut on his head as if someone had clubbed him. The injury looked real. *Looked.* However, Cash figured it could be a clever fake and part of whatever this sick plan was that had already been set in motion.

"We can't leave him out here," Delaney insisted, already reaching down to take hold of her father's arm.

No, they couldn't, but that didn't mean Cash intended to trust the man. After all, if it hadn't been for Gil, Cash would have a phone and would have already called for backup.

Cash let go of Delaney so he could grab Gil. "If you try to hurt Delaney," he warned her father, "I'll kill you. Understand?"

Gil mumbled something that he didn't take the time to catch, but Cash kept his eye on their surroundings and then threw open the barn door and practically tossed Gil inside.

Just as the dogs reached them.

Cash felt the gut punch of fear that Delaney could be mauled to death, and he fired a shot over the dogs' heads. The sound of the blast stopped them long enough to shove into the barn. Together, they slammed the doors shut.

The dogs continued to bark and growl and began pawing at the door. Cash slid the board latch in place and whirled back around to make sure Gil wasn't about to attack them. The only light in the barn came from a battery-operated bug zapper, but it was enough for Cash to see Gil. He was still on the ground and wasn't making any attempt to get up.

Good. That was where Cash wanted him to stay.

Cash didn't have any cuffs with him, but he grabbed some hay baling twine and used it to tie Gil's hands. It might not hold, and it darn sure wouldn't prevent the man from trying to run, but at least Gil wouldn't be able to pick up something and try to bash them with it.

"Are you working with Ramone?" Cash asked him. "Did the two of you set all of this up?"

Gil moaned again and shook his head. "Set up what? What's going on?"

Cash wanted to know the same damn thing, but this wasn't the time to play twenty questions with Gil. He had to take some precautions and take them fast.

"This way," Cash said, and he caught on to Delaney's hand to lead her behind some stacked hay bales. It wasn't much cover, but it was better than nothing. "In case there's another grenade."

Even in the dim light, Cash could see the terror in Delaney's eyes. He cursed that terror. Cursed himself for not having kept her safe.

Delaney reached out for him when he started to move away and go back to Gil. "You should be behind cover, too," she pointed out, and her gaze flicked to her father. "Him, too. He can tell us who's trying to kill us."

Probably, but at this point having a name wasn't nearly as important as stopping the person. Still, Cash dragged Gil away from the barn door. But he put the man yards away from Delaney.

"Cash?" someone called out.

Ramone.

Cash was sure of it. He didn't respond, and he motioned for Delaney to stay quiet. Of course, it was possible that Ramone already knew they were in the barn, but in case he didn't, Cash didn't want to make this easy for him.

"Cash?" Ramone called out again. "Delaney? Are you all right? What the hell happened to your porch?"

The dogs stopped barking, and Cash could hear them running away from the barn. Probably heading toward their owner.

"Go get in the truck," Ramone said, and Cash hoped that meant he was calling off the dogs—literally. But if Ramone had been the one to set the Dobermans on them, why would he do that?

Maybe as part of the ploy to draw them out of the barn?

If so, Cash wasn't buying it. He shifted his attention to the front barn doors, took aim with his gun and waited.

"Cash, I got a call from one of your hands," Ramone shouted. "He didn't give me his name, but he said my dogs were over here and that I should come and get them right away. I'm really sorry. I don't know how they got out." He paused. "Are you two okay? Was there some kind of explosion in your kitchen?"

Ramone's concern sounded like the real deal, but Cash still didn't answer.

"I'm calling 911," Ramone finally said, and a few moments later, he cursed. "Hell, one of your ranch hands is on the ground."

There was the sound of running footsteps, and Cash grumbled some profanity. If Ramone was the killer, Cash couldn't just stand by while he murdered Stoney.

Cash snatched up a pitchfork and handed it to Delaney. "Use it if you need to," he told her.

Of course, that had to cause her fear to soar, but Delaney stood, gripping it like a weapon. She looked plenty ready to defend both of them if it came down to it.

Cash hurried to the front barn door, eased it open and leaned out enough to take aim at Ramone. "Stop where you are," he warned Ramone.

Ramone whirled around, and he must have had no trouble seeing Cash's gun because he cursed and lifted his hands in the air. He had his phone in his right hand, but his left one was empty. No signs of a weapon. Of course, he could have one tucked in the back waist of his jeans.

"I don't know what you think I've done," Ramone snarled on a huff. "But the only reason I'm here is to get my dogs. I'm pretty sure someone let them out of their pen."

"And who would have done that?" Cash fired back.

"I don't know," Ramone repeated, tipping his head to Cash's house, "but I'm guessing it was the same person who did that to your porch." His forehead bunched up. "Are you and Delaney okay?"

Cash ignored that question and went with one of his own. "Did you call 911?"

"Not yet. You want me to do that now?"

"Why don't you toss me your phone, and I'll make the call?" Cash countered. That way, he'd be sure it would actually go through and not be part of Ramone's ruse to make Cash believe that help was on the way.

"Okay." Ramone's voice and expression were now all caution.

Or pretend caution anyway.

But with his left hand still in the air, Ramone inched closer. Cash didn't plan on letting him get too close. When Ramone was a couple of yards away, he'd have him throw the phone toward him. If Ramone had had no part in this attack, then Cash could snatch up the cell and call for help. However, if Ramone was up to his eyeballs in this, then he'd likely use this latest incident with the dogs to get closer to Cash. Maybe so he could try to kill him. However, if he tried that, Cash would take him out.

Even though Cash didn't want to take his attention off Ramone, he glanced at the barn to make sure Delaney was okay. She was. For now, anyway. She still had hold of the pitchfork, and Gil hadn't moved an inch from where Cash had put him.

Ramone was still moving toward him when Cash heard the swooshing sound. Not a gunshot fired from a silencer. This was bigger than a handgun. And Cash quickly saw what it was.

Someone had launched another grenade.

And this one landed right next to Ramone's feet.

FROM THE MOMENT Delaney had heard Ramone's voice, she'd suspected there'd be more trouble.

And there apparently was.

Ramone yelled out, "What the hell?" a split second before Cash ducked back into the barn.

Much to her shock, Ramone was right behind Cash, and Cash didn't stop him from bolting into the barn. The two men slammed the door shut and continued running to the side of the barn where she was. Both of them dived behind the hay bales with her, with Cash positioning himself between Ramone and her.

Before she could ask what was happening, Delaney heard the third explosion. This one was louder than the other, and it shook the barn, causing bits of hay and dust to spill down from the hayloft.

"He's playing with us," Cash growled. He gave her a quick glance as if to make sure she was okay, and then he shifted his attention to Ramone.

"Did you have anything to do with this?" Cash demanded.

"What the hell is *this*?" Ramone demanded right back, and even though Delaney couldn't see his expression, the man certainly sounded shocked and scared. "Was that really a grenade?"

"Yeah," Cash verified. "And if you helped set that up, then I swear that you'll pay hard for it."

"Set it up?" Ramone challenged. "I could have been killed, and I sure as heck didn't launch a grenade at myself. It landed right by my feet. If it'd gone off just a couple of seconds sooner, I'd be a dead man."

Since Cash didn't disagree with that, Delaney got a mental picture of what'd happened outside the barn. Ramone had called off the dogs, but while he'd been talking with Cash, someone had fired a grenade at him. Someone who wasn't her father. Wasn't Ramone.

And that left one person from their suspect list. Byers.

"He wants us all in here," Cash said as if talking to himself. He cursed. "Call 911," he added to Ramone. "Ask for backup."

She heard Ramone punch in the numbers on his phone and then relay Cash's order and their situation. It wouldn't take long for the deputies to arrive, but if their attacker had more grenades, then he could toss one at the barn. That would only take a couple of seconds. And she doubted the barn was strong enough to withstand a direct blast.

"We have to get out of here," Cash muttered. "He plans to kill us all."

"He?" Ramone asked when he finished the call.

Cash didn't get a chance to answer, because someone called out to them.

"I'm betting you're all at each other's throats right about now," the man shouted. "I'm going to give it a minute or two and see if you off each other for me."

Byers. He was the one behind this. The one who'd been trying to kill Cash and her.

That realization slammed into her like a Mack truck. She'd been the one to invite Byers into their lives by hiring him. Of course, she hadn't asked for this, but if she'd never...

Delaney stopped the guilt trip and rethought everything. Fitting the pieces together like a puzzle.

"Byers set this up," she said.

"Yeah," Cash readily agreed. "And we have to get out of here. Because I'm betting Byers has another grenade."

"Byers?" Ramone repeated, shaking his head. "Why the hell would he do something like this?"

Delaney intentionally answered in a loud enough voice for Byers to hear. "Byers wants to kill me because he thinks I got your brother a break when Webb wasn't convicted of first-degree murder."

"Webb got manslaughter," Byers snarled, confirming that he had indeed heard her. "Webb should have gotten the death penalty, and you managed to get him a slap on the wrist."

A twenty-year sentence wasn't exactly a slap on the wrist, but Byers wouldn't want to listen to that. Nor would he want to hear that there simply hadn't been enough evidence to prove premeditation for a first-degree murder conviction.

"A jury gave Webb that sentence," Cash pointed out.

"A jury that heard only what Delaney wanted them to hear. And don't tell me she was just doing her job. She made sure a killer would get out of jail so he could kill again. Too bad Webb didn't manage that when he escaped," Byers said.

No, but he'd come close. But so had Byers. Considering the grenades, it wasn't much of a stretch to believe Byers was behind the other explosion, but Delaney had to ask.

"You put that bomb in my house?" she called out. "And left me that message?"

He didn't answer, but she could tell from the look in his eyes that it was a yes. And Delaney started to work out why he'd set up the attack that way. Byers had tried to make it look as if her father had caused the explosion, especially since Gil had been at her house earlier, and Byers could have done all of that so that Gil could take the blame.

And maybe that's what was going on here tonight.

"Byers wants my father to take the fall?" Delaney asked.

Cash made a sound of agreement. "Byers is almost certainly going to try to set this up as murder-suicide," he muttered. "After we've all been blown to bits, he'll make it look as though Gil got drunk and went off the deep end. I'm betting there's a letter or something that'll back that up."

Delaney was betting the same thing. While her father was drunk, Byers could have easily manipulated him into doing something like that.

"We have to get out of here," Cash repeated.

While he kept an eye on Ramone, Cash hurried to her father, hauling him to his feet. Gil was still wobbly, so Delaney threw down the pitchfork and took Gil's other side, shouldering him while they went to the back barn door.

"Wait a minute," Ramone interrupted. His voice was shaky and he swallowed hard. "What stops the SOB from just killing us when we go out there?"

"Nothing," Cash answered without hesitation. "But I'm betting this barn is about to blow."

Cash raised the board lock, easing the door open a fraction. "Help Delaney with Gil," he told Ramone. "And remember—if you double-cross us, you're a dead man."

"I'm not double-crossing you," Ramone insisted, hurrying to take Gil from Cash. "But I still don't think this is a good idea."

"It's not a good idea," Cash agreed, "but we don't have a lot of options. Unless we can get away from Byers and a grenade, either we can get shot or die in an explosion." Then Cash stopped, his gaze zooming to Ramone. "Can you call back the dogs? I want them to go to Byers, not my ranch hand who's lying unconscious on the ground by the shed."

Ramone's head whipped up, and he nodded. "They'll go to Byers since he's likely moving around."

Delaney prayed that was true. If not, Stoney could be mauled.

Cash was obviously having a debate with himself

about that very thing, but he finally said, "Do it, Ra-mone. Call the dogs."

Moving fast, they went closer to the door, and Ra-mone gave a loud whistle. Within seconds, Delaney heard the dogs begin to bark.

"They'll attack Byers without any other command?" Cash asked him.

"Maybe. I got the Dobermans from somebody who'd rescued them. I'm not sure what they'll do since they obviously still need a lot of training. That's why I've been keeping them in the pen."

Yes, they did need training, but maybe they could distract Byers enough for them to escape. Delaney only hoped Byers didn't shoot or hurt the dogs. She was ter-rified of them and thought they were dangerous with-out the training, but she didn't want the Dobermans to suffer or die, especially since it wasn't their fault they were trying to attack like this.

She listened for Byers to shout or make any sounds of distress, but the only thing Delaney heard was the frantic, agitated barking of the dogs. And her own pulse throbbing in her ears.

Cash opened the door wider, easing out while he whipped his gaze and his gun from one side to the other.

"Delaney, take the pitchfork with you," Cash in-structed.

Ramone shifted, taking her father's weight so she could do that. But Delaney hoped it didn't come down to her having to use it. Still, she would. If it meant keep-ing them alive, she'd fight. Even if it meant fighting off Ramone. She didn't think the man was part of this at-tack, but just in case she was wrong about that, she'd keep an eye on him.

"Run for that big oak," Cash told them, and he tipped his head to the tree that was about twenty yards away. "Get down on the ground on the other side of it and cover your heads."

The oak was pretty much the nearest cover, but twenty yards gave Byers plenty of room to shoot them. Of course, from the sound of it, Byers was dealing with the dogs by ordering them to sit and stay.

Delaney paused long enough for her gaze to connect with Cash's. "What about you?" she asked.

"I won't be far behind you." He dropped a quick kiss on her mouth.

She wanted to make him swear that he wouldn't take any unnecessary risks, but at this point, everything was necessary.

"Call off these dogs!" Byers shouted, and he added some vile profanity to his demand. "Call them off or I'll shoot them."

Cash ignored him, and without looking back into the barn, he motioned for them to come out. When Ramone hesitated, Delaney used her free hand to help with her father, and she got them moving.

"Byers," her father muttered. "He's gonna try to kill you."

Yes, he would. Delaney had no doubts about that. But she kept moving, and the moment they were outside, they started running. Well, running as fast as they could considering her father was practically deadweight.

Each step seemed to take an eternity, and she focused on getting to the tree. And on watching Ramone. However, her thoughts—and fears—were with Cash. They had to make it out of this alive. They just had to.

The night air was heavy and humid. Smothering.

And the smoke and stench from the burning porch made it hard to breathe. Still, Delaney dragged in as much air as she could and made a beeline for the tree. They were still a few yards away from it when all of her fears came true.

The explosion.

It came from behind her. The sound, heat and blast ripping through the night. It propelled them forward, tumbling them to the ground and knocking the pitchfork from Delaney's hand. She landed hard, her head smacking into a rock.

The dizziness came, the ground swirling around her, and Delaney couldn't move. Couldn't make her eyes focus. But everything inside her was screaming just one word.

Cash.

She had to get to Cash. She had to make sure he was okay.

Moaning, Delaney pressed her hands against the ground, trying to get up. She failed, but then someone was lifting her. She looked up into Cash's eyes.

He was alive.

But he was hurt. There was a gash on his head, and blood was sliding down the side of his face. However, that didn't stop him from running with her to the oak. He put her behind it and raced away. Delaney tried to take hold of him, to pull him back to safety, but she couldn't stop him.

She blinked hard, trying to will away the dizziness and clear her eyes, and she finally saw what Cash was doing. He was hauling her father to the tree. Cash had gone back to save him.

Ramone was limping along behind Cash and her father, but the man looked back over his shoulder. Delaney looked, too, and saw what was left of the barn. Which wasn't much. Byers had obviously used a grenade to blow it to bits.

"The dogs ran off," Ramone muttered, dropping down beside her father. "I hope they ran off."

So did she. But it was possible they'd also been hurt in the blast. Then again, if the dogs had still been close to Byers, he probably would have made sure he was out of range of the blast.

But where was Byers now?

Delaney didn't have to wait long for that answer. Byers stepped through the smoke, and in the moonlight, she could see the gun in his right hand. A grenade was in his left hand, and he had his fingers poised on the pin. If Byers pulled it, she was pretty sure the grenade would explode in a matter of seconds.

"If you shoot me," Byers warned them, "I'll have just enough time to toss it at you. You'll all die."

Delaney figured that was true, but with everything Byers had already done, she knew in her heart that he had no plans for them to walk away alive.

The black smoke swirled up around Byers, and the milky moonlight shone on his face. A face gone mad with the need for revenge. He looked like a demon who haunted people's nightmares.

"You were going to set up my father to take the fall for this," she said.

"Yeah." Byers's tone was flippant, but he cursed when he heard the sirens. His eyes narrowed. "He will take the fall. But Cash and you can save him by stepping out and letting me finish this."

Finish this by killing her.

If Delaney had thought for one second that Byers would be satisfied with just her death, she might have considered it, but there was no way he'd leave witnesses. Especially a cop like Cash. No. She figured the moment she stepped out, he'd fling the grenade, killing all of them.

"You're not going out there," Cash told her.

Her gaze met his again. The muscles in his jaw were tight. His mouth, in a grimace. But there was no madness here. What she saw was his fierce determination to keep her safe. However, this was out of his hands now since Byers was the one with the grenade.

"I have to do something before my deputies get closer," Cash added. "Get down and cover your heads again. I'm going to shoot Byers."

"You won't be down, and your head won't be covered," she reminded him.

Cash kissed her. "I'll be okay. Promise."

She was about to say that wasn't an assurance he could keep, but the growling sound stopped her. Delaney whirled back to Byers to see one of the Dobermans leap through the smoke. The dog's powerful jaws locked onto Byers's arm.

Cursing, Byers twisted his body around. He lifted his gun, but he also pulled the pin.

Byers threw the grenade at them.

"Get down!" Cash yelled.

But he didn't do that. Cash remained standing, took aim.

And he fired.

Chapter Seventeen

The moment Cash fired the shot into Byers's chest, the man dropped to the ground. Cash didn't wait to see if his shot had killed Byers, because every second counted. He had to try to stop the blast from killing him.

"Cash!" Delaney called out.

He prayed that she hadn't started running toward him, but there was no time to tell her to stay put or get down.

Because the grenade went off.

The explosion sent a slam of heat and pressure right at him. A hard punch to every part of his body. Cash covered his head with his forearms and hands, but there wasn't much he could do for the rest of him. He had to lie there while the debris battered him as it flew from the blast.

Delaney called out his name again, and he cursed because she sounded closer than she had been just seconds earlier. He wanted her behind the tree, away from the fiery fragments coming at him like missiles.

While still keeping his head covered, Cash rolled to the side so he could see her. She wasn't behind the tree but rather to the side of it, and judging from the look of horror on her face, she thought he'd been hurt. Heck, maybe he had. Right now, it was hard to tell because his nerves were firing from the impact of the blast.

"Stay put," Cash told her. "Get down."

He did the same, but he had to turn back and make sure Byers wasn't coming after them again. However, it was hard to see anything in that direction because now there was a wall of smoke, dirt and heaven knew what else.

In the distance, Cash could hear the sirens. His deputies, no doubt, and maybe an ambulance and fire truck. They'd likely all be needed, but he didn't want any of the first responders hurt or killed. Something that could happen if Byers was still alive. The PI might take out any number of people while attempting to escape.

When the debris finally began to die down, the dogs started to bark and growl, and Cash heard Ramone belt out a loud whistle. "The truck," he ordered.

Cash thought the Dobermans obeyed because he heard them hurrying away. He couldn't tell how many of them were doing that, but maybe they'd all survived.

"You're hurt," Delaney said, and her voice was shaking.

"No, I'm fine," Cash answered, and to test that out, he forced himself to a sitting position. He took aim at the spot where he'd last seen Byers, but he still couldn't see the man.

Wincing from the bruises and cuts he'd gotten in the fall, Cash got to his feet and fired glances all around. Looking for any signs of another attack. Hard to tell that, though, when his backyard looked like the aftermath of a war zone.

Hell.

Smoke and debris filled the yard. The barn had collapsed, sending boards and beams as far as the eye could see. The ground was torn up, and there was a gaping hole where the last grenade had exploded. Cash suspected the back of his house would have similar damage. In fact, there might not be much left of his place.

One bright spot, other than them being alive, was that there'd been no livestock in the barn. Cash also didn't hear any sounds to indicate any of the dogs had been injured. He wanted to keep it that way. They'd all dodged a bullet, but that didn't mean more *bullets* weren't heading their way.

"Ramone, call 911 again," Cash instructed. "Tell the first responders to hold at the end of my driveway. I don't want them to approach until I'm sure the threat's been neutralized."

Cash wanted to go looking for that threat. For Byers. He also needed to check on Stoney and his other ranch hands to see if they needed help. Or if they were even alive. But first he needed to make sure Delaney would stay put while he did that.

"Don't move yet," Cash reminded her.

With his gun ready, he went closer to where he'd shot Byers. There wasn't a clear path to reach the man, and Cash had to kick aside some debris and maneuver around the crater caused by the blast.

And then he finally saw Byers.

Cash's hand stayed on his weapon, but he was certain of one thing. Byers was dying. The man was sprawled out, his arms and legs at awkward angles, and the front of his shirt was covered with blood.

Byers moaned and then muttered some profanity.

"You might have won, but Delaney still paid some. Not enough but some."

The man was wrong. Delaney had paid plenty. And why?

"Why did you do all of this?" Cash demanded. "Was this payback because of Webb's light sentence?"

"He got a slap on the wrist," Byers spat out. "I was going to let it go, but then Webb escaped. He was a free man, and that wouldn't have happened if he'd gotten a harder sentence to start with and gone to a prison where it wouldn't have been so easy for him to sneak out."

Cash could have pointed out that none of that was Delaney's fault, but he didn't bother to respond. Unlike Byers who was obviously still seething with anger.

"After Webb was free, I wanted Delaney to pay and pay hard," Byers said, his tone full of venom. "I wanted everyone to think she'd lost it, that she was delusional, and then she would have been an easy target for Webb. Webb would have killed her, but he would have made her pay first."

Yes, Webb would have, and Cash was thankful both Webb and Byers had failed. Thankful, too, when Byers finally dragged in the last breath he'd ever take. Seconds later, the man's now lifeless eyes stared up at the night sky.

So there had been a casualty. A loss of life. Which wasn't much of a loss at all as far as Cash was concerned.

Cash didn't see any other grenades, but since it was possible that Byers had more on him, he didn't go any closer to the man. Once his deputies were on scene, he could have one of them get in a bomb squad. No use taking any unnecessary chances.

He turned when he heard the moan, and he looked past Byers and at Stoney. The ranch hand was sitting up and rubbing the back of his head.

"You okay?" Cash called out to him.

Stoney squinted against the smoke and gave a shaky nod. "Yeah. Somebody hit me with a stun gun."

Byers, no doubt, was responsible, and Cash hoped that meant Byers had done the same to the other ranch hands. Being stunned wasn't any fun, but it was far better than being killed. Maybe Byers had used the stun gun rather than shoot them because the shots, even those fired through a silencer, might have alerted someone. This way, Byers could sneak up on the hands and quickly disable them.

"Stay put for a couple more minutes," Cash told Stoney.

He didn't want Stoney stumbling around, tripping on debris. Or worse, stepping on a grenade. Plus, Stoney needed to be checked for injuries he might have gotten when he fell after being stunned.

Cash turned and headed back to the oak tree. He tried not to limp when he walked toward Delaney, because he knew it would alarm her even more than she already was, but he figured he failed big-time. His knee was throbbing like a bad tooth, but he could deal with the pain.

Yeah, he could deal.

Because Delaney was all right.

He didn't see any blood on her. No bruises or other visible injuries. That was something of a miracle, considering all the debris that had been flying around, and Cash would make sure she got a thorough examination since she'd hit her head when she fell.

"Byers is dead," he let her know right off.

"Dead," she repeated on a rise of breath. The sound she made was one of pure relief.

Cash made it to her as fast as he could and pulled her into his arms. He needed this contact, needed to know that she was truly okay, but that need didn't blind him to taking precautions. That meant checking to make sure Gil and Ramone weren't about to launch their own attack. One look at the men, though, and Cash knew they had no intention of doing that.

Gil was sitting up, his back against the tree. There wasn't any fresh blood on his head, but he looked shell-shocked. Ditto for Ramone. His hands were shaking hard while he spoke with the 911 operator. If Ramone had had any plans to try to hurt them, he would have done it when Cash had been down in the yard.

"Go ahead and tell the responders they can come on the scene," Cash instructed Ramone. "They'll have to be careful, though, because there might be other grenades."

That put some fresh alarm in Ramone's eyes, but he relayed the information to the emergency dispatcher. Soon, they might be able to clear the grounds so they could get in an ambulance.

"You're really not hurt?" Delaney asked, drawing Cash's attention back to her.

"Just banged up a little. Nothing serious," he assured her.

That was the truth. If something had been broken, he was certain he would have felt it by now.

Cash leaned in and kissed her. Because he needed that, too, as much as he'd needed to hold her. He'd nearly lost her tonight, and it might take him a couple of lifetimes to get over that she'd nearly been killed by a madman hell-bent on revenge.

He felt the dampness on her mouth and realized she'd been crying. On a sigh, Cash eased back, wiped away her tears and gave her another quick kiss. One that he hoped held the promise that he'd give her a much longer one once he was certain she was safe.

"Why'd you do it?" Gil muttered.

Cash pulled back enough from Delaney so he could look down at the man, but he kept his arm around her. He didn't want to let go of her until they'd both settled some more. Which, again, might take a lifetime or two.

"Do what?" Cash asked.

Gil pulled in a long breath. "Why'd you save me? You saved my life when you got me out of that barn."

Cash probably had kept him from dying, and he nearly gave Gil the line about it being his job, that it was just part of being the badge. And that was indeed true. But it'd been more than that.

"You're Delaney's father," Cash said simply. "She loves you."

Gil blinked hard, and the moonlight showed the tears pooling in his eyes. "I do love her." He groaned, shook his head. "And I nearly got her killed."

"I'm okay," Delaney insisted. She went to him and pulled him into her arms.

"No thanks to me. I didn't know what Byers was going to do. I swear it."

"I believe you." Delaney eased back to meet her father eye to eye. "Did Byers talk you into coming here tonight?"

Gil nodded. "He got me drunk, and I don't think straight when I'm drunk. Byers convinced me to come here."

"And do what?" Cash asked when Gil stopped.

"Demand that Delaney leave you." Gil looked up, stared at Cash. "He said as long as Delaney was with you, she could be killed. I wanted to believe him because I didn't want Delaney to be with you. But I can see I was wrong about that. You and Delaney belong together."

Well, that was a concession Cash hadn't thought he'd ever get from Gil, and he hoped that meant Delaney's father wouldn't give them grief about being together. Because Cash was going to do his best to talk Delaney into staying with him.

Delaney sighed. "I was the one who put Cash in danger."

"Not true." Cash hitched his thumb toward Byers. "Byers is the one who did this. He's the reason for the danger." He paused, kept his attention on Gil. "How'd Byers get to you? Did he find you after you left your house?"

Gil winced, probably regretting that he'd sneaked out on the bodyguard Delaney had hired for him. "I'm not sure. I was walking from my house, and Byers was just there."

Byers had likely had Gil under surveillance, maybe hoping that he could use Gil to get to Delaney. And it'd worked. When Cash had let Gil into his house tonight, Byers had obviously put his sick plan into motion.

A plan to kill Delaney, Ramone, Gil and him.

Hell, maybe that plan had included anyone and everyone on the ranch if they got in his way. But the moment Cash had that thought, he heard Buck call out to him.

"Boss, you okay?" Buck asked.

He spotted the hand making his way from the bunkhouse, and Cash felt another wave of relief. "We're fine. How about you and the other hands?"

Buck staggered a little, but despite being unsteady, he still made it to Cash. "We all got stunned. We got some bumps and bruises in the fall, but we're okay. Where's Stoney?" Buck added.

"In the yard. He's all right, too, but I don't want him walking over here until the area's been checked for grenades."

Which would be soon, since Cash heard the fire truck and cruisers pull into his driveway.

"Wait here," Cash told Ramone, Gil and Buck. "I need to talk to my deputies."

"I'm going with you," Delaney insisted, taking hold of his hand.

Cash could have probably talked her into staying put, but the truth was, he didn't want to be away from her. "Stay right next to me," he instructed.

Delaney was already doing just that. She slipped her arm around him as they made their way around the remains of the barn and into the side yard. There was no damage here. No sign that Byers had even been on this part of the property.

When they made it to the front of the house, Cash spotted Jesse, who was already out of the cruiser. He'd brought three other deputies with him.

"What the hell happened?" Jesse asked, eyeing first the damage and then giving Cash and Delaney the once-over.

"Long story short, Byers tried to kill us," Cash explained.

Cash gave them a quick update, and they sprang

into action, fanning out over the yard to check for any other explosives.

"Your house is burning," Delaney muttered. "I'm so sorry."

It was indeed on fire, and Cash had to accept that it might burn to the ground before the fire department could move in. It was a loss for sure, but at the moment, he couldn't feel any regret over it. He could always get another house. The same couldn't be said for the woman in his arms.

Because Delaney was the only woman he wanted.

"I'm in love with you," Cash told her. Yeah, the timing sucked, but he didn't want to go another minute without letting her know how he felt about her.

She looked up, and her eyes were surprisingly clear, considering they'd just gone through hell and back. "Good."

Delaney smiled. Kissed him. A long and deep kind of kiss that nearly made him forget that her "Good" was not the response he'd wanted to hear from her. Well, not the only response anyway.

"Good?" he managed to ask.

"Good," she verified, and distracted him with another kiss.

Cash decided to get in on that distraction. He hooked his arm around her, pulled her closer and added some heat to the kiss. Again, bad timing, but it felt *good*. It felt right.

The kiss went on way too long, and got way too hot, considering they had an audience what with the fire department and EMTs having arrived. Still, even when Cash finally tore his mouth from hers, he didn't let go of Delaney. He kept her in his arms.

"I'm in love with you, too," she muttered.

Now, *that* was the response he wanted. The response he needed. Just as he needed Delaney.

"Promise you'll tell me that often?" Cash prompted.

Delaney's smile widened, and he could almost taste that smile when she kissed him again. "Promise."

* * * * *

SCENT DETECTION

LESLIE MARSHMAN

To the Lunch Bunch.
May our friendship and encouragement last forever!

Chapter One

The truck careened through the night, its driver hell-bent on his objective.

Angry blades of rain slashed across the windshield, cutting visibility to almost nothing. On this lonely stretch of State Highway 95 in Idaho's northwest backcountry, landslides were frequent, streetlights rare. Only wicked forks of lightning, strobing every few seconds off the inky peaks of the Seven Devils Range, revealed the dangerous ledge where the pavement ended and the cliff's steep drop began.

Another blinding flash illuminated a sharp curve up ahead. Exhausted, fueled only by caffeine and adrenaline, the driver's grip tightened on the steering wheel. The truck hydroplaned, spinning across the rain-slick road before stopping on the asphalt's edge. For several long seconds, the vehicle teetered at a precarious angle.

Thunder cracked and shook the ground. The truck's nose dipped farther, held for a moment, then tumbled into the black abyss. Glancing off trees. Plowing over saplings, scrub and rocks. He jammed down on the brakes in a futile attempt to stop the frenzied descent.

Icy fingers of death reached for him, and his gut crawled into his throat as the truck continued its downhill plunge. His head smashed into the steering wheel before crashing against the side window. Once. Twice. After that he lost the ability to count. To see. To concentrate.

But not to feel pain.

The airbag deployed, ramming into his chest and face like a concrete wall. Air whooshed from his lungs. He fought to take a breath. His face throbbed; blood ran from his nose across his lips. And still, the truck pinballed down the hill, the seat belt digging a sharp groove into his shoulder and torso.

One last hard bump, another crack on the head and the truck came to a jarring halt. Steam hissed from a busted radiator. High-pitched ringing filled the inside of his head, inviting madness. Clouded by pain, he fought the mental chaos until one concept came into focus.

Danger. Must keep moving.

He fumbled to release the restraint cutting across his shoulders, then brushed away shattered windshield glass from his lap, his chest. A warm and sticky wetness streamed from his scalp, over his ear and down his neck. Crushed metal blocked his escape. He found a handle. It wouldn't budge. He rammed his shoulder against the obstruction. Agonizing pain shot up his spine and exploded inside his skull.

Fighting waves of nausea, he continued to throw himself against it until the door gave way with the groan of a dying beast. He tumbled out, landed hard in the mud. Rocks cut his fingers. He groped like a blind man, grabbing small boulders and trees to pull himself up. His hands and feet slipped with each attempt. More ground-shaking thunder. More pain.

Lightning illuminated everything like the ominous sweep of a prison searchlight. Movement drew his gaze uphill. Something black and thick and powerful rolling toward him. Like a gelatinous demon, it consumed branches, rocks, small trees, everything in its path.

Mudslide.

The mix of dirt and rain formed a deadly flow, and he scrambled from its path of destruction. One foot got tangled in the muck and it tried to swallow him. He panicked. Pulled and pulled. With a sucking squelch, a bare foot broke free.

He fell away from the mud. White pain blinded him as he hit his head once more. After clambering to his knees, he crawled sideways from the slide. At a hideous screech of metal, he turned back to look. A flash of lightning spotlighted the flow of mud engulfing his truck and carrying it over a ledge he hadn't known he was sitting on.

The close call paralyzed him.

The barrage of pain muddled his brain.

Keep moving. Hurry.

Clawing his way up the slope, he fought for every inch, lost traction, slid backward, pushed on. Punishing rain stung his face, but the cold eased the throbbing that raged inside his skull. He topped the hill, made it to the pavement. He stumbled like a drunkard down the middle of the road, wind lashing at him with no mercy. A stray tree branch struck him in the back. He fell forward, hands flailing, scraping his face on the pavement.

One breath. Two breaths.

Danger. Keep moving. Danger everywhere. Anywhere.

He lurched up, regained his footing, staggered back to the edge of the road. Fell again, this time sliding downhill. His exhausted body crumpled, landing in a water-filled culvert alongside the road.

One breath. Two breaths. Three.

Get up.

Keep moving.

Danger.

His muscles refused to cooperate. His eyelids refused to stay open. It was all he could do just to keep his head above the water sluicing through the natural ditch.

One breath. Two breaths...

Danger.

The strobing lights behind his eyes dimmed, the ringing in his ears dulled. His last thoughts before losing consciousness were to hurry, to keep moving.

But why?

DESPITE HAVING TO dodge broken branches and patches of mud, remnants from last night's unprecedented storm, Marie Beaumont headed south from town on her normal early morning run. Since settling in Jasper five years ago, she'd honed her list of preferred routes for maximum safety, the only way to guarantee the most enjoyment from her favorite pastime. The metronome-like slap of her shoes on asphalt quieted troubled thoughts and lowered her ever-present anxiety. Even today, watching every step to avoid tripping, it was worth it.

The mountain breezes that flowed into the canyon never smelled fresher than after a summer storm. The temporary reprieve from August's heat lifted Marie's mood, even if the cloudless blue sky foretold the rising temperatures to come.

"More storms coming. Should help with the heat." She glanced down at her running companion, who'd looked up at the sound of Marie's voice. "Right, girl?"

Astrid, her Doberman-beagle mix, bounded alongside in a running version of "heel." Trained at the DCA—Daniels Canine Academy—located on several acres just north of town, the brown-coated beauty rarely left Marie's side. Despite having cause, Marie had vowed not to live her life in fear. However, cowardice and caution were two different things, and Astrid was as much guard dog as loving pet.

Rounding a bend in the road, Astrid froze, sniffing the air, her tail no longer wagging. Marie skidded to a standstill.

Astrid was in her alert, nonaggressive stance, but that could change in an instant if the situation warranted. "What is it, girl?"

Marie's heart rate kicked up a notch as she surveyed the area. Other than butterflies flitting among the wildflowers and a breeze teasing the tall pines, nothing moved. Nothing unusual caught her eye. Still...

Astrid continued to stare at the far side of the road, whining.

"Search." At Marie's one-word command, Astrid tore across the asphalt and disappeared over the edge of the road, her progress marked by tall, swaying weeds and grasses.

Marie waited until insistent barking told her Astrid had found something. Pulling out her pepper spray, Marie inched toward the side of the pavement with caution. She peered over the road's shoulder and gasped when she saw what had Astrid so worked up.

A man, covered in filth and blood, lay crosswise in a runoff ditch, his eyes closed.

As Astrid paced in agitated circles, Marie dropped all pretense of caution and scurried downhill, tossed her phone on the ground and slide into the wet muck beside the man. A large, well-muscled man, maybe early thirties, whose skin bore a whitish-blue tint that caused Marie's stomach to churn. She reached for his neck, praying to find a pulse.

All hope evaporated the moment she touched him. Despair gripped her insides and twisted. His skin was cold.

Deathly cold. And he hadn't moved an inch, not even a slight rise and fall of his chest. With two fingers lightly pressing on the artery in his neck, Marie waited to feel the tell-tale pulsing of blood. Nothing.

"Come on, mister. Wake up!"

Astrid stopped her pacing, approached the man and licked his face.

In that moment, Marie felt a pulse.

He was alive.

She'd already had far too much contact with death, and Marie took a deep breath, grateful that today would not lay more at her feet. Then, she swung into motion.

Astrid wasn't the only one with training, and Marie wasted no more time. As Jasper's one and only veterinarian, she worked with both large and small animals and was no stranger to moving heavy, unresponsive patients. Something had dammed up the ditch farther down from their position, and the pooling water crept toward the man's face.

Running muddy hands over his body, she checked him for broken bones. His head and neck were aligned, a good sign. Ribs okay. Arms and legs, check, check.

The water continued rising, lapping at his chin. Injured or not, she had to move him. She got behind him and shoved him to a seated position. Feeling along his spine, she found no obvious breaks or injuries.

Kneeling on the edge of the ditch, she hooked her elbows beneath his armpits and pulled with all her strength. He barely moved. She slid down behind him, braced her feet and wrapped her arms around his chest. She tugged. Her feet sank in the muck. She braced again, pulled again. She couldn't get traction in the wet, muddy ground. He slid down even lower than before.

The water kept rising. His mouth would soon be covered. Then his nose. Overwhelmed by a strong certainty that she was meant to save this man, Marie called for Astrid. Pulling the shoulder of the man's shirt up, away from his skin, she let Astrid grab it with her teeth.

"Pull, girl!" There would be no drowning on her watch.

She again looped her arms under his shoulders, and together she and Astrid hauled until his chest cleared the water. Grabbing his belt with both hands, Marie planted her feet and dragged his torso out of the culvert. Astrid took over belt duty to keep him from tumbling back into the water as Marie worked one of his legs up and over the edge.

She issued the pull command again. Gripping the belt tighter in her mouth, Astrid yanked. Marie hopped back down and put her shoulder into shoving the rest of the man up and over the lip of the ditch.

"Good job, Astrid."

Marie climbed out of the culvert, sweaty, muddy, trying to catch her breath. Moving with speed, she rolled the man onto his back, confirmed his breathing passage remained clear, then checked his pulse again. Weak, but there. Unconscious, but still alive.

With hands shaking from exertion and the subsiding rush of adrenaline, Marie reached for her cell phone. Only 5 percent juice, but enough. With the power out during the storm, she should have remembered to check it before she left this morning. She dialed 911.

Astrid sniffed the stranger from head to foot, then sat back on her haunches.

Relieved help was now on the way, Marie sank to the ground next to the man and inspected his head wound. "Well, mister, it's not deep, but it's still going to need stitches."

Astrid cocked her head to one side, as if questioning Marie's professional opinion.

"Oh, hush. Just because I'm a vet and not a people doctor doesn't mean I don't know about cuts."

Astrid woofed in reply.

"Really? You think you know better? Listen here, a cut's a cut, no matter how many legs the patient has."

A contrite Astrid came up to her, placed one paw on Marie's arm and slobbered a kiss on her chin.

"Yes, baby. I know. I love you, too." Marie scratched behind the dog's ears.

Astrid settled down, and Marie's attention returned to the man. Her gaze moved from his ripped polo shirt to his mud-soaked jeans, then down to his feet, one wearing only a sock, the other completely bare. "How the heck did you wind up in this situation?"

She looked around but didn't spot a vehicle. She frowned at Astrid. "A hiker?" Astrid tilted her head. "Okay, you're right. Not dressed for it. A tourist maybe?"

Astrid had no response to that question, and no wonder. Marie steered clear of strangers. Other than the few people in Jasper she did know, most thought her stand-offish. Someone with trust issues, she'd heard whispered, which she supposed was true, although that wasn't why she avoided strangers. Not by a long shot.

She gave a mental shrug. Whatever people thought about her, she was not the kind of woman who could let this guy, or anyone for that matter, drown in a ditch.

Smoothing back his dirty brown hair, she studied his face, as if by looking at him she could tell what kind of character he had. "Once the blood and mud are washed off, I have a feeling you'll clean up good." She twisted her lips, amused at her train of thought. "Not that I care about that, mind you. What I really care about is, are you a good person?" She continued to caress his forehead with the same gentleness she used on injured and abandoned animals.

It didn't surprise her that what drew her most to this man was the helplessness of his situation. Imagine being discovered alone, unconscious and nearly drowned in a water-filled ditch smack-dab in the middle of Nowhere, Idaho. Whatever had befallen him, his plight reeked of the loneliness Marie lived with every day.

His eyelids fluttered open, and just that fast Marie's empathy vanished as her instinctual wariness reared up. Gray eyes met hers with an eerie intensity that seemed to reach for her darkest secrets. That gaze, somehow so knowing, punched an icy blast of foreboding through Marie's chest and froze the breath in her lungs.

A second later, Astrid jumped up as the distant wail of an ambulance siren grew louder. The man's eyes drifted closed, and Marie breathed a sigh of relief. What a strange, unnerving moment that had been.

"Stay," she told Astrid before dashing up the incline to wave down the EMTs.

The ambulance stopped and two paramedics jumped out, one smiling when he saw her. "Hey, Doc. Didn't know you were the one who called this in. What can you tell me about our John Doe?"

Marie knew Eddie, which calmed her jangled nerves even more. She relayed to both paramedics what she knew, which wasn't much, and within minutes the patient was triaged, stabilized and loaded in the ambulance.

"You riding in with us?" Eddie asked her, eyeing her soaking-wet, mud-splattered jogging gear.

Marie looked down. "Oh, wow. I'm quite a mess, aren't I?"

"The uniform of heroes if you ask me. Besides, we have towels for just such emergencies."

Marie patted Astrid's head. "Can my muddy companion come, too?"

Eddie's smile broadened. "You think I'd leave Killer's sweetheart behind? Muddy or not?" He opened both passenger doors of the ambulance's four-door cab. "Even have a harness she can use."

Eddie's Chihuahua, Killer, was a patient of Marie's, and the pint-sized pooch had developed a mastiff-sized crush on Astrid. Marie and Eddie always shared a good laugh whenever the two dogs were together, joking that Killer would need a ladder to take the relationship any further.

Marie got Astrid buckled into the backseat, then climbed in to ride shotgun. Definitely one of the perks of small-town living.

Lights flashing, siren screaming, they sped up the road to Jasper Memorial. During the short ride, Eddie, bless him, rambled on about this and that, oblivious to Marie's noncommittal murmurs and nods. Her focus was squarely centered on the man in the back, no doubt getting hooked up to an IV and being covered in a heat-generating blanket.

She had no reason to fear the stranger. Anyone could have found him. It was just coincidence that she and Astrid happened to. But coincidence was simply not something that existed in Marie's world, and she couldn't stop herself from imagining the countless ways her Good Samaritan act today might come back to haunt her.

Borrowing trouble, her grandmother had called it.

As much as she hated what it might mean to her well-ordered life, it was time to call George Murphy.

THE HOSPITAL ADMISSIONS nurse tapped a tuneless beat with her pen against the desk. "You must have *some* relationship with the patient. You rode in the ambulance with him."

Marie summoned her patience. "I promise you, I *don't* have a relationship with him. I found him on the side of the road and called 911. I'm happy to give you my contact information, but I don't know the man from Adam." She handed the nurse her driver's license. "As long as you're adding me as a contact, would it be possible to keep me informed of his status?"

Until she spoke to George, the most important thing would be keeping an eye on the mystery man. Her safety might depend on it, after all. And as a caring person, of course Marie was concerned about his medical status. She always followed up on her patients. Even the tall, handsome one with gray eyes whose life she saved.

The admissions nurse lifted her gaze from her computer screen and gave Marie a somewhat disapproving look, then handed her license back. "Unless the patient gives us permission, we can't release his medical information. But no doubt the police will want you to stick around. They'll need a statement, I would imagine. Maybe they could check with his doctor for you."

"Thank you."

Marie found a chair in the corner of the waiting room where Astrid would be less noticeable. When they had trailed through the ER door behind Eddie, the nurse began scolding her for bringing a dog into the hospital. Eddie had simply said, "Service dog," on his way past the desk and that seemed to mollify her. While it was true that Astrid was a sort of service dog, Marie felt more comfortable keeping a low profile.

Her phone battery was down to 2 percent. Before it went dead, she checked her messages. None. Pretty typical unless there was an animal emergency. Then she dashed off a quick text to Liz, Marie's office manager, letting her know she'd be late getting in to the office, deciding last-minute that the why-she-was-going-to-be-late explanation was too much for a text. She'd just pushed Send when Officer Jason Wright of the Jasper PD strolled up to her.

With cropped black hair, dark brown eyes and a charming smile, the six-foot, muscular rookie officer was engaged to Tashya, the vet tech employed at the Daniels Canine Academy. Which meant Marie saw him often and knew him better than most of the local cops.

"Hi, Jason. I was hoping they'd send you."

He favored her with a sly grin. "Why? 'Cause you like my biceps?" He curled his arm and gave her a flex.

Marie couldn't help it. She grinned back. Extending her arms, placing her wrists together as if in handcuffs, she said, "You busted me. Just promise you won't tell Tashya." For the first time since finding John Doe, Marie felt a measure of calm. Jason had that way about him, a way of brightening a room and easing tension just by being in it.

"I make no promises. Tashya can always tell when I'm lying, so I find it best not to do it."

Wouldn't that be nice. A stab of jealousy pierced Marie. What would it be like to live in a world not consumed by lies?

Jason pulled a small notebook and pen from his pocket. "So, you found our John Doe, huh?"

Nodding, she filled him in on the particulars. He asked a few additional questions, which she answered while he jotted down notes, then he snapped the notebook closed and pocketed it. "That's one lucky dude, if you ask me. Hey, listen, if I have any follow-up questions, I'll just call you, okay?"

"Sure thing."

"You heading home? Need a lift?"

"Thanks, but I think I'll wait here a bit longer. I want to make sure he's okay."

"You might want to rethink that," Jason said with a knowing wink, giving her an up-and-down once-over. "You look a bit like the Creature from the Black Lagoon."

Marie chortled when she glanced down at herself. "What? Is soggy and mud splattered not my best look?"

"Well…"

"Don't answer that. Wouldn't want you lying."

"Whew!" He laughed with her, and then said, "Look, I'm not planning to stick around much longer, but if he wakes up before I leave, I'll let you know."

"Thanks, Jason." She watched him walk away. When he and Tashya tied the knot in a couple of weeks, they would be one of the lucky couples who makes it. Love like theirs gave others in town hope for their own eventual happily-ever-after.

She scoffed.

Not you, Marie. Get a grip.

She probably should leave, grab a shower, forget all about John Doe.

But she wouldn't. Not yet, anyway. She couldn't ignore that look he'd given her, and how it had stirred something within her. Curiosity, certainly. Caution, that was a given. Maybe even a touch of fear. But there was more, something akin to desire, and that was absolutely a path she couldn't afford to go down.

So instead, she worked to convince herself this was just her normal MO. Since early childhood, she'd felt a calling to take in wounded animals and nurse them back to health. And that's what this man reminded her of. A wounded stray who needed her. Well, maybe not her, but someone.

"Dr. Beaumont?"

Startled, Marie looked up at a nurse in scrubs. "Yes?"

"The patient is waking up. Officer Wright and Dr. Saul wondered if you'd join them in the ER."

"Okay if Astrid comes with me?" She grabbed hold of the harness.

"Absolutely. Dr. Saul happens to be a big believer in the

power of four-legged companionship." Yet another perk of small-town life.

With Astrid at her side, Marie followed the nurse through the hands-free doors of the ER.

The man at the center of her consternation lay propped against several pillows, his bed partially elevated. He was hooked to an IV bag, a bandage covered the side of his head and most of the mud had been cleaned from his face.

Marie almost sighed in delight. John Doe most definitely cleaned up good. Maybe too good. She stepped closer to his hospital bed, taking in his five-o'clock stubble that gave him an outdoorsy look. Wispy, abstract streaks of white filled the irises of his gray eyes, pulling her in like a black hole in space. She took a deep breath, then exhaled to try to slow her pulse.

His brows pinched into a frown above an unsmiling mouth. Hardly the reaction she expected. Could be as simple as him noticing her less-than-tidy appearance. Or perhaps he was sizing her up, as she had done him. *Hmm.* Just so long as his penetrating stare didn't hide anything more sinister.

Dr. Saul looked up from his clipboard. "Ah, here she is." Wearing a white coat over green scrubs and with a stethoscope dangling around his neck, he was average height, bald and bespectacled. Possibly in his sixties, but Marie never had been good at guessing ages.

The doctor tucked his clipboard to his chest and spoke to the patient. "Do you mind me discussing your medical condition in front of this woman? I was hoping she might help fill in the blanks, as it were, since she was the one who fished you out of a water-filled ditch this morning. According to Officer Wright here, you would have drowned if not for her."

The man, whose name she still didn't know, said nothing. Only gazed at her with the same disturbing intensity as he had on the side of the road. Finally, Marie grew warm with discomfort.

"Glad to see you're awake. And I don't deserve all the credit. I had a little help this morning." She looked down at Astrid and gave her a pat.

"Sorry, I don't remember." His eyes lingered on her face. "Apparently, I don't even remember *me*."

Dr. Saul rested a sympathetic hand on the man's shoulder. "Our patient is suffering from retrograde amnesia, or the loss of existing and previously made memories. This type of amnesia tends to affect recently formed memories first. Then, if the condition persists, it affects older memories, such as those from childhood. I'm working on transferring him to St. Luke's Hospital in Boise to see a neurologist there who specializes in this sort of thing."

The man with no name continued to stare at Marie, as if paying no attention to the doctor's words. You'd think someone facing such a diagnosis would be more interested in what the doctor was saying than in puzzling out her role in things.

"Seems he can't remember anything before waking up in the ER," Dr. Saul went on. "Not his identity, not how he came to be out in the storm, not even how he received his wounds. And as he said, he doesn't remember being rescued, either."

"He didn't have any ID in his pockets, but he was wearing this." Jason held up a man's watch. "The back is engraved with the name Jack."

"Then I guess we'll call you Jack." Marie smiled and held out her hand toward him. "I'm Marie."

He returned her smile, but it seemed like an automatic response rather than anything genuine. "Nice to meet you, Marie." Jack clasped her hand and held on to it longer than necessary. His touch, warm and strong, sent a pang of loss through her. It had been a long time since she'd experienced a man's touch. Then she raised her chin and shoved the foolish sentiment away. She'd made her own decisions. No point wishing for what she couldn't have.

"Thank you for saving my life." His smile faded, replaced by another disconcerting frown.

Tipping his bandaged head to one side, he studied her face as if trying to piece together a puzzle. But his next words left Marie reeling.

"Didn't you used to be a blonde?"

Chapter Two

Jack's question played on an endless loop in Marie's head as she and Astrid jogged home from the hospital.

Didn't you used to be a blonde?

Her blondes-have-more-fun days ended five years ago when she entered witness protection, WITSEC, after testifying against domestic terrorist Abel Gaines. Marie wasn't even her real name. Neither was Beaumont. As soon as she'd stepped off the witness stand, she left behind everything—and everyone—she loved. She'd chopped off her waist-length ash-blond locks, read the directions on a box of Rich Chestnut hair color and gone into hiding. In Jasper, Idaho.

The instant Marie got home and locked her front door, she reached for the charging cord and plugged in her dead phone. Seconds later she dialed Deputy US Marshal George Murphy, her witness protection case deputy. It went straight to voice mail. *Great.*

"George, this is Marie Beaumont. Call me. SOS. I repeat, SOS."

By the time she ended the call, the phone had recharged enough to show a missed call from Emma, owner of Daniels Canine Academy. In her voice message, Emma left an urgent plea. A pregnant stray had wandered in from the storm last night with a broken leg and needed her attention ASAP.

What was it about this storm and wounded strays?

Marie took a quick shower, decided not to bother with makeup and tied her *brown* hair—thank you very much, Mr. I Can't Remember Anything Except You Used to Be a Blonde—back into a damp ponytail. She and Astrid made it to the academy in record time.

Before turning off her ignition, she tried her case deputy again. It went to voice mail again. For a man supposedly available twenty-four/seven, his absence troubled her.

Marie's fingers curled around the steering wheel as the past, which she fought so hard to forget, drew her back to what a sweet-talker Abel Gains had been. In the beginning, anyway. How carefully he'd shielded her from his twisted side until it was almost too late.

Oh, there'd been clues, if she hadn't been too smitten to notice. But then, she'd always sucked at picking men. Still, even for her, falling for a delusional domestic terrorist in charge of a band of more delusional domestic terrorists had been the cherry on top of her disastrous dating life.

A rap on her window startled her. Emma Daniels peered through the dark tint, her brows pulled together in concern. "You okay?"

Nodding, Marie turned off the engine, unbuckled her seat belt, then Astrid's. Trained as a guard dog at the academy, Astrid fidgeted with pent-up eagerness, but stayed.

"Patience, girl." Marie pushed the door open. The well-trained Doberman struggled to contain her excitement and only leaped from the car when Marie gave the command. Sitting at Emma's feet, Astrid looked up at her, waiting… waiting…

Emma finally took pity on her. "Come here, my sweet girl." Although strong, Emma staggered under fifty pounds of enthusiastic dog greeting. "Good girl, Astrid. I'm happy to see you, too." She commanded Astrid to sit, then turned to Marie. "Okay, it was kind of weird seeing you sitting here in your car, looking all serious. Are you sure you're all right?"

Emma's concern plucked at Marie's loneliness chord, and the truth longed to come out. Marie hated lying, especially to the people she considered friends. But she'd told the truth, the whole truth, nothing but the truth once before. About Abel and his compound full of fanatics, and now her life was one endless lie. WITSEC had its rules, and to stay alive, Marie followed them. No matter how much she hated it.

She pasted a smile on her face. "Just a little rattled, is all. During our run this morning, Astrid found a man unconscious on the side of the road." She reached into the back of her RAV4 and grabbed her vet bag. "I called 911, then rode with him to the hospital." Marie shrugged. "I wanted to make sure he was okay, you know?"

Emma's eyes rounded in sympathy as she reached for Marie and gave her a warm hug. "Of course, you did. You never pass up a chance to help an injured creature." Standing back, Emma gave her a knowing smile. "Does he happen to be young and good-looking? Single, perhaps? I happen to know a vet who is young, good-looking and single."

Marie's cheeks warmed. "You know I'm not looking for a man."

Emma huffed. "I don't see why not. And you've never bothered to explain it to me, either. Your reticence is one of the most annoying things about you if you ask me."

With one eyebrow cocked, Marie held Emma's gaze for a beat before speaking. "And I didn't."

"Okay, okay." Emma raised both hands in surrender.

"I'll back off. For now. How's he doing, anyway, your two-legged stray?"

Astrid heeled along Marie's left side as they all walked toward the kennel, knowing if she behaved now, she would be let loose once they got inside.

"No broken bones, but a serious concussion. And amnesia, apparently."

"Amnesia?" Emma whistled, which had Astrid's ears twitching. "I didn't think that was really a thing. Just a plot device they use in books and movies."

"Oh, no. It's real enough. Just not very common."

Emma opened the door to the kennel and Astrid looked up at her with round, pleading eyes. "Free." Hearing her release word, Astrid ran off to sniff around and get reacquainted with the other academy residents.

Marie followed Emma toward the last stall on the left. Although the building could handle twelve dogs at one time, with six inside stalls and connected outdoor runs on each side of the building, it wasn't at full capacity right now.

Emma unlatched the stall door. "Here's our little mama-to-be. I found her out behind the barn when I checked on the horses last night." A small, emaciated black Lab cowered in the corner of the space, shivering despite the warm day.

"Aggressive?" Marie asked.

"Nope. Not so far. Just the opposite, in fact."

Marie noticed the bowls of food and water. "Has she eaten anything?"

"Not a bite, but she did take a bit of water. She hasn't had anything since midnight, though."

Marie crouched and held her hand out, palm up. The dog stared at her with plaintive eyes. "You must have been terrified in that storm. Where'd you come from, I wonder?"

Emma's words turned hard, though her tone remained calm. "Well, wherever it was, based on her injuries, I don't want her going back. Between the broken leg and abrasions on her sides, my guess is someone tossed her out of a moving vehicle. Either that or she was unrestrained in the bed of a truck and flew out."

The dog quivered with fear, so Marie let her sniff her hand for a few minutes before she started the exam. Her front right leg was bent at an odd angle due to the fractured bone. Bloody patches of matted hair and raw scrapes that looked like road rash covered her. Aside from the fresh wounds, old scars from previous injuries told a story of abuse.

"Poor girl. You've had it rough, haven't you? Not to worry. I've got you now. You and your babies are going to be just fine." Marie glanced up at Emma. "I'm going to sedate her so I can move her to my office and properly set the leg. While she's out, I'll check her for internal injuries and clean up her other wounds. I might have to take the puppies instead of waiting for natural labor. Hopefully, I won't have to."

Turning her attention back to the dog, Marie stroked the soft fur on her head, one of the few places not bloodied. A wave of déjà vu swept over her. Just a few hours earlier, she'd smoothed hair back from the man's—no, *Jack's*—face. Were the two somehow connected beyond the circumstances of the storm? Or had fate simply placed the same healer in the path of two injured parties in one morning?

"Well, you know how I feel about animal abuse." Emma picked up the dog's dishes to keep Astrid from having a midday snack. "So, you just add the surgery and whatever care she needs to my tab."

"Don't be silly. This one's on the house." True, Marie's

tight budget meant she could ill afford the cost, but she often treated strays pro bono.

"Hmph. Unless someone can prove they're the owner and that they weren't responsible for this girl's injuries, I'll soon have a whole litter of future search and rescue dogs that you'll need to be tending. So, I *insist* on paying."

Marie, still focused on the Lab, couldn't help but smile at just how stubborn Emma probably looked right now. She may not be able to tell Emma the entire truth of her life, but she thanked her lucky stars to have her as a friend. "How 'bout this? I'll take care of the surgery, then bring her back here and Tashya can handle her aftercare." Marie finally looked over her shoulder at Emma. As expected, Emma's hands were on her hips.

"All right, all right." She dropped her hands to her sides. "Thank you. I don't know how we got along before you moved to town."

"Can you come keep her calm?"

Emma did just that while Marie took a syringe from her medical bag and injected the dog, who was soon asleep. "Let's give her a few more minutes before we move her."

After some well-earned free time, Astrid followed her nose back to Marie. Coming alongside her owner, Astrid approached the injured dog one sniff at a time. She stopped about a foot away, lay down on the floor and whined in sympathy.

"You got it, Doc." Emma stood and leaned against the wall. "So, about your two-legged rescue, any more to the story?"

Marie refused to break one of her cardinal rules. But if she couldn't tell Emma the whole truth, she could at least allude to the possible danger the man presented. "There's something odd about his situation. I mean, beyond the whole amnesia thing. The guy said he had no idea where he was from. When Jason asked him where he thought he might have been heading, he wasn't sure about that either. But here's the strange part. Right after that, he said somehow 'this place' felt right."

"This place? As in the hospital?" Emma's nose wrinkled in puzzlement.

Marie gestured with her arm in a large arc. "No. *This* place, as in Jasper. He seems to think Jasper is where he belongs. But Jason told me in confidence there aren't any missing person reports on anyone fitting his description."

Emma frowned. "Okay, that's a little weird."

Then she tilted her head, reminding Marie of Astrid.

"But try thinking about it from his point of view," Emma continued. "It's got to be strange. To know things, but not understand the context."

Marie conceded her friend's point with a small nod.

Emma crossed to a stack of freshly laundered dog towels and folded the top one. "He doesn't remember anything about his past?"

Marie shook her head. "Nope. Nothing. The only thing he had with him was a watch engraved with a name on the back."

"Wait. He has a name?"

"Yeah. Well, maybe. Jack."

"Hmmm, Jack," Emma said, trying it on for size as she folded more towels. "Nice enough. What's going to happen to him?"

"His doctor's going to transfer him to St. Luke's in Boise, to see some neurologist who deals with memory loss and claims of amnesia." Marie repacked her vet bag. "Said it's the best option for him."

And for me.

After being convicted, Abel had sworn she'd never be safe again. And he was the type of man who made good on his promises. That threat had taken her into witness protection and given her reason to avoid strangers.

Given that Jasper was a year-round tourist town, from skiing in the winter to fishing and white water rafting in the summer, avoiding strangers was a full-time occupation. No matter how hard she tried to live a quiet life, she couldn't help but wonder if every unknown set of eyes that lingered on her just a bit too long might be one of Abel's men. Made sense that getting Jack out of town, and off her mind, gave her one less stranger to worry about.

Emma cocked a brow. "What do you mean, 'claims of amnesia?' You think this guy is faking it?" She left the stall, returning a minute later with a pet carrier.

"Could be." Marie's shrug felt a bit defensive. "Like I said, amnesia is pretty rare." She hefted her bag from one hand to the other. "I mean, think about it. How would anyone know if he was telling the truth?"

Emma chuckled. "You really are the most untrusting person I know."

"And you're entirely too trusting," Marie countered, even knowing her friend was right. She lined the carrier with some of Emma's clean towels, then lifted the stray in. "Can you bring my bag? I'll carry the dog."

Astrid whined and Emma scratched behind her ear. "Aren't you getting enough attention, girl?"

"Oh, she never gets *any* attention. I completely ignore her all day." Marie crouched down and rubbed Astrid's chest. "You poor neglected thing, you."

She stood and lifted the carrier with both hands, waiting for Emma to open the door for her. Astrid dashed out and was waiting next to the RAV4 by the time the women arrived.

Marie loaded the carrier into her car. "I'll call you tonight and let you know how our girl is doing. And in a few days, when she's recovered enough to move her, I'll bring her back."

"When you do, would you mind looking at Elton's foot for me? I thought I saw him favoring it this morning, but I might be wrong."

Elton, a black-and-white Appaloosa, was one of Emma's two rescue horses. The other one, a brown American quarter horse, she'd named Presley. Marie wondered which singer was up next if Emma rescued a third horse.

"Sure. Want me to do it now?"

Emma shook her head. "The dog's injuries are much worse and way more time-sensitive. I'll keep an eye on Elton."

Marie stuck her hand out the window and waved as she drove away. On the way back to town, she focused once more on her two-legged stray. She recalled how Granny Mae used to tell her curiosity killed the cat and that if Marie wasn't careful, it would get her, too.

And so it had. Sticking her nose into someone else's business was exactly how her life had taken a dangerous, unexpected detour. To Jasper, Idaho. A place where the stranger insisted he belonged.

Didn't you used to be a blonde?

MARIE BEAUMONT.

Cooped up in a hospital room for three long, frustrating, boring days, Jack—at least he thought he was Jack— could conjure little else in his otherwise blank head. Why, when he could remember nothing else, did she seem familiar to him? Especially puzzling given that she couldn't say the same about him.

His natural inclination—and yes, he'd apparently retained inclinations—was to distrust her. Amnesia be damned. She was hiding something. He knew that for certain. Down deep in his gut, where instinct was ingrained and not dependent on memory, he knew. Wouldn't that mean she knew him, too?

The patrolman, Jason, confirmed she'd been the town's vet since moving to Jasper five years ago. If they had known each other, it was in a past Jack couldn't remember. According to the friendly cop, Dr. Marie Beaumont was a bit of a loner, and no one knew much about her life before she'd shown up in itty-bitty Jasper, Idaho, out of the blue and with no relatives to draw her here. Well, regardless of the reason that brought her here, Jack owed her his life.

And speaking of Jasper, why Jack felt a connection to the place when clearly no one here knew him was anyone's guess. Maybe it wasn't a person, but the place itself that called to him. He'd borrowed Jason's phone and scrolled through pictures of the town, but nothing triggered his dormant memories. Talk about maddening.

Then there was Jason, himself. The young officer made it a point to visit him each day. Like a friend. Only they weren't. Not that Jack was about to look a gift horse in the mouth. His physical injuries were healing, but conversations that didn't involve his medical chart were a breath of fresh air.

A rap sounded on the door, and Dr. Saul came into his room. *Speaking of walking, talking medical charts.* "Afternoon, Jack. How are you feeling today?"

"Okay, Doc, except for the headaches. But no memories yet, and I'm starting to worry."

Setting his clipboard on the edge of the sink, Dr. Saul washed his hands then bent to examine Jack's bandage-wrapped head. "Well, son, it's as I told you, brain injuries are tricky things. As long as you're retaining new memories, just give it more time. The swelling in your head has gone down, and the MRI revealed no aneurysms. In most cases of retrograde amnesia, the memories eventually return. Sometimes in pieces. Sometimes all at once. With one or two holes, maybe, but nothing overly concerning."

"You sound encouraging." Jack sat up straighter in the bed. "That makes me feel better."

Dr. Saul clapped him on the shoulder. "You'll be fine. And I think we can safely remove this." Dr. Saul pulled off the tape and bandage. "The stitches look good, and you're healing nicely. You'll have a scar, but with your hair, no one will ever see it."

"Thanks, Dr. Saul. I appreciate you making sure my brains didn't ooze out."

"Ha. We always try to avoid oozing brains." He tossed the gauze into the biohazard trash container, then sat in the visitor chair and faced Jack. "Now, what's this I hear about you refusing to go to the Head Trauma Institute in Boise? Dr. Huber is tops in his field. He's already reviewed your case and is willing to take you without the benefit of insurance. The institute is state funded and has resident patients, which means while you recover, you won't have to worry about a place to live. It's a no-brainer, if you ask me."

Jack laughed. "I think I'm the no-brainer here."

Dr. Saul chuckled. "Poor choice of words, but don't let that detract from the soundness of my advice. While I have every expectation that you'll recover, head trauma is nothing to mess around with, especially in cases like yours. Go to Boise, Jack. Find out who you were. Who you *are*."

The doctor made complete sense. Of course, he did. Any reasonable person would heed his advice, but apparently Jack wasn't reasonable. *Good to know.* Besides, what possible reason could he give for not wanting to leave Jasper that didn't make him sound more unhinged than someone with amnesia?

And why hadn't he told Dr. Saul about the one memory he did have?

Marie Beaumont.

Every time he turned around, whether sleeping or awake, her image flashed before his eyes. Sometimes like a photo, flat and one-dimensional. Sometimes in motion. But in every instance, she appeared alone and fearful. And in every instance, she was a blonde.

"Look, Doc, I appreciate everything you've done for me. I mean that. But if I want to get my memories back, then Jasper is the place I need to be."

Dr. Saul perked up at this. "So you're remembering things, then? Something to do with Jasper?"

"Cool your jets, Doc. It's just a hunch, but it seems… well, it seems right somehow. I don't know how else to explain it, other than my gut insists I should stay here." *So, how lame did that sound?* He massaged his temples, trying to ease the thundering drum solo in his head.

Dr. Saul *tsked* with resignation. "Suit yourself. I'll order something for the headaches."

"Thank you." Jack smiled in relief. As long as he had something for the pain, he could keep trying to figure out his life.

Dr. Saul picked up his clipboard and scratched out some quick notes. "Since you're determined not to go to Boise, you need to understand something. With the improvement in your physical condition, I'll have no choice but to release you tomorrow. Have you at least spoken to the hospital social worker? Figured out what you're going to do, where you're going to go?"

He hadn't, but another rap on the open door saved him from lying about it.

"Knock, knock." Jason stuck his head in. When he saw

the doctor, he said, "I can come back in a few minutes, if you need to finish up."

"No, we're done." The doctor turned back to Jack. "If you're absolutely sure about not going to Boise, promise me you'll speak to the social worker. Today."

"Ten-four, Doc."

The doctor's brows raised in doubt.

"I promise." Jack gave the doctor a genuine smile and hoped the social worker could help him get a roof over his head and a job. Without those, staying in Jasper would most likely be impossible.

"I'm holding you to that."

When he'd gone, Jason set a can of icy cold Coke and a bag that smelled of carbohydrate heaven on the tray table. "Still no missing person reports that match your description, but I've widened the search area to include the surrounding states." Jason plopped into the visitor chair. "So, what was that about you not going to Boise?"

"Yeah, I've decided I like Jasper so much that I'm going to stay a while."

"And why's that?" Stretching his legs out, Jason yawned. "Is our small town helping your memory come back?"

"I wish." Jack chuckled at his wistful tone. "But I'm pretty sure if I stay here, it will. Thanks for the grub, by the way. I owe you, man." He unwrapped the burger Jason had brought him and bit off a huge chunk.

"Forget it." Jason stood and walked over to the window. "I find it interesting that a man who can't even remember his own name is suddenly an amnesia doctor."

Jack didn't take offense at the teasing sarcasm. "It's a hunch, okay?" He popped open the can of Coke and gulped half of it.

Jason shrugged. "A hunch, I understand. So, what did the doctor mean about a social worker?"

"It means I need to figure out where I'm going to live and how I'm going to pay for it when I get out of here. Tomorrow." Jack used his teeth to rip open a ketchup package, squeezed it out onto his burger wrapper, then dipped several warm, salty fries, darn near salivating in anticipation. *I should start keeping notes. I'm definitely a burger and fries man.* "Come to think about it, I probably owe a pile of cash to the hospital and Doc Saul." Jack popped the fries in his mouth and sighed with happiness. After swallowing, he continued, "In a nutshell, I'm broke and homeless."

"Oh, snap." Jason leaped from the chair. "I might have just the ticket. Need to make a call first. Back in a sec." And with that, he zipped out into the hallway.

Jack dragged another fry through the ketchup and chewed it as he pondered his situation. No name, no home, no past. But he was alive, saved by a beautiful woman. He had a new friend who was trying to find him a place to live. All in all, he was a very lucky man.

Now he just needed to fill in all the blanks.

Chapter Three

True to his word, Dr. Saul released Jack the next day. Because Jason's plan came through, Jack didn't even have to meet with the social worker. Seems a woman Jason knew, Emma Daniels, owned a spread north of town where she trained search and rescue dogs, and had horses there, as well. Ms. Daniels offered him room, board and a small stipend in exchange for his labor. She'd also promised to deduct from his wages the debt Jack was racking up. He'd insisted on that. Seems he didn't like owing people.

According to Jason, he'd be living in an RV while staying at Emma's, which had the added benefit of helping out some guy named Shanc, whose girlfriend was mighty glad to get the monstrosity out of her driveway.

"Ready to blow this joint?" Once more, Jason was uniformed and ready to lend a hand. The young cop, who Jack owed a bigger debt than money could repay, would be going in to work after dropping Jack off. He scurried out of his police cruiser, which was parked in the circular drive in front of the hospital, and opened the passenger door.

"You have no idea." Dressed in a T-shirt, jeans and sneakers, which Jason had dropped off the day before, Jack waited while the nurse locked the wheelchair so he could stand.

"Then your chariot awaits."

Jack got in the car. He checked out the equipment console and comm system up front out of idle curiosity. He felt no connection to the squad car, but he couldn't deny a sense of déjà vu. Then he turned and looked through the steel mesh cage to the hard plastic seats in the back. A flash of memory came. Sitting in the back of a different squad car. Struggling with someone…a cop? The glint of handcuffs. A grunt of pain. Then it was gone.

Nausea hit Jack. Not from his persistent headache, but from wondering if he'd been that man. He tried to expand that brief flash of insight, but his head just throbbed in answer.

He buckled his seat belt as Jason got behind the wheel. "You're positive this is okay with your friend Emma? I mean, me staying on her property?"

Jason buckled up and started the car. "I told you, man. Everyone gave a thumbs-up."

"And they know about my condition? Heck, I could be an ax murderer, for all they know." The images flashed through his mind once more. "For all *I* know."

Well, maybe not a murderer. But possibly someone who belonged in the back of a cop car.

And that thought made him recall Marie's guarded reaction to him. Did she know more about him than he did? Maybe that he was some sort of criminal?

His head throbbed to the beat of his escalating heart rate.

Don't force it, Dr. Saul had told him.

Jack massaged his temples. *Easier said than done, Doc.*

Looking in his side mirror, Jason waited while a car pulled up alongside and double parked, boxing them in. "Trust me—Emma was all for it when I suggested you move out to the DCA. Of course, she'd already heard about your situation. Probably from Marie, who's out there all the time. Both of them were worried about where you'd wind up."

Jack adjusted the vent nearest him for a better blast of cool air. "You don't say."

So Marie was worried about him. He kind of liked that idea. Tons better than having her afraid of him. And maybe an indicator that she did not, in fact, have secret information about a nefarious past he couldn't remember.

They pulled away from the hospital into a cloudless morning with a wide sky, bluer than blue. The sun was cheerful and warm with the promise of real heat later in the day. An altogether gorgeous day Jack struggled to enjoy, because the glaring brightness had his head throbbing like a jackhammer.

As he and Jason drove through town, the Jasper PD officer pointed out various local landmarks. The town hall here, the police station there. The fire station, library, and at the intersection of Main and Elm, a picturesque town square complete with a gazebo.

They even drove by Marie's vet practice, which was an old, converted house, the second floor an apartment where she lived.

He made note of that, just as he made note of the street names, the distance between buildings, the general layout of the town. Like he was mapping out escape routes. He noticed something else, too, when they stopped at the drug store where Jason fronted him the money to pay for his headache script.

At strategic points in the building were large round mirrors, and video cameras aimed at the checkout registers and pharmacy counter. Cameras Jack pegged as fakes, meant to scare off amateurs, except for the one in the back by the drugs. That camera not only filmed but stored it digitally without recording over it.

Jack frowned at the security camera, his fading head-ache now a solid drumbeat. How did he know that? *Why* did he know that?

Jack didn't like the first answer that came to him. The way he cataloged the entire security setup in less than twenty seconds felt like he was casing the joint.

About fifteen minutes later, they drove away from the pharmacy, Jack not even waiting for water before pop-ping a pain pill, hoping it would settle the pounding in his head. "Thanks for these." He shook the pill bottle. "Add it to my tab?"

"Emma paid for them. She'll keep track of it and de-duct it from your paycheck." Jason continued acting in the role of a Jasper tour guide. "There's Millard's Diner. That's where your burger came from yesterday, and a block down, over there is the Bartwell Brewing Company. You ever come into town with an appetite, Millard's or Bart-well's are your best bets."

"I doubt I'll be coming into town very often."

"Oh? Why not?"

"No identity means no driver's license means no driv-ing."

"Man, don't you know by now, I got your back?"

"Oh, yeah. And how's that?" Jack laughed. "A permis-sion slip from the cops to drive without a license?"

Jason chuckled. "Wait and see."

As they headed north out of town, Jack tapped his fin-gers on his knees, impatient for the pill to work its magic. The brick and mortar of town gave way to rolling foothills, and he began to relax.

He'd learned something else while waiting in the phar-macy for his script to be filled. Something positive, for a change. Without thinking, he'd reached for a magazine and started flipping through the pages, barely looking at them. But then his attention focused, and his gut reacted in a way he was coming to recognize. Tightening, then relaxing, then growing a bit tingly with a sense of…familiarity, he supposed.

Holding up the magazine at the checkout, he'd asked Jason, "Mind if I add this to my tab?"

"Not at all. Rafting and kayaking, huh?"

Jack shrugged. "No flood of memories, if that's what you mean." But the images had certainly captured his attention, and he intended to go with his gut. What else did he have?

Eventually they turned onto a long dirt road, then drove under the framed entrance of the Daniels Canine Academy, formed by two round posts and a wooden sign emblazoned with a German shepherd silhouette across the top. Jason parked in a large open area between a one-story white brick house and a small white barn.

Some distance from the barn sat the kennel, which was brown with a green roof that matched the one on the house. Even with the fenced runs along the sides of the kennel, there was enough room to park the RV between it and the barn.

"About time," called an attractive woman who came out from the barn, tugging off thick work gloves and then tucking them into the rear pocket of her well-worn jeans. Her light brown hair was pulled back, and as she approached, Jack noticed clear blue eyes that reminded him of Marie. Although, Emma's were light, like a cloudless summer sky. Marie's eyes were a much darker blue, more like a storm-tossed ocean.

"Hi. I'm Emma Daniels. You must be Jack."

"That's what they tell me." He smiled and shook her hand. "Appreciate you letting me stay here."

"Don't thank me yet. Earning your keep is going to be hard work. You're not afraid of hard work, are you, Jack?"

"I don't think so." He chuckled and rubbed the back of his neck, uneasy over being less than sure of himself. "Guess we'll find out together."

Her expression softened. "Tactless of me. Take no notice. As long as you give me a fair day's work, you can consider this your home until you're ready to move on. However long that might be." Emma gave him a friendly smile, but there was steel there, too. No pushover, this lady.

Turning her attention to Jason, she morphed into a mother role. "Shoo. Off to work with you. I got it from here."

"Yes, ma'am." Jason gave her a quick kiss on the cheek, then handed Jack the bag with his prescription and magazine. "Oh, I almost forgot." He pointed to where a serviceable old blue bicycle with a wire basket between the handlebars leaned against the side of the barn. "There's your transportation." He nudged Jack with his elbow, a smirk on his lips. "See, no license required."

Jack chuckled for the second time in less than five minutes. "I can deal with that. Thanks, man." Out of the sterile four walls of his hospital room and being offered a chance to move around and talk without medical supervision, he was starting to feel like his old self again.

Or what he hoped his old self felt like—relaxed and grateful.

"Protect and Serve. That's me." Then Jason headed out.

"He's a good boy," Emma remarked absently, watching Jason's disappearing cruiser with a faraway look. When the dust of his leaving settled, she snapped to. "One of my foster child success stories." She tilted her head in Jack's direction. "Hope you'll be one of my successes, too."

"Yes, ma'am."

"Well, come on, then. No time for dawdling. Before I show you where you'll be working, let's get you set up in Shane's RV." She threw him a pleased look. "I think you'll be surprised."

She set off at a quick pace, and Jack trotted to catch up with her, each footfall sending a thread of pain up his spine and into his head, hot needles stabbing behind his eyes.

She halted before the RV door, unlocked it, then handed him the key. "Take care of this. I've got a spare, but I expect—" She stopped herself. "You'll have to forgive me. I'm used to dealing with teens, not full-grown men."

Jack smiled. "No apology necessary. I'll take good care of the key." He slid it into the coin pocket on his jeans.

Emma opened the door, and he followed her inside.

And surprised he was. The interior smelled new, the cabinets and furnishings extravagant, lavish even. If not for the fact it was so cramped that only a runway model could squeeze through, he might have called it perfect. "This is amazing." He'd get used to walking sideways.

Emma seemed to know what he was thinking. "Trust me. You'll fit. These buttons here work the slides."

In minutes, the slides opened up, expanding the living room by a good three feet. The bedroom opened up, as well. A good thing, since he wasn't exactly a small man. "Kitchen and bathroom are stocked. Bed's made up. Shane said you were to help yourself to the clothes until you can afford some of your own. He also asked that you keep the place clean and no smoking."

"Yes, ma'am. I'm pretty sure I didn't smoke before. And if I did, guess now's a good time to quit, right?" He followed her back to the front.

"For having your world turned upside down in an instant, you've got a good attitude." Emma laughed. "I hope everything here is acceptable to you."

"Totally acceptable. In fact, I can't thank you enough."

"You already have." Emma opened the door. "Dinner's at six at the house, and I imagine you'll have worked up an appetite by then. Just don't overdo, or Dr. Saul will have my hide. I'll give you a few minutes to catch your breath, then meet me in the kennel for your introduction to poop patrol." She winked at him. "Wear work boots. Shane left a pair for you in here, somewhere." And she was gone.

So far, so good. He'd wanted to stay in Jasper and here he was, in a luxury RV no less. He'd wanted to learn more about the pretty lady vet, and apparently she spent a lot of time here at the DCA.

Now he just needed to figure out his identity, why Jasper was so important to him and whether he was a good, or a very bad, person.

Hope for the best—prepare for the worst.

IT WAS ANOTHER warm sunny morning, three days after setting the broken leg of the stray. Raoul, a vet tech interning for Marie through a college program in Boise, had christened the dog Amaya. In her SUV, taking the recovering Amaya back to the DCA, Marie should have been engulfed in the warm-and-fuzzies.

She and Raoul had performed a near-miraculous surgery. The X-rays revealed a much worse break than Marie had originally thought. If the surgery hadn't been successful, the dog would have lost her leg. And if Emma hadn't found the poor thing and called Marie, Amaya and her pups would have died.

But worry overshadowed any sense of triumph. True, her two-legged stray, Jack, was long gone to Boise by now. But Deputy Murphy still hadn't returned her multiple calls and texts. What if Jack really was a threat to her and had stayed in Jasper, making her emergency real and immediate? What then? Murphy had never failed to respond when she'd reached out in the past. Something must be wrong. And not knowing scared Marie like she hadn't been scared since…since the last time she'd seen Abel Galnes.

Sensing her distress, Astrid woofed. "You're right, girl. Nothing I can do right this minute." But Marie wondered if maybe she shouldn't just drive to Boise and find out what was going on for herself.

Shutting off the engine, she worked to shed her anxiety. "Come on, Astrid." She climbed out of the SUV and Astrid hopped out right behind her, following Marie around to the back. Opening the hatch, she left the carrier in the car, opting instead to carry the dog. "Here we are, Amaya. Home sweet home." She hefted the pregnant stray into her arms and strode toward the kennel.

Stepping into the kennel's cool, dark interior brought instant relief from the sun's heat. The impatient dog struggled to get down. "Knock it off, Amaya. I'm trying to help you here."

"Need a hand?"

Marie froze. Her mouth went dry, and her heart rate ratcheted up. Astrid drew near, ears twitching and tail up, stance alert.

Turning in a slow spin, Marie peered through the gloom. "Jack?"

About ten feet away, his shadowy form leaned on a shovel handle. "DCA poop patrol, at your service."

Based on his words and light tone, he meant to be funny. But nothing about this situation struck Marie as the least bit amusing. "What are you doing here?" Her words carried a sharp edge. "I thought you were going to Boise."

"I was. Plans changed. And at the moment, I'm cleaning the kennels. Why don't you let me help you get that dog settled?"

"Her name is Amaya, and I can manage."

Think, Marie, think.

A stranger who had shown up a few days ago out of no-where, supposedly with no memory, standing in Emma's kennel instead of a hospital in Boise. At the same time that Deputy US Marshal George Murphy had suddenly gone AWOL. Coincidence? Maybe. If you believed in them. And Marie did not.

Sensing her mistress's concern, Astrid stayed by her side as Marie walked to the last stall, bent her knees and set Amaya down. The poor stray didn't seem at all happy about being forced into the small pen Emma had prepared in order to limit her movement. But then, being forced to endure things one didn't like happened to everyone from time to time.

"Just for a little while, girl." Marie calmed Amaya, then stood and did a quick search for a weapon just in case she needed one. The only thing available was a metal dog bowl. Not nearly as effective as her pepper spray, which she had conveniently left in her car.

Stupid, stupid, stupid.

Well, if it came to it, Astrid was trained to attack if Marie gave the command.

Her eyes had adjusted to the dim lighting of the kennel enough to see tousled brown hair brushing against impossibly broad shoulders. The white T-shirt he wore stretched tight across his chest and showed off arms defined by corded muscles. An unlikely mixture of tempered fear and cautious pleasure filled her. He was a pretty one, all right. But Abel had been pretty, too.

Jack had put down the shovel and moved closer. Marie tensed.

He must have sensed her discomfort. "Have I done something to offend you?"

If he'd come here to kill her, he would have already. Unless he really did have amnesia and forgot he was supposed to kill her. In which case, each recovered memory of his might bring her one memory closer to death. She gave herself a mental eye roll. Until she spoke to George, all she could do was try to figure out Jack's identity while working to get him out of Jasper. Out of her life.

"No, I'm just tired." The lie came easily. Well, it wasn't as if she hadn't had plenty of practice.

"What happened to her?" Jack asked, indicating Amaya.

"We think she was tossed from a moving vehicle during the storm. Broken leg, road rash all over and she's pregnant. Not to mention quite a few old scars."

"That's rough. She going to be okay?"

His concern seemed genuine. But she wasn't exactly the best judge of men, or the validity of emotions they expressed. "Should be, but I can't be sure about the puppies."

"When's she due?"

"Any day now. That's why I wanted to get her back here so fast."

"So, she came out of the same storm as me?"

"Apparently so."

Jack squatted and looked Astrid in the eyes. "And who is this beauty?"

"Her name is Astrid. She's the one who helped me get you out of the culvert." And Astrid was an excellent judge of character.

She gave the dog a slight tap, releasing her from Marie's side. Astrid woofed in pleasure and, tail wagging, went up to Jack and sniffed him. He remained still, his hand extended, and Astrid, the little traitor, licked his palm.

Then Jack did something unexpected. Something Marie had seen Emma, a professional trainer, do countless times. He slapped the flat of his hand against his chest in invitation. Astrid responded by jumping up on two legs, front paws planted on his shoulders.

Jack laughed, a rich, warm baritone sound. A genuine laugh. He ruffled Astrid's ears. "Nice to meet you, too."

Marie couldn't help but smile. "Astrid, down."

"She's definitely well-behaved. Was she trained here?"

Marie nodded. "As an attack dog." *Just putting that out there in case you get any ideas, buster.*

"Really?" Jack scratched Astrid's tummy, now that she was stretched out on the floor. "A lot of crime in Jasper?"

"No more or less than any other place." Marie checked Amaya's bowls for fresh water and food. "So why aren't you in Boise trying to sort out this memory loss thing?"

"Decided I'd rather stay here. As odd as it sounds, my gut's telling me that if I want my memories back, I need to be in Jasper. And thanks to Jason, Emma was kind enough to offer me a place to stay." He nodded in the direction of the shovel. "And a job. Cleaning kennels isn't much, but when you're broke, it's everything." He shrugged, the movement doing great things for his shoulders. "So, here I am. Thanks to a lot of nice people in this town."

Marie blinked to keep from reacting to the heart-stopping smile on Jack's face. "Yeah, Jasper is great like that."

The kennel's atmosphere changed in a flash, as if an electrical current whipped through the room. Jack stared at her again with that all-knowing intensity she remembered from the side of the road.

"Marie?"

She swallowed. Her pulse stuttered. "What?"

"Thank you." He ducked his head, then raised his eyes to meet hers. "For saving my life."

She let out a silent sigh of relief. "No thanks necessary."

"You say that like it was nothing." He straightened to a standing position, and Astrid followed his cue. "But it wasn't nothing. It was my life." He beat a fist against his chest one time, his voice breaking with emotion. "I can never repay you for that. But I'd like to try. For starters, maybe you'll let me take you to dinner?"

Marie appreciated his gratitude, but going to dinner together? Not gonna happen. "Thought you were broke." She tempered her words with a teasing tone.

"We might have to wait a couple weeks while I save up my allowance." He gave her a mischievous grin that took her breath away.

As her guard around Jack began to slip a little and her attraction to him grew, it would still be best to nip this in the bud. *Remember Abel.* Even if Jack hadn't been sent to kill her, he was dangerous to her self-control.

"Not to worry. No repayment needed." She latched the door on Amaya's stall. "But maybe you can answer a question for me."

"I'll try, but lately I seem to have more questions than answers, myself."

She crossed her arms over her chest. "That first day in the hospital, you asked me if I'd been a blonde. Why?"

"I'm not sure. I guess you must look like someone I know who's blonde, but I have no idea who." He shrugged. "*Did* you used to be blonde?"

Marie ignored his question but considered his answer. It could be the case, but how would she know if he was lying? "Well, have fun on poop patrol. I've gotta go. I need to take a look at Elton's hoof." Her voice came out in a rush, and she hustled from the kennel, calling Astrid to her side. She had to get rid of him, and she had to do it now. To accomplish that, she would need Emma's help.

She found Emma sweeping the central area in the barn. "There you are."

"Marie, watch out." Emma motioned her out of the way

as she sprinkled water on the floor and swept dust into a pile. "You bring my stray back?"

"I did. And by the way, her name's Amaya."

Emma snickered. "Amaya, huh? Let me guess. Raoul?"

"Of course." Marie chuckled. "It means night rain in Basque."

"Aw, I like that." Emma's face softened. "Fits her perfectly. Is she settled in? Was the pen what you needed?"

"Yes, and yes." Marie looked around the empty barn. "Um, I thought I was going to check Elton's hoof today."

"Darn it." Emma stopped sweeping and slapped a palm to her forehead. "I completely forgot. Hugh and Kyle came out today to work, but I already had Jack mucking stalls and scooping the paddock. They asked if they could exercise the horses instead, and Elton didn't seem to be favoring that foot. I thought maybe I'd just imagined him limping."

Hugh, Kyle and William worked afternoons and weekends for Emma through a co-op program for at-risk kids at the local high school. Wanting to make sure they also stayed out of trouble during the summer, Emma offered them part-time jobs.

"Tell you what. I have a light day at the clinic tomorrow, so I'll just come back in the morning and take a look. I'd rather catch it early, if he does have something wrong."

"Perfect. Thanks." Emma went back to her sweeping.

Marie perched on a bale of hay and tried to keep her tone neutral. "You want to tell me how Jack ended up here?"

Emma's broom froze midsweep. She straightened her back and met Marie's questioning look with one of resolve. "He needed a place to stay and a way to earn some money. I can never have too much help. Figured it was a win-win situation." Her lips curled into a sly smile. "Besides, I thought you might appreciate having him around. You seemed quite taken with him, and girl, you weren't exaggerating about him being good-looking."

"I'm not taken with him, or anybody else for that matter." Marie crossed her arms to emphasize her denial. "In fact, I think you should send him to Boise. There's a brain trauma specialist there willing to take him without insurance. He'd have a place to stay, and money wouldn't be an issue. Dr. Saul is really worried about him. By giving him a place to stay here, you're not helping him. You could be hurting him."

Emma shook her head. "Give me a little credit. I spoke to Dr. Saul before making the offer to Jack. True, he doesn't agree with Jack's decision to stay here, but he doesn't think it will harm him, either."

"And what if he ends up being some serial killer? I get strange vibes from him. I'm telling you—you're not safe with him here."

"'Methinks the lady doth protest too much.'" Emma's words came out in a singsong version of a bad English accent.

Marie stood. "What are you talking about?"

"If I didn't know better, I'd think you have a crush on him." Emma sprayed more water on the floor. "Not that I'd blame you."

"Oh, please." But Marie's heart sank. Emma would not be her ally in this. If she was going to get rid of Jack, she'd have to come up with Plan B.

"You know," Emma went on, "it wouldn't kill you to have a social life."

You never know, Emma. It actually might.

JACK MAY BE missing most of his memories, but reading people seemed to come easily to him. Doc Saul, Jason,

Emma—piece of cake. But Marie? She was the proverbial onion with lots of layers. Jack stood outside the kennel, following her progress as she practically ran to the barn to find Emma. But he couldn't tell if she was running to Emma or away from him.

What reason did she have to act so skittish around him? True, he was a man from nowhere with nothing, not even a name. But no one else seemed bothered by that. She actually appeared to be afraid of him, and that rankled.

The first time he met her, in the hospital, she'd been touted as his savior. So when he was unconscious, she had no problem saving his life. But awake, he apparently seemed poised to leap from his bed and bite her head off.

Today, she came into the kennel happy and talking to dogs, until the moment she'd become aware of his presence. Then she'd gone all starchy and hard. He'd even maintained a safe distance, spoken in soft, nonthreatening tones, even made a joke. She might have even been softening, but then, like a bolt of lightning, she'd practically run out of the kennel as if fleeing the hounds of hell.

One minute friendly, the next wanting nothing to do with him. Not that he blamed her, entirely. She'd found him in a muddy ditch. And now he was mucking horse stalls and shoveling dog runs for a living. He was not a catch for the sexy vet. He got that. But someone to fear?

Marie Beaumont—a woman with wintry blue eyes and full, ever-so-kissable lips. A woman with dark hair who haunted him as a blonde. A woman who championed strays but didn't always trust them.

Marie Beaumont made his head hurt.

Despite that, he was inexplicably drawn to her. Not just sexually attracted, though there was that. He wanted to know everything about her. As much as he hankered to unearth his own past, he wanted to discover hers even more.

He finished up the last of his indoor kennel chores, cleaned the shovel, then grabbed a muck rake and started for the paddock on the far side of the barn. He stopped short when Marie went speed-walking from the barn to her vehicle, Astrid right on her heels. Jack's gaze followed the trail of dust left by her speeding SUV as she drove away down the dirt road.

And that sudden, razor-sharp pain struck him with an intensity so powerful, he bent double and grabbed his head in both hands. Behind his eyes he saw another trail of dust, from another time, another place. A place thick with trees. Men shouting. The *pop, pop, pop* of automatic gunfire. He flinched and bucked as if dodging live bullets. Then his wrist was on fire, the burning pain overshadowing the pain in his head.

In the next instant, his mind went dark, and the horror-filled memories retreated back behind the walls of his amnesia. He panted, trying to catch his breath. Cool, clammy sweat covered his skin. He straightened, massaging his temples, checking his body for bullet holes he knew weren't there. Examining his left arm, he stopped cold. Thick, fibrous ridges and slick indentations covered the wrist and forearm. Burn scars.

All this time, he'd assumed the undercurrent of danger he sensed when he was around Marie had something to do with her. But now, with these memories, maybe he was the one in trouble.

"Oh my gosh, Jack. You look pale as a ghost. You okay?" Piper Lambert, a dog trainer at DCA, stood in the kennel doorway. A tall woman with long dark red hair, her green eyes reflected genuine concern. She had a harnessed dog, her latest search and rescue trainee, on one side. On her other side was a corgi mix puppy she'd adopted recently. It was kind of cool that every day at the DCA was *Bring Your Pet to Work* day.

"Just another one of my headaches," Jack assured her. "It's already passed."

"I don't happen to think it was just another one of your headaches. You should see yourself. Sit, will you? Before you fall."

He dropped onto a nearby bench.

"That's better. Do I need to call Emma, or maybe Dr. Saul?"

"Absolutely not." They might send him to Boise. He needed to stay in Jasper. He had to give Piper something to make her back down. "Okay, you got me. It wasn't just another headache. I got a flash of memory."

She gave him a broad smile. "That's outstanding. Can you remember your name? Who you are?"

"Nothing like that, unfortunately. Just a dirt road. Some trees. Well, lots of trees. Nothing I recognized." He swallowed that half-truth he'd just told. "No big deal, really."

"Of course, it's a big deal. Wait until I tell—"

"Do you mind not saying anything about this? Not yet anyway. I want to tell people in my own time. You know, once I get my head wrapped around it."

"Sorry, I wasn't thinking." She dropped her gaze. "Of course. I won't say anything."

And despite only meeting Piper a few days ago, Jack believed her.

"Thanks." That's when he looked down. Muddy boot steps and equally muddy paw prints crisscrossed the concrete floor he'd just washed. He blew out an exasperated breath.

Piper snickered. "Sorry about that, but you might as well get used to it. It's a never-ending job." She ushered her trainee into one of the stalls, removed its harness and gave the water dish a quick look. "At least you remember to clean and fill their bowls. The after-school kids took a while to learn that one."

"After-school kids?"

"Yeah, there're three of them this year. Hugh, Kyle and William. Have you met them yet?"

"No, but I saw two teenage boys earlier. They disappeared into the barn."

"That would be Hugh and Kyle. They're out exercising the horses right now." Her mouth screwed up into a droll smile. "I bet they were *so* disappointed to find out you've taken over as head poop scooper."

Jack chuckled. "It's a crappy job, but someone has to do it."

Piper planted her hands on her hips in a battle stance. "I like your can-do-doo attitude."

Jack held up his hands in surrender, chuckling. "Enough. You win."

He'd met Piper when he first arrived at DCA, but they hadn't had much of a chance to chat it up yet. With well-practiced ease, she hung the harness on the wall and crossed her arms, studying Jack as she might a dog about to become a new trainee. "You settling in okay?"

Jack waggled his hand from side to side in a so-so gesture. "I could be doing a lot worse. I really appreciate you and Shane letting me use your RV."

"Technically, it's just Shane's. And I should be thanking you. At first, I loved it when he parked that huge thing in my driveway, because I knew it meant he was staying." She shrugged. "But after almost four months, I'm so ready to have my driveway back."

"Glad I could help out." Like some nervous tick, Jack scuffed his boot against the floor. "It's been nice getting to know folks around here. Marie just left." *Smooth, Jack, real smooth.*

"Yeah, I saw her tear out when I was coming in. Probably some clinic emergency. That gal loves animals, which is saying a lot around here. She told me once that from the time she was a little girl, she felt a calling to heal injured critters."

"I guess you know her pretty well, then?"

Piper shrugged again. "As well as anyone, I suppose. Nice as they come, but she doesn't open up much." Amaya whined, and Piper ambled down to the last stall.

Hoping to learn something, anything, about the enigmatic Marie, Jack followed her. "Why is that?"

"Who knows?" Piper opened the stall door and crossed to Amaya's pen. "And to be honest, I don't need to know about someone's past in order to like them for who they are now. Or not like them, as the case may be."

"Glad you feel that way. Otherwise, there'd be no chance for me."

Crouching down, Piper reached in and rubbed Amaya's head. "Hey, with me, you're in until you're out. But with Marie? Well, you best count on being in the getting-to-know-you category for quite some time."

"Gives me something to strive for. Full acceptance in Jasper, Idaho." He left the stall, refilled the bucket with water and grabbed the mop, ready to clean up the muddy footprints after Piper left.

Piper laughed. "We're generally not a tough crowd. I'm sure you'll fit in just fine." She leaned toward him and stage-whispered, "Unless the law's after you. You're not the leader of some fringe group hiding out in the hills, are you?" She hooked a thumb over her shoulder. "Ruby Ridge is just up the road, you know." With a wink and another laugh, she headed out the door.

And just like that, Jack knew Ruby Ridge. In Boundary County, Idaho. Site of an eleven-day siege in 1992. Three people dead, including one deputy US marshal. Of all the things to remember, and with such clarity and detail.

He shook his head. Bizarre. And even more bizarre, the memory had returned without pain. When that standoff happened, Jack was pretty young. It wasn't a true memory, but something he'd learned from a book or TV.

His stomach cramped into a cold ball of dread. The mention of Ruby Ridge triggered a recall of something learned, just minutes after a dusty dirt road triggered a painful flash of true memories. Memories of gunshots and burns. There had to be a connection.

But the connection was far from clear, and as Jack struggled to find it, his headache returned in earnest.

Chapter Four

After practically fleeing the DCA, Marie eased up on the gas pedal. She tapped her hands-free console and rang George Murphy. Still no answer. No point in leaving another message. Frustrated at not being in control of her own life, she opted for routine and called her office.

"Anything I need to come in for?" Marie asked her office manager through the car's speaker phone.

Liz Jellis had worked for a small law firm in Jasper until a car full of partying tourists mowed her down as she crossed the street on her lunch hour. Multiple surgeries later, her right leg had more metal than bone. Her boss sued the driver on her behalf, handed Liz her share of the settlement and promptly retired for parts unknown.

A few years later, her settlement money gone and still without a job, Liz had brought in her sick cat right at closing time. Marie, who could never say no to an ill or injured animal, had invited Liz in after hours. After hearing the woman's story, she'd treated her beloved tabby at no cost and hired Liz on the spot, never once regretting it.

"Nothing you need to be here for, but aren't you supposed to be working on Elton?"

"I was, but there was a mix-up. If my schedule's clear, I plan to go back tomorrow." Marie tried to ignore the sudden cramp twisting her stomach.

"Let's see. You have a couple appointments in the afternoon, but tomorrow morning is free."

"Great. And what about my schedule for the rest of today?"

"Free and clear." Liz's tone turned serious. "And you shouldn't sound so happy about that. You have some pretty big bills coming in."

"Don't I always make bills?"

"You do, but I would be remiss if I didn't remind you. Where are you off to?"

"To pick up some fudge, and then I'm heading over to Hemlock Hills. I haven't seen Dotty all week."

"Then you better get on over there. And tell her I said hi, will you?"

"You bet."

"I'll never understand why they named that place after hemlock, even if it *is* for the *non* poisonous trees nearby." Liz scoffed. "Every time I hear it, reminds me of 'Hotel California' by the Eagles. You know, the part about checking out but not leaving."

Marie chuckled. "Well, that's a bit morbid, but the residents don't seem to mind. They even joke about it."

"Oh, don't forget the fundraiser at Bartwell's Friday night."

"Got it on my calendar. See you tomorrow."

TAKING A DEEP, cleansing breath, Marie inhaled the hint of fresh lavender as soon as she and Astrid walked into the airy, sunlit foyer of Hemlock Hills. The staff here had no need for plug-in scent diffusers meant to hide the stench of bodily functions, nor did they use that eye-watering pine cleanser that made everything stink like a morgue. No, Hemlock Hills was a far cry from the corporate-run facility where her grandmother had spent her final days.

After Marie had been orphaned in a car crash at the age of three, Granny Mae had raised her. As an adult, Marie had cared for her grandmother when cancer ravaged her body. Since she was an immediate family member, Granny Mae could have accompanied Marie into witness protection. But her grandmother had been too sick to travel, and insisted she'd be just fine in a nursing home. And the woman Marie owed everything to had died alone with no one to mourn her. Marie's guilt over leaving her grandmother behind was something she grappled with every day. But her friendship with Dotty helped salve the pain.

"Hi, Dr. Beaumont." Kim, the young woman who manned the reception desk, smiled. "Miss Dotty has been asking after you and Astrid."

"Oh, no. She's not mad enough to throw anything at me, is she?"

Kim snickered. "You go on in and let me know."

"Coward."

Marie hurried through the large family room with plump couches, shelves packed with books and a large-screen TV quietly broadcasting the news. At a table next to a large window, four women sat playing bridge. They exchanged waves with Marie, then returned to their game.

The Hills, as it was sometimes called, was a sprawling one-story ranch-style home on the northern edge of town. It had been converted into an assisted living facility with ten small private rooms. Not long after moving to Jasper, Marie had been called to the Hills about a stray cat. Seemed the residents had fallen in love with Sassy Cat, as she came to be known, and asked to adopt her. The only way the owner would agree was if the cat was current on shots and rendered sterile.

As always, Astrid accompanied Marie during the back and forth with Sassy Cat and became an instant favorite of the feisty older woman in 5A, Dotty Hazzard. And Dotty Hazzard became an instant favorite of Marie's, filling the gaping hole left by her grandmother's passing.

Marie knocked.

"That better be Astrid and her never-comes-to-see-old-Dotty-anymore owner. Well, come on in here before I croak."

Marie opened the door of the cheerful space and released Astrid just as Dotty hit Mute on *Judge Judy*. Astrid went straight to the easy chair where Dotty sat and laid her head in the woman's lap. Dotty's collection of bangle bracelets jingled on both arms as she scratched and petted and cooed. "Here's my good girl. At least *you* love me, don't you, Astrid?"

Marie perched on the tie-dye quilt on Dotty's bed. Each resident was allowed to decorate their room however they wished, and Dotty, an original flower child, Woodstock attendee and once-upon-a-time commune resident, had gone full-on hippie, bohemian in her decor. Colorful batik hangings covered the walls, rattan chairs with bright cushions sat on a paisley rug and plants hung in macramé holders.

The lady herself wore her long gray hair in twin braids and got scolded on a regular basis for playing her classic rock favorites too loud. "Fetch me the jar, hon."

No need to specify which one. Marie got up and reached for the dog biscuit container, a purple glass jar hand-painted with a gold Moroccan design. She handed the jar to Dotty, who unscrewed the lid, and soon Astrid was chomping away.

Dotty put the lid back on and squeezed the jar onto the side table next to her that also held her TV remote, tissue box, one pill bottle and a glass of lemonade. "So, life must be keeping you real busy these days."

Smiling at Dotty's rebuke, Marie dropped into the chair

next to her, sinking into the pink-and-orange cushions with a grateful sigh. "It has, actually." She pulled the scrunchie off her ponytail and sighed again when her hair fell around her face. "The morning after that big storm we had last week, Astrid and I went jogging as usual, and I found a guy along the side of the road. Well, Astrid found him."

Dotty leaned forward, rubbing her arthritic hands together. "Was he murdered?"

"What?" Marie's shock at the old lady's morbid excitement made her voice louder than usual. "No."

"Oh." Disappointment colored Dotty's tone. "I thought maybe we'd have an intriguing mystery to solve. Something to activate the old brain cells."

"I think you've been watching too many true crime shows."

Dotty waved off Marie's suggestion. "Okay, okay. So he wasn't murdered." She folded her arms across where her breasts used to be. Burning her bra decades ago, along with the undeniable force of gravity, had relocated them somewhere between her sternum and her belly button. "Was he at least dead?"

Marie rolled her eyes. "I called 911, and they took him to the hospital."

"Is that all?" Dotty complained with a phony pout. "I can see where *you* might consider that mildly newsworthy, you being so young and lacking any real-life experience, but it's hardly reason enough for not visiting me. Anything else?"

"Actually, there is. I think he might be—" Marie caught herself. It was too easy to relax around Dotty.

"He might be, what?" Dotty probed.

"Well, he hit his head pretty hard. That's why he was unconscious. When he woke up, he couldn't remember anything about his past. Retrograde amnesia, his doctor called it."

"Go on with you now. His name wouldn't happen to be Jason Bourne, would it?"

"Ha-ha. Very funny. His name is Jack." Marie shrugged. "Least, we think it is. And for your information, he doesn't look anything at all like Matt Damon, if that's what you were fishing for."

"So what *does* he look like?"

Marie fiddled with the fringe on one of the throw pillows. "Handsome, I suppose, when his face isn't covered with mud."

"Uh-huh."

Marie didn't need to meet Dotty's eyes to know she was getting a thorough once-over.

"So tell me what your plans are for this handsome guy you found in a ditch. Not the usual way to meet men, but hey, if it works, more power to you."

"I have no plans for him." Marie forced herself to stop pulling on the pillow tassel before she yanked it right off.

"Don't pass up this chance, kiddo. You saved the life of a hunk, and now he owes you. I say take him home and keep him." She slapped her hand on her thigh and cackled. When Marie didn't bite, Dotty's playfulness fell away and her tone grew serious. "Oh, come on. Face it, sweetheart. You need a man in the worst kind of way. Far as I know, you haven't had one since you hit town. It ain't right for a woman your age to be alone."

"I have Astrid. Besides, my life is just fine as it is." Sometimes, she really did miss having a man around. What she didn't miss was the anxiety that came with them.

"No offense to Astrid, but a dog isn't a man. Look at me." Marie flicked her gaze up, and Dotty leaned forward, resting her hand on Marie's arm. "Maybe a man who can't remember his past is perfect for a woman trying to forget hers. Maybe you should try not to worry so much about who he used to be and just get to know the man he is now."

"I'm not sure I can do that. Besides, I don't have the best track record when it comes to judging men."

Sitting back in her chair, Dotty shifted around until she seemed comfortable. "So, tell me more about this Jack."

Marie filled Dotty in, careful to keep to the facts.

"And so now he's staying in Shane's RV out at the DCA, and you don't like it."

"I never said I didn't like it."

"Well, your face surely did. What is it about this Jack that you don't like?"

Marie stiffened, and like a pressure cooker, all her pent-up fear bubbled to the surface. "I don't like that he came out of nowhere. I don't like that everyone seems to trust him without knowing a single thing about him. I don't like that he refused to go to Boise and be treated, for free I might add, by a head trauma specialist because his gut tells him he should stay in Jasper. A place, incidentally, where not one person knows him."

Eyebrows high and forehead wrinkles deep, Dotty stared at her. "Feel better now?"

A laugh erupted from Marie. "Actually, I do."

"Always a good thing, getting that stuff off your chest. Want to get high?"

"Dotty." Marie swatted her friend's leg with the pillow she still held.

Dotty doubled over, laughing. "Ah, you know I was only pulling your leg."

"You're incorrigible." Marie laughed along with her, knowing the old woman loved that joke.

"It's what keeps me young." Dotty's expression turned somber. "You know, sweetheart, I doubt this Jack is someone to worry about. But don't forget that half the police force is out at the DCA a lot, what with their dogs being trained and all. In a pinch, those high school kids are out there, too."

Astrid moved beside Marie and butted her head against Marie's knee until she got a dog biscuit.

"And even you've said so yourself, Emma is an excellent judge of character. But I get you. You have a hard time with things that aren't neat and tidy. And you think this man Jack is about as messy as they come." Dotty opened a container of breath mints and shook one out, then passed them to Marie. "Just see how it goes, and if he does anything that scares you, you report it. Okay?"

"Okay," Marie lied.

Dotty hmphed. "This has something to do with your past, doesn't it? That dark place you never talk about."

"It does, and I'll work through it like I always do." Marie straightened her spine, refusing to let this get her down. "Talking to you helps."

"Well, I'm glad to hear it, although I'm not sure how. No one should go through this life alone, kiddo. You got to have someone to talk to. And laugh with. Someone to help you get those doggone fitted sheets onto your mattress." She drained her lemonade. "Now then, what's going on at Bartwell's this weekend? I heard they're having some sort of special social thing."

Glad to be back on safe ground, Marie jumped on the topic. "One of the brewery's seasonal employees, I think her name's Millie, was diagnosed with cancer and she doesn't have insurance. The Bartwells decided to host barbecues once a week and donate the proceeds to offset her skyrocketing medical bills."

"Good people, the Bartwells. They always look out for their employees. Are you going?"

"I'm thinking about it. Do you want to go with me?"

"Nah, but thanks for asking. I'll probably be asleep by the time the dancing starts."

"Oh, I almost forgot." Marie rummaged in her bag. "I brought you some fudge."

"You know me so well. Thanks, kiddo."

"Now, what about *your* news? I thought you were working on the mystery of the missing clothes." Apparently, some items had gone into the laundry room, never to be seen again.

"Oh, shoot. I forgot to tell you." A satisfied smile spread across Dotty's face. "We solved it."

"We?"

Dotty nodded. "We. Us. The ones with the missing clothes."

"Well, don't keep me in suspense. Who's the culprit?"

"Betty Turnbull." Dotty rolled her eyes. "She showed up at movie night wearing Edith's blouse and my shawl, then claimed it was an accident. Can you believe the gall?"

Marie closed her eyes, a running profile of the female residents filtering through her mind. "Which one is Betty?"

"She's new. You haven't met her yet. She's the one I told you about who eats the fresh rose on her table every night at dinner. And then picks her teeth with the thorn." With an indelicate grunt, Dotty pushed up from her chair. "They must get those flowers awful cheap, 'cause the stems *always* have thorns. Come on—let's walk and talk. Every time I sit too long, I get stiff."

Dotty's limp was more pronounced than usual and her gait slow as they wandered into the family room, where the TV news droned on and the Hemlock Four, as Dotty called them, were still at their game of bridge. Across the room, near the large fireplace, sat a drink station with coffee, iced tea, lemonade and water.

Marie couldn't miss Dotty's grimaces during the short distance they'd walked. "Why don't you sit, and I'll get you more lemonade." She set her bag on the couch and told Astrid to stay.

"You're too good to me." With a grateful sigh, Dotty edged down on one of the couches and took the glass of cold lemonade when Marie brought it over.

After taking a long draw on the sweet drink, she smacked her lips. "Stay 'til the news is over?"

The plea tugged at Marie's heart. "Watching the news with you is one of my favorite things to do."

"I don't believe you, but I'll let you lie to me about it." Dotty reached for the remote and turned up the volume, waiting for the commercials to be over. "Dang lemonade. I need to use the can."

"Charming as ever." Marie chuckled as she rose to help Dotty get to her feet.

After that, Dotty swatted her away. "I got it from here." She shuffled toward the restroom near the lobby.

With nothing to do but wait, Marie turned to the TV when the news anchor announced a breaking alert.

"In a daring early morning escape, survivalist Abel Gaines escaped the US Penitentiary, Hazelton in West Virginia…"

At the name Abel Gaines, everything went cold. At the word *escape*, the nursing home faded from view as shock hit her. Abel's face, his mug shot, stared back at her from the screen.

No, no, no. Astrid whined, and Marie realized she'd spoken out loud.

Marie curled in on herself. She wrapped her arms across

her churning stomach, barely noticing her icy hands as they cupped her elbows.

"...serving multiple life sentences for the deaths of five civilians and FBI Agent Mike Winston. Convicted as a domestic terrorist, Gaines was also charged with treason when plans to blow up several federal government buildings were discovered along with an arsenal of small arms and a cache of C-4 explosives."

Astrid nuzzled into her, the dog's stable heartbeat and warmth grounding her enough to catch the rest of what the news was saying.

"Gaines reportedly killed one prison guard and seriously wounded another during the escape. It's believed he was assisted by at least one of his original co-conspirators, and unconfirmed sources in the FBI say it's most likely his older brother Seth Gaines. The youngest Gaines brother, Isaac, was killed during the shootout five years ago when several law enforcement agencies attempted to serve arrest warrants at the Gaines family compound in the Allegheny Mountains. Gains was reportedly seen fleeing west, so the manhunt has expanded to include Ohio and Kentucky. More news as—"

A high-pitched buzz in Marie's ears drowned out the TV, and her gaze darted around the room, each item it touched coming in and out of focus like a drug-induced hallucination.

Dotty materialized in front of her. "Why, honey, you look like you've seen a ghost."

I have.

Marie parted her lips to speak, but her mouth seemed filled with cotton. She reached for her lemonade and drained the glass. "I...it's nothing." Standing, she grabbed her bag and Astrid's harness. "I know I promised, but I really need to go. I feel a stomach bug coming on."

"Go on, then. Take care of yourself." Dotty lowered herself onto the couch. "Keep me posted on your fella. And if you're still unsure about him, bring him by. Let me get a feel for him."

"Will do. See you soon." Marie kissed the top of Dotty's head, then for the second time that day, forced herself to walk, not run, to her car.

Abel Gains escaped. George Murphy was MIA. The unexpected arrival of Jack, who just happened to have no memory.

After turning the ignition key and locking the doors, Marie pulled out her phone and jabbed her case deputy's number for the umpteenth time. Instead of hearing his gravelly voice, a female recording informed her that this number was no longer in service. She slammed the phone down on the center console.

Fine. She would handle this herself.

Chapter Five

Dirt road. Dust flying up. Lush green trees. Maple, poplar, ash. Rolling hills. Afternoon sun. Heat. An idyllic scene that was anything but.

Blue-and-red flashing lights. Law enforcement. Uniforms everywhere. A barrage of gunfire. Handguns. Semiautomatics. The thwunk *from a tear gas canister. Trailing white smoke. Shouting. Men running. More shots. More shouting.*

A room, small, rustic, messy. Windows barricaded. Shell casings littering the floor. Sunlit dust motes. Still bodies. Sightless eyes. Blood everywhere. On the floor, the walls. On the living. The dead.

Flames raced along the dry wood siding of a building. A hand reached out. Fighting. Voices yelling. A body.

Pain blacked out the scene.

Jack bolted upright in bed, gasping for breath. As the horror show faded, he struggled to get his bearings. Bedroom. Shane's RV. The DCA. Marie.

Angry, confused and drenched in sweat, Jack flipped away the sheets and headed to the cramped bathroom. Cupping water from the faucet, he splashed his face then scooped a handful into his parched mouth, slushed it around, spit it out. A foul taste still lingered.

He brushed his teeth, looking at himself in the mirror.

Was the face he stared at the face of a killer? What he'd experienced in his sleep, what he remembered now that he was awake, was a whole lot of death. He winced. Even his head was killing him. He reached for his pill bottle, shook one out and swallowed.

Flipping on the shower, he stepped in without waiting for the water to warm. He hoped the icy needles of water would help drive away the pictures in his mind. Just as he had every morning since moving to the DCA.

What Jack had seen was nothing he'd learned about from a book or on TV. He was remembering. The pain in his head confirmed that. The images were spotty and incomplete, but he recalled the verdant smell of the trees, the metallic stench of blood as he walked among the corpses.

The skylight above him displayed a bright, cloudless sky. But the sunny day did nothing to erase the evil scenes still tormenting his mind. What kind of depraved person dreams of such malevolence?

Who the hell am I?

MARIE PASSED THE night in a tangle of sheets, tossing and turning, until insomnia finally got the better of her and she shouted, "I give up!"

Startled to wakefulness, Astrid barked. And then kept on barking.

"Shut up!" Marie flipped off the sheets, turned on every light in the apartment and dressed in her running gear. As she laced up her shoes, her muscles tight, guilt over how she'd treated Astrid ate at her. "Sorry, girl. You know I didn't mean it."

Astrid sat, looking at Marie with round, glistening brown eyes.

"I'm sorry, okay?" Astrid only cocked her head, and Marie felt worse than ever. "Even if some crazy man is on the loose, I shouldn't have yelled at you." She hugged Astrid around the neck. "Wanna go for a run?"

Checking to make sure her phone was fully charged and her pepper spray within easy reach, she trotted downstairs, out the side door and into a beautiful, cool morning. She set out at a record-breaking pace with Astrid loping beside her, and the cloud of fear fogging her mind began to clear.

She formulated a plan.

AN HOUR LATER, fresh from her shower, Marie was recharged and primed for action, while at the same time relaxed. Emotionally, calm. Mentally, focused. Running always had this affect. She went over her plan's checklist in her head.

Step one—George Murphy.

Not expecting a reply, Marie tried calling him one more time, to no avail. But hey, this was the twenty-first century. Cell phones and texts were not the end-all methods of communication. Though direct contact with a field office wasn't allowed, her situation qualified as an emergency. She penned a note to George. VETSOSDR.MB. George would understand it, and she hoped if he wasn't around, someone else would, too.

She would stop by the grocery store's shipping center on her way to Emma's and send it overnight to the Boise office. It was a risk. But a necessary one.

Step two—Research.

After half an hour online reading every news article or update on Abel Gaines she could find, Marie gave up on learning anything new about him. She spent a few more minutes on amnesia. Seemed retrograde amnesiacs often experienced sharp headaches and limited epileptic seizures. While conditions could resolve in less than twenty-four hours, they could also persist for a lifetime. There were multiple methods of treatment.

Step three—Work on Emma.

It wouldn't solve the actual Abel Gaines issue, but getting Jack out of town would give Marie one less thing to even think about. Although Emma was a softy when it came to hard-luck cases, she was also sensible. If Marie could just convince her that Jack's headaches were clues that he needed serious professional care, hopefully Emma would rescind the offer of a place to stay and a paying job. For his own good, of course.

Step four—Soften Jack up, then convince him to go.

She'd have to just wing it on this step.

"Ready, girl?" Marie grabbed her vet bag, purse and mail and led the way to the SUV. Astrid followed, woofing with excitement.

Driving down the alley behind her building, Marie smiled. "Everything's gonna work out perfectly, Astrid."

In her backseat harness, Astrid fidgeted.

"I'm not being underhanded." Marie looked at her dog in the rearview mirror. "This is self-preservation, plain and simple."

Astrid's tongue lolled out and she panted.

"I know you like Jack, but don't judge me."

Astrid let out a low howl she'd inherited from the beagle side of her ancestry.

A short while after mailing the note, Marie passed under the entrance to the DCA and, despite Astrid's not-so-silent objection, had the plan firmly fixed in her head.

All she had to do now was put it into action.

THOUGH JACK'S FLASHES of memory this morning hadn't included Marie, now he was even more certain they had been acquainted in the past. Just gut instinct. Maybe she feared he might remember something about her, what she was hiding. And she *was* hiding something. Another gut instinct.

After his shower, he dressed and poured a bowl of cereal. While he crunched on milk-soaked granola nuggets, he analyzed what little he knew about himself. His past seemed terrifying. That didn't mean his future had to be. This led him back around to what he was certain about.

I may not know my life's details, but at least I have a sense of who I am now.

He didn't harbor uncontrollable rage. He didn't hate, or hear the call to violence. In fact, what filled every corner of his being was desire.

Marie Beaumont.

A desirable woman, with her deep blue eyes and well-toned curves, what attracted him most was her air of mystery. He had no desire to break down those daunting walls she'd built around herself. Only she could do that. What he wanted was the chance to see what she hid behind them once they were down.

He'd learned over dinner last night that Marie was expected this morning. One of the horses had an abscess in its foot. Jack tugged on his work boots, then headed out.

Maybe today he'd have a chance to find out what the lovely Dr. Beaumont was hiding.

"ELTON, STOP THAT!" Marie blew out an exasperated breath, tucking a loose tendril of hair behind her ear. Planting both fists on her hips, she glared at him. Each time she tried to pick up his foot, the cantankerous horse jerked it from her hand. "You're not going to get the best of me, you stubborn mule."

Elton nickered and swished his tail.

"If you don't like being called a mule, then don't act

like one. Now, hold still. I'm trying to help you." She bent down and grabbed the Appaloosa's front foot again.

"Would you like a hand?"

She'd been waiting for him to come into the barn, and still she jumped. Astrid barked and Elton pulled away again, giving her a mocking whinny.

She couldn't stand it when people materialized out of thin air and scared her out of her wits. She wanted to freeze Jack out, but she remembered *the plan*.

Knowing it was too soon to do a complete about-face, Marie remained aloof. "No, thanks. I've got it."

She tempered her refusal with a frank and hopefully flirty appraisal. *Good lord.* It just wasn't right that a man looked so good in grubby work clothes. And whether she liked him or not, Jack had an impressive set of muscles.

He was checking her out, as well. His head tilted at a jaunty angle, his eyes twinkled with mischief, his grin was wry. Her cheeks flamed and she dropped her gaze. Her plan to soften Jack up sucked. She had no game, whatsoever.

Finally getting ahold of Elton's foot, she set to work cleaning out the sole with a hoof pick so she could check for an abscess. Elton jerked his foot away and tried to lunge against the rope he was tied with in the barn aisle. In the process, he slammed into her, and she fell backward into the wall behind her. Trying to catch herself, she wound up tripping over her own feet and coming down hard on the corner of the muck cart handle with her chest.

Astrid ran to her as Marie struggled into a sitting position on the floor, her breath stuck somewhere between her mouth and her lungs.

Jack was at her side in an instant, squatting so he was eye level with her. "Are you okay? Marie? Say something."

She shook her head. Back and forth, back and forth, her

hands fluttering in front of her like hummingbird wings, trying to tell Jack what was wrong. Her lungs burned and her head seemed ready to explode. Tears leaked from her eyes as she struggled to breathe.

"Marie!" Jack grabbed her forearms as she still fought for air. "Calm down—you'll be okay."

Okay? She was dying and he wasn't helping. She tried pulling away.

He took hold of her face, warm palms cupping her cheeks. Earnest gray eyes locked on hers. Their noses practically touched. "Breathe, Marie. It's okay. That's right. It's coming back now, isn't it?"

She nodded, still afraid, then her nostrils flared, and sweet, sweet air flowed down her windpipe. Her lungs expanded, her chest rose. "Ahh, my chest. It hurts." She looked down at her cleavage, where a bruise was already purpling between her breasts.

"We need to take care of that. Can you stand?"

"I don't know." Her voice wobbled; her hands shook. Astrid pushed her muzzle against Marie's arm and whined. "I'm okay, girl. Just need to catch my breath."

"Take a second." Jack took her hands between his and rubbed warmth into them. "Try taking slow, deep breaths."

"It hurts to breathe. But I just hit the edge of that handle there." She pointed at the muck cart, tipped over on the floor now.

"I know, baby, but you need to have that looked at."

He called me baby.

She nodded and he helped her up. "Thank—thank y—"

Marie's legs crumpled like cooked spaghetti. Before she could hit the ground, Jack swung her up in his arms and in that moment, the sting of loneliness hurt far more than her chest. She'd forgotten what it felt like to be held, cared for. Her fingers brushed against his soft, thick hair at the nape of his neck. The unusual light whorls in his stormy gray eyes hypnotized her. How wonderful it would be to wallow in the scent of sun and warm hay from his skin, staying wrapped in his embrace forever.

How's that for softening him up?

What an idiot she was. She hadn't learned one thing since Abel, because if anyone was softening, it was her.

"This is ridiculous. I can walk." One arm wrapped around his neck, the other hand rested against his chest, quite comfortable right where she was.

"All evidence to the contrary." With Astrid following on his heels, Jack carried her to a bench near the barn door but continued holding her, his gaze moving across her face as if memorizing every detail. His mouth parted and Marie touched a finger to his full bottom lip. Soft, especially compared to his perpetual three-day beard.

When he closed his lips around her finger and teased it with his tongue, Marie's insides tightened like a full-body Kegel. She pulled her hand away. "Set me down. I can't leave Elton like this."

Jack placed her on the bench. "Stay. I'll put him back in his stall."

Oh, no, he didn't just issue an order to me.

"I appreciate the offer, but he might have an abscess, given the way he reacted with the pick. I've got to check that hoof."

"You sure?"

"Positive. I'm fine."

"Uh-huh." But Jack didn't argue, to her surprise. "Ready to try standing?"

"Ready or not." Marie stood up and stayed up this time. She walked to where Elton was tied. He was still put out about her messing with his foot and tugged his halter a few times to let Marie know. By way of an apology, she rubbed his neck. "I'm sorry I hurt you, but I think we're even, don't you?"

Elton snorted in response.

"I know you don't need any help," Jack said, "but do you *want* some?"

Marie smiled at him and grabbed the pick. "That would be nice. Can you stand by his head and hold on to the halter? Try to keep him quiet?"

Glancing at Jack, she found his intense gaze on her again. But with a smile this time, the effect beguiling her. As he held Elton's halter, his eyes stayed on her as if no one else in the world existed. It was intoxicating.

Get a grip. The plan to soften him up was meant to get rid of him, not become infatuated with him. With the extra pair of hands, Marie finished cleaning Elton's sole. As she suspected, he had an abscess that hadn't yet broken, so she applied a poultice to help it drain.

Although Marie stood straight and tall, her insides softened into mush. How long since she'd had a partner, someone to share the workload, lighten the burden? Someone who carried you when you couldn't walk and cared when you were hurt? She blinked away a burning dampness behind her eyes.

After ten minutes, she removed the poultice. She packed up her vet paraphernalia while Jack led Elton to his stall. "Thanks, Jack. I mean it."

"Any time. And I mean it, too."

Now what?

"Well, I guess I better get going. I've got patient appointments at the office this afternoon."

With Astrid on one side of her and Jack on the other, she walked from the barn into the midmorning warmth of a typical August day, pulling the neckline of her tank top down in a V just enough to see the bruise.

"Maybe you should put a bag of ice on that before you go." He waved his finger in the general direction of her chest. "For the swelling."

She turned to face him while walking backward toward her vehicle. "Nah, it's mostly just a bruise. I'll ice it when I get to the clinic." She waved and spun back around.

"Lucky ice," Jack muttered.

"I heard that," she called over her shoulder.

Driving home, Marie talked to Astrid. About her plan to get rid of Jack, which was failing miserably. About her feelings toward him, which fluctuated often enough to make her dizzy. About Abel Gaines, who was on the lam and had sworn to kill her.

Maybe it was time for her to run, too. Pack some clothes, take Astrid and disappear. She wasn't supposed to, according to WITSEC rules. But according to those same rules, there would always be a case deputy to help her if she was in danger. So much for that.

It was time to start playing by her own rules.

Chapter Six

Two young boys chased each other around Marie's legs Friday evening at the Bartwell's fundraising barbecue. "Will you kids please stop pestering this nice lady?" A harried woman jumped up from a picnic table and came after them.

"It's all right." Marie laughed. "They're just blowing off steam."

The woman grabbed each boy by an arm, puffing a loose strand of hair from her face. "Sorry about that. Too much sugar, I'm afraid. Boys, tell the lady you're sorry for bothering her."

"Sorry," the boys said in unison, looking anything but apologetic.

"Not a problem." Wearing a genuine smile, Marie's heart warmed as she watched the young mother direct her rambunctious offspring back to the family's table.

The boys' enthusiasm infected Marie, and an effervescent tingle raced across her body. The owners of Bartwell's had taken full advantage of its location to host these fundraising shindigs. Sawhorse barricades blocked traffic at both ends of the Third Street alley, where the huge warehouse-turned-brewery loomed. They'd filled the space with picnic tables, a play area for the kids, even a portable dance floor where a local bluegrass band had just started playing.

Before coming out tonight, Marie decided to set aside her worries and simply enjoy the revelry. For just one night this week she'd be alert, but relaxed. Free to relish the savory scents of barbecue, the twinkle of colored rope lights and the promise of toe-tapping tunes. And perhaps Jack would show up. Not that she cared, beyond the opportunity to work toward her plan to get rid of him.

That she'd changed into a colorful cotton blouse, shorts and strappy sandals no way implied she was dressed to impress him. Not in the slightest. Appropriate dress for a muggy evening, that was all. Marie ignored the subtle hint of expensive perfume she wore as she mingled with Jasper's townsfolk and exchanged brief pleasantries before moving on.

Get-togethers of this type, she could handle. Casual small talk. No deep conversations or probing questions that forced her to lie. But despite the festive atmosphere and the promise she'd made herself, Marie maintained situational awareness.

She had to, since she'd left Astrid in the apartment tonight. The crowds, loud music and mouthwatering food on the grill would send the poor dog into sensory overload. Last time Marie had brought her canine protector to a party like this, Astrid had eaten something she shouldn't have. It had been touch and go for a few days, and Marie swore she'd never endanger Astrid's life in exchange for her own.

Liz caught Marie's eye and waved at her, then disappeared into Bartwell's with a group of her friends. Although a few different beers were featured on tap outside for the party, anyone wanting a more artisanal brew could slip inside and request it in a plastic cup. Proceeds still went to the benefit. Liz and her book club, which did more drinking than reading, leaned toward the fancier ales.

When a heavy arm encircled Marie's shoulders from

behind, she reacted immediately, twisting loose from the hold and spinning toward a man she'd never seen before. Her mind shouted danger, and her body responded accordingly, muscles tightening, fists balling and her flight instinct poised at the ready.

In the next heartbeat, Marie reappraised the threat level. The guy, a tourist by the looks of him, did not have the appearance of one of Abel's men. He leered at her with bloodshot eyes, his gaze traveling the length of her and back, stalling at breast level in both directions. His tongue crept out and circled his lips with moisture before disappearing back into his mouth. Marie's nose crinkled with distaste. Did he honestly think that was sexy?

"Hey, babe. Wanna dance?" Judging by his slurred words, the beer he held wasn't his first of the evening.

Marie's fear diminished until only disgust remained. Not wanting to engage with him at all, she turned and took a step away.

His heavy hand came down on top of one shoulder, pulling her back toward him. "Come on, babe. Don't do me like that."

Man, did you pick the wrong woman to mess with.

Harnessing every bit of nearly a week's worth of pent-up fear and frustration, Marie rammed her elbow straight back into his solar plexus. His hand fell from her shoulder, and she looked back to see his beer cup hit the ground as he grabbed his lower chest with both hands. His eyes narrowed to slits. "You bi—"

He jerked backward as if by invisible strings, bellowing. Jack, towering over him, jammed an elbow in his back under the shoulder blade, locked his arms and made any movement impossible. The violence of Jack's response happened so fast, it stunned Marie. Sure, she'd hoped to see him here tonight, but not like this. And again, she questioned who Jack really was. Why he'd been found in Jasper. How he knew she had once been a blonde.

"This guy hurt you?" Over the concern in his question, Jack's voice carried a frightening edge of anger.

"No. I took care of it myself." Okay, she sounded like an unappreciative harpy, but it aggravated her to be in a situation where Jack assumed she needed a savior. On the inside, though, in that secret place where she was most vulnerable, Marie was charmed by his gallantry. "But thank you."

Jack frog-marched the guy past Marie, shoved him against the wall of the brewery and kicked his feet into a wider stance.

Jason emerged from the crowd, holding Tashya's hand. "Whoa, dude. You looking for a job with the JPD? We do have an opening coming up soon."

Jack looked over his shoulder. "Huh?"

"We have a rule around here that the citizens leave the arresting to actual cops." Jason smirked and gave Jack a friendly punch to his arm. "I appreciate you wanting to save the day, but if this guy needs to be booked, I'll take it from here." He swung a questioning gaze to Marie.

"He doesn't." Marie stepped closer. "Unless he's planning to drive. He's drunk." She laid a hand on Jack's forearm. "Let him go. He didn't hurt me."

"He could have," Jack said, firm but with less anger.

"But he didn't." Marie hooked her hand in the crook of his arm and tugged him away. "Come on—let Jason handle him. I'll buy you a beer for being my extraneous protector."

He let her pull him only a couple feet before he stopped. "Extraneous?"

"Yes. It means—"

"I know what it means." He twisted his mouth to the

side, his wry sense of humor apparently returning. "It means I'm irrelevant."

Marie chuckled. "Not exactly. In this case, it means I can take care of myself, but I still appreciate your concern."

"Hmph. Well, don't get offended by my concern in the future. Seems I lead with it."

"I'll do my best." Marie smiled to herself. She liked to boast about how self-sufficient she was, but having a US marshal on speed dial put the lie to her claim. And now that George had disappeared, and assuming Jack was on the up-and-up, she wouldn't complain about a little chivalrous concern.

As they strolled in the direction of the outdoor bar, Marie kept hold of his arm, pleased that he didn't pull it away. His skin was warm, and despite the night's heat, she edged closer to his body.

To the right of the platform where the band played, she caught sight of Emma, Piper and Shane. Emma's widened eyes focused on Marie, shifted to Jack, then back to Marie in exaggerated movements. She smiled, mouthed the words "I told you so" and gave Marie a thumbs-up.

Rolling her eyes, Marie returned the gesture, but not with her thumb.

JACK SURVEYED THE alley while they waited in line for beers. "I didn't expect anything this big. The only thing missing is a traveling carnival with rides and game booths."

"Too much of a liability, and it would cut into the profits. Besides, we've got games." Marie pointed past the picnic tables to an area set up for kids. "Cornhole, ring toss, Jenga Giant, even a basketball hoop." She nudged his arm with her shoulder. "What more could you possibly want?"

Jack looked at her, his gaze lingering on the lips he'd

wanted to kiss yesterday. Still wanted to kiss, for that matter. "Oh, I can think of a thing or two."

Glancing up and meeting his eyes, Marie blushed. The peachy hue suited her, and her shy smile caused his chest to puff out. *I want to make her smile like that every single day.*

Beers in hand, they watched kids lobbing beanbags into holes and tossing rings over spikes. A little girl, maybe five years old, started crying when the boys with the basketball wouldn't let her play. Marie set down her cup and went over to comfort the child. When Jack aimed a full-force frown at the boys, they went from derisive laughing to dropping the ball and running away.

Marie helped the girl get into position near the basket.

"I want to be back there." The tiny thing insisted on throwing from where the bigger boys had been standing.

"Okay, we'll stand there." Marie glanced over at Jack, shrugged her shoulders, then moved to the throw line.

After several unsuccessful attempts, Jack came over. "You know, you're not as tall as those boys were."

"So?" The girl pouted. "Doesn't mean I can't play."

"Oh, you can definitely play," Marie said. "But I think he's going to tell you about an advantage you get." She looked up at Jack, her eyes filled with hope.

"Yes, I am." Jack squatted down next to Marie, so he was face level with the child. "When you're at a height disadvantage, you get what's called an assist." He picked the little girl up under the arms and swung her around onto his shoulders.

Marie handed her the ball. "Now, dunk it."

Jack danced his way toward the basket as if avoiding other players on the court. He stopped next to the basket. The girl giggled, raised the ball in both tiny hands and flipped it through the hoop.

"Woo-hoo! Good shot!" Marie danced around like a cheerleader on hot coals.

After a few more dunks, Jack lowered the girl to the ground. "Know where your mommy is?"

"Still eating, I guess." She bounced the ball. "Can we go again?"

"I think we better check on your mom first. She might be looking for you." Marie took the girl's hand and led the way toward the food.

The future hoops star's mother was indeed looking for her daughter and grateful to have her back.

Jack patted his own stomach. "I'm getting hungry, too. You ready for some barbecue?"

"I'm starving." Marie checked out the blackboard menu for food options. "Hamburger, hot dog, smoked brisket—"

"Ladies and gentlemen, we have a winner. I can't remember the last time I had smoked brisket." Jack paused. "Of course, I can't remember my own name, so…"

Marie snickered. "At least you're developing a good attitude about it."

"It is what it is. I just have to believe my memory will come back one of these days." He conferred with Marie on her dinner choices, then ordered two plates of brisket, potato salad and baked beans. "Why don't you save a couple seats at a table? I'll bring the food."

"Um, didn't you say you wouldn't get paid for a while?" She spoke in a low tone that only he could hear.

"Emma gave me an advance. Said she wanted me to have fun tonight."

"Okay, then I'll get us another couple beers and meet you at the table."

Jack watched her bounce away on the balls of her feet, like a barely contained bundle of energy. A few minutes later, plates in hand, he took the bench across from Marie.

He would have liked to sit close beside her, but this way he could study her face without contorting to do it. A natural beauty with her brown hair loose, framing her turbulent eyes and sexy-as-all-get-out mouth, staring at her posed no hardship. But he also hoped her face would jog a memory for him. Where he'd seen her before. Something. Anything.

"It's nice that the whole town comes together to help someone like this." He sipped his beer.

Marie nodded. "Anytime someone needs help, we all try to pitch in however we can. Sometimes it's baby things for new parents who've lost their jobs. Sometimes it's paying medical bills for a cancer patient."

"Did you ever know anyone with cancer? Anyone else, I mean?"

"My grandmother. She fought for years." Her voice trembled and she closed her eyes for a moment.

"Were you two close?"

"I guess you could say that."

Talking to Marie was like talking to an iceberg. For every few words voiced above the surface, an entire mountain of unspoken thoughts and secrets stayed hidden underneath.

Jack set his fork down and focused on her eyes, hoping they'd reveal more than her words. "I'm sorry. Did she live here in Jasper?"

Marie popped a potato chip in her mouth, chewing longer than necessary before taking a long, drawn-out drink of beer. "No. She was too ill to travel when I moved here."

"That sucks. Must have been hard, leaving her behind." He piled onions and pickles on top of his brisket and forked a bite into his mouth.

"It *was*. But I had an opportunity, so I took it."

What a sad timbre to her usually melodic voice. *Why*

won't you talk about your past? Switching tactics, he asked, "So, where are you from originally?"

She shrugged. "Here and there. Nowhere in particular. What about you? Beginning to remember anything yet? Like maybe where *you're* from?"

He wiped his mouth with a paper napkin, then tilted his head. "A little here and a little there. Nothing in particular."

"Ha-ha. Very funny." She grinned, and it lifted some of the sadness from her eyes.

"You know, it wouldn't kill you to share a little. Like this grandmother of yours. Surely her name isn't a state secret."

Silence. Ten seconds, twenty, forty. What on earth made her so reticent about a mere name?

"I just called her Granny. She raised me."

So, a beloved grandmother fell victim to cancer and was left behind when Marie moved to Jasper to become a vet. Not that Jasper wasn't a great town with great people, but she could have opened a practice anywhere. Why not stay with her granny? Was it guilt that caused Marie to be so hesitant to open up?

"You must miss her very much."

Marie's eyes filled with unshed tears. "I do." She grabbed a napkin and made a pretense of wiping her mouth but managed to dry her eyes at the same time.

"I'm sure she wanted you to seize that opportunity and be happy."

"She did."

"And are you?"

She rested both arms on the table and met his eyes with an unblinking stare. "Enough about me. What exactly are you remembering?"

Okay, we'll play it your way for now. "It's not like

normal remembering. I get flashes of places and scenes. Sometimes when I'm awake, every night when I sleep."

Marie sipped her beer. "Flashes of what?"

It was his turn to hesitate. How much could he share without scaring her? "I haven't wanted to talk about it, because, well, so far very few of the images have been pleasant."

"That sounds ominous. How about telling me a few? You never know, it might help." She leaned forward, elbows on the table, a posture intended to invite confidence. Was she a bit too eager? Did he trust her? Did he have a reason not to, besides once upon a time she might have changed the color of her hair? And realistically, how could he expect her to share if he wasn't also willing?

"I see men fighting, and I hear gunfire. I'm pretty sure someone dies." More than one, but he didn't mention that. He also left out the fire and the blood splattered everywhere. As if his words conjured the very images he desperately wanted to avoid, the pain in his head increased. His stomach roiled. Jack grimaced against the onslaught and closed his eyes to block out the sights.

Marie took hold of his hand. "Is it one of your headaches?"

Her cool fingers acted like a soothing damp cloth laid across his brow. His pain lessened, his stomach settled. "It's passing." Jack opened his eyes.

"Jack, these headaches can't be good for you. It might be a sign of something really wrong. Why don't you go to Boise and have that specialist help you? It's not like there's anything holding you here."

Nothing holding me here. The sting of those words surprised him. To avoid embarrassing himself, Jack looked past her shoulder to where people were milling around the dance floor, waiting for the band to start back up after a break. "Look, I have no intention of going to some specialist in Boise. I wish everyone would just drop it."

Marie's crestfallen face stung him even more than her earlier comment. Staggered by her hold over him, Jack stood and gathered their plates and napkins. "I'm going to dump our trash."

As the band began their warmup, a crowd pushed toward the dance floor and Jack lost track of Marie. Not wanting to force his way to their table, he wound through the throng, working his way behind the food service counter to loop back around.

As he passed the smoker, the man in charge tossed more cedar chunks in and fanned the flames. The wind shifted. The scent of burning wood hit Jack square in the face, and the images returned with the brutal force of reality. Agony split his brain as if he'd been cleaved in two by a medieval battle axe. He was barely aware of the sweat rolling down his face as he relived the horror. The burning building, red-orange fingers curling into fiery fists that punched out windows, tendrils crawling over sills and blanketing the exterior wall like an ivy of orange flames. The kiss of volcanic heat on the skin of his wrist.

"Jack!" Marie's voice, so distant, broke through his pain-filled stupor but he didn't answer. Couldn't answer. If he opened his mouth he would scream, and he doubted he'd be able to stop. She grabbed his arm and gave a small shake. "Jack. Jack! Are you all right?"

He nodded. Her face shimmered into focus, banishing the heat, the stench, the fear of the fire. Marie's wide, frightened eyes were filled with worry as she tightened her grip on his arm. As before, her touch pushed back the pain. He let her tug him away from the smoking grills and the loud band, down the alley where only a lone dumpster could eavesdrop on them.

Marie dropped her hand. "What happened back there? I had to yell to get your attention."

He took several deep breaths. *Get a grip, Jack.* "The smoke. It reminded me of a fire. Another of my flashes. This one was just more...intense."

"But you're okay now, right?"

"Besides being a little sweaty, I'm fine." He tried smiling, but Marie didn't appear reassured.

"More intense. Does that mean you remember where or maybe when the real fire happened?"

Jack shook his head. "I have no idea." But he did know two things for sure. One, each headache he suffered was worse than the previous one. A lot worse. And two, Marie's touch eased that pain. Made no sense. Absolutely no medical justification for it. But there it was. Another reason not to go to Boise—as if he was considering it.

They wandered down the alley, and Jack took Marie's hand. "It's nice to be able to talk about this with someone. Other than a doctor, I mean."

"I'm glad I can help, but I worry that your brain injury might be worse than Dr. Saul thought." She paused and turned to face him. "I know you don't want to talk about Boise, but what if you never get your memory back?"

"Would that be so bad? It might even be a good thing."

"You might have family worried sick about you. Parents. A wife. Kids." A bittersweet smile took over her lips. "You were awfully good with that little girl back there. Almost like you're a natural."

Every day since he'd awakened in the hospital, he'd wondered who might be missing him. Parents, if they were alive. His job, if he had a legitimate one. Wife and kids? He didn't feel like he was married with children. But who knew?

He leaned against the wall and pulled Marie against

him, pleased when she didn't protest. Like she'd been made for him, she laid her head on his chest and wrapped her arms around his middle. "I can't think any more about my past. Not tonight. It hurts too much. Just hold me a minute. Let me get my bearings."

For several long, wonderful minutes they stood still in each other's embrace. Jack couldn't imagine he'd ever felt so content, and he didn't want the moment to end.

"Jack," she whispered.

"Yes?"

"I can hear your heartbeat. It's slowing." She looked up at him, her mouth parted and inviting. "Does that mean you're feeling better?"

He cupped her cheek with one hand and lowered his mouth to hers. He began with a slow, sweet kiss, not wanting to scare her away. Her lips on his were tentative at first, shy but curious, then grew hungrier. He teased with his tongue. She kissed, licked, nipped his bottom lip. Weaving his fingers in the silky strands of her hair, he eased her head back and tasted her mouth. Spice, hops and something so incredibly alluring.

Pop! Pop! Pop! Bang! Bang! Pop! Pop!

Jack threw Marie to the ground, covering her with his body. Guns. Shooting. Blood. Death. Raging pain in his head. Too much pain. Danger everywhere. More pain.

A group of kids escaped from behind the dumpster, pointing at Jack and Marie and laughing as they ran back to the crowd.

"Are you all right?" Marie's voice, in his ear.

He lifted his head and looked around. *Alley. Barbecue. Party.* He looked down. *Marie.* Beneath him, looking up at him with wide blue eyes. Her lips, only inches away, tempted him. Hell, the entire length of her body, pressing against his, tempted him.

"What just happened, Jack?" She reached up and took his face in both her hands.

"I thought…gunfire…so real."

"It's okay. It was just some kids with firecrackers."

As her touch soothed away the pain, humiliation overcame him. He rolled off Marie and stood.

Marie sat up. "Better now?" Her words were kind, her eyes concerned.

"Fine." He reached out a hand to help her up.

She laid a hand on his arm. "You don't really seem fine."

"I'm just frustrated. Tired of not remembering anything important about myself. Fed up with dreams and images and reactions to things that make no sense."

"I'm sorry you're having to go through this." She glanced around at the party. "Do you want to go inside, where it's quieter? Get a couple beers and talk?"

He knew Marie was trying to be kind, and he appreciated it. "I'd like nothing more, but I think I should call it a night. I need to…" Jack shrugged.

"Recenter yourself?" Marie still held on to his arm, her touch warming his skin.

"I'd need to know my center before I can do that." He chuckled. "I just need to get some space, try to understand everything."

"I get it. But if you want to talk…" Her blue eyes sparkled with invitation.

Jack nodded, then cradled her face in his hands and kissed Marie as if she were his salvation. "Thanks." As he walked away, he glanced over his shoulder at her. She stood rooted to the spot, an indecipherable look on her face.

And Marie Beaumont was near the top of his list of things he wanted to understand.

But how?

Chapter Seven

Saturday evening, Marie lounged in her favorite couch potato attire, cuddling a throw pillow while stewing on Jack's behavior at the barbecue. With the benefit of space and time, she realized his reaction mimicked what she knew about PTSD. Clearly, he'd endured some sort of trauma. Something to do with guns and a fire. And it wasn't like she hadn't seen the scar on his wrist, the one that looked like a burn. So, the real question was, did his trauma have anything to do with Abel Gaines, and had Abel sent Jack to deal with her?

Her knee-jerk reaction said no way. He may not know his past—and by now she believed the amnesia was real—but the Jack she was getting acquainted with had to be who he was at his core. And that Jack skewed toward protective, not homicidal. Someone accepting and courteous. The only time he'd exhibited violence was when he thought she was in trouble.

She pointed the remote at the TV and changed the channel to some comedy show. Didn't matter which one, she wasn't paying attention. But the background noise took away some of the loneliness of a Saturday night spent in an oversize pink T-shirt and sloth-covered leggings while eating a pint of coffee ice cream straight from the carton. She dropped the remote on the couch, scooped another spoonful into her mouth and continued thinking about Jack from every angle.

One thing for sure, he was handsome. And he could kiss the starch right out of her knickers. Still, with George Murphy ghosting her, why take a chance by muddying her life with such a complicated man? Under the circumstances, her plan to get rid of him still seemed the safest course. With his headaches worsening, she should keep trying to convince him that Boise was his best option.

Her phone rang. Caller ID read DCA. "Hello?"

"Marie, this is Jack. Amaya's in labor, and I think something's wrong." His words came fast, hinting at panic.

Marie tossed away the throw pillow and sat up. "Okay, slow down. Tell me why you think something is wrong?"

"She's been pacing, seemed to have contractions, but no pups. I don't know. Something told me that isn't normal."

"Okay. Keep her calm. I'm on my way."

Fifteen minutes later, plagued with worry, Marie raced into the kennel with her vet bag in hand and Astrid on her heels.

Amaya was gaining strength, but some birth complications could be too much for her body to handle. After everything the poor dog had endured, Marie refused to lose her now.

"Where are Emma and Tashya?" She opened the stall door and went directly to the mother-to-be, who lay on her side, panting. Astrid trotted in behind Marie, who commanded her to sit. As if sensing she should stay out of the way, Astrid retreated to a corner of the stall and watched.

"They took off midafternoon for McCall. Some wedding-related errands, I think." Jack, sitting cross-legged on the opposite side of Amaya, soothed the dog with a gentle hand. "Tashya checked her temperature yesterday and said everything looked fine. Then right before they left for McCall, she checked her again, predicted she'd give birth sometime today."

Marie kneeled next to Amaya. "There, there, pretty girl. I know it hurts, but soon you'll have a brand-new family who will keep you so busy, you won't have time to remember this pain." After opening her bag, Marie pulled on vinyl gloves and checked the birth canal. "She's definitely dilated. How long has she been in stage one?"

"Um, define stage one." Jack had been avoiding direct eye contact since the moment she arrived.

"When did she stop pacing?" Marie felt along the dog's abdomen.

"A couple of hours ago. Then she started straining. Nothing happened and eventually she lay back down. Later she did it again but strained for a lot longer, and I figured maybe a pup got stuck." He finally met her eyes. "That's when I called you."

A small wooden table near the door held a stack of clean towels cut into twelve-inch squares. Marie rose and brought it over near the dog, then turned the whelping box so Amaya was in a better position for Marie to help her.

"Is she going to be okay?"

Marie looked up at Jack's concerned tone. "We're going to make sure she is." She grabbed some towel squares from the table. "The first pup's breech."

"How can I help?"

Marie gazed across at him, once again caught in the high-beam intensity of his eyes. She blinked, breaking the spell. "I'm not sure you can."

"I may not be a vet, but I'm an extra pair of hands." He got up, walked around to her bag and pulled out a pair of gloves for himself.

Marie ran her hand along the dog's flank. Amaya lifted her head and looked back at her.

"It's okay, girl. This first one's decided to come out bottom first, that's all. You do your part, and I'll help it along."

Using her fingers and the towel, Marie started to pull the tiny puppy from Amaya. With all four legs facing forward, there wasn't much to grab on to. But she continued pulling, slow, steady, and Amaya's contractions kicked in.

By the time Marie held the whole puppy in her hand, clearing his face of liquid and stimulating him to a soft cry, Amaya had gotten up and was straining again. Marie glanced at Jack, again sitting opposite her. With some of the towel squares on his lap, he held both hands out toward Marie, and she handed the puppy to him.

While Jack wrapped him in a dry cloth and warmed him, Marie felt for the next pup. This one also planned on backing out of its mother, but its hind legs and tail were appearing first. A more normal position than the breech. Keeping a close eye on its progress, Marie sat back and allowed Amaya some time. When the dog flopped onto her side, Jack placed the first puppy near Amaya's face.

Studying Jack, Marie's curiosity finally got the best of her. "How did you know to put him in with his mother right away?"

"I think I had a dog when I was a kid." Jack's gaze drifted up toward the ceiling as if searching for answers. "And I'm pretty sure she had puppies. I kind of remember watching, and my mom explaining what was happening."

The second puppy emerged with no help needed. Amaya grabbed it in her mouth and did the cleaning herself. Marie and Jack both sagged with relief, releasing loud sighs like two deflating birthday balloons.

Amaya licked both of her babies, easing Marie's fear of the first one not being accepted.

"Is that it? Only two puppies?" Jack leaned over the box and examined the tiny, squirming creatures.

"Not by a long shot." Marie shifted so she could stretch her legs out straight in front of her. "But she may take rest breaks between births."

Jack copied her position but propped himself up with his arms out behind him. "So what do we do now?"

"We wait to make sure she has no more complications." She pulled off her gloves and set them next to her vet bag. "Or I can wait. Probably no sense in both of us sitting here." She kept her tone neutral, but she hoped he would stay, too.

"I'm not leaving until this is done." His facial features smoothed out. "It's nice to remember something good. Something that doesn't make my head throb."

"Have you had any other memories like that? Just normal stuff, instead of death and destruction?" Marie checked Amaya again, satisfied that she merely needed to rest.

Jack shook his head. "Maybe death and destruction *are* normal for me."

Astrid crept toward them in an army crawl, like they wouldn't notice her if she approached in tiny increments.

"Astrid? I thought I told you to stay." Marie gave her an admonishing look.

"Actually, you told her to sit." Jack's mouth kicked up at the corners when Marie turned the look on him. "Maybe she wants to help, too."

Astrid eyed Marie, then continued crawling over to Jack, licked his face and tried to climb into his lap. She was too big, so she lay down next to him, her head resting on his thigh. Jack wrapped his arms around her and loved her up.

With downcast eyes, Marie pretended to check on Amaya while she sneaked a look at them. Astrid, normally an excellent judge of character, rolled over for a belly rub. Apparently, Marie was the only one who doubted the man's integrity.

Amaya began straining again, and the next two puppies came out headfirst, one right after the other. Needing no human help with these, the new mama licked them until they were clean and breathing.

The next few hours passed with the dog resting, straining, then birthing a fifth pup.

Vehicle lights shone through the windows, then disappeared. Voices, followed by the slamming of truck doors, drifted from outside.

The kennel door squeaked as it opened, followed by quick footsteps crossing the floor.

"What's wrong?" Tashya came into the stall, her broad smile fading.

"Breech birth with the first pup." Marie looked up at the tech. "Thanks for having the towels ready."

"I hoped they wouldn't be necessary." Tashya came closer and peered in at the puppies. "Are they okay?"

"So far, so good. I'm just sticking around to make sure everything goes well."

"And I'm helping." Jack grinned at Tashya.

Tashya raised her brows at Jack, then at Marie, her mouth curling back into a smile.

"Jack realized Amaya was in distress and called me." Marie folded and unfolded a square of cloth in her lap.

"Uh-huh." Tashya smirked. "Well, I'm back now and can help, if you want to get out of here, Jack."

"Tashya." Emma stood near the stall door. "We need to go over our notes on the centerpieces for the reception." She grabbed Tashya's arm and pulled her from the stall. Tashya's laughter faded away as they closed the kennel door behind them.

"What was that all about?" Jack asked.

"Nothing." Marie's cheeks burned. "Emma likes to tease me about…things." She leaned over Amaya, checking the birth canal again. "Just one more, I think."

She allowed the new mama to rest a while longer, but anxiety over the last pup grew. When the new mama finally stood and began to strain, Marie pulled on a fresh pair of gloves and grabbed a few cloths. The ordeal was a lot for the exhausted dog, and Jack scrambled onto his knees and supported her with a hand under her chest.

"I see the last one." Marie held a cloth beneath the tiny head being pushed out into the world. As Amaya strained and the puppy fell onto the cloth, her heart sank.

"No, no, no." Cleaning away fluids and checking for breath, Marie whispered, "Breathe. Breathe."

But the stillborn pup would never take its first breath. Marie wrapped it in a clean towel, placed it next to the pen, and moved so she could sit cross-legged with her back against the wall. She pulled off her gloves and dropped them on the floor.

Jack came over and sat next to her. "I'm sorry." He set his gloves on top of hers, then put his arm around her shoulders.

"This is ridiculous." She blinked against hot tears. "Death is part of the profession. I never react like this. It's just been a crazy week, and I'm tired and…"

Jack wrapped his other arm around Marie, pulling her against him.

The human contact pushed her over her emotional edge. With her face against his chest, Jack tightened his hold on her, smoothing her hair and whispering that everything would be all right.

Marie tipped her head back and looked up at Jack. "Thank you for being here tonight."

He brushed the lingering dampness from her cheeks,

ran his thumb over her lips. She lost herself in his stormy eyes until he covered her mouth with his. Slow and sensual. Warmth filled her, spreading to every nook and cranny in her body, even those she'd thought long dead.

Astrid crawled onto both of their laps and pushed her muzzle into the middle of the kiss.

"No, Astrid. Get down." Marie pushed at her.

Astrid pulled her brows into that "don't ignore me" expression and whined.

Jack laughed. "She makes a pretty good chaperone."

Marie tousled Astrid's ears. "Too good." She must be losing her mind. Get rid of Jack. Kiss Jack. Fear him. Like him. She had to decide once and for all about him. Emotionally exhausted, Marie gave up on trusting her own judgment. It was time to phone a friend.

And just in case I'm way off base, Dotty will have his number in nothing flat.

Chapter Eight

Jack was surprised when Emma waved him over to the house early Sunday morning. It had to be close to eight, but he'd been up for more than an hour, taking care of the kennel dogs and checking on Amaya and her pups. He'd never appreciated how much work went into caring for and training animals. Well, at least he didn't think he'd appreciated it. This amnesia business was for the birds.

Jack entered the house through the mudroom, toed off his boots, went straight to the sink and scrubbed his hands. "Smells amazing in here," he said to Emma, who he could see through the doorway leading into the kitchen. She hummed while pouring pancake batter on the griddle, and the mouthwatering scent of cooked bacon filled the room.

"Good morning." She greeted him with her signature smile.

Jack dried his hands. "Morning to you. What's up? Didn't think breakfast was for another half hour."

"It's not, but Marie called for you. I told her I would have you call back as soon as I could wrangle you into the house. How you get along without a cell phone is beyond me. Would drive me bonkers."

Jack's mind went on high alert. So Marie had called him, had she? That was something new and different.

"Well, when you don't have anyone to call, who needs a phone? Besides, can't afford one."

Emma sighed. "There I go again, being thoughtless. Just ignore me. About the phone thing, that is. Not about Marie calling. Her number is on the pad by the phone."

He walked to the phone, an old-fashioned rotary type, hanging on the wall with a cord that looked two miles long. He picked up the receiver and dialed the number, marveling each time at the *click-click-click* as the dial rotated back to its starting position.

He couldn't stop himself from glancing at Emma, who stared at him with brazen curiosity, then favored him with an all-knowing female grin. Right about then, he wished he wasn't about to have this conversation in so…public a place.

"Marie? This is Jack. Emma said you called." Good. Nice and neutral sounding. So far, he hadn't embarrassed himself.

"Hi, Jack. Thanks for calling me back."

"No problem. What's up?"

"So, um, I wondered, and of course you're in no way obligated, but I wondered, if you're free that is, well, I'd like you to meet someone."

The tiniest breeze could have knocked him over. Not at all what he'd been expecting. "This morning?" He tried to buy himself time to gather his thoughts.

She *tsked*. "I know it's short notice, but yes, this morning. I realize it's just about breakfast time over there, so I was thinking I could pick you up around nine thirty. If you want me to, that is."

The most guarded woman in town wanted him to meet someone. Who? "Sounds great. See you at nine thirty."

"Okay. See you then."

"Looking forward to it."

"Me, too."

Okay, nothing witty or sparkling as conversations went, but since he hadn't known what to expect, he'd take it.

Emma held her peace about the call during their meal and the cleanup afterward, but she couldn't hide her Cheshire grin. And that's when Jack understood what was really going on. Marie was taking him to meet someone who mattered to her, someone to look him over. He was about to be tested.

IF JACK PASSED the Dotty test, then Marie would feel much more comfortable about, well, about things. She'd called Dotty right after she spoke to Jack and told her surrogate grandmother that she'd like to come by for a visit, and if it was okay, she'd like to bring a friend.

"Of course, it's all right. The more the merrier. I surely do hope that by 'a friend,' you mean that two-legged stray of yours. Been hearing some fanciful tales about how handsome he is, and I would love to judge that for myself."

"Well then, you're about to get your chance."

"Yay. You just made my week. Or at least my day."

"Gee, thanks."

"Ah, give an old lady a break, will you? Not many handsome men come around the Hills."

Marie laughed. "We'll see you at ten."

"With bells on, my girl. With bells on."

An hour and a half later, after taking more than a little effort with her appearance, Marie and Astrid pulled up to the DCA. Wearing a cheesy grin, Emma dashed over to the car and poked her head in through Marie's open window. "Hi, Astrid, you big, beautiful girl." Astrid gave a pleased bark from the backseat. To Marie, Emma said, "I'm so glad you're finally going out with someone. It's been way, way, way too long."

"I'm not going out with him. We're just going…we're going to… I'm not going out with him, okay?"

"Ooh, I see. Wink, wink." She gave Marie an exaggerated blink with one eye.

Marie shook her head. "You're impossible."

"Maybe, but that doesn't make me wrong."

Marie flicked her hands in a shooing motion. "Go train a dog or something."

"Gotcha. Need some alone time, eh?"

"Did you hear the part about you being impossible?"

"I did." Emma's silly smile faded a tad. "Listen, go easy on him, okay?"

Startled, Marie asked, "What did he tell you?"

"Relax, oh mistrustful one. He didn't tell me anything. This is me talking to you. All I know is, this is highly unusual Marie Beaumont behavior, and Jack—" she thumbed behind her back "—hightailed it back to the RV to freshen up, if you get my drift."

"Don't be ridiculous." But secretly, Marie was pleased.

Emma shrugged. "All I'm saying is, you know how he's struggling with the return of his memories and with those terrible headaches of his. I can tell he feels lost a lot of the time, and you've become like an anchor for him. I'm just saying be careful with him. He's more fragile than he looks."

I'm his anchor?

"Hey, are you sure you don't mind staying here next weekend while the rest of us go to Tashya and Jason's wedding?" Emma frowned. "It doesn't seem fair, but you're one of the few people I trust with my animals."

"Of course I don't mind. It would be silly for you to drive back and forth to McCall instead of spending Saturday night at the resort there. I'd love to see them get married, but I know you'll take plenty of pictures."

"Thanks. You're the best." Emma waved and ran back into the house just as Jack came up to the car.

"Subtle as a herd of elephants, isn't she?" He climbed into the passenger seat.

Marie gave a snort of laughter. "*Stampeding* elephants, in Emma's case."

"I stand corrected." Jack chuckled.

The car ride was quiet, but not awkward. At least not for Marie. The peace gave her a chance to shore up her defenses, while at the same time prepare to possibly let them down. Which was all very confusing to her.

Liz was a friend, almost like a mother to her, but Marie had never taken her to visit Dotty. Nor had she taken Emma. Jack would be the first. He'd gotten under her skin, but he was also an anomaly. In her world, that could spell disaster. Besides her secrets and lies, Marie feared making another mistake where men were concerned. Dotty's opinion of Jack would be her litmus test.

Fifteen minutes later, Marie pulled into the small circle drive in front of the assisted living facility. Jack leaned forward and stared at the sign through the windshield.

"Hemlock Hills? Sounds like something out of a Tim Burton movie."

Marie smiled as she turned off the car engine. "Tell me about it, but you'll be pleased to learn that it's named after the non-poisonous variety of hemlock."

"Didn't know there *was* a non-poisonous variety."

"Few people do, which is why most people refer to it as the Hills." Marie climbed out of the SUV. "Some of the residents joke about it, but it's usually best to let them start that conversation."

"Note to self."

They walked inside the ranch-style home, greeted as

usual by the scent of lavender and a friendly welcome from Kim Stanford behind the reception desk.

"Marie. It's good to see you and Astrid back again so soon."

"Thanks. Kim, this is Jack."

"Hi, Jack. Welcome to Hemlock Hills."

"Don't you ever get a day off?" Marie asked.

Kim looked down. "Nope, they've got me chained up back here. You here to see Dotty?"

"Yes, indeed."

"I do work a lot of hours," Kim said as she signed Marie and Astrid in on the guest list. "But then, they don't mind that I use any down time to study for my LSAT."

Jack perked up. "LSAT, huh? When's your test date?"

"In October."

"Do you know what kind of law you want to practice?" he asked, and Marie cocked her head in curiosity.

"I'm not sure I want to practice law in the traditional sense. I'm thinking I want to go into law enforcement. Eventually parlay that into a political career, maybe. Who knows?"

"Well, good luck to you. The LSAT is no cakewalk."

Marie gave him a look that asked how he knew that.

He shrugged.

"Jack, what's your last name so I can add it to the guest register?"

"Yeah, about that—"

Marie cut him off. "He doesn't have a last name."

Kim's facial expressions segued from confusion to understanding. "Ooh, so he's *that* Jack."

Jack's brows shot up. It appeared that somehow he knew his way around the LSAT, but he didn't quite understand the nuances of living in a small town where everyone knew who you were, even if they didn't know *you*.

Kim scribbled on the guest list. "I'll just leave it as Jack. Enjoy your visit."

"Thanks."

Marie reached down and stroked Astrid's head, but her eyes stayed plastered on Jack. "Come on—it's this way." She and Astrid led him to the bright, airy family room. The TV was off, and next to the large bay window, the bridge table was as empty as the room. "Between the worship meeting and the special Sunday breakfast selections, the Hills' residents tend to get a later start on the Sabbath."

"I see." Jack looked to his right, then his left, down each respective hallway. "From what I saw on the outside, I was expecting the inside to be dark and depressing." Then adopting an announcer's voice with a faux microphone pressed to his mouth, he added, "Although Hemlock Hills, hemlock in this case being of the non-poisonous variety, might be described as lacking curb appeal, it more than makes up for it with a bright, sunlit inside, affording its residents plush, comfortable seating."

Marie pasted on a smile. His attempt at humor wasn't the best, but he *was* trying. "You might have a future hosting a home reno show on HGTV."

"Ah, but then I'd have to quit my poop patrol job."

"It's tough, making decisions when life throws so many opportunities at you. To your left," she said, although with Astrid already trotting that way, directions weren't needed.

"There are so many doors, and none of them have room numbers. How do you know which one is which?"

Marie stopped and turned to look at one of the doors. "Oh, that. I totally forgot. They're about to do some fresh-up painting, so they removed the door numbers before the painters arrive. Not to worry. I know where I'm going." She continued down the hall to where Astrid sat patiently outside the last room on the right.

"Good to know. You going to give me a clue about who I'm here to meet?"

"Her name is Dotty Hazzard. She's my adopted grand-mother, a good friend and an excellent judge of character."

"And I'm here to be judged?"

"You're here to meet the most important person in the world to me."

"I'M HONORED." JACK meant it. Sharing parts of herself didn't seem to come easily for Marie. Actually, it mostly didn't come at all. That she was willing to share with him was an amazing leap of faith.

Her reaction was not what he'd anticipated. Arm up, hand fisted, about to knock on the unmarked door, she stopped midmotion and snapped her head around. "Are you making fun of me?"

"Seriously?" But she made it clear by her narrowed eyes that she was entirely serious. "Marie, I'm not making fun of you. I really am honored. You don't know a hill of beans about me, and yet you trust me enough to meet—" Darn, he'd already forgotten the adopted grandmother's name. "Um, someone you love. Why wouldn't I be honored?"

For several interminable seconds, Jack waited while she deliberated with herself. Who would have thought the phrase *I'm honored* would set her off? What he wouldn't give for just one minute inside that lovely head of hers, to learn what or who had scarred her so profoundly. She finally inhaled, then exhaled on a slow breath. "Sorry. I guess I'm just not used to people talking like that."

"Like what?"

"About honor."

With no idea what to say in response to that sad state of affairs, Jack opted for a bit of levity. He cocked his head and grinned. "Gee, I didn't think I'd be meeting the family so soon."

"Cute. Real cute." But at least she smiled.

"I hear you two out there, and that's just plain rude. Get in here, Marie, and introduce me to this man you're all—"

Marie pushed the door open. "Dotty, I was just about to knock." She headed for the woman sitting in her easy chair, but Astrid beat her there.

Dotty offered up love to the cherished canine. "Who's a good girl? You be sweet to Sassy Cat, and I'll give you a treat before you go. Yes, I will."

"Sit," Marie said, and Astrid sat, allowing Marie *her* time for affection. Bending down, Marie wrapped her arms around Dotty. "It's good to see you."

"You too, my dear. You know how much I look forward to your visits. Now, introduce me to your friend."

Marie straightened and turned to face him. "Dotty, this is Jack."

"Ma'am," he said, and held his hand out for Dotty to grasp. "It's a pleasure to meet you."

Dotty smiled as she took his hand in both of hers. "Goodness. You might not know your last name, but I guess manners must be genetic because they seem to come naturally to you. It's certainly a pleasure to meet you. Sit, sit. Take a load off. Not you, Marie. Reach up on the counter and get Astrid her treat."

Jack took a seat on the far side of the small couch that sat at a right angle to Dotty's chair.

Marie reached into a glass jar. "I thought you said Astrid wouldn't get a treat until we left."

Dotty flicked her hand. "Bah! Astrid knows I didn't mean it. Don't you, girl?"

"You're just using bribery so Astrid will love you more

than me." Marie handed a couple of biscuits to Dotty and then sat on the couch next to Jack.

"So what if I am? It's not like I have that much time left." She fed Astrid a treat. "You'll have this pretty girl all to yourself after I'm gone."

"Please. You're only seventy-four. You have decades more to live."

"Or I could be dead next week."

"Only the good die young." Marie sat back with a satisfied smile on her face.

"Bah," Dotty said again, leaning forward to speak around Marie. "Isn't she mean? I bet you'll treat me better than she does, won't you, Jack?"

He enjoyed this playful side that Dotty brought out in Marie. He also leaned forward and placed his hand to the side of his mouth and whispered. "Yes, ma'am. I'm bound to treat you better, because Marie over here—" he said as if she couldn't hear him "—can be one cantankerous creature."

"Ha!" Dotty slapped her hand on her thigh. "See, there. Both your dog and your man like me better. What do you have to say about that?"

Marie folded her arms across her chest. "I have absolutely nothing to say to such utter nonsense."

"Hmph." Dotty's slow and appreciative appraisal of Jack would've turned him pink if he'd been a blushing man. Apparently satisfied, she said, "So tell me, Jack, what do you think of my little piece of paradise?"

"I think your room is…far out." The phrase sat unfamiliar on Jack's tongue, but it best described the older woman's style.

Dotty's eyes went round, and she nodded. "It's totally groovy, right?"

Marie snorted.

"Trust me—you kids don't know what you missed during the Summer of Love."

Jack, who had just leaned back, sat forward again. "You were in San Francisco?"

"Of course. I crashed with some friends in an apartment right near Haight-Ashbury. Then in '69, we hitched all the way to New York for Woodstock."

"Really?"

Marie rolled her eyes. "Oh, boy, here we go."

But Jack could tell she didn't mean it. She was enjoying herself, and so was he.

Dotty regaled them for nearly an hour on her adventures during the sixties. "Marie, be a dear and go get us some lemonade."

"Jack, will you come with me? I don't have enough hands."

"Oh, for heaven's sake," Dotty said. "Marie, be a dear and make yourself scarce. I want to have a little talk with Jack."

"Well, I guess that's plain enough." Marie levered herself up from the couch and left them alone.

Dotty relaxed against the back of her chair. "Okay, Jack, I know you have manners, but what else can you tell me about yourself?"

"Not much to tell."

"Don't kid a kidder. I know about your amnesia. What I want you to tell me is, since the accident, what you've learned about the man you are, deep down." She patted her heart. "Where it matters."

"Well, I know I don't like bullies. I seem to have a strong work ethic and a sense of fair play. I believe I have honor and integrity, and I know that truth matters." He paused, then added, "And I like dogs."

As if sensing her species being praised, Astrid leaned her body against his leg.

"That's a fine start. Anything else?"

Jack debated, then just let it all out. "I know Marie is hiding something, and she seems scared all the time. It brings out this urge in me to protect her. I don't know— it's like I have this pull toward her that's more than—"

"Sexual?"

He grinned. "Yeah, that."

"Well, don't stop now. You were on a roll. And if you're worried, I ain't the gossipy type. What you say to me will stay with me."

"All right, then. I can't explain it, but I feel like she lies about things despite being a basically honest person. She has a protective wall around her that I doubt anyone will ever be able to break through."

"Do you want to try?"

"I think I want to see what's behind it, but—"

"You're afraid, too. Of all the things you don't know about yourself."

And the things I do know.

"I am. For one thing, what if I'm married?"

"What does your gut tell you?"

Dotty was the first person who not only asked him about his gut feelings but seemed ready to trust them. "I think not."

"I see no reason not to trust your gut on this. What else bothers you?"

"I get these flashes of memory, and they hint of violence." *And death.*

"And yet here you are, no more violent than I am. Means either you're a profoundly changed man, or you were never violent in the first place. Tell me—what other insights do you have about my girl?"

"I know how much she loves animals. Kids, too, from what I've seen. Seems like she'd make a great mother. She keeps herself apart from everyone, even those she's closest to. I don't understand it. I also know she saved my life and now feels a sort of responsibility for me, even though sometimes she seems scared of me."

"And?"

"And I know I care about her."

"Ah, there it is."

There it was. He cared about her. More than cared. Dotty allowed him a moment of congenial silence while he wrapped his head around the notion.

"Well, Jack, seems to me you know a lot more about yourself than most folks who have never lost their memories."

"Means a lot to me that you think so."

Banging came from outside the room. "My hands are full. Could someone open the door?"

Jack jumped up and opened it just as Marie was about to kick the door again. He grabbed two of the three cups of lemonade, handed one to Dotty and sipped from the other as he sat down.

"What'd I miss?" Marie reclaimed her place on the couch.

Dotty sipped her lemonade. "Not much, dear. Jack and I were just getting to know each other."

After downing the rest of his lemonade, Jack asked, "Where's the guest restroom?"

"Bah, use mine. It's just through there." She pointed at a partially closed door in her room.

"For heaven's sake, Dotty. Be a dear and tell me where the guest restroom is so Marie can talk about me behind my back." Jack aimed a mischievous smile at the septuagenarian.

"Ah ha ha!" Dotty cackled, slapping her thigh. "You're

a hoot. Just go out the door and turn right. You'll see it. It's just down the hall."

"Thanks. I'll be right back."

As he was closing the door, he caught Marie whispering, "What do you think?"

He shut the door without hearing Dotty's reply and looked down a hallway with several closed, unlabeled doors. Great. He could just imagine walking into someone's room when they least expected it.

Shrugging, he started with the doors at the end. The first one was full of brooms, mops and cleaning supplies. The door next to it was an exit with a keypad requiring a code to open it. The next door coming back toward Dotty's room had oxygen canisters with a large refilling machine along the back wall. He should have started with the door between that room and Dotty's. It revealed the small guest bathroom, which he gladly availed himself of, taking great pains to give Marie time to grill Dotty.

After judging he'd been gone long enough, he returned and knocked on Dotty's door.

"Thought you fell in," the older woman teased.

"Took me a while because none of the doors were marked."

"Shoot, forgot about that. Sorry."

"Not to worry. Found it on the fourth try."

"Good for you. I like a man who doesn't give up when he's going after something he wants." She aimed a quick wink at him. "So, what are your plans for the rest of the day?" Dotty asked them both.

Jack shot a questioning glance at Marie, who shrugged. "I thought maybe we could grab lunch somewhere," he said. "I don't need to be back to DCA until late afternoon."

"Then you should get going before the lunch rush starts.

And I have to get ready for my PT." Dotty stood, followed by Marie and Jack. "It was nice meeting you, Jack."

"The pleasure was mine. I hope we can visit again soon."

"Any time you like." Dotty tipped her head toward Marie. "If she won't bring you by, you just come alone. We'll give all these old fogies something to talk about, me with a gentleman caller." She cackled again.

Smiling, Jack nodded. "It's a deal."

Dotty hugged Marie, then waved for Jack to come closer and give up a hug, too. He did, enjoying the maternal-like embrace. With no idea if he even had parents or grandparents still living, Dotty's hug brought him a sense of family.

"Now, you two scoot. Go have some fun." Dotty winked again. "Then come back soon and tell me all about it."

Jack held the door open for Marie and Astrid to precede him. After the door swung shut behind them, he asked, "Did I pass the test?"

"Test? I don't know what you're talking about." Marie's dazzling smile couldn't be much bigger, and her step had a fresh spring in it.

"Fine, play it your way. But I know she liked me. Old ladies like me." A wet snout pushed its way into Jack's hand. "And dogs. Old ladies and dogs like me." He petted Astrid's head.

"I'm assuming you're basing that on your limited experience with Dotty and Astrid, since you couldn't possibly remember that from before." Marie's smile turned smug. "And it's too bad for you I'm not an old lady or a dog."

"You," Jack said, sliding his arm around her waist, "are in a category all your own. And you like me, too."

Marie laughed. "In your dreams."

Marie didn't belong in his dreams. No one good did. His dreams were reserved for evil and malevolence.

But maybe, like his memories, his dreams would get a second chance, as well.

Chapter Nine

A blast of noonday heat greeted them when Marie, Astrid and Jack walked out of the Hills, and she raised her arm to shield her eyes from the sun's glare. On the walk to her car, Marie's elation ran the gamut, from happy to grateful to relieved. She hadn't been sure what to expect, bringing Jack to meet Dotty.

She tapped her key fob and unlocked the RAV4. Bottom line, Jack had absolutely nothing to gain by coming here today, but he had come anyway. In her book, that counted. "Seriously, thanks for meeting Dotty. She did like you. I could tell." The rub was that Marie liked him, too. More and more. That hadn't been part of her original plan.

"I enjoyed meeting her. She's great. Feisty as all get-out and sees a lot more than she lets on."

Amazed that he had sized up her surrogate grandmother so quickly, Marie melted a little more on the inside.

Marie buckled Astrid into the backseat, then Jack held the driver's door open for her and her brows went up. Not something she was used to. Great, just great. Handsome, muscular, good with animals and the elderly, and also a gentleman. Oh yeah, that plan to get Jack out of town was going up in smoke, all right.

He rounded the hood and climbed in. "You hungry?"

"Starved. What are you in the mood for?" She cranked the engine.

"Anything is fine, only…"

"Only what?" The inside of the car was hot, so Marie turned on the AC.

"Well, I know we just ate at Bartwell's, but when we were there on Saturday, I saw something I think I'd like to try."

"Don't keep me in suspense."

Jack reached around his shoulder and drew the seat belt across his middle, clicked it in place. "Idaho ice cream potato."

Marie laughed. The Idaho dish sounded bizarre, true enough, but she'd defy anyone to take a bite of the tasty creation and claim they weren't hooked. Vanilla ice cream crafted into the shape of a potato, covered in cocoa and topped with whipped cream, made it look like a potato with a dollop of sour cream. "Bartwell's it is."

"But what about Astrid? We can't leave her in the car. It's too hot."

"Ah, just one more great thing about Bartwell's. They're dog friendly."

They entered through the main door, and Marie watched Jack's expression as he checked the place out again. The owners had kept the concrete walls and floors, just as they'd highlighted the high ceilings and exposed pipes and fixtures. Each wall featured at least one large-screen TV, every one of them tuned to either a Sunday sports show or a twenty-four-hour news channel.

"I didn't realize they had pinball machines." Jack pointed toward a corner of the space, beyond the high-top tables and stools.

"And darts, too." Marie indicated a board on the wall.

"Some people are begging them to put in pool tables, but I doubt they will."

A young server led them to a table in the back dining area and placed two menus in front of them. "What can I get you folks to drink?"

"You ought to look at the blackboard behind the bar," Marie told Jack as she grabbed her menu. "This place has a lot of great craft beers."

While Jack squinted at the list across the room, Marie smiled at the server. "I'd like your Blood Orange IPA. And a bowl of water for Astrid, please." Marie ordered Astrid to lie down next to her chair.

"And I'll try the Seven Devils Grog."

The server made a note on his pad. "I'll get those for you while you look over our menu." He headed for the bar.

Jack skimmed the menu. "Man oh man. These sandwiches sound good."

"It didn't used to be this way. When they first opened, the food was pretty basic. But when their craft beers developed a cult-like following, tourists started coming to Jasper specifically to visit Bartwell's. So the owners upped their game."

"God bless the tourists." Jack shut his menu.

The server reappeared with their drinks. "Have you decided what you'd like?"

Marie ordered the grilled ham, Gouda and caramelized onions on light rye. Jack settled on the smoked brisket torta with chipotle aioli on a telera roll.

The server picked up the menus. "Make sure to save room for dessert."

Jack and Marie looked at each other and started laughing.

"We forgot about dessert," Jack said.

"The whole reason we came."

They sipped their beers.

"Good." Jack nodded toward his glass.

"Mmm-hmm," Marie replied.

Silence fell. Not exactly uncomfortable, but…expectant. She contemplated which way to take the conversation next. In for a penny, in for a pound. "At the risk of ruining this beautiful day, why did you leave so abruptly Friday night?"

Jack nursed his beer.

"Look, if you don't want to talk about it, tell me to mind my own business. I just hope it wasn't because of me."

"It wasn't." Jack gripped his pint with both hands, holding it tight enough to whiten his knuckles. Whatever he was holding back was hard for him to talk about, and that was something she knew a whole heck of a lot about. "But I *was* upset."

"About what? That jerk who got too friendly with me?"

Jack looked up. "Him? I was at first. I've never liked bullies."

Marie set her beer glass down a bit too hard, sloshing golden brew on the table. "See. That's what Dotty was talking about. You may not know the exact details of your past, but you know who you are. What kind of man you are."

Jack unwrapped his fingers from his glass and pushed it away. "She tell you that? Maybe she has more faith in me than I do."

"I don't think so." Marie took another sip of beer and relaxed against her chair. "Like I told you earlier, she's an excellent judge of character. So, why don't you tell me what happened at the barbecue?"

"I threw you on the ground. I lost it over some stupid firecrackers." The moment the words passed his lips, his shoulders sagged and his broad back rounded into a slump.

Oh, my gosh. It all made sense now. She reached across

the table for his hands. He jerked back. She laid hers on the table, palms up. "Give me your hands, Jack."

He didn't move.

"You know what I saw the other night? I saw a man whose first instinct was to protect me. A man willing to take a potential bullet for me." She leaned toward him. "You shielded my body with yours, thinking we were in danger. That makes you a hero in my book."

Jack looked embarrassed, but now for the entirely different reason of high praise.

"Give your hands to me." She slapped her hands on the table for emphasis.

And he did. Large, thick hands, slightly calloused, with blunt clean nails.

"What happened to you was PTSD. Sometime in your past, you suffered something traumatic. That's all. It doesn't make you a bad person, and I don't think any less of you."

He looked at her with that intense gaze that had come to define him in her mind. "What if I didn't suffer trauma? What if I caused it?"

Oh, wow. She certainly hadn't considered that angle. "Think about what you're saying. You're talking about a man who Dotty approves of, who birthed puppies, who extraneously saved me from that jerk." Her mouth twisted into a sideways grin. The same man who somehow made her feel safe, who held her like she mattered, who kissed her until she couldn't think straight. *The man I want to stay in Jasper.*

Jack gave her a smile in return, small, but genuine. His shoulders squared and his back straightened as he once again became a man to be reckoned with. That her words encouraged the transformation made Marie happy.

"Grilled ham and gouda." The server seemed to appear

out of nowhere. Their hands separated as he set Marie's plate down, then slid Jack's in front of him. "And the brisket torta for the gentleman. Can I get you anything else?"

They told the server they were fine, and he hurried off to attend other tables as the place filled up with craft beer enthusiasts and sports junkies. For golf fans, the Wyndham Championship in Greensboro, North Carolina, flickered on one large screen, while on another, local sports jocks offered their take on the coming college football season.

And, of course, no respectable sports bar in Idaho would fail to feature the Steelheads, Boise's hockey team, as the talking heads discussed upcoming exhibition games before the season started. Other screens featured preseason football and trout fishing while two played the news, the commentators discussing some debate raging in the halls of Congress.

Marie lost herself in a mouthful of gooey melted cheese and sweet, caramelized onions. Checking to see if Jack was pleased with his choice, she found him watching her, his lips quirked into a smile.

"What?" She put down her sandwich and dragged a napkin across her mouth, assuming she must be wearing some of her lunch.

"You were kind of dancing in your chair."

Self-conscious about enjoying her food so much, she tried to shrug it off. "This sandwich is *that* good. What about yours?"

He took a bite, then gave her a thumbs-up while making agreeable sounds. "Mm-hmm."

Marie froze with her sandwich halfway to her mouth. Five of the seven flat-screen TVs flashed pictures of Abel Gaines.

"...the fugitive was reportedly spotted near the Utah-Idaho border..."

The rest of the story faded to white noise. Abel. Heading for Idaho. Coming for her. What else could she think? He'd sworn to get even with her, and now, despite her every precaution, he'd found her. But how? George? Was that why he wouldn't answer her calls? Maybe.

Then the bile in her stomach bubbled up, and she watched Jack from the corner of her eye.

"…AUTHORITIES SAY HE is traveling with at least one other person and is considered armed and dangerous. Those with information should report it immediately to the tip line."

Jack's appetite drained away as the announcer continued with Abel's prison escape and then played footage from his criminal past. All too familiar scenes of a wooded area showed on the screens. Black SUVs with flashing lights drove up on the Gaines compound, billows of dust rising in their wake.

It can't be.

Men in FBI jackets crouched behind cars, being fired upon from people inside an old farmhouse. Footage from a helicopter gave a bird's-eye view of the structure, situated in a low-lying area between the rolling hills of West Virginia. Smoke drifted upward, windows exploded and flames licked the wooden siding.

Sweat popped on Jack's brow. His pulse sped up and his stomach dropped. Pain erupted in his head. He knew that place. Those trees. That house. The flames, the heat, the terrible burning pain. When the footage showed a US marshal slapping cuffs on a man, spinning him toward the camera, Jack remembered that face.

Abel Gaines.

Jack's right hand touched the scars on his left wrist and forearm. He could deny the truth all he wanted, but he'd been in that farmhouse. He'd been there with Abel Gaines. Was the fugitive headed this way because of Jack?

The life he'd only just begun to imagine with the gorgeous vet shriveled in the face of what he truly must be. A criminal. A killer. He looked at Marie and found her staring at him with wide, haunted eyes.

Chapter Ten

"Doc, I can't wait a second longer for Raoul to finish up. Watch the desk for me while I dash down the hall, will you, dear?"

"Go, go. I got you covered," Marie said.

"It's the curse of getting older," Liz grumbled as she hurried to the bathroom.

It was late Wednesday afternoon, three days after her Sunday lunch with Jack. The clinic waiting room was empty, the phone quiet, and Marie, glad for the moment to be alone, rested one elbow on the check-in counter and dropped her chin into her open palm. Her other hand reached down to absently tug Astrid's ear.

Since that awful moment at Bartwell's, when she'd learned Abel had been spotted near the border of Idaho, Marie had drawn three conclusions.

The first, Abel was coming to Idaho for only one reason. He was coming for her, as he promised he would. Whatever noxious mix of psychopathic traits comprised Abel Gaines, including lying about every single little thing, when he set his mind on something, he didn't quit. He'd sworn he would kill her, and according to the news, he seemed intent on keeping his word.

Deep down, Marie had known the truth at Bartwell's the moment she heard the news report. The pleasant Sunday lunch turned awkward, the food tasted like ash and she and Jack finished their meal mostly in silence. Relieved beyond measure when he decided against ordering the ice cream potato, Marie couldn't drop him back at the DCΛ fast enough.

Sunday night she'd tossed and turned like splattering grease on a hot griddle, terrified for her safety. Astrid spent the night pacing and whining. Monday, the newscasts reported that federal, state and local authorities were convening in Boise to set up a dragnet. But Abel was clever, and Marie spent the day anxious, short-tempered and jumping at every sound.

Liz, bless her, had given Marie space, not once questioning her out-of-character behavior, but poor Astrid refused to eat, sensing her human's distress but unable to find the source.

By Tuesday, she'd had enough. Instead of living in fear like some helpless victim, better to look at her problem rationally, like a disinterested third party. When Abel escaped, he could have fled anywhere in the United States, but he chose to head straight for Idaho. No way could that be construed as a coincidence.

Did he know she was in Jasper? Hope for the best but plan for the worst. A bit of Granny Mae's wisdom. Marie needed to plan how she would protect herself based on the assumption that Abel knew exactly where she was.

And that led her to her second conclusion.

She didn't know what happened to Deputy US Marshal George Murphy, why he'd failed to answer her calls or respond to the FedEx SOS message she'd sent. But whatever the reason, Marie was as sure as she could be that George's AWOL status didn't mean he was colluding with Abel Gaines.

While case deputies made a point to keep their private

lives to themselves, over the last five years Marie had learned a few things about the man tasked with keeping her safe. For one thing, George was a family man, married with a couple of grown children. In his sixties and nearing retirement, he'd mentioned a few times how much he was looking forward to taking it easy, maybe getting in some rounds of golf and spending time with his grandkids.

Even more compelling, George had lost a friend during the siege at the Gaines compound. Taken with everything else she knew about the man, she couldn't see her way clear to believing George would have helped Abel, either with his escape or by sharing the knowledge of Marie's whereabouts.

At this point, it really didn't matter how Abel knew where she was. He knew. End of story. A small chance remained that he might not know her as Marie Beaumont. But realistically, if he'd had her tracked to Jasper, a false name presented no real obstacle. He already knew she was a veterinarian, and in the town of Jasper, there was only one vet. Not much of a leap.

She ticked off the inferred facts on her fingers. Abel was coming for her. He knew she was in Jasper, and her false name wouldn't slow him down. When he found her, and she had to assume that he very well might, Marie couldn't count on the US Marshals Service to help her.

That led to her third and final conclusion. This one about Jack. The evidence that he was in cahoots with Abel was certainly damning. A stranger, showing up in Jasper right when Abel escaped from prison. The whole "my gut is telling me to stay" thing. The convenience of his amnesia. All highly suspect.

Even once she believed Jack's amnesia was real, the recounting of his memory flashes troubled her just as much.

Add in his reaction to the news alert at Bartwell's, and Marie's cynicism seemed justified.

Anyone in her position, and with half a brain, would have mistrusted Jack. When you pushed aside emotion and examined only the facts, things didn't look good on the surface. But after five years of castigating herself for her poor decision-making when it came to men, Marie finally admitted that she had learned a thing or two. A man could paint himself any way he wanted on the outside. Abel had been a grand master. But on the inside, only a true psychopath could hide his reality.

When Marie peeled back the layers of Jack's external complications, underneath were values opposite of Abel Gaines in every way imaginable. Kindness to the less fortunate, a willingness to lend a hand, humility, gratefulness, respect for life and strength without the need to oppress those weaker. Jack could never be Abel's creature.

Despite how it looked, Marie concluded that Jack was a good man, one she was coming to care for. A lot.

"Earth to Dr. Beaumont? Marie! For goodness' sake, where are you?"

Marie snapped upright. "What? What did you say?"

Liz shook her head in a motherly way. "You're a million miles away. What on earth is the matter with you? You've been out of sorts all week. Are you coming down with something?"

"Just got a lot on my mind."

"Well, I'd say it had something to do with that handsome man with no memory, but you don't have the giddy schoolgirl look about you. Are you sure you're not feeling sick?"

"I promise. Thanks for the concern, and sorry I've been cranky. Tell you what—since no one is in the waiting room, how about we close up early?"

Liz grabbed up the office keys. "You don't have to tell me twice." She hustled around the reception desk, locked the front door and flipped the open sign to closed.

Marie arched her back and stretched. "Raoul should be finishing up with Whiskers any minute. Can you think of anything else we need to do?"

Liz began straightening her desk and putting files back in their places. "Barring any emergencies, we're in the clear."

"Good. Think I'll take a hot bath and get to bed early. I'm pooped." Marie straightened a stack of canine dental health care brochures on the counter. "Oh, before I forget. Are there any calls I need to return?"

"No. We're in the clear there, too. But there was this one weird call. Earlier. While you were in the back."

"We really need to get brochure holders for these." Marie picked up another pile of catawampus pamphlets and began straightening them. "Weird how?"

"Well, for one thing, he asked to speak to Megan, not Marie or Dr. Beaumont. When I—"

The brochures flipped from Marie's grasp and sailed everywhere, like a giant game of Fifty-Two Card Pickup. Her skin chilled as if she'd been coated in a glaze of frost. But it didn't stop there. Cold spikes of fear bored their way inside, numbing everything in their path. In another life, when she'd been another person, Megan had been her name. Very few people knew that.

Could it have been George who called? She knew the answer to that before the question fully formed in her head. George never called her except on her cell. Squatting, she began retrieving scattered brochures.

Liz rounded the counter to help clean up the mess from the floor. "Goodness. I'll order holders for these first thing tomorrow. So anyway, I told the guy on the phone that he had the wrong number, that no one named Megan worked here. Then he said he'd mixed up the names, that he meant Marie."

Breathe. In. Out. In. Out. Forcing herself to take a breath, then another, Marie fought for composure. For clarity. For control.

"I don't know why, but I got suspicious when he said that. Maybe it was the way he said it." Liz looked up at Marie, her brows knitted together in a frown. "I can't explain it. I just got the feeling he was lying, but that's not even the weird part. I gave him my standard line when you're in surgery or not in the office, that you were temporarily unavailable. And I could have sworn he said that was about to become a permanent situation. It sounded sort of threatening if you ask me, but it was hard to tell since he was mumbling. Gave me the creeps, though. You don't have a stalker, do you?"

If you only knew. "Not that I'm aware of," she lied.

Lies, lies and more lies. She hated that part of her secret life more than anything else. *Keep your poker face on, Marie. Think about this rationally.* Prior to her disappearance, she'd gone through weeks of WITSEC preparation where they drilled into her what to do in situations like this. Unfortunately, the first step would be contacting her case deputy, who she still couldn't reach. *Get a grip. Stay calm.* Mentally, she slapped her face, knocking herself into action. She picked up the few remaining brochures.

"Here's the last of them," she said, handing the bundle to Liz. "And I wouldn't worry about the weirdo. Probably just a client, upset that I didn't drop everything to take his call. Did he leave a name, a number? I'll just call him back, straighten things out." She braced herself for the name that had haunted her for five long years.

"I asked, but he hung up on me. Talk about rude. Caller ID showed unknown, so I have no idea who he was."

"Well then, that's that." Marie stood, watching Liz straighten the pamphlets and set them in a neat pile back on the counter. "I guess if he wants to reach me badly enough, he'll call back. You go ahead and punch out. I'll lock the back door when Raoul is done. See you tomorrow."

Liz grabbed her purse and pulled out her car keys. "I have enough time to grab an extra bottle of wine before my book club tonight. We just finished reading this exciting, action-packed romantic suspense called *Resolute Justice* and I can't wait to discuss it. A fairly new author, I think. Oh, what is her name? Something like Marshmallow, Marshland. I really need to remember it so I can buy the next book in her series. Well, good night." She waved as she hurried out the back door.

Fifteen minutes later, Raoul had settled Whiskers in the kennel for the evening and was headed home for some much-needed study time. Marie locked up and flipped off the downstairs lights. "Come on, girl. Let's you and I have a girls' night in."

Astrid's tongue lolled from her expectant, happy-dog smile.

Halfway up to her apartment, Marie paused when the office phone's shrill bell broke the silence. What were the odds? She took another step up, wanting to ignore the call. But like a death knell announcing her own demise, the ring called her back down the stairs.

Hoping whoever it was would give up, Marie shuffled into her office and closed the door. Then locked it, as if the flimsy wood barrier would protect her. Taking a slow, deep breath, she picked up the receiver. "Dr. Beaumont."

"Been a long time, Megan. Oh, wait. It's *Marie* now, isn't it? You should go back to using *Megan*—it suits you so much better." A raspy chuckle came through the line. "Miss me, my sweet?"

Marie's blood ran cold and her hands began to shake, but she'd been preparing herself for this. She would not allow Abel Gaines to detect so much as a hint of fear in her voice. "What do you want?"

"What I've wanted ever since you turned traitor on me." The menacing, thorny tone belied his soft voice.

"Then I guess that will be one more thing you'll fail at." Marie sat in her office chair before her knees could give way, proud that her voice, at least, didn't quiver.

"Grown a spine since we last spoke, I see."

"And I also have a concealed weapons permit." For once, telling a lie felt good.

"My, my. What a turn-on, but tell me, my sweet, ever kill a man?"

"I won't have to. The FBI will have you back in custody long before you reach me."

"Will they? You sure about that?"

"If you have nothing more to say—"

"Oh, but I do. I asked you once to be my wife, a mistake, I realize now. But instead of loving me as I loved you, you betrayed me. And the result of that betrayal was the death of my baby brother, now lying in the cold, hard ground. Seems only fitting that I share my pain with you. Since that old witch grandmother of yours is already moldering under six feet of dirt, and you have no other family, I wracked my brain for a solution."

"I'm hanging up."

"Fine. But don't forget to tell your canine friends hello for me, my sweet. I'll be by soon with a special treat for them. Real soon."

The line went dead.

Chapter Eleven

The instant Abel ended the call, Marie grabbed her keys from the top of her desk and raced to the back of her building where recuperating animals were kept. Only Whiskers was there, Whiskers, and she was fine. Although she'd locked the back door herself after Raoul left, she checked it again. Still locked.

Marie could set the alarm when she left to protect her patients, and she'd keep Astrid by her side to keep the dog out of harm's way. But maybe the creep was threatening her friends and the dogs at the DCA. It was one thing to have her own life threatened. Marie found herself in this predicament because of her own actions. But it's an altogether different thing to have her friends' lives endangered. Emma was innocent, and even worse, she had no idea what might be heading her way.

Marie shivered. *Don't let Abel be there already.*

"Astrid, come."

The Doberman came to her side, ready to heel. Marie unlocked and opened the door with caution. The setting sun still offered plenty of daylight to see by, and the parking area seemed clear. Marie set the alarm, closed and locked the door and ran to her vehicle with Astrid next to her.

In record time, Marie buckled Astrid into the RAV4

and then herself. Rolling through stop signs and exceeding speed limits, she raced for the DCA. "Call Emma," she said to her hands-free Bluetooth. The phone rang and rang and rang. She muttered a curse as it went to voice mail. "Emma, this is Marie. Call me as soon as you get this."

There may be an escaped homicidal terrorist coming after you. How do I know? Yeah, about that. Not allowed to say.

She tried Piper, to no avail. No answer from Tashya. Even Barbara, DCA's administrator, didn't pick up. Marie tightened her grip on the steering wheel and tried to control her shaking hands. Erratic breathing, sweat rolling down her back, she recognized the symptoms of panic.

You're letting him win. Calm down.

Her logical side insisted there was no way Abel had made it through countless roadblocks set up all over the state. If he had, then he traveled through the backcountry and over deer trails, a much slower way to move. He couldn't already be in Jasper. Still...

She turned down the dirt road leading to the DCA, fishtailing, sending up billowing dark clouds of dust trailing behind her car like ominous thunderheads. She scanned the buildings as she drew to a stop and jumped out of the vehicle. Nothing seemed out of place, and yet...where was everybody? She unbuckled Astrid. "Come."

She ran to the house first. "Emma!" In through the unlocked back door. Not unusual. Emma rarely locked her doors. The mudroom. Clear. Kitchen, too. "Emma!" Master bed and bath, nothing. No one in the other bedrooms either. The whole house devoid of life. She tore out the front door, Astrid on her heels.

Running for the barn, her panic notched up. Astrid outpaced her and reached the building first. "Search," Marie called to her, and Astrid sprinted inside.

When Marie heard barking, her heart nearly stopped. Reaching the barn, she slowed her pace as she entered, dreading what she might find. Stopping just inside, she bent over, hands on her thighs, and tried to catch her breath. Astrid pounced and nipped with Amaya, who appeared equally pleased to see her playmate.

"Astrid…" Marie panted. "You scared the life out of me. And you," she crouched down and rubbed Amaya's ears. "What are you doing out of the kennel? Why aren't you with your pups?"

Inside their stalls, Elton and Presley turned big brown eyes on her with complete indifference. She pushed upright, and commanded Astrid. "Come." They ran through the barn, out the rear door, and headed for the kennel. Astrid tore ahead of her, and Amaya limped along at a slower pace. Both dogs raced past the RV and disappeared inside the kennel.

Marie reached the RV, pounded on the door. "Jack!"

No answer. She opened the door, peered inside. Everything neat and tidy, but no Jack. She stepped down and slammed the door. Her breathing turned rapid and shallow. She couldn't get enough air. Her hands shook and her heart thundered in her chest.

She sprinted to the kennel. Terrified by the silence. No barking. No whining. No human voices.

No, no, no.

Marie reached the door and flung it open.

THE DOOR OF the kennel slammed against the side wall. Jack looked up from scratching Astrid's neck, Emma from scratching Amaya's. The sun's last rays shadowed the figure who had just thrown open the door like a wild woman. He recognized Marie's lean curves. What he didn't recognize was the chaotic look in her eyes and the heavy panting, like she'd just run a six-minute mile.

Astrid took off like a shot, sniffed the ground around Marie, then sat at attention beside her.

"Good grief. What's wrong?" Emma hurried to the entrance where Marie remained standing like a frozen zombie, staring at them both as if seeing something unbelievable. Unbelievably good or unbelievably bad, Jack couldn't decide.

"Um, everybody's okay?" Marie finally rasped.

"Of course, we're okay." Jack straightened from his crouch. "Why wouldn't we be?"

"Nobody answered their phones."

Emma smacked her forehead. "Left mine in the truck. I hate when I do that. Better go get it." As she passed Marie, Emma drew up and gave her the once-over. "You're soaked in sweat. How far did you run? This is more than me not answering my phone. Tell me this instant what's going on."

Jack watched Marie transform before his eyes. One moment an out-of-control whirlwind, the next a shuttered woman who seemed to be searching for a way to cover her uncharacteristic display of emotion.

Ever since Bartwell's, when he'd caught the news report about Abel Gaines and then turned to see Marie's surprising reaction to the same story, Jack was certain about two things.

He and Abel Gaines were connected.

Abel Gaines and Marie were connected.

And now, Gaines was on the loose. In Idaho, if you believed the TV. Heck of a time for Jack to be missing his memories.

"Um, I thought something was wrong. I came to make sure everyone was all right."

Jack walked closer to her, stopping alongside Emma. "Why would you think we were in trouble?"

She met his eyes, and reflected in those twin blue pools was unadulterated fear. Her secretive nature had made him wonder, but now he was positive that whatever secrets she held, they terrified her.

"Clearly it was nothing." She turned to go.

"Oh, no you don't." Emma reached out and grabbed Marie by the arm. "You're not leaving without telling me what made you think something was wrong out here. So much so that you raced here to save us. Thanks for that, by the way."

As was her habit, Marie rested one hand on Astrid's head. The other was down at her side, fingers rubbing back and forth, back and forth, small movements not meant to be noticed. Jack noticed. Her face bore a closed expression; her eyes shifted to focus on the ground. Marie was about to lie.

"I got a prank phone call. It worried me, so I came by to make sure everyone was all right."

Emma raised her arms as if talking to the heavens. "What a terrible thing to do. I wonder who it was. I'd like to wring their neck."

In Jack's opinion, Emma was asking the wrong questions. "Marie." He kept his voice soft. "What did they say that worried you?"

"It doesn't matter. Astrid, come." She was shutting him out as surely as if she'd slammed down the gate of an impenetrable fortress, and for some reason that infuriated him.

He raised his voice a notch. "It does matter. What did they say?"

Emma stopped ranting and returned her gaze to Marie.

Marie looked miserable. "I already feel like a fool. Why can't you just drop it?"

"Because we have to report it," Emma said. "Jason is due here soon. We'll wait for him and then report it. Who knows—he might catch the little miscreant."

"I'm not waiting and I'm not reporting it. I'm telling you it was no big deal, so I'd appreciate it if both of you could stop making it one."

Jack frowned. Since day one, she'd been probing and prodding, poking at his memories like a young boy with a stick poked at a dead animal discovered on the side of the road. He had no intention of letting her off so easily. Turnabout was fair play.

"So you received a prank phone call that scared you so much that you raced here and ran helter-skelter to find out if we were okay, but for some reason you don't think what the prank caller actually said is important enough to share with us. Or to report to Jason. And don't bother telling me it's no big deal, because your actions clearly say otherwise."

Marie pulled her shoulders back, and Jack could practically see her adding another two feet to her already high protective wall. What on earth could have happened to her to make her so fearful of opening up? Could it have something to do with Abel Gaines?

"I need some air." She stepped outside, Astrid glued to her side. Like Jack, the dog sensed something not right with her mistress. Also like him, Astrid was in the dark as to what that something was.

Amaya and Emma followed Marie outside. "That doesn't look good." Emma pointed with one hand, shielding her eyes from the setting sun with the other.

Marie followed her gaze toward town, where a thick, vertical stream of black smoke reached into the sky. "Oh, my gosh, no! Come, Astrid." She and Astrid dashed for her car.

"Go," Emma said to Jack. "Whatever is going on, she's in no condition to drive."

Overwhelmed by the need to protect Marie, Jack raced after her.

Chapter Twelve

Tell your canine friends hello for me, my sweet.

"Not the clinic!" None of Marie's "canine friends" were there, but Abel wouldn't know that. And Whiskers *was* there. She couldn't leave the poor cat to burn alive.

Jack beat her to the car and blocked her way to the driver's side door. "Give me your keys. I'll drive."

"Get out of my way!" She squared off with him. "You don't have a license. You can't legally drive."

He held out his hand. "And if you get behind the wheel like this, you'll most likely kill yourself. Astrid, too. Along with innocent—"

"*Fine.*" Speed mattered now, and she *was* shaky as all get-out. She threw him the keys, dashed around to the passenger side, buckled Astrid in the backseat and then hopped in the front. Jack was already strapped in with the car started. He gunned it the second she slammed the door and reached for her seat belt. They raced toward Jasper.

Without taking his eyes from the road, Jack said, "Are you going to tell what's going on, or do you plan to let me walk into something blind?"

"What are you talking about? Nothing's going on. There's a fire. I'm going to help. That's it."

For the second time in as many minutes, Jack raised

his voice. "So all of a sudden you're a trained firefighter. Gee, where's your Dalmatian?"

She flashed an angry glare his way, but his eyes faced forward. Well, he wasn't the only one who could shout. "What's your problem?"

"You're my problem. You are—"

"I didn't ask you to come. That was your choice, so get off my case."

"You're lying to me. You've been lying to me since the day we met. Tell me what has you so scared."

"Look out!"

Jack jerked the steering wheel, swerving to avoid a jackrabbit crossing the road. Tires squealed on the pavement, and a hint of burning rubber wafted in through the open window. Quickly righting the car, Jack continued down the road.

"Your driving is what's scaring me."

"Whatever. Can you tell where the fire's coming from?"

Marie snapped to. Instead of fighting with Jack, she should have been paying attention. As they approached the city limits, she could tell the smoke wasn't in the right place for the clinic. Her heart stopped.

"Oh, no, no, no. Jack, hurry. It looks like the smoke is coming from Hemlock Hills."

They drove up on a scene of frightening pandemonium. Two fire trucks, lights flashing. Firefighters held hoses from which white arcs of water attacked a blaze out of control. The entire structure was engulfed. The fire captain's car, two police cars and an ambulance scattered around the perimeter like blinking Legos. First responders everywhere, some running, some shouting, some helping soot-covered residents away from the danger.

"Where's Dotty? I can't see her anywhere."

"Marie, don't panic. You can't go over there," Jack said

with maddening calmness, pointing with one finger to the scene of the fire. "They won't let you. Dotty is probably already out. Look, they're taking residents over to the lawn of that house. Let's ask about her over there."

Marie feared this fire was no accident. If Abel proved to be the arsonist, then he would have known about Dotty and would have targeted her. Dotty's room was on the far side of the building where the fire seemed the worst. "Stop the car! Let me out!"

"No. It's not safe."

Spaced between the emergency vehicles, parked cars lined the street leading up to the Hills, and clustered in bundles, gaping pedestrians stood watching the melee. Jack slowed to a crawl and Marie didn't wait for him to stop. She leaped from the slow-moving RAV4.

"Marie, no!"

But her fear for Dotty's safety was so intense, she didn't even unbuckle Astrid. She sprinted for the building.

When they saw her coming, Jasper PD Lieutenants Cal Hoover and Margaret Avery spread their arms. "Dr. Beaumont, stop. We can't let you through."

Fear and panic exploded into a scream. "Dotty's in there! I have to find her!"

"Doc, calm down. You can look for her over at Jim Nance's house. They've set up a staging area and triage on his front—"

If one more person tells me to calm down... She backed up as if in compliance with the officers, but she instinctively knew Dotty wasn't on Jim Nance's front lawn. When Hoover and Avery let down their guard just enough, Marie darted left, flanking them.

"Doc!"

She ignored them, and they didn't follow her. They had to man their post. She tore around the side of the building and pulled up short. Three firemen on a hose blocked her path. Even if they hadn't been there, Marie could go no farther.

The rear of the house was an inferno, scalding heat sending her backward. She gasped for air stolen by the raging fire. What little she managed to find seared her throat. She fell back more.

This was no pleasant hearth fire crackling in the winter. This fire roared at the top of its lungs. And mixed in with the roar were pops and snaps, like bones breaking. The left half of the building collapsed. A shower of orange sparks flickered up into the rising dark smoke like lightning bugs in a midnight sky.

Marie fell to her knees, her hands covering her mouth. She shook her head and wept. *This is all my fault. Oh, Dotty, I'm so sorry.*

Another team of firefighters raced over and brought a second hose to join the effort. Ignored by the first responders, Marie watched the black smoke war with boiling-hot white steam as water began conquering fire. As the flames died, Chief of Police Doug Walters, Lieutenant Avery and Fire Chief Rich Newcomb stood nearby in a huddle, oblivious to Marie's presence.

"We've had one too many fires lately for my liking," Chief Walters said.

Newcomb nodded. "We have, indeed. But what we have here is a heck of lot different than forest fires in the hills."

"Agreed." Chief Walters turned to Lieutenant Avery. "We get everybody out?"

"It wasn't easy to double-check, with no numbers on any of the room doors." She gave a nod in the direction of the makeshift triage area. "Haven't gotten the official head count yet, but the Hills' director just showed up and

Cal's working on it. Should have the count to you in a few minutes."

"Good." Walters turned to his counterpart in the Jasper fire department. "Your guys sure about the body?"

Chief Newcomb nodded. "Hundred percent sure. Near the site of the explosion."

Body? Explosion? What little hope Marie held vanished on a puff of smoke.

"Any chance this was an accident?" Walters asked.

"Sure, but only a slim chance."

Avery folded her arms across her chest. "Why's that?"

"Even accounting for the explosion of the oxygen tanks, the fire damage was extensive and quick, suggesting the use of an accelerant."

Marie gasped. The oxygen tanks exploded. The oxygen tanks that were stored near Dotty's room. And...there was...there was a body. A harsh sob escaped.

Chief Walters turned at the sound. "Son of a... Avery, get her out of here."

Lieutenant Avery bent down and wrapped her arm around Marie's shaking shoulders. "Come on, Marie. We have to get you out of this area. It isn't safe."

Dotty's death had been her fault, and defeated by her guilt, Marie simply didn't have it in her to move.

"You know somebody who lives here?" Avery asked, gripping Marie's shoulders tighter.

Unable to speak, Marie nodded.

"I'm going to help you up and take you to the triage area. Dollars to donuts we'll find your friend there."

"But, but the body?"

"No way to know who it is until the autopsy, but odds say we'll find...what's your friend's name?"

"Dotty."

"Odds say we'll find Dotty over at Jim Nance's place. You ready to try standing?"

Marie nodded again and got to her feet, swaying a little. True to her word, Avery kept her arm around Marie and led her away from the smoldering wreck that had been Dotty's home.

They rounded a corner.

"There are a couple of people over there who look like they're waving you down." The lieutenant pointed toward the crowded front yard of Nance's house.

Marie's gaze followed Avery's hand and she couldn't believe her eyes. Dotty, wearing her shiny gold sneakers, her face filthy with soot, held a bundle of singed fur in her lap. She sat in a lawn chair, waving one arm in the air like an inflatable tube man in front of a car dealership. Jack stood at her side, his large hand resting possessively on Dotty's shoulder, his intense look melting Marie's heart even from this distance. Astrid sat in front of them, as if on guard.

"Oh, my gosh." Marie waved back.

"Go," Avery said.

Marie didn't need to be told twice. Still a bit wobbly, she started off at a slow pace but picked up speed. When she reached the chair, she dropped to her knees next to the precious woman sitting there and threw her arms around Dotty.

Sassy Cat gave a low growl but endured Marie's trespass.

"I thought… I thought… I can't believe you're all right." She wiped at the tear tracks running down her cheeks.

"Hush, now. Everything's fine. I'm a bit shaken up is all. Not even a broken nail." She ran her fingers through Marie's hair, soothing her.

"I don't know what I'd do if anything happened to you."

Dotty laid her gentle hand on Marie's damp cheek. "I'm perfectly fine, and thanks to Jack, so is Sassy Cat."

"I really didn't do anything. A firefighter was leading Dotty away from the backyard, and the cat was fighting to get away from her. I just took the cat and brought them both over here."

"Oh, fiddlesticks. This is my rescue story, and I'll tell it how I want to." Dotty whispered to Marie, "He saved us both. He *carried* us over here."

Marie looked up at him, still standing at Dotty's side like her sworn protector. "Thank you," she mouthed, afraid that if she spoke her gratitude aloud, she'd disintegrate into a sobbing mess again.

For the next two hours, while the firefighters made sure the fire was fully out and then began their investigation, the police finally got an official head count, finding all the residents and staff of Hemlock Hills accounted for.

Night fell, almost unnoticed as the sparks dancing in dark smoke segued to a black sky filled with stars. The Hills' director had already made phone calls, ensuring his residents would be well taken care of. Marie and Jack helped see Dotty and the others settled in temporary quarters at the Salmon River Motel.

Since it was an open investigation, no one mentioned the charred remains, but Marie dared to hope it had been Abel, killed in the act of his own mischief.

If it wasn't him, who that Marie cared about might be next on the evildoer's hit list?

WHILE DRIVING BACK to the DCA, Jack glanced at Marie. She was disheveled, smudged with soot and zombielike. *Not good.*

His eyes went back to the road. He recognized the symptoms of shock, and it worried him. Luckily, she kept a poncho in the car, which he'd wrapped around her for warmth. He'd stopped at the convenience store for electrolyte water and protein sticks, but she sipped and nibbled only when he prompted her.

This was not the stubborn, fiercely independent Marie he knew. Once they'd seen Dotty settled, she had agreed without protest when he'd insisted on driving. More telling, she'd forgotten to buckle Astrid into the car. Now she sat in the passenger seat without talking, pale, knots of tension in her shoulders and upper arms, her jaw clenched.

The prank phone call, the rush to the DCA followed by the rush to the Hills, then the horror of thinking Dotty was dead, had wiped her out. Coupled with the drop in adrenaline, she could barely keep her eyes open. He pulled up to the RV, knowing he couldn't let her drive home until her blood started flowing again. Until the life came back into her eyes.

He unbuckled Astrid, then opened the RV door. But instead of going inside, the dog stayed in the backseat, unwilling to leave Marie. Jack opened her car door, reached over and undid her seat belt. Sighing as if the weight of the world was on her shoulders, Marie swung her legs out and stood, rousing from her stupor.

Jack steered her up the steps and into the RV. Astrid bounded after them, sitting next to Marie's feet when she dropped onto the small couch. After he closed the door, Jack retrieved the bottle of whiskey that Shane had left in the RV as a gift. He poured a small amount into two glasses, then handed one to Marie and sat next to her, their legs almost touching.

She held it in both hands, looking at nothing with a thousand-yard stare. A few minutes later she blinked, her head jerking back slightly, and glanced around. "Where am I?"

"Shane's RV, where I'm staying."

Marie nodded. Noticing the glass in her hands, she took a sip, then set it in the armrest's cup holder. "If I'd lost Dotty…" Tears welled in her eyes.

"You didn't lose her. She's fine."

"But if she'd been hurt in that fire, I'd… I'd…oh, Jack." Marie leaned her head on his shoulder and wrapped her arms around him, clinging to him. At last the tears came, heart-wrenching and agonizing. Jack held Marie as her pain tore at his gut.

After crying herself out, she lifted her head and looked at him with wide, sad eyes. She touched her lips to his as her tear-spiked lashes began to lower.

Jack's heart raced, and every muscle in his body went taut. He shifted on the couch, pulling her against him. Her breathing was quick and shallow; her breasts pressed into his chest. Again and again, every time she breathed.

Through his thin T-shirt, he felt her hard nipples pushing against him, and he went hard himself.

She gasped, licked her lips. "Jack," she whispered.

And there was the permission he needed. Passion broke the dam of his restraint, and he crushed his mouth to hers. She opened to him immediately, her tongue sparring with his. Panting like he'd climbed a mountain, he couldn't seem to catch his breath. Suffocating never felt so sweet.

They stood while she tugged frantically at his shirt, and he hurried to help her remove it. He pulled hers off and began guiding them to the back of the RV, their mouths never breaking contact. Moving as one, they bumped into the kitchen counter, got held up by the bathroom door. Jack slammed it closed and propelled them into the bedroom.

They fell on the bed as one, facing each other, kissing each other. He fumbled with her bra strap. When he finally removed it and held her bare breasts in his hands,

Marie moaned. Warm, soft mounds, capped by pinnacles of desire. He thumbed the twin peaks, and she arched against his palms.

He rolled her onto her back, unfastened her jeans and slid them down her legs. Standing, he stared down at her from the foot of the bed, fumbling with his fly.

Marie, naked and waiting for him with greedy eyes… nothing had ever looked so enticing. He ached from wanting her. Apparently impatient herself, she sat up and moved to the edge of the bed. As soon as his jeans hit the floor, Marie slid her warm fingers beneath the waistband of his boxer briefs. She didn't take the time to tease him with her hands or mouth. Instead, she tugged his shorts down past his knees. They dropped the rest of the way and he stepped out of them.

Biting her bottom lip, Marie looked at him with a longing that nearly undid him. He lowered himself on top of her, and they resumed their kissing.

They rolled across the sheets, stopping with her on top, Jack loving the weight of her. They rolled again, this time with him on top. Her legs fell open to cradle him and he pressed himself against her slick opening, using every drop of willpower to hold back from entering.

She groaned, thrashing beneath him, her hands latching on to his buttocks, pulling him closer.

"Marie," he groaned. "Protection."

"I've got it covered. Jack…please."

No force on earth could have stopped him then. He thrust inside her and the world tilted on its axis. She tightened around him. Hot. Wet.

Marie gasped and bucked. "Harder."

He levered himself up on his arms and did her bidding. Taking her, possessing her, giving her all of him in return.

Fisting the sheets in each hand, Marie arched again

and cried out, her muscles taut, her body quivering. Jack plunged deep within her, groaning with pleasure as Marie tightened and squeezed, again and again. He finally could wait no longer and shouted his own release.

He collapsed on top of her, each of them struggling to catch their breath, their bodies slick with sweat, desire pooling where they were joined. Though loath to separate, he rolled off her, spent and fulfilled at the same time. She cuddled into his side, and he brushed a tendril of hair away before kissing her forehead. They lay like that until their heat dissipated and Marie shivered.

"You okay?" His voice came out raspy.

"Mm-hmm," she murmured. "Except, I'm thirsty."

"Water or whiskey?"

"Whiskey, I think."

He got up, walked naked to the other room and grabbed their glasses and the bottle. When he returned to bed, he found she'd wiggled under the sheet and propped herself up against the pillows, watching him with eyes that still sparkled with desire.

He got in bed beside her, topped off each glass and handed one to her.

She took a sip. "You know what I was thinking?"

"I'm surprised you can think at all. More than I'm capable of." He sipped from his glass, enjoying the liquid heat burning down his throat and into his stomach. "So tell me, what were you thinking?"

She set her glass on the bedside table. "I was thinking that if you and I, here, like this—" she spun her index finger around to encompass the bed and the two of them in it "—had been a scene in an old movie, we'd be smoking cigarettes right now."

He stared at her, not comprehending.

"You know, like they used to do after a particularly

steamy sex scene. Of course, we don't, but if we smoked, what we just did would definitely be cigarette-after-sex worthy."

Jack laughed.

She smiled. "What?" Then she started laughing, too, and punched his arm. "Stop laughing at me."

He responded by doing an exaggerated parody of smoking, which made them both laugh harder.

It took a while, but eventually the laughter slowed to hiccupping chuckles, finally leaving them both silent and smiling.

He pulled her into his embrace and kissed her whiskey-glazed lips. Taking his time this go-round, Jack replaced the frantic groping and desperate need with gentle exploration. Skimming his fingers across her satiny skin, learning her peaks and valleys, making note of what pleased her, was not something to be rushed.

His fingers sought her center, where he massaged, rubbed and probed until she shook with climax after climax. Only then did he enter her. Only then did he seek his own release. They chased each other to unknown heights, peaking together, then drifting back to earth in each other's arms.

Sitting back against the pillows, processing what had just passed between them, they turned to each other as if on cue and puffed on invisible cigarettes, smiling at the type of private joke only lovers shared.

"Come over here." Jack moved so that Marie could nestle against his side. "How did Dotty come to be your adopted grandmother?"

She held her glass before her lips, and he thought she was about to clam up on him.

"Sassy Cat," she said, and told him about her house call on behalf of the residents' adopted feline.

Pleased Marie was sharing, Jack kept his mouth shut and enjoyed her story. The longer she spoke, the more animated she became. When she paused for another sip, he asked about her real grandmother.

"Oh, Granny Mae was the best. I wish you could have met her. She put her life on hold to raise me. And then, when it should have been her time to travel or do whatever she wanted, she was diagnosed with cancer." Marie raised her eyes to meet Jack's. "Life can be so unfair."

"I didn't mean to make you sad."

"You didn't. I'm glad you asked. I don't get many chances to talk about her."

And she chose me to listen. A warmth spread throughout his chest that had nothing to do with the whiskey. "Want to do something fun this weekend? Just you and me?"

Yawning, Marie asked, "Like what?"

"White water rafting."

"As long as we don't go down any hard ones. I'm not very good at it."

"But you'll go?"

"I'll go if you let me sleep now."

He kissed the top of her head, gratified that she was staying the night, that he would wake with her beside him.

They slid down in the bed, Marie snuggling next to him. As exhaustion overtook him, he marveled at the turn his life had taken. And yet, insidious seeds of doubt ate at the edges of his newfound joy. Dreading the specter of his unsavory past that was sure to visit him in his dreams, Jack focused on their night of lovemaking. But even as he did, an uncomfortable question pecked at his brain.

Why does something so good feel so wrong?

Chapter Thirteen

Early the next morning Marie left a note for Jack, and she and Astrid slipped out of the RV without waking him. He deserved his rest after last night. A grin took over her mouth and her cheeks flushed with warmth.

She glanced in the rearview mirror, coming eye-to-eye with Astrid. "Oh hush. It's not like I do this all the time." *But last night with Jack definitely made up for the long dry spell.*

Astrid huffed.

Marie parked outside her office, and she and Astrid dashed up the outside stairs to her apartment. After a quick shower and change of clothes, she fed Astrid and asked Liz by text to please walk the dog when she got to the office.

Then she locked up and walked toward Millard's Diner, intent on unearthing information about the Hemlock Hills fire.

The diner's policy was to sit wherever you wanted, so when Marie entered, she grabbed an empty booth near the front.

Vera Millard stopped at the table with an empty mug and a full carafe of coffee. "You need a menu?"

"No thanks. Just coffee." Marie smiled up at her.

"Something happen to Liz?" Vera set down the mug and filled it. "She always picks up your coffee, doesn't she?"

Shaking her head, Marie said, "No, Liz is fine. I just felt like popping in this morning."

"Hmph." Well-known for her cantankerous demeanor, Mrs. Millard seemed to be in true form today.

After Vera moved on with her carafe, Marie relaxed against the vinyl back of her bench seat, nursing a cup of coffee and biding her time. When the diner's door swung in, its chime announcing another arrival, Marie looked up. *Finally.*

Officer Ava Callan joined three other JPD officers sitting at the blue Formica counter. Marie was better acquainted with Ava than the other cops who'd come in so far. This would be her chance.

"Ava." Marie raised her voice to be heard over the din of the other diners.

Ava turned and Marie waved her over. The policewoman said something to the cop next to her, grabbed her coffee and joined Marie.

"This is a nice surprise. I thought Liz picked up your coffee on her way in." Ava slid into the booth.

"Good grief. Does everyone know my habits and schedule?"

Ava chuckled. "Small towns. After living in Chicago, the hardest thing to get used to here is having everyone all up in your business." She shrugged. "But you've been here longer than me. It gets easier, right?"

"Ask me in another ten years. I might know by then." But chances were, in ten years Marie would still be walking the tightrope between loneliness and safety. The main reason she didn't frequent Millard's was the same reason she didn't date or join a book club or go dancing. The less she hung out in the same places with the same people, the fewer probing questions about her past she had to fend off. She'd already learned that once you got past the small talk, once you forged a bond with a group of people and once that group started baring their souls to you, they expected you to reciprocate.

And that could never happen. The only reason Marie was in Millard's now was to find out what she could about the fire and the burned body. She should have come up with a better plan, since apparently her appearance in the diner was headline news.

She gave Ava a warm smile. "How's Lacey doing?" Marie had operated on Ava's K-9 partner a couple months earlier, after the dog was injured in a bomb explosion.

"Great. After her last follow-up with you, I started easing her back into her duties. She's good as new now."

"Glad to hear that. Thank goodness she wasn't burned in the explosion." Marie cringed internally at her awkward segue to yesterday's incident.

"That would have been horrible." Ava stirred sugar into her coffee. "Speaking of fires, I saw you at Hemlock Hills yesterday, didn't I? And who was that fine man you brought with you?"

But the segue worked.

"I saw the smoke and wanted to make sure everyone was safe." Marie shook her head. "I can't believe Dotty managed to save that darn Sassy Cat and still get out unscathed."

Ava arched a brow. "And the fine man?"

"That would be Jack. Astrid and I found him injured outside of town a couple of weeks ago."

"That's the guy with amnesia? Dang, girl. When you're out finding strays, you don't mess around." Ava gave her a sly grin. "You two an item already?"

With her cheeks warming, Marie scoffed. "Hardly. We barely know each other." She took a sip of coffee. "But we're going rafting this weekend."

"That should be fun."

"I hope so. I've only gone a few times, so I want to make sure we stay on the easier rapids."

"Maybe you can just fall over the side and let him rescue you." Ava pretended to swoon in the booth, fanning herself with one hand.

Marie shook her head. "My two main goals are to not look stupid and not drown. Maybe not in that order." She waited for Ava to stop laughing, then switched back to their original topic. "So have they figured out what started the fire? I heard some of the guys talking about an explosion. It wasn't another bomb, was it?"

"I'll tell you this—Dotty was lucky she went looking for the cat as soon as she smelled smoke." Ava leaned over the table and lowered her voice. "And no, it wasn't a bomb. The fire started in the restroom just past Dotty's room. If she'd still been at that end of the building..."

Dotty was the last resident on that hall. A chill raced down Marie's arms, leaving goose bumps in its wake.

"So what caused it? A visitor sneaking a cigarette in the restroom?" The few residents who refused to quit knew they had to go outside for a smoke.

Ava shook her head. "The fire chief brought in an arson investigator from Boise. The fire was started deliberately. From what I understand, the guy started it with a liquid accelerant in the restroom between Dotty's room and the oxygen room. Apparently, when Hemlock Hills was built, the workers left small gaps between the floors and the bottom of the drywall sheets. And as the house shifted with ground settlement, the baseboards loosened too.

"So when the arsonist poured the accelerant, it flowed under the walls into the rooms on either side, taking the flames with it. The oxygen tanks began to overheat. They're still piecing it together, but they think the guy didn't realize that and opened the oxygen room door searching for an unlocked exit. A lot of the doors in there aren't marked because the Hills' manager was repainting. Before the arsonist could turn around and get out, the tanks started to explode from the increased pressure due to the heat. And when all that escaping oxygen hit the flames, kaboom." Ava imitated something blowing up with her hands.

"They think the body they found was the arsonist?"

"No doubt about it." Ava, still leaning across the table, waved Marie to lean in, too. "The arson investigator took some of the remains back to Boise with him. The Boise PD has one of those Rapid DNA machines that can develop a profile in less than two hours."

"Refill, ladies?" Vera stood over them, a coffeepot in one hand, the other planted on her hip.

Marie and Ava sat back in the booth while their cups were topped off.

"You two talking about that fire at the old folks home?"

Ava crinkled her forehead as if confused. "Hemlock Hills? Oh, no, I was telling Marie a story about my days in Chicago when I worked narcotics."

"Looked like it was pretty top secret, you ask me." Vera smirked.

"I was trying to keep my voice low so I wouldn't gross out anyone else." Ava stage-whispered to Vera, "I mean, who wants to eat breakfast while hearing about some guy who crammed so many vials of heroin up his—"

"I know you haven't been in town long, Officer Callan. But we don't allow that type of talk in here. If you want to continue enjoying our world-famous coffee and home cooking, I expect you to curb your graphic crime details."

"Yes, ma'am." Ava looked appropriately contrite until Vera stalked off toward the counter. Then she screwed her mouth to the side. "Dang it, Marie. Now I'm probably going to get sent to detention."

"Not my fault. I didn't say a word." Marie held her hands up in surrender. "But seriously, Ava, don't tell me anything that you shouldn't. I don't want to get you in trouble with Chief Walters."

Ava waved her in again and they resumed their heads-together positions. "There's going to be a press conference later today. You're just finding out a little sooner than most. But everyone on the force has been talking about it, so it's hardly confidential."

Thanking her lucky stars that Ava wasn't about to stop talking, Marie prompted, "So they ran a DNA test?"

"Yes. And based on the test results, they think the arsonist was that fugitive who was on the news this week. The guy who broke out of prison and was spotted near Twin Falls."

Stunned, Marie just blinked while emotions fought within her. Elation that Abel was dead. Guilt that he'd tried to kill Dotty to hurt Marie. Relief that she's safe. Dread that there might be more of Abel's accomplices still out there. Still coming for her. But with Abel dead and unable to direct anyone's actions, would they even bother with her now? Especially after all the attention directed at Jasper after the fire.

Oblivious to the turmoil raging inside Marie, Ava continued talking. "The forensic lab in Boise is convinced it's him, and they're turning the remains and evidence over to the FBI. Technically, it's their case, anyway." She leaned back, her brows drawing together. "Don't you think that's bizarre? A felon breaks out of prison and travels halfway across the country to set a nursing home on fire?"

Marie dropped her gaze to the tabletop. "Yeah, that's weird all right." And why hadn't George or someone else from the Boise US Marshals' office been alerted to what was going on in Jasper? George's absence was becoming more and more puzzling. Marie had lost her faith in the WITSEC program. She was on her own.

Ava checked her watch. "I've gotta go. Catch the news tonight if you can. They'll probably have more details than I do."

"I will. And in the meantime, I promise not to repeat what you told me to anyone." Marie had been intent on finding out what she could, but not at the expense of Ava's career. That would have meant more guilt to pile on and carry around with all the rest.

"Don't worry. Like I said, it's unofficial, but not confidential." Ava slid to the edge of the booth and stood. "We should meet for lunch one of these days. I don't want Lacey's vet visits to be the only time we catch up."

"I'd love to. Give me a call when you know your schedule." Marie smiled to herself. Maybe now she could actually have friends to meet for lunch.

She paid her bill and left the diner. Instead of heading straight back to her office, Marie strolled to the town square and sat on a park bench. People rushed past on their way to work in downtown businesses. Shop owners unlocked their doors and flipped window signs from closed to open. Flowers planted throughout the park bloomed in a riot of colors.

With Abel gone, perhaps she could leave witness protection. She could continue on as Marie Beaumont since that's how everyone here already knew her. Or maybe she would reclaim her real identity, Megan Burnett. She'd have to make a pros-and-cons list to decide, but at least she had options now.

Well, not *right* now, but soon. She still needed to contact her case deputy. If not George, anyone would do. She wanted the go-ahead that she could leave the program. If she didn't hear from him soon, she'd drive down to Boise herself and take matters into her own hands.

How great would it be, not to have to lie anymore? To anyone. Without the lies, and now that she finally trusted Jack, maybe they could see where things went between them. After five lonely years, she was ready.

Marie's lips curved into a satisfied smile. Last night had been full of revelations, and aftershocks still swept through her, muscles tightening, other parts tingling. Like someone freed from prison, she'd luxuriated in the attention she'd received from Jack. A considerate lover, he'd taken things slow until she made it clear she'd already waited way too long.

His kindness to Dotty, his compassion for animals, his tenderness toward Marie, all sealed the deal. Despite her original apprehension about Jack, she felt at ease with him now. She wasn't at all ready for him to leave Jasper.

Leaning back against the bench, Marie inhaled a deep breath of fresh mountain air. Shifting her perception, she surveyed the town as if it were her home. A place where she belonged, with friends she could talk to. Not a place of exile, for a lifetime of loneliness and fear. On this glorious, sunny morning, anything seemed possible.

THE PRESS CONFERENCE Ava predicted had aired Thursday evening. The Boise stations all sent reporters and featured the story on their local five o'clock newscasts. The three main networks also mentioned it on their evening national news shows.

According to Liz, it had been the main topic of conversation everywhere in town on Friday. Marie took her word for it. Other than visiting Dotty at her temporary lodgings and delivering a wedding gift to Tashya, Marie had spent the day in the clinic. She'd avoided talking to people because her emotions were too extreme, too involved, too personal.

But now it was Saturday morning, and she was ready to let go of her tension and try for a little fun. If anyone could help her relax, it would be Jack. It was almost like they were the perfect couple, Marie trying to forget her past, Jack unable to remember his.

After parking in front of Emma's house, Marie released Astrid and hauled her duffel bag out of the SUV. Astrid started for the kennel and Marie called her back. "We're going in the house first, girl." Setting down her duffel, she crouched by Astrid and ran her hands through the dog's short hair. "While everyone is away this weekend for Jason and Tashya's wedding, we get to stay here and play with the animals."

"Can I be one of the animals you play with?" Jack stood in the open doorway, a huge grin splitting his face.

Marie's cheeks warmed as she straightened. Astrid whined, her big brown eyes bouncing between Marie and Jack as if watching a tennis match. Jack joined in. "Please can she come to me?"

"Honestly, between the two of you." Marie laughed. "Astrid, free."

Jack knelt and patted his chest. Astrid ran to him and soon they both went down in a pile of legs, arms and floppy ears.

Smiling, Marie sidled past them and took her bag to Emma's guest room. By the time she returned to the front door, Jack had disengaged himself from Astrid. He slid his arms around Marie and for a long moment they stared into each other's eyes. Leaning into him, she lowered her gaze to Jack's mouth. Traced his lips with her finger. Remembered the things his lips, his tongue, had done to her just a few nights ago.

Holding her against him with one arm, he cradled her cheek and tipped her face up toward his. As his lips touched hers, barely a whisper of contact, every nerve ending in her body sizzled. Marie rose on her tiptoes, intent on capturing his mouth. But Jack pulled back, making her wait. Driving her crazy. By the time his gentle kisses turned demanding, Marie met them with equal force. When they finally separated, Marie gasped for breath as her legs trembled.

"Are we sure we want to go rafting today?" Jack's wicked grin made her laugh.

"Yes, we're definitely going rafting." Marie looked down at Astrid, who'd been watching them kiss. "But not you, girl. You're staying home today."

"I've rarely seen you without her."

Marie walked out to the porch with Astrid. "I don't want to worry about her falling in the river."

As they all headed to the kennel, Astrid's head and tail hung down.

"I don't think she's happy about it." Jack pointed out the obvious.

Marie put Astrid in the same stall as Amaya and the puppies. "You two behave." Marie squatted and loved up Astrid.

As they closed the kennel door, a forlorn howl started up and Jack's eyes widened in mock horror.

Marie laughed. "That's the beagle part of her."

Jack wrinkled his nose and chuckled. "Now I see why you don't leave her behind much. What a racket."

"I know, right?" Marie laughed along with him, even though howling wasn't why she usually never left Astrid behind. But for the first time in a long while, Marie felt safe not taking Astrid with her. Especially with Jack at her side. "Just don't tell *her*. I think it might hurt her feelings."

"If hurt feelings sound like that, not a problem."

Marie drove them through town toward Blaze's River Tours and Rafting. The morning was fair, a warm sun and a blue sky dotted with hundreds of fluffy white clouds. As they drew near the popular rafting spot, the crowds increased. Marie peered in the rearview mirror at the empty backseat. No Astrid. She suddenly felt exposed and agitated, scanning the crowd for someone who didn't belong, someone paying too much attention to her.

"Have you done much rafting?" Jack asked.

She exhaled. Slowly, so Jack wouldn't notice. Abel was dead. Her life had become her own again. She made a concerted effort to smile and relax her grip on the steering wheel. "I'm not much of a swimmer, but I've gone a few times, though only on Class II and III runs, and only with a guide. Class IV, or heaven forbid a Class V, no way, not ever. Every year it seems at least one or two people die on one of those excursions, and I have no intention of that being me." *Not with the kind of luck I have.*

"Then thanks for trusting me."

Marie drove around until she found a parking spot. "Come to think about it, why is that? Why am I trusting you, that is?" She turned off the engine and climbed out.

Jack unbuckled, got out and stared at her across the top of the RAV4. "I'm going to tell you why."

"First," Marie countered, jabbing her index finger in the air, "you're going to stop staring at me like that." Those eyes. Worse than any Siren's song. If she was going to get on the water, she needed her wits.

Jack shrugged, tipping his head and grinning in a way that could only be described as charmingly arrogant. "Like what?" he asked, all innocent-like.

"As if you didn't know, Mr. Hypnotic Staring Man."

Jack burst out laughing. "Seriously?"

"I'm not kidding. Cut it out or I'm not going."

"Okay, okay. How's this?" He crossed his eyes.

"Ha-ha, funny man."

"Well, if I'm Mr. Hypnotic Staring Man, you must be Miss Chicken to Get on the Water and Using Any Excuse Possible Not To. Nice to meet you."

Marie rolled her eyes, slammed the front car door closed and got her bag from the backseat. "Remind me again why I'm trusting you?"

"The more I flipped through my rafting magazines, the more sure I became that I've done it before." Jack followed suit and retrieved his bag. "So yesterday, I rode Ol' Blue down to the river and watched for a while. And guess what?"

"Ol' Blue?"

"My bike."

"You named your bike Ol' Blue?"

"He's blue. I wasn't going to name him Ol' Red." Jack drummed his fingers on the car roof. "Stop changing the subject. Are you gonna guess or what?"

"No. Just tell me."

"Spoilsport. I had some memory flashes. And they didn't bring on a headache. It seems like happy memories and things I remember that didn't actually happen to *me*, don't hurt me at all. Anyway, I've done this before. Rafting, I mean. Kayaking, too. Lots of times. But I wanted to be sure. So Blaze and I had a long talk. Great guy, by the way. Heard all about his problem with that bomber. Told me you saved the life of one of the heroes who helped catch the guy."

Marie frowned. "Ava's dog, Lacey. Yeah. Terrible what happened to her, but she pulled through."

"Thanks to you."

"I had something to do with it, sure." She shook her head as she remembered. "But that dog. She had one strong will to live. Amaya reminds me of her. But what did you learn from Mr. Blaze?"

As he spoke, Marie couldn't help but be infected by Jack's enthusiasm. That stare of his changed. His eyes became animated, sparkling with pleasure and his grin was warm and genuine. "That's the thing. When he started talking, I knew what he was talking about. You know, things like eddy fence, throw bags, dry bags, swimmers."

"What're all those things? I don't know what *you're* talking about."

Jack chuckled. "An eddy fence is the swirly water line between an eddy and the current. A throw bag is a piece of rescue equipment, and a dry bag is just what it sounds like. It keeps water out and hopefully keeps the stuff you put in it dry."

"And swimmers? People swim down these rapids?"

Jack hoisted his bag over one shoulder. "No. Well, not that I know about. A swimmer means someone who has fallen out of the raft."

"That's not going to happen to me, right?" Marie held her bag by the straps and met him around the back of the vehicle. Together they headed for Blaze's.

"No, and that's why Blaze and I decided that a tandem kayak would suit us better than a raft. Easier for us to control by ourselves."

"Why don't we go with a guide?"

They edged their way inside the newly opened Blaze's River Tours and Rafting, crowded with people checking in, gearing up, slathering on sunblock.

"A kayak can be more fun. And we don't need a guide. I'll be your guide." He puffed out his chest in a comical pose.

"Jack!" Blaze hollered from across the room and barreled his way through the throng. "You made it, and with the vet in tow. Good, good. Got your gear all set." He turned to Marie and grabbed both her hands in his. "So glad to see you." He squeezed her hands and then let her go. "It's a great morning to be on the river. You're going to love the pools between the rapids, with waters deep enough to soothe the soul. And then the drops, where the rapids pick up again and are the real reason you're here. Water temps are warm, so you won't need to rent wet suits."

"Just as you predicted," Jack said.

Blaze placed his finger on his nose. "I've got a nose for it. And you're in luck with Jack, here. Knows his stuff," Blaze said to Marie with a firm nod of his head. "He'll be a fine guide."

"Glad to hear it." *Because her life would be in his hands.*

Blaze turned to Jack. "Stow your gear in the lockers over there. I've got you a dry bag already packed, and the shuttle bus is arranged for your return trip. When you reach the bottom, look for the bus named Greenleaf. They'll be expecting you. Your kayak is already in the water out back. Head that way," he said, pointing. "You can pick up your PFD and other gear, then you're off. Now, go! Enjoy your day."

Marie gave Jack a quizzical look. "PFD?"

He grinned. "It's the term we professionals use for a personal flotation device."

"Professional, huh? Well, thanks for the education. And Jack?" She waited until he met her eyes.

"Yeah?"

"Thanks for this day," she said, and she meant it. She couldn't remember the last time she felt this relaxed and excited at the same time, the last time she allowed herself a whole day for nothing but fun.

"You're welcome." There was a weight of meaning behind the soft reply.

"Oh, Jack. I forgot to mention," Blaze said, stopping them. "Make sure you're off the river by midafternoon. Weather report says those fluffy little darlings outside are going to form up. Predicting severe thunderstorms this evening."

"Good to know," Jack said, seemingly unconcerned.

"Got to run." And like his name, the owner was gone in a blaze.

Marie stopped in her tracks. "Thunderstorms. Um, maybe—"

"Don't even think about backing out. Come on. Everything's going to be fine."

Jack took charge. He saw to it that they were outfitted with life jackets, full-cut helmets and neoprene booties for their feet.

"The water is nice when you're out in the sun," he explained. "But your feet will probably be wet the whole time. I think paying a little extra for these makes for a more enjoyable ride."

"You *think*, do you? I'm not going to ask you about all these memories just now, but I reserve the right to question you about them later."

"And I promise to tell you everything, even though I have no clue how I'm remembering some of these things." He shrugged.

He helped Marie get into the front seat and showed her the handles along the edges of the kayak. "If you fall out, just grab on to one of these or the side of the kayak, and I'll pull you back in."

"That in no way reassures me."

He laughed, and it was rich and full-bodied. "Stop worrying." He handed her a paddle, grabbed the dry bag and got situated in the back.

"That's not in my nature."

"How about you try it for just one day? Heck, how about for just a few hours?"

She twisted around and gave him a fake, cheesy smile. "Here you go. This is me, totally not worried."

"Whoa. Now, I'm the one who's not reassured."

"Not so easy, eh? Hey, listen, I've only kayaked once in my whole life, and it was by myself on a very small lake. I'm not sure how two-person rowing works."

"Tandem works the same way. We paddle together, same side at the same time. If we need to maneuver around anything, I'll make the calls."

"Aye aye, Captain." Marie gave him a sharp salute.

They practiced in the calm water at the launch point until Marie felt comfortable with the motion and paddling. Then they traveled across the river and entered the downstream current, the rapids easy, with still pools between.

Marie tipped her face toward the sky, smiling at the sun. She was happy. Safe. And her feelings for Jack? They went way beyond like, and unless she was off the mark, he seemed to feel the same way.

Drifting farther downstream, they hit a few spots that made Marie's heart skip a beat, but Jack kept control of the kayak, and except for his occasional shouted directions, the hustle and splash of the river made conversation difficult. They were getting tossed around a little, but Jack worked to keep them away from large rocks.

Farther down the river there would be a fork on their left that led to a Class V run. Just the idea of the chaotic water, crashing as waves against rocks and forming whirlpools with deadly undercurrents, made her queasy.

But Marie relaxed in the knowledge that Jack knew

what he was doing. He'd promised to take care of her, and she trusted him. She looked back at him and smiled. He raised his oar and grinned back.

Today was going to be a fantastic day.

Chapter Fourteen

As soon as Jack was in the water with the paddle in his hands, muscle memory kicked in. If he felt comfortable on the river, sitting in the kayak was like coming home. His lost memories weren't coming to him in a rush; they were creeping in. At least the pleasant ones were, and the joy he derived from challenging the river filled him.

As for the rest? Jack pushed aside thoughts of the nightmares that still came every night. The flashes of that one, horrific scene in the West Virginia woods where Abel Gaines had his shootout with law enforcement. Jack even pushed aside the possibility that he'd been on Abel's payroll. According to the news, Abel Gaines was dead, and as far as Jack was concerned, whatever his connection to the terrorist might have been, it was just as dead.

Instead, he cast his eyes on Marie sitting in front of him. A rope of braided hair came out of the bottom of her helmet, its tip resting at the edge of her pink tank top. Well-toned shoulder blades moved easily as she paddled. She seemed happier than he'd seen her, and he was willing to take at least partial credit for her relaxed mood. Making love to her had rocked his world, and he was pretty confident it had rocked hers, too.

So today would be about her, about teaching her to relax and just have a little fun. Then maybe, just maybe, she would relent and open up to him. To that aim, yesterday he and Blaze had mapped out the route he would take. About an hour from now, he would take the right fork at Push-off Rock to avoid the Class V.

In the meantime, this day would also be about him. He needed to relax as much as Marie did, and he concentrated on the muscle burn from paddling. He enjoyed the clear water, wide pools and drops that nature provided. He laughed out loud when they roller-coastered through the splashy waves.

As he navigated the river, taking in the wilderness of steep hillsides, deep gorges and dense forests, the peace and quiet of the atmosphere brought forth another memory. In his mind, a man was speaking. At first, he couldn't quite remember who, but then the story formed clearly in his head.

One evening during World War II, Winston Churchill was dining at 10 Downing Street when the air raid sirens went off. Allegedly, his gut warned him of impending danger, and he told his staff to leave the kitchen immediately. A short time later, a bomb landed exactly where his staff had been.

Like Churchill, Jack's gut began to churn. His grip on the paddle tightened as he scanned the river. No seams, where two currents flowing in opposite directions meet and form an unstable line in the current. No keeper holes, thank God. The powerful backwash of one of those could suck a kayak in and keep recirculating it until long after the rider drowned. Nothing at all to give him pause. He looked to his right, then left, checking each riverbank. Nothing there, either. Glancing up, he checked out the heights on either side of the river. Nothing.

What could have possibly set his senses on high alert? The oar suddenly jerked in his hand, so hard that he nearly lost his grip. At the same time, a piece of plastic from the paddle splintered off and hit him in the face. He felt the sting on his cheek. "What the...?"

In the hills to his right, he saw a glint of sun reflecting off something. But no noise followed the hit of his paddle, like he'd expect if it had been a gunshot. Had he somehow snagged his oar under a rock without realizing it? He didn't think so, but that made more sense than someone shooting at them.

The current took them near a rock jutting up to the left. Push-off Rock, Blaze had informed Jack. The marker just before the fork. If he pushed off the rock to its right, they would continue down the easy Class II, which was exactly where they wanted to go.

Go around the rock on its left, and they'd enter the foaming rush of the Class V. In an inflatable kayak. With an inexperienced rider. And Jack with a damaged paddle. That was where they definitely *didn't* want to go.

As they approached the rock, Jack held his paddle in both hands and leaned toward it. Just then, a bullet sheared off a slice of stone right in front of his face. It sailed across the kayak and into the river. Once again, he couldn't hear anything. The shooter was using a suppressor.

Jack dug his oar into the water, twisting his torso to add more torque. The bow of the kayak edged to the left, and he didn't have time to explain to Marie why their course was changing.

"Jack!" Marie screamed.

They weren't on a Class II anymore.

THE INSTANT THE kayak committed to the Class V fork of the Salmon, Marie knew she was going to die. Her mind swirled with possibilities. Abel might be dead, but apparently not all his followers were. Abel had escaped with the help of others. He had been seen at the Idaho-Utah border in the company of another man. Jack had an airtight alibi for both; he'd already been in town then. But someone had to locate her for Abel, and Jack *could* be that someone.

Jack was going to kill her. What other explanation could there be? He'd lulled her with honeyed words and sweet lovemaking so she'd lower her guard. Then, when Abel had died, Jack must have decided to finish the job for him. He took her to the one place where he could be guaranteed to get away with killing her.

She had to be some kind of deeply flawed individual to yet again miss seeing a man for who he really was. Didn't matter that Emma had missed seeing it. Dotty, too. Even Astrid had missed it.

Already, the kayak was being tossed around in ways that frightened the hell out of her. She chanced a quick look behind her. Jack's biceps bulged as he paddled like a mad man, fighting to keep them upright. She turned forward again. When the kayak lurched to the left, Marie shrieked, slid her paddle under her feet and grabbed hold of the edge of the kayak. They spun in a circle, a vortex grabbing hold and threatening to pull them under. They finally broke free and shot forward. Straight into the middle of the Class V.

"No!" she screamed. They spun between rocks the size of cars. They bounced over waves and dropped down, getting swamped. Then they were caught up in a spot where two different currents battled for control. It pulled them to the aerated backwash of what looked like a recirculating geyser that exploded upward, then sucked back into itself.

Jack yelled something at her, but she couldn't make it out. She looked over her shoulder.

He yelled again, and again his words drifted away. He held up his paddle, and for the first time she saw that it was broken. He pointed at his, then hers, then himself.

Marie could handle a lot without losing it. But apparently, Class V rapids, the betrayal by Jack and a fear of dying pushed her past reason.

I'll give you my paddle, all right. She picked it up and swung it at him. Only a quick last-minute duck saved him from a blow to the head and perhaps losing his memories for good this time. Jack managed to grab hold of the handle and yanked it out of her hand.

Almost losing her balance, Marie faced forward, grabbing the sides of the kayak again. They hit the hole she'd seen, where the water flowed over rocks and toward the bottom of the river, then reversed onto itself in an eruption of whitewater.

The kayak went airborne. Her grip on the sides slipped and when the kayak dropped, Marie sailed forward over the bow and into the river.

And like a dog with a new toy, the river played with her. It sucked her beneath its surface and trapped her there until her lungs threatened to explode. She broke free and came up sputtering and coughing out water.

She managed to get her legs out straight in front of her, the safest way to go downstream. But the river tugged her sideways, then spun her, slamming her head into a rock. Her full-cut helmet protected her brain as her head bounced against the foam padding.

Straightening her legs on top of the water again, arms crossed over her chest like a corpse, Marie shot down the rapids, cursing every smack into a rock, every plunge beneath the surface. Where the loop reconnected to the main branch, churning waters shot her into a still pool halfway across the river.

Marie swam to the far bank and dragged herself out of the water, gasping for air. Although her arms hung like broken rubber bands at her sides, she worked her helmet off and unbuckled her life jacket. After resting a minute on her back, she stood. Shaky, but her legs would hold her.

It was happening to her again. The man she cared about was trying to kill her.

JACK'S FEAR AS he fought the rapids was nothing compared to seeing the bow seat empty. "Marie!" His gaze swept over the churning water; he was hoping for a glimpse of her head or her arms flailing in the spray. Not even a spot of neon yellow from her vest was in sight.

Was she held captive beneath the power of the swirling water, subjected to a slow death by drowning?

"Maa-riee!" Her name hung in the air for a moment before the furious rapids swallowed it, just as they'd swallowed her. Jack bent to the paddle and maneuvered out of the hole that had trapped them. The kayak lurched forward. He tried in vain to stop his downstream momentum so he could find her.

You idiot.

With her body weighing less than the kayak, Marie had likely cascaded down the river and could be as much as a half mile ahead of him already. He paddled for all he was worth, constantly scouting for signs of her.

Why had she tried to hit him with her paddle? True, she most likely didn't know they were being fired upon or that he was trying to save their lives. Even he couldn't hear the shots, and by the time he was sure, they were on the part of the river where you couldn't hear yourself think, let alone talk. He'd sworn there'd be no rough rapids, yet they wound up on a Class V. When she'd turned around and looked at him, the naked hatred on her face had stunned him.

He battled to stay upright as the tumultuous water swept him around a bend. The main river banked left, and Jack shot through the last dangerous whirlpool and into still water. Pushing past his exhaustion, he paddled to the thin crescent of sandy beach closest to him. He stumbled out of the craft, his overworked muscles cramping until he fell forward on his hands and knees. Scrambling up, he grabbed the kayak and pulled it out of the water. A few yards up the beach sat a large boulder formation. He ran for it, climbed and scoured the river. No neon yellow life jacket or helmet.

A cauldron of fear and anger, like the river itself, bubbled through his veins. She blamed him. Of course, she did. He'd promised to keep her safe, and he'd failed. Completely. He'd made the wrong call, steering them away from the shooter. By trying to save her life, had he sentenced her to death?

Cursing his lack of a cell phone, he slid down the rocks and ran back to the kayak. Where was the dry bag? There was a flare inside.

"No!" Just like Marie, the bag was gone. Miles from here by now, or buried in the underwater silt.

He pushed the kayak back into the water and leaped in. The landing area couldn't be much farther. The faster he got there, the faster he could report her missing, and the faster the police could start hunting for whoever had targeted him from the hills.

Abel Gaines was dead, but clearly someone connected to him nursed a grudge against Jack. He paddled hard, ignoring the pain of his overexertion. All this time, he'd worried about the wrong thing, so sure he was a man with a violent past. Not once did it occur to him that he might not be the perpetrator of violence, but the target. Possibly both. Anyone foolish enough to be caught in the crosshairs with him was fated for collateral damage.

"Marie!" His plaintive cry bounced off the canyon walls

until he heard only condemnation echoing back at him. He'd fallen for her, fallen hard. And he'd been so close to chipping away her armor. Now the mysteries of her past lay silent at the bottom of the roiling river. For Marie, he was too late in every way that mattered.

Chapter Fifteen

Concealed in the shade of a pine tree, Marie peeked between its branches, searching for Jack. A bright flash of orange caught her eye, their kayak coming out of the same loop where she had. But instead of paddling toward her, Jack swung around to beach on the far side of the river.

Marie turned around and leaned her back against the tree. Curling her fingers into fists, she pounded them against her thighs.

Stupid, stupid, stupid.

Even the extra rules she lived by now hadn't prevented a repeat of her worst mistake. She'd been attracted to Abel's charm and intelligence. He'd treated her with respect. Until she'd walked into his war room, its walls covered with maps, pictures of government buildings and whiteboards detailing bomb attacks, she'd even thought he might be the one.

And here she was again. Charmed by Jack, already falling for him. The first man in years she'd kissed, let alone made love with. Inhaling a cleansing breath, Marie stopped chastising herself. She shifted her focus back to surviving.

Another glimpse through the branches revealed Jack digging through the kayak. Marie seized the opportunity to skedaddle.

The beach area on her side of the river ended at a gentle slope of trees and plants. Working her way upriver and upslope at the same time, Marie used trees for cover as she climbed toward safety.

Sorry, not sorry, Jack. Today's not my day to die.

MARIE PULLED HERSELF up over the edge of the slope. The road lay just beyond the trees, and she trudged toward the landing spot downriver, hoping someone there could give her a lift back to her SUV at Blaze's. A glance at the sky, filling with dark storm clouds, made her hustle.

More people than she'd expected milled around at the landing. Two police cars were parked just off the road, and she made her way down to where the cops were talking to some men.

"What's happened?" she asked. As all eyes turned toward her, Marie looked down at her bedraggled appearance.

A river guide came over to her. "What happened to *you*?"

Unwilling to involve anyone else in this mess, and having no proof that Jack tried to kill her, Marie shrugged. "I fell out. Lost my grip and over I went."

"Were you on a raft?" The guide seemed upset that she might have been left behind by a Blaze employee.

"No, a kayak. The friend I went with is still on the river with it. I'm sure he'll be here any minute." She needed to get out of here before Jack showed up. Figure out how to protect herself. "I'm sorry to put you to any trouble, but could one of you give me a ride back to Blaze's, where I'm parked?"

One of the police officers stepped closer. "I'm Officer Hampton, ma'am. I'd be happy to give you a lift."

Thanking him, Marie climbed into the squad car with Hampton. As he reached the road and turned north, Marie looked through her window at the river. An orange kayak approached the landing area.

As soon as Jack learned she was alive, he'd be coming after her again.

But this time she'd be ready.

And this time *he* wouldn't see it coming.

As JACK BEACHED the kayak, he noticed a police officer talking to one of the Blaze guides. Jack rushed over and interrupted them.

"My friend fell out of our kayak and I couldn't find her. We need to start a search right away. Someone was shoo—"

"Whoa, slow down, buddy," the cop said. "Take it from the top, but calmly."

Jack gave the guide a pleading look. "Please, if we don't find her soon, I'm afraid it'll be too late."

"What's her name?" the guide asked.

"Marie Beaumont. She flipped out as we were—"

"I know Marie. You can calm down. She was just here, and she's fine."

Jack didn't know whether to laugh, cry or kiss the guide. "You're sure? She's all right?"

"A little waterlogged, but she seemed fine otherwise."

The officer stepped away and keyed his shoulder mic. Static crackled over an unintelligible reply. "Hey, Jenny, what's the name of the guy you wanted me to bring in?"

"Jack." This time the dispatcher's voice came through loud and clear.

"Hang on a second," the cop said to his shoulder. Then to Jack, "Hey, buddy, what's your name?"

"Who wants to know?" Jack's relief that Marie was alive deflated with the police wanting to know who he was.

The mic squawked again.

"What, Jenny?"

Jenny's voice crackled to life again. "If it's Jack, you need to bring him in to the station, Nugent."

"Why?" Jack asked.

Officer Nugent let go of his mic. "You heard the lady. Let's go."

"You don't even know if I'm the person she wants."

"You're the guy with amnesia, aren't you?" This from the river guide.

The cop was paying attention. "Unless you show me some ID that proves you're not Jack, I'm taking you in."

"You can't just—"

"I *can* just." Nugent unhooked his cuffs from his belt. "Come on, buddy. Don't make me use these." He waggled the handcuffs in his hand.

Jack backed away from the cop, who grabbed Jack's arms, pulled them behind his back and cuffed him. Jack found himself being put in the backseat of the squad car.

The day Jack awoke with amnesia had been the most frustrating day of his life, until now. Today, Marie disappeared but was apparently safe. The police wanted him at the station but wouldn't tell him why.

He pushed the pieces around like a giant jigsaw puzzle. His nightmares and jagged memories. Recognizing Abel Gaines's picture. The certainty of a connection between himself and Marie. Jack's worst guesses as to his identity seemed to be coming true.

He'd been one of Abel's lackeys, here to do the fugitive's dirty work for him.

And he was about to wind up behind bars.

Chapter Sixteen

Officer Nugent marched Jack into the police station, arms still cuffed behind his back. Memories of other police stations, or similar places, poked at Jack's mind. Smells of paper, mold, gun oil and leather. And always the hint of either urine or vomit. Stabbing pain tore at the backs of his eyes.

Just when he thought the unpleasantness of his past was over with, something came along and triggered the damn headaches. Was he doomed to suffer these for the rest of his life?

He was escorted across the lobby floor just as a uniformed Asian woman stormed out from behind the front desk.

"Why is this man cuffed?"

"Jenny, you told me to bring him in, so I brought him in."

"Bring him in, sure, but I never said anything about cuffs. Get those off of him this minute." Then to Jack, "So sorry about this. I guess you know almost everyone in the department is in McCall for Jason's wedding. Some of the McCall cops were kind enough to volunteer to cover the weekend shifts. But what can I say?" She shrugged apologetically.

Nugent stepped behind Jack to remove his cuffs.

"It happens," Jack said, but he wasn't sure it did. "You must be Jenny Dix." At her raised brows, he added, "Jason mentioned you."

"Ah. Yes, Officer Dix, at your service. Call me Jenny."

With the cuffs removed, Jack rotated his shoulders and rubbed his wrists. "Well, Jenny, at the moment, you're my new favorite person. You want to tell me why I was brought in?"

"Not here. Follow me. Nugent, watch the desk for me. I'll be right back." She led Jack through a bullpen to a small interview room. "Have a seat. I have something for you."

Jack dropped into a chair. Resting his arms on the table, he folded his hands and closed his eyes. Taking deep breaths, he readied himself for whatever came next.

Less than a minute later, Jenny returned, carrying a box, which she carefully set on the table. It was a used supply box, brown with old shipping labels on the outside. The top flaps were bent, some frayed at the edges. Not a box he would associate with the care Jenny was taking in handling it.

She took the chair opposite Jack, placing one hand on the top of the box. Employing the compassionate tone used to convey horrible news to crime victims, she asked, "Does the name Finnegan mean anything to you?"

Jack clenched his jaw. "Should it?"

"Maybe not yet, but it will." Jenny smiled. "It's your last name."

They'd found out who he was. Jack Finnegan. The two names together nudged a corner of his brain.

And Jenny had ordered cuffs removed. He wasn't wanted, then. Not a known associate of Abel Gaines. Jack felt the tension in his shoulders give.

"It almost sounds familiar. But I...how do you know it's my name?"

"This morning a hiker came in. He'd been hiking the gully below where you were found, and he came across a black pickup truck. It was pancaked, apparently from falling off the cliff above it." Jenny stood and opened the box flaps. "Inside the truck, he found your duffel bag. When I looked through it, I realized it belonged to you and sent Nugent to find you at the river."

A pickup truck. Duffel bag. Finnegan.

"How did you know I'd be at the river?"

Jenny shrugged. "Small town. I'm going to give you privacy to go through this. I'm not sure if it will help you remember, or what'll happen if you do, but if you need anything, I'll be right outside."

"Thanks." *I think.*

I hope.

"Listen, maybe it's none of my business, but I think you'll be happy with what you find." She closed the door behind her when she left.

Jack stood and looked down in the box. Inside was a duffel, coated with dried mud. He opened it. Lying on top of soggy, mildewed clothes was a wallet. He removed it and sat back down to go through its contents. Everything was damp, so he worked with care to not rip anything.

A Washington driver's license with Jack's picture. Address in Seattle. "Jack Finnegan." It rolled off his tongue in a familiar way. Credit cards in his name. A couple pictures stuck together. The top one was of a woman, two young girls and a young boy. Pain, like a sword through his chest, gripped him. He recognized his mom and sisters, all murdered by Jack's father.

Also in the duffel, a leather case, which Jack pulled out.

He flipped it open. And almost dropped it. A deputy US marshal badge. The ID proved it belonged to him.

He cradled his forehead in his hands as an onslaught of memories came from all directions. He was a freaking deputy US marshal. Not part of Abel Gaines's crew. What he knew of the shootout in West Virginia was from the law enforcement side.

Marie! He no longer had to hold back his feelings for her, thinking he had a criminal past. Jack opened the door and Jenny appeared.

"Everything all right?" she asked, her brows drawn together in concern.

"Better than all right. Thank you for finding me as soon as you could. But before I leave, I'd like to file a report. I don't have much information, so I'm not sure if it'll even do any good, but I'd rather have a record of it."

"Sure. What type of report?"

"While Marie and I were kayaking today, someone shot at us from the top of a cliff. Hit the end of my paddle, and then just missed us again when he hit the rock we were next to." Jack touched his cheek where the piece of his oar had hit him.

"That's awful. Is Marie okay?" Jenny waved at him to follow her to her desk.

"He didn't hit us." Not exactly answering the question, since he doubted Marie was what he'd call okay.

Jenny took down what little information Jack could give her. "Well, it's not much to go on, but I'll get someone out there as soon as I can to check for shell casings, any other possible evidence. Might have been stray bullets from a hunter, but he shouldn't have been aiming at the river. I'll let Fish and Game know too so they can keep an eye out for hunters on those cliffs, just in case."

"Thanks." Jack hoped Jenny was right and the shooter

hadn't been targeting him. But the idea that he'd almost caused Marie to drown for no reason made him sick to his stomach. "Is there a chance someone can give me a ride to the DCA?"

"Officer Nugent's about to go off the clock. He can take you on his way home." She followed Jack into the room while he picked up the box. "Your gun was in the truck, too. The hiker found it on the floor of the cab, packed with mud. We're hanging on to it for now. The chief needs to release firearms himself."

"No problem. The last thing I need right now is a gun."

Chapter Seventeen

As predicted, the early evening Idaho sky turned gunmetal gray from the buildup of massive thunderclouds. In the distance, Marie saw the flicker of fork lightning, and the wind, which had been quiet all day, kicked up a notch. The day's warmth fell away, and the heavy scent of rain permeated the air. Like a soldier on the eve of battle, Marie was beset both internally and externally by forbidding expectations, adrenaline shakes and a roiling stomach.

A plume of dust alerted her that someone headed her way. Her pulse ramped up and she rubbed her sweat-damp palms on her jeans. She didn't want to shoot Jack. She just wanted him to go away, get arrested, whatever it took to get him out of her life.

She'd been sitting cross-legged on top of the RV, waiting. Now she swung her legs behind her and lay on her stomach near the front edge of the vehicle, positioning Emma's loaded Winchester so she could look through the scope.

She may have been fooled by Jack's good guy routine, but she had no intention of playing the meek victim. Emma kept the rifle to scare off coyotes and the occasional mountain lion. Marie was using it to scare off a snake. A yellow-bellied, two-legged snake.

Whose kisses were sweet as cotton candy.

"Bring it, Jack," she muttered, her anger stoked when re-membering how the day had begun. What a fool she'd been.

Pressing the stock snug against her shoulder, Marie squinted, sighting the red compact car as it came through the DCA's front gate and up the long dirt drive.

Her two-legged snake sat in the passenger seat, lean-ing forward to peer out the windshield. "You can't see me, but I can see you," she murmured. She placed him in the crosshairs. "If you think you're going to catch me unaware a second time, you've got another think coming."

She didn't recognize the driver. Maybe one of Abel's men, maybe some unwitting person who'd picked up a hitchhiker. She'd worry about him later. As the car stopped in the circular drive, facing the RV and barn, Marie turned her head and shouted down to her backup. "Astrid, stay." She'd positioned the dog at the rear of the RV where the ladder was located so no one could climb up without her knowledge.

The passenger door swung open.

Her pulse ramped up.

Jack stepped out of the vehicle.

After leaning back in to speak to the driver, he closed the door and walked to the trunk, which popped open. Jack carried a large brown box around to the driver's win-dow and spoke to the other man again, then headed to-ward the RV.

Marie aimed the rifle. Wrapped her finger around the trigger. Inhaled. Blew out half her breath and pulled the trigger.

The kick was painful, hard and sharp. Her ears rang. The bullet hit the dirt in front of Jack, spraying him with dust, the report echoing like thunder.

He dropped the box and slithered like the snake he was to the passenger-side door, pulled it open and crouched behind it. At the same time, the driver tumbled out of his side and followed suit, but unlike Jack, he aimed a gun at her.

She hadn't counted on that.

"Marie!" Jack shouted, looking around as if he didn't know exactly where she was.

"I've got you in my crosshairs, Jack, and my first shot was just a warning. If I'd wanted to hit you, you better believe I would have. Now, get back in that car and leave." Her voice carried in the quiet evening air.

Jack's face contorted in feigned confusion. "Crosshairs? Marie, are you the one shooting at me?"

What an actor.

She fired again. "How's that for an answer? I want you and your minion out of here. I mean it!"

"Marie, for God's sake, tell me what's going on!"

That was rich. "You tried to kill me today."

"You mean the river? That's not what happened."

"You're a liar. I'm only going to tell you one more time. Leave."

"Give me one minute and I can clear all of this up."

"I'm not—"

The driver held up his hand. "Marie, I'm Officer Nugent of the McCall Police Department. I need you to put down the gun and come down from up there with your hands up." In a quieter voice, she heard him ask Jack, "Did you try to kill her on the river?"

"No! Someone was shooting at us. I filed a report with Jenny when I was at the station."

Marie turned the scope on the officer and saw the badge he held.

"I don't believe either one of you."

"Marie, he's a real cop." Cautiously, Jack straightened to a standing position. He spoke to her as if she were a skittish, cornered animal. "They found my personal effects from the night of the storm. Jenny, the dispatcher, gave them to me this afternoon. My name is Jack Finnegan and I'm a deputy US marshal." He moved out from behind the car door, hands up.

She couldn't believe she was waffling. "Prove it."

Jack walked to the box he'd dropped and pulled out a badge. He held it up, but she could make out little more than its shape. Could be from a box of Cracker Jack for all she knew.

"Don't move." Marie pulled her phone from her back pocket. She found the main number for the marshals' office in Boise. At the after-hours recording, she punched the option to speak to a live person. When the operator came on the line, Marie asked to speak to Jack Finnegan.

"Who's calling?"

"It doesn't matter who I am. I need to know if there's a Jack Finnegan there."

"Ma'am, I'm sorry, but I can't provide information on whether someone is or isn't an employee. If you'd like to leave a message—"

Dang it. Marie hung up. She'd gone through the same routine when she'd tried reaching George through the main number.

"Ma'am?" the "cop" called out from behind the safety of his car door. His gun was still trained on her. "Call the Jasper PD. Ask to speak with Jenny. She can confirm what we've been telling you."

Why not? Marie dialed the number.

"Jasper Police Department. Is this an emergency?"

"Is this Jenny? It's Dr. Beaumont."

"Marie? What can I do for you?"

"I have a question for you. What is Jack with-no-memory's last name?"

"Oh, you haven't heard." Excitement colored Jenny's

voice. "We recovered his personal belongings. His name's Jack Finnegan. Turns out he's a deputy US marshal. Can you believe it?"

"Jenny, I can't explain right now, but my life depends on how sure you are that he's legit."

"Are you all right? Do you need—"

"I'm fine. I just need to confirm he's with the Marshals Service."

"Yes, he's legit. I went through his things before we brought him in, to make sure who they belonged to. I recognized his picture on his driver's license. I even ran a check on him to make sure, and his record is stellar."

"Thanks, Jenny. I appreciate it. I promise I'm okay, and I'll talk to you later."

Not sure if she should be embarrassed, still wary or just plain relieved, Marie climbed down the RV's ladder. But she kept hold of the Winchester and commanded Astrid to heel as she confronted the two men.

Officer Nugent already had his badge and ID out to show her. "You mind putting the rifle down?"

Marie thanked him and set the rifle on the ground. Nugent talked to each of them separately, finally satisfied that both were okay and neither intended to shoot the other.

"Well, it seems you two will resolve this with a conversation, so I'm going to take off. The weather looks like it's about to turn nasty."

"Sure," Jack said, looking to the sky. "Thanks for the lift."

Nugent shook his head, chuckling. "No, thank you. Most interesting day I've had in a while."

Marie shrugged. "I had to be sure. You understand."

"Not the details, but I'm sure you two will sort things out."

Marie nodded, and Nugent climbed in his car, waving as he drove off.

She remained standing where she'd been, staring at Jack. Apparently, there was a limit to how many emotions she could deal with at one time before being rendered speechless and brain dead. Astrid whined and looked up at her, but Marie wasn't quite ready to release her.

Jack's intense gaze looked haunted. "I'll explain what happened on the river today, then you can tell me why on earth you thought I wanted to kill you. But first, can I show you my stuff?"

Blowing out a long breath, Marie picked up the rifle and put it in safe mode. "You use that line on all the ladies?"

Chuckling, he picked up the box. "Nope. You're the first one. And hopefully the last."

That brought a smile to her lips.

"Let's go in the RV. Nugent was right, looks like it's about to rain." There was a hesitancy to Jack's steps as he walked over to her. Astrid looked up at him, issuing a low growl and wagging her tail at the same time. "And maybe call off your enforcer? I'd like to keep all my appendages. Especially the ones at chomping height."

"Astrid, free." Marie waved her hand toward Jack. "Free."

Jack held his hand out for Astrid to sniff. "Just until she knows for sure I'm not the bad guy."

Twisting her mouth to the side, Marie snickered. "She knows. She knew before I did."

"Good girl, Astrid." Jack knelt on one knee, set the box back down and patted his chest. Astrid was on him in a flash, licking his face.

"Jack, I'm sor… You have no idea how… There's a good reason. I mean for thinking that you were… I mean, what else was I supposed to think? The Class V, and—"

"Someone was shooting at us on the river. Jenny thinks they might have been stray bullets from a hunter, and I hope she's right. But if she's wrong, I don't know which one of us he was shooting at."

"Tell me why someone might want you dead."

Marie shook her head. "I…" She shrugged.

"So even now, knowing who I am, you can't open up to me."

"I want to. But I can't."

He grabbed her hand and led her to the door of the RV. He took the first step up, then stopped. Turning, he stared down at her. Powerful, intimidating, demanding. "I want the truth from you, or we'll have nothing more to talk about." The finality in his statement made it clear he meant it.

She was sick of the deception, the lies. No more. At least not with Jack. "Okay, the truth," she said.

"Did you used to be a blonde?"

The tension of the day exploded in a laugh of incredulity. "That's what you want to know?"

"For starters."

He smiled and her insides melted.

INSIDE THE RV, Jack set the box that held his whole life down on the kitchen counter. He waited while Marie got Astrid settled on the small couch. Then, like a recalcitrant child, she faced him, standing by the door as if poised for flight.

"I'll have that rifle, if you don't mind." He was generally a trusting sort, but there were limits. She handed it to him without protest. He checked to make sure the safety was on, then reached around her, resisting the urge to fold her into his arms, and laid the Winchester across the driver's seat, out of the way. "Where'd you learn to shoot?"

She hesitated.

"The truth, Marie. I mean it."

"I learned from a guy named George."

"Now there's an earth-shattering revelation." He shook his head, smiling again despite trying to keep a stern expression. "I'm going to have to drag every detail out of you, aren't I?"

She shrugged. "What can I say? A leopard doesn't change its spots."

"Well, there's a cynical viewpoint. But let's get back to my original question. Were you ever a blonde?"

She smiled shyly, and some of the stiffness left her posture. "I was."

Why do I know that?

Jack leaned against the kitchen counter, crossing his arms over his chest to hide his frustration. Much of his memory had returned. He remembered his mom, his sisters, where he grew up, his childhood. He remembered college and the allure of law enforcement. He remembered past cases, and he definitely remembered what happened during the shootout at the Gaines compound.

But there were gaps. For one thing, he had no idea how he got the burn on his arm. He didn't know what a marshal from Seattle was doing in Jasper on the night of the storm that had robbed him of his memories. And most frustrating of all, he didn't know how Marie fit into all of this.

"Did you know Abel Gaines? Not from TV, but in person?"

Marie shivered.

"You're cold. Here, let me get you something." He walked to the master bedroom in the back of the RV, and rummaged through the closet, pulling out a red-and-black flannel shirt.

She'd changed clothes since their river excursion, but the T-shirt Marie had pulled on over jeans was inadequate for the sharp drop in temperature from both the oncoming night and the approaching storm.

She slipped into the shirt with a grateful sigh. "Thanks."

"So, about Abe—"

"My turn. Let me see what's in your box."

He hesitated. Her mysteries were far more enticing than his. Still, he had promised. Pushing away from the counter, he turned to the box and lifted the lid. "Have a look."

Marie went through the contents of his wallet, hefted his badge and peppered him with questions. He identified his mom and sisters in the only picture he kept on him and promised to tell her about them someday. No, he wasn't married, never had been. No fiancée, no girlfriend. No kids. Not even a pet.

"I knew Abel Gaines. In person." She took a step away from Jack and wrapped her arms around her middle. Her head dropped forward, and she refused to meet his eyes. Jack recognized the body language. Shame. "I took care of his horse. And I sort of dated him, for a little while."

Laser-like pain jabbed behind his eyes, and he drew in a sharp breath. Reaching up, Jack massaged his forehead. The connection. She knew Abel. As a blonde. She took care of his horse. She'd *dated* him. He dropped his hand away from his forehead, and looked at Marie, *really* looked at her, seeing her as a blonde. In a photograph. In a case file.

Memories teetered on the edge of remembrance. Why had a field agent from Seattle been in Jasper? Because... he no longer worked in Seattle. He'd been transferred to Boise. Yes, that was right. But why? Because there was an opening. Someone, a deputy named George something or other, had died unexpectedly. A heart attack. Jack was his replacement.

Where'd you learn to shoot?

I learned from a guy named George.

"Marie, are you in WITSEC?"

"Yes," she whispered. "That's why I couldn't tell you anything."

He moved to her and grabbed her shoulders in excitement. "I remember now. George Murphy had a heart attack and passed away. I was assigned as your new case deputy. The night of the storm, I learned of Abel's prison escape. I was coming to Jasper to find you, move you to safety."

Marie's eyes widened. "That's why I couldn't reach him. I've been trying to contact him since the day Astrid and I found you." Her voice turned somber. "I knew he had health problems, but I'd hoped that wasn't why I never heard back from him."

"I'm sorry about George. It must be hard losing someone you depended on. I know life in Witness Protection isn't easy."

Nodding, Marie took a small step back and out of his grasp. "I told you how I knew Abel, and I'm sure you know the rest from my file." Lowering herself onto the couch, she asked, "Do you know what's been causing your headaches?"

Jack sat next to her. "I was at the Gaines compound for the siege." He quickly added, "As a marshal, involved in the take-down of Abel and his followers." He blew out a breath. "Starting with when I woke up with no memory, every time a vision from that day has tried to rear its ugly head, the headaches come. As well as nightmares of blood, bodies, fire. Everything I saw there."

Marie ran a finger along the scarred tissue on his arm. "Is that where this came from?"

He looked down at the grisly mass of melted flesh, realizing that siege *was* when it had happened. "I tried to save another marshal when a piece of burning wood fell on him."

"Tried?"

"He made it to the hospital. But his injuries were too extensive." Jack looked into Marie's eyes. "He died the next day."

Marie rested her palm against his cheek. "Jack." The word left her lips on a whispered sigh.

That was all the invitation he needed. He crushed his lips to hers and invaded her mouth. She opened to him without hesitation, her arms stretching up and encircling his neck. His arms wrapped around her, pulling her tight to his body. Tighter still. He never wanted to let her go.

He understood her now. Her reticence to know people, to share her life with them, her crippling fear, all of it rooted in being the hunted prey of Abel Gaines. And when Jack turned up in Jasper with no memory right when Abel escaped, it wasn't so farfetched for her to think he might be one of Abel's accomplices.

Adding to the confusion, his transfer to the Boise office happened shortly before his vacation was scheduled to start. As of the day Marie had found him, he was supposed to be on a three-week fly fishing trip, unreachable in the Montana wilderness. But when he caught the alert that Abel had escaped, he'd put the vacation out of his mind and rushed to move Marie to safety. He'd planned on calling in to the office from the road. No one from his office was expecting him back yet. They didn't even know he'd been missing.

Taken with the fact that Marie didn't know why George never answered her pleas for help and didn't know Jack was her new case manager, he'd been lucky she hadn't turned that Winchester on him right from the beginning. How alone, how confused, how afraid she must have been.

Yet, despite all that, and even with her mile-high walls, she had let him in. A little, but in.

He broke their kiss, his nostrils flaring, his chest rising and falling rapidly. She was panting, as well. The man he used to be had been unhappy. In his job. In his life. For far too many years. He hadn't realized that he'd been searching for that elusive *something* to restore his zest for living. In Jasper, Idaho, of all places, he found what he'd been missing. Marie was his happiness.

He cradled her cheeks in his palms and gave her his best, most intense Mr. Hypnotic Staring Man look. "Marie, I love you."

Chapter Eighteen

The intoxicating scent of lovemaking filled Jack's nostrils. Warm and sated, Marie lay naked beside him, tucked into the crook of his arm like she belonged there. For all time. Nothing had ever felt so right. Using his free hand, he reached across his chest and brushed a tendril of hair away from her face and tucked it behind her ear.

The only thing that would have made this moment perfect was if she had admitted to loving him, too. But he got it. It was going to take a while for her to get to the same place he was, and he was prepared to wait for as long as that took.

The rain had started, not heavy, but a solid downpour punctuated by the occasional flash of lightning and a rumble of thunder. The effect was insulating, like they were the only two people on the planet. He enjoyed that they could spend time with each other in companionable silence, especially after sex.

Sex. Now, that was a wholly inadequate word for what had passed between them. The first time, after the fire, it had been amazing. Two people who really liked each other, and who answered the strong pull between them. But ultimately, it had been sex.

This time was as different from that as night was from day. This time he'd known who he was, and he'd known why Marie was the way she was. This time there had been openness and vulnerability. He'd willed his soul to her, and it felt like she gave back in kind. This time it had been lovemaking. At least for him.

Marie lifted her lazy gaze to him and smiled. Heaven help him. He could spend the rest of his life looking at that beautiful mouth. "Why the smile?"

"As if you didn't know."

"Maybe, but a man likes to hear his woman tell him, to be sure."

"So, I'm your woman?"

"If you'll have me."

"I think I could be persuaded. I have a lot of reasons to smile, my man." Marie ran her toes up his leg. "And I'm in bed with the best one."

Jack's lips met hers in a quick kiss that took a passionate turn. Then he pulled away with a moan.

"What's the matter?"

"You're going to kill me. I need a little recovery time."

She chuckled. "Women are definitely superior to men in that regard."

"You'll get no argument from me." He pulled his arm out from under her head and rolled to face her. "You're so beautiful."

"Please, I must be a total mess."

He stroked her cheek. "Not to me."

She ran her fingers through the hair on his chest. "Jack?"

"Yes?"

"Don't give up on me. About being in love."

"Only if you promise that you won't push me away."

"Deal."

When he committed, he committed. But that was his fear now, that in his quest to make her love him, he would smother her. Time to change the subject. He looked over at one of the small bedroom windows. "Listen. Do you hear the wind? Sounds like it's really kicking up out there."

"Word on the street is that you're a big, bad lawman. Not afraid of a little weather, are you?"

"No, ma'am. Just offering up a friendly observation." He kissed her again just as the electricity went out. "What is it with this place and storms?"

"The power outages around here usually don't last long." Marie sat up and pulled on her jeans. Groping on the floor, she felt around for the rest of her clothes. "If this one does, Emma has a generator for the house and another for the kennel."

"That's good, because it sounds like the dogs aren't digging the dark." Jack pulled his T-shirt on and stood.

"I'm going to check on them. I don't suppose you have a slicker or maybe a windbreaker I could borrow?"

"Not sure." He dug through the closet. "How about this?"

An old, faded hunting jacket. "Why not? Better than nothing."

She slipped it on, slid her phone into the jacket's pocket and walked toward the door. "You don't have to go. No sense in both of us getting wet."

"Just give me a sec, will you? I need to take a leak."

"It's okay. I'll be back in a couple of minutes." And she was out the door, Astrid on her heels.

"Stubborn woman," he muttered.

While he took care of business, it seemed like the dogs ramped up their howling and barking. He was pushing his feet into his boots when he heard a gunshot blast.

His head swiveled to the driver's seat where the Winchester still lay. His fear when Marie had been swallowed by the river this morning paled to the fear he felt now.

Whoever had been shooting at them earlier had found them. And it sure as hell wasn't any wild game hunter.

Jack grabbed the rifle and raced out after her.

WHEN SHE DASHED from the RV, Marie encountered a storm much worse than she'd expected. Rain pelted her like tiny marbles, and the wind ripped at her jacket and turned her hair into whips. Without the outside kennel light to see by, she stumbled blindly through the inky darkness.

Astrid had disappeared, her agitated bark still audible over the roar of the storm. Marie was getting a bad feeling, and her old protective instincts geared up.

Slogging through mud, swinging her arms for balance, she headed for the kennel, telling herself she was acting the fool. Abel was dead and Jack was a good guy. He might be wrong about someone shooting at them on the river. Maybe Jenny was right, it was just a hunter who should have his license taken away. She still needed to be careful until they were sure, but she was ready to start living her life instead of just existing. *So* ready.

A flash of lightning revealed the kennel, the gate to the outside runs and a man pointing a weapon at her. Darkness reclaimed the sky. Marie screamed. A gun blasted. A burning sensation sliced through her left arm.

She pivoted toward the RV when she heard the pitiful yelp of an animal. She turned back, hightailing it to the kennel, slamming shut the front door the same instant a second bullet punched through.

The kenneled dogs continued their racket as Marie spun to the side, taking shelter against the concrete wall of the building. Touching her arm with care, she winced and brought away fingers coated in blood. She'd been shot.

"I can't believe I left the Winchester in the RV."

She pulled out her phone, dialed 911. The recording informed her there was no service in her area. "Perfect. And no landline, because no power."

She didn't bother to wonder who had shot her. She'd been wrong about Jack working with Abel, but she'd been right that someone was. About to peek out the window, hoping to see Jack coming, the door burst open and slammed shut.

"Marie? Are you all right?" Jack stumbled against her.

"Yes. It's just a flesh wound in my arm. But I left the rifle in the RV."

"I've got it. Grabbed it as soon as I heard the shot." He crouched next to her and helped her take off the jacket. "Give me your phone." Jack examined her arm by the phone's flashlight. "Looks like a through-and-through in the fatty part of your arm."

"Did you seriously just call my arm fat?"

"Just meant no bone or muscle damage." Jack pulled his T-shirt over his head and wrapped it around Marie's arm. "Where's Astrid?"

"She took off. I heard her barking, but then I got shot and just ran for it." She tried to ignore the pain while he tightened the makeshift bandage. "I've got to find her."

"You're not going back out there."

"Jack—"

"We'll call her. Get her to come in here." He moved to the other side of the door, still protected by the kennel's concrete construction.

Marie followed him. While Jack cracked open the door and held it against the wind, she whistled and called Astrid as if her life depended on it. Astrid's, anyway. Having a dog that was trained to protect you was all well and good until the dog was endangered. Pushing the thought from her mind, Marie grabbed the edge of the door and yelled again. Astrid's barking sounded closer.

"Come, Astrid. Come!" Followed by a long whistle. A louder bark. "Here she comes, Jack."

Jack pulled Marie behind him, away from the door, and opened it wider. A very wet, very muddy Astrid dashed through the opening. Jack slammed the door shut and Marie collapsed on the floor, checking Astrid to make sure she hadn't been hurt.

"Thank goodness, girl. I was so worried about you." Marie hugged her, then flinched when Astrid shook rain and mud everywhere.

"Are there any lanterns, anything in here we can use for light?" Jack put his arm around Marie and moved her back under the window, where there was more wall space. Astrid followed.

"Emma might store some flashlights or LED lanterns out here. Let me check." Marie stood just as lightning branched across the sky. She looked out the window, screamed and dropped back to the floor. "It's Abel!"

"They said he died in the fire."

"Well, they were wrong. I just saw him out there, as alive as you and me."

Jack grabbed the rifle and flipped off the safety. "We need to wait for another flash of lightning so I can see him."

They moved back to the side of the door with the handle. Jack knelt on one knee. Waiting, watching for light from Mother Nature when the window they'd just been sitting beneath exploded into the room. Marie locked the door handle while Astrid huddled next to her. The poor dog had been trained to attack threats, not deal with broken glass raining down.

"Stay here." Jack moved to the window and stood next to it.

When lightning struck, he poked the barrel through

where the glass had been, paused a moment, then took a shot. Another bullet flew through the kennel as Jack pulled back, then just as quickly, he resumed shooting.

Frustrated, Marie let out a string of curses that had Astrid tipping her head from side to side. "Do you see him?" she asked Jack.

"I did. Can't see anything now. Too dark." Jack glanced at Marie. "Your arm okay?"

"Other than hurting, it's fine."

"Is the back door locked?" He peeked past the window frame, only to duck back as Abel took another shot.

Panicking about the back door, Marie scurried in a crouch to check it. She squat-walked back. "It's locked."

Another shot came through the window, followed by a barrage of bullets through the wooden door, splintering sections of it.

"We've got to set a trap for him. Right now, he's got the advantage." Jack hunkered down. "And we're out of ammo."

Marie reached into her pocket and pulled out the extra cartridges she'd brought. "No we're not." She handed them to Jack.

"I love a woman who's prepared." He reloaded the rifle. "Can you shoot this with your arm hurt?"

"Yes." Whatever it took to bring down Abel Gaines.

"I'm going to grab the shovel and unlock the back door. You stay up here and shoot through the window. If he thinks we're both still up here, firing, maybe he'll go round to the back, where I'll be waiting for him."

"What if he doesn't?" Marie took the Winchester from him.

"I'll figure out a way to lure him back there." Jack slid his hand around the back of her neck and kissed her.

"Be careful. You're not shooting to hit him, so don't take any chances."

Marie nodded and Jack went to find the shovel with Marie's phone light. When he called to her that he was in position, she propped the barrel on the windowsill and fired. Abel must have moved, because his returning shot smacked into the window frame. Marie dropped to the floor, her back to the wall, and covered her head while more bullets came through the door.

When they stopped, Marie popped up, fired and dropped back down. Fearing Abel might sneak up and just lean in through the window, she scuttled backward across the floor until she could see him if he came. From her new position, she propped her sore arm on her knee, the rifle on her arm, and sent bullets through the window at irregular intervals, continuing even after the incoming shots paused.

The kenneled dogs still barked at full volume and the rain poured down on the metal roof, making it impossible to talk quietly. Marie ran to where Jack stood. "Be careful. He might be circling around. He's not shooting at the front now."

"I'm ready." Jack stood to the side of the back door, holding the shovel by the handle with the blade in the air. "Get in Emma's office so you're out of the line of fire."

"No way. I'm going to keep watching the front." She returned to her previous position.

Astrid ran between Marie and Jack, ready for whoever needed her help. With everything quiet in the front, Marie crept down the short hall to the corner of Emma's office, where she could peek around at the back door. A low growl started deep in Astrid's chest, breaking into a ferocious snarl as she charged toward Jack. Abel stood on the other side of the back door, framed in the window.

Marie screamed as Astrid jumped through the glass, attaching herself to Abel's left arm. Drops of blood stained the sharp edges of window glass still in the frame. Astrid's blood.

Jack threw open the door, brandishing the shovel. Yelling and turning in circles, Abel tried to get Astrid off him. Unable to hit the man without possibly hurting the dog, Jack backed into the building. Abel followed, swinging the gun in his right hand and hitting Astrid with it. She yelped and fell to the ground.

Marie went into mother-bear mode for her fur baby. Jack swung the shovel toward Abel. The fugitive raised his gun toward Jack. Marie pulled the trigger on the Winchester, hitting Abel in the chest. Falling inside the door, Abel dropped his gun and lay still. Jack grabbed the gun and held it on him while Marie jumped over his body and through the door.

Astrid lay on the ground, covered in cuts from the broken window. A gash on her head from being pistol-whipped oozed blood that mixed with the rain as it ran into the mud. Marie dropped to her knees and cradled Astrid. She was conscious, whimpering, and when she looked at Marie her eyes were filled with pain.

Jack appeared at Marie's side. "Is she okay?"

"I need to take care of these cuts." Marie stroked Astrid's ear. "Is he…"

"Dead. We don't need to worry about Abel Gaines ever again." Jack bent down and picked up Astrid. Carrying her like a young child, he brought her inside the kennel.

"Take her into the indoor training area. There's a table in there you can put her on." Marie headed toward the supply cabinet in the stall area, where she grabbed clean towels. She ran them over to Jack. "I've got to get my bag from the house. Be right back."

"Marie, no! We don't know if anyone else is out there." That stopped her.

"Tell me where it is, and I'll get it for you. Dammit, trust me, will you?"

She told him its location, as well as that of a gallon bottle of distilled water Emma used for ironing, and he returned with both. With Jack holding her phone for the light, Marie opened her bag and removed bandages and tweezers. "I understand bull riders now. That was the longest eight minutes of my life."

"Princess, a bull ride is eight seconds, not eight minutes."

"To-mato, to-mawto." Her left arm hung limp at her side. Her right rested on Astrid. Jack took the water bottle and set it on the floor.

"Do you need to sedate her?" Jack asked.

"I'm going to try to do it without. See how she does." Marie removed the cap from the water jug. "Can you pour some of it over the head gash and the cuts on this side?"

Jack did as she asked while Marie kept a hand on Astrid, calming her.

"The gash is the only one still bleeding. If you hold a towel against it with some pressure, I'll check these other cuts for glass." Marie put on a pair of magnifying glasses and tweezed tiny pieces of glass out of the many cuts.

The lights blinked on in the room, and Marie realized the rain on the roof had tapered off. When she was sure she'd gotten all the sharp fragments, she disinfected the cuts. Most were narrow enough that they would heal on their own. She repeated the process on Astrid's other side, then cleaned and bandaged cuts on her legs.

The head wound's bleeding had slowed, and it wasn't as deep as it had seemed. They rinsed it again, then Jack continued to hold a clean towel against it while Marie packed up her bag. Standing on opposite sides of the dog, Marie met Jack's intense gaze.

"Thanks for helping with Astrid. With my arm, I'd never have been able to do it alone."

Jack lifted the towel to find the wound no longer bleeding. He walked around the table and wrapped his arms around Marie. "Thank you for saving my life." He bent down and kissed her.

"I think we were all kind of saving each other, so…"

Shaking his head, Jack pulled her into a tighter hug. "Uh-uh. That's the second time you've rescued me, and this time you risked your own life to do it."

She smiled up at him. "Well, considering I practically tried to kill you twice, trying to hit you with the kayak paddle and shooting at you earlier, I think we're sort of even."

With her head pressed against his warm skin, his heart beating beneath her ear, Marie couldn't deny her feelings. She'd been wary, careful, hesitant, determined to not get attached. But the attachment happened despite every effort to stop it. She mumbled against Jack's chest.

"What did you say?" Grasping her shoulders, Jack held her a few inches away from him so he could see her face.

Marie lowered her eyes. *This is stupid.* She'd faced off with the bane of her existence and won, but voicing her own emotions out loud scared her. *Stupid. Stupid. Stupid.* She lifted her head and looked Jack straight in the eye.

"I love you," she repeated. There. She'd said it. Out loud. To Jack.

"Was that so hard?"

"Yes." She wrapped her right arm around him and hugged as tightly as she could.

"Then it means even more." Jack rested his chin against her head.

Astrid whimpered and Marie let go of Jack to check on her.

Jack checked Marie's cell for service. "Looks like the towers are still out."

"The landline should work now that the power's back on. Check in Emma's or Barbara's office." Marie continued to comfort Astrid while Jack called the police. When he returned, she said, "The wedding party is going to be upset when they learn we have a better story to tell about this weekend."

With one arm around Marie and the other hand stroking Astrid's snout, Jack smiled. "Yep. And the ending makes it all worth it."

Chapter Nineteen

"I love this awning." Marie sipped her wine.

After the pandemonium of Saturday, Sunday afternoon drew down in serene comfort. The sun was low in an orange-hued sky. A slight breeze stirred a carpet of green-and-brown grass, while chirping bluebirds added to the ambience. She and Jack sat in lawn chairs outside the RV, enjoying nature's display, a large, motorized awning open above their heads.

"Blocks the sun, and if it drizzles again, we won't get wet," she said. "How'd you figure out how to work it?" She set her glass down on the small table brought out from the kennel.

"Shane showed me last week when he stopped by, but this is the first time I've had a chance to use it." Jack reached over and threaded his fingers through Marie's uninjured right hand. "Much nicer with company." A playful smile kicked up at the corners of his mouth.

"I'm finding quite a few things are nicer with company." Marie chuckled as she stretched her bandaged left arm and moved it around to ease the stiffness.

After Abel had been killed and once power was restored, they'd called in the cavalry, and pretty much every police and emergency vehicle in Jasper arrived, lights flashing and sirens blaring.

Eddie, the paramedic who'd helped Marie the morning she'd found Jack beside the road, wanted to take her to the hospital. She'd refused. Astrid had been hurt trying to save them; no way would Marie leave her side. No way would she leave Jack's side. The gunshot wound hurt like hell, but even she could see it wasn't serious.

With reservations, Eddie had sterilized and bandaged Marie's wound at the scene. "All right, Doc. I get it. I remember how I was when Killer was hurt, but promise me that first thing Monday, you'll see a doctor."

Now, lying on a pallet between the lawn chairs, a recovering Astrid kept watch on the drive. Emma, Piper and Shane would be home soon from the wedding, and Astrid seemed to know that. Marie reached down and gave her ear a tug. "Ready for things to get back to normal, eh, girl?"

Astrid's tail thumped the ground in response.

"Me, too." Although Marie was still trying to wrap her head around the fact that her normal was about to be redefined in a profound way.

She faced Jack, struck, as always, by the intensity of his intriguing eyes. When bound by secrecy, she'd feared his ability to deep-dive into her soul. Now that she was free, she hoped she'd be able to overcome her ingrained reticence. Buried inside her was a need to share her life. With Jack. And to share his in return.

"I still can't believe you're my case deputy." Not necessarily a good thing. No fraternization allowed. A situation guaranteed to put the kibosh on a relationship between the two of them. "But not for much longer." She gave his fingers a quick squeeze.

Jack's eyebrows rose. "You're definitely leaving the program?"

"Abso-freaking-lutely. I decided that as soon as I heard Abel—who wasn't Abel—died in the Hills fire."

Jack shook his head. "I won't lie—I thought you were seeing things last night when you said he was the one shooting at us."

"I don't blame you. Thank goodness the FBI identified Abel's brother as the burned body, or I'd think I was deluded myself. I guess those DNA tests aren't always 100 percent perfect" Marie picked up her wine glass. "I'm glad the Jasper police found those shell casings up on the cliff and matched them to Abel's rifle. It'll be nice not looking over my shoulder all the time."

The FBI had also informed them, via Jasper PD, that all key players with Abel at the compound that day five years ago were either in prison or had cut ties with him. "You gonna stick with the name Marie or go back to using Megan?" Jack stroked Astrid's ear, still the best place to pet her amidst all the cuts and bandages.

Picking up her glass, she ran a finger around its rim. "Haven't decided. But to be honest, every time I so much as think the word *Megan*, I hear it in *his* voice. Besides, everyone here knows me as Marie."

And I like hearing you say Marie when we make love.

"Sounds to me like you've already decided."

She rewarded him with a sardonic grin. "I'm not sure I like someone knowing me so well."

Jack chuckled. "I'll have to notify the office. Since all your IDs and papers are in the name of Marie Beaumont, they may have some suggestions on which name to use going forward."

"I hope whatever they have to do to cut me loose doesn't take long, since case deputies can't fraternize with their witnesses." Marie waggled her brows.

Jack slapped a palm to his temple. "I'm such an idiot." He dropped his hand and looked at Marie. "The night of the fire, when we made love, I had this strange feeling we were doing something wrong. Subconsciously, I must have known it wasn't allowed."

"Well, I'm glad you managed to ignore the feeling." Marie sighed. "But I guess now we'll have to behave until I'm officially out of WITSEC."

"Um, about that."

Marie's heart curled into the fetal position.

"I made a decision, too."

He's going to tell me we're over.

"I'm going to resign from the Marshals Service."

Exhaling in relief, Marie realized what that meant for him. "You can't quit the job you love just so we can have sex. It won't take that long to—"

Jack laughed. "I'm not quitting for sex. I haven't been happy in my job for quite a while. I remember that now." He rubbed his palms on his knees. "Since the Gaines compound thing, in fact. It's funny—I never made the connection between what happened there and PTSD until you mentioned it. I don't think I have actual PTSD, because the only times I had symptoms were during the amnesia. But I doubt I'll ever enjoy the job again." He took Marie's hand. "And then, of course, there's the sex."

Marie gave him a playful swat. "I won't lie and say I'm disappointed about that, but what will you do? Find something else in Boise?" It would be okay. Boise was only three hours away. Maybe she'd even move there.

"Oh, no, I'm not staying in Boise." He leaned closer to her. "See, there's this beautiful vet who lives in a teeny, tiny town called Jasper. And I intend to woo her until she agrees to spend the rest of her life with me." He turned Marie's hand over and kissed the palm. "Since I'll be living here, I think I'll take Jason's suggestion and apply with the Jasper Police Department."

Marie felt her throat tighten. "You'd do that for me?"

"I'd be doing it for both of us. I really like Jasper and the people here. One in particular." Astrid raised her head and whined. "I like you, too, Astrid."

A small cloud of dust rising in the distance brought the three of them to their feet.

"Ah, the return of the wedding party," Marie said. "I bet Tashya made a beautiful bride. And Jason in a tux? I wish I could have seen them."

Jack chuckled. "And miss all the excitement around here this weekend?"

"Well, it wasn't *all* horrible." She squeezed Jack's hand, which was still holding hers. "And at least the parts that *were* horrible are over now."

They watched until Emma's car pulled across the drive and stopped near the RV. Emma, Piper and Shane climbed out, all smiles.

"Oh, Marie, you missed the best wedding," Piper said. "Everything went off without a hitch."

"Except the bride and groom, I hope." Jack's grin faded as three sets of eyes turned toward him. "Without a hitch? The bride and groom…got hitched?"

Emma groaned at the bad joke. "I hope your sense of humor returns with your memory."

Marie exchanged a small smile with Jack, then said, "Tell us all about the wedding."

Emma and Piper shared the important highlights, even teasing poor Shane about when he and Piper would be walking down the aisle.

"So the reception was magical and very romantic," Marie said in recap.

"Oh, yes. Great food, lots of champagne and tons of dancing." Piper turned to Emma. "Go on, tell her. Tell her about the dancing."

Emma wore a big cat-ate-the-canary smile. "Turns out Chief Walters can really cut a rug on the dance floor."

"The best part is *who* he was dancing with." Piper looked at Marie as if expecting her to guess. When she didn't, Piper blurted out, "Teresa Norwood."

Marie knew the name. "The police department's secretary?"

Emma nodded. "That's the one. She's been flirting with him for years, but the man was oblivious. Well, this weekend he finally noticed. They danced nearly every dance together."

Piper added, "It was so cute. And then this morning, Shane ran into...you tell them, Shane."

Shane crossed his arms over his chest. "I refuse to stand here and gossip."

"Fine. I'll finish telling it." Piper rolled her eyes. "This morning Shane got up early to work out in the resort's exercise room. He was walking down the hall toward the elevator, and here comes Chief Walters, sneaking out of Teresa's room."

"I didn't say he was sneaking," Shane said.

"Whatever. He was leaving Teresa's room at, like, five o'clock in the morning." Piper's enthusiastic smile grew even larger. "But there's more," she told Marie. "Guess who caught the bouquet?"

"Teresa?" Marie guessed.

"Chief Walters?" Jack tried.

"No and no." Piper moved into the stance of a game show beauty displaying the grand prize, and her hands went to Emma. "Ta-da!"

"Really? You caught the bouquet?" Marie's grin turned mischievous. "Now we just need to find *you* a man, Emma."

Emma's cheeks turned red. "I really don't want to discuss this."

"You know, it wouldn't kill you to have a social life."
Marie enjoyed tossing Emma's words of advice back at her.

"All right, enough about the wedding. Sorry you two
got stuck here," Emma said to Jack and Marie. "How did
everything go?"

"Well, we got shot at while we were kayaking," Jack
said.

Shane, Piper and Emma looked at him, their mouths
open in a row of perfect Os.

"Then I almost drowned on a Class V rapids," Marie
added.

They turned their Os toward Marie.

"We had another really bad storm." This from Jack.

"But before that, a hiker found Jack's truck and his
stuff. His memory is back. Turns out he's a deputy US
marshal."

The other three finally closed their mouths, but they
still followed the conversation like a ping-pong match.

"Marie's been in witness protection for the last five
years."

"And Jack's actually my case deputy."

Still not a peep from the three wedding guests.

"Abel Gaines didn't die in the fire at the Hills, and he
ambushed us here last night," Jack said. "Busted out two
of the kennel windows and shot the front door up. Sorry."

"Abel shot me in the arm, pistol-whipped Astrid and
almost shot Jack."

"But Marie killed Abel and saved my life."

Emma stared at Piper, who stared at Shane, who stared
at Marie and Jack.

"Now she's leaving WITSEC." Jack put his arm around
Marie's shoulders, and she nestled closer to him.

"And he's leaving the Marshals Service." Looking up
at Jack, she smiled. "And moving here."

"Yeah, I might apply for the opening at the Jasper PD."

Marie shrugged. "You know. Just another boring, run-of-the-mill weekend in Jasper, Idaho."

* * * * *

COMING SOON!

We really hope you enjoyed reading this book.
If you're looking for more romance, be sure to
head to the shops when new books are
available on

Thursday 4th August

To see which titles are coming soon, please visit
millsandboon.co.uk/nextmonth

JOIN US ON SOCIAL MEDIA!

Stay up to date with our latest releases, author news and gossip, special offers and discounts, and all the behind-the-scenes action from Mills & Boon...

 @millsandboon

 @millsandboonuk

 facebook.com/millsandboon

 @millsandboonuk

It might just be true love...

GET YOUR ROMANCE FIX!

Get the latest romance news,
exclusive author interviews, story
extracts and much more!

MILLS & BOON
MODERN
Power and Passion

Prepare to be swept off your feet by sophisticated, sexy and seductive heroes, in some of the world's most glamourous and romantic locations, where power and passion collide.